WHERE THE NIGHT CONSUMES

THE BLOOD OF EITH, BOOK TWO

GILLIAN GRANT

www.GillianGrant.com

DEDICATION

To my family, both blood and found.

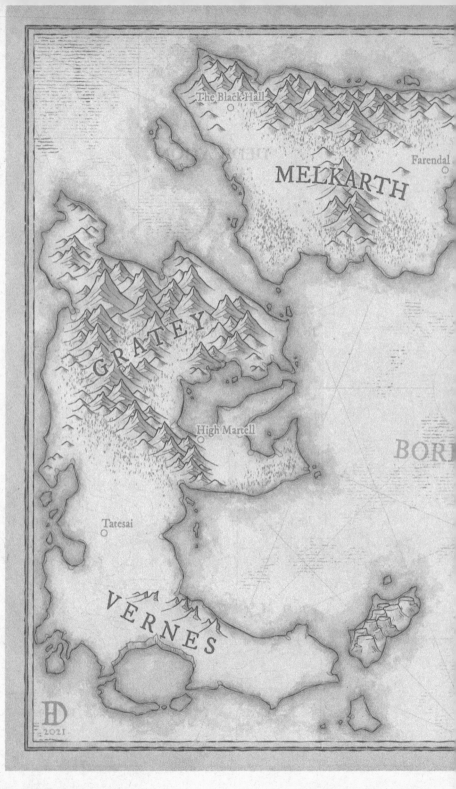

The Black Hall

MELKARTH

Farendal

GRATEY

High Martell

BORI

Tatesai

VERNES

HD
2021

Dirn-Darahl

ETHERAK

Linston

TERERVAS

Rhienwall

SEA

AMRUTHAN

EITH

PRONUNCIATION GUIDE

People and Creatures:
- Sahar Al Fazil: Sa-**har** Al **Fuh**-zil
- Nerezza Quill: Ner-ehz-uh
- Drystan: **Drih**-stan
- Eirunn: **Ai**-roon
- Keres: Keh-**ruhs**
- Mortova: **Mor**-tow-vuh
- Ikedree: **Ike**-dree
- Evren: Eh-v-r-eh-n
- Gyda: **Gee**-da
- Sorin: Sor-en
- Abraxas: Uh-**brak**-suhs
- Arke: ar-**kuh**
- Solri: Soul-**ree**
- Viggo: **Vee**-go

Places and Countries:
- Etherak: Eh-ther-ahk
- Vernes: **Ver**-nes
- Terevas: Ter-eh-vahs
- Boreal Sea: **Baw**-ree-uhl

- Melkarth: Mell-karth
- Gratey: Grah-**tay**
- Orenlion: **Ore**-ren-lee-on

Things:
- Xirstine: Zir-stine

Terms:
- krevas: kruh-**vas** - a dwarven term for dishonored one, coward or traitor
- levenya: lev-en-**ya** - elven word for family, clan, or group
- foya: **foy**-ah - Ikedree term for father

The Banished Faith:
Once a nearly universally worshipped religion, the Banished Faith is now solely clung to by those in Etherak and few others. Once, the Divines were able to give their closest worshippers great power, and their absence has left the once powerful kingdom of Etherak crippled.
- The Banished Divines:
  - Haphion, God of Light and Flame
  - Nutvian, Goddess of Ice and Order
  - Vuhione, Goddess of Honor and Justice
  - Holtia, Goddess of Love and Healing
  - Emion, God of Music and Dance
  - Mandros, God of Knowledge
  - Elos, God of Change and Freedom
  - Eitrix, Goddess of Industry and Money
  - Roania, Goddess of Nature
  - Zelmis, Goddess of Darkness and Chaos
  - Nomien, God of Wrath and Fire
  - Mituna, Goddess of Tempests and Seas
  - Vyone, God of Death
  - Nuris, Goddess of Illness and Envy

1

It was the dead of a long winter's night, and Evren Hanali was singing.

The tune, and the half-elf that sang it, were entirely out of place. The shadows of the night were thick and grasping as they clung to the towering pine trees of the Enrial Wilds. What little moonlight crept from behind the heavy blanket of clouds illuminated the thick layer of ice over the needle-covered ground. Ice and snow crunched under her feet, a bow devoid of an arrow dangled leisurely from her hand as she walked deeper into the Wilds.

"Take to the stars ye lost soul of water,
Where your salt-laden spirit cannot falter.
Oh, spirits to ash, and bones to thunder,
We wait for the day our souls meet in wonder."

Evren's voice was wobbly and untrained, yet pleasant. It carried far through the crystalline forest but wasn't the type of voice to grace a tavern or stage. It was a voice made for lulling children to bed, for lovers in the dead of night, for a kitchen when there was nothing but flour and sugar beneath her fingernails.

She was not that type of woman.

"Leave behind your home of salt and the sea,
Forget the ending of life you didn't foresee.
The Bond that holds us has never been stronger,
I wait for the day our souls meet in wonder."

Ice-covered branches snatched at Evren's heavy cloak but snapped musically as she pulled away. Her breath clouded the air in white puffs, silver in the moonlight. Behind her, something in the trees stalked her.

"Swim in a sea of stars and ride waves of wind,
Your brilliance in life such death cannot dim.
Just don't forget who waits for you under,
I cherish the day our souls meet in wonder".

The words left her lips in a final puff of air as she stopped between two pines. Her throat ached from the cold and the song, and she took a soft gulp of air. She could start all over and keep walking. A fourth time through couldn't hurt much beyond her patience. She kept her body loose and relaxed as she leaned against the tree and closed her eyes.

The smell of pine and ice filled her nostrils. The darkness behind her eyes was not so different from that of the night surrounding her. Plenty of dangers lurked in the shadows, but her fear of the dark had long since been trumped. The Yawning Deep had a gloom unrivaled by anything on the surface.

Besides, one could not hunt a hunter.

A twig snapped.

Evren kept herself still. It wasn't behind her anymore. It was circling. She kept her eyes closed and started to sing again.

"Take to the stars ye lost soul of water,"

She'd sung these words for so long they were starting to lose all meaning. The Vasa funeral song felt numb on her lips. But there was something in the steady rhythm that kept her calm. It kept her fingers from twitching towards her quiver, bristling with arrows. It kept her stiff legs from bolting into action.

It kept her still. The perfect bait.

Her borrowed words lilted across the frosty Wilds, and she

kept her eyes closed. She could hear the crunch of ice beneath its feet. She could picture it watching her, circling her, waiting. She ignored all her instincts that tried to drive her into action. To nock an arrow and join the hunt as predator, not prey. She licked her chapped lips. She could do none of that.

Evren leaned her head back against the tree's cold bark. She forced herself to focus on the music, on the smell of the earth around her. She wouldn't be afraid.

She took another deep breath, a new verse on the tip of her tongue, and then stopped. Thick silence descended over the forest, unbroken by creaking tree limbs or cracking ice. The air smelled less of pine needles now. It smelled of rot.

Something warm and wet dripped on Evren's cheek. She forced her eyes open.

Nothing. Nothing but ice-laden branches and chipped bark. But she could smell it now. She could feel it's hot breath on her face. A moment too late, she saw a sliver of its fangs shift in the air.

The ice wraith's invisible body slammed into Evren from above. Jagged claws dug into her shoulders and dragged her to the ground. Snow and dirt flew up around them as Evren tried to roll away, and her bow slipped out of her grip. The wraith clung stubbornly to her shoulders and pinned her to the frozen ground. Snow slipped into her armor and down her back. The wraith hissed in her ear, a tune eerily similar to what she had sung earlier. Mocking her, taunting her. As it had countless others before.

Evren fought back the panic crawling up her throat. She brought her arm up to keep the invisible beast back. Hot breath in her face, gurgled vibrations humming through her sleeves; she had its throat. She was already shaking from exertion; the wraith was stronger. It was winning. She could just make out the shimmering outline of its fangs, several inches long and sharp as daggers, closing the distance to her throat.

Evren let its throat go and slammed her wrist into the

wraith's mouth. The fangs cut through her armor like butter, and white-hot pain laced through her as the teeth almost met bone. She swallowed back a cry of pain. It was better than her throat.

She could use this.

Her blood rushed down her arm, the coppery scent filled the night. She watched, her breathing calmer, as her blood coated the wraith's mouth. It dripped down its neck, tangling in its matted fur. A spike of adrenaline shot through her. She smiled.

Evren ripped her arm out of the wraith's mouth and, with the same arm, elbowed it square in its bloody jaw. It reared back, snarling, bubbles of bloody foam at the corner of its mouth. She took her brief window and kicked her legs at the wraith's stomach. She rocked backwards and rolled onto her feet, a hand still on the ground for balance.

The wraith had recovered, and she could see the translucent spikes along its spine bristling in the frigid air. It paced back and forth in front of her. Her bow was behind it. She was eye level with it still, and her veins were humming with the special kind of fire she'd recently come to welcome during fights.

The tense moment between two predators could've lasted hours, but one of them needed to crack, to blink. The wraith started hissing the Vasa tune again, and a shiver that had nothing to do with the cold ran down Evren's spine. She could've sworn she saw it smile.

She waited for it to pace again, all the while singing its song, before she lunged for the bow behind it. Quick as lightning, it lunged at her. She pulled back at the last minute and took off in the opposite direction. The wraith screeched of frustration, and the bounding footsteps behind her let her know it was following.

Finally.

Her arm was stinging as she ran through the woods, the wraith hot on her heels and her bow getting farther away with each step. A calculated risk she hoped she wouldn't regret later.

Evren skidded on some ice and grasped a tree trunk to swing around and continue her momentum. Seconds later, she heard the tree crack and groan as the wraith slammed into it. The midnight forest blurred past her in shades of grey and silver. The cold air stung her lungs and throat, and her arm throbbed with every footfall. But she was grinning like an idiot anyway. If the wraith could see her face, perhaps it would've turned around and ran back. Perhaps it would've made the smart decision and waited for her to come back to it. Instead, all it tasted was her blood, and her running away was far too tempting.

The trees thinned out suddenly into a small clearing barely lit by the moon. Evren ran to the opposite edge of the tree line, her voice raw and piercing as she screamed, "NOW!"

She turned around just in time to see the shimmering, bloody outline of the wraith leap at her. It twisted in the air, jaw open and claws outstretched, until it was jerked backwards and yanked out of the air. It yowled in pain and its claws dug at the metal reinforced rope lassoed around its neck.

Behind it, a dark-haired elf kept the rope taunt, his eyes not moving from the wraith's writhing form.

"A second pair of hands, Sol?" Abraxas yelled to the trees.

There was barely a murmur of movement before a large net made of the same rope came down on the wraith from above. Its screams of outrage echoed throughout the previously silent Wilds. Evren looked up to the treetops and couldn't contain her grin as the pale blonde dwarf waved at her from above.

"Quite an entrance there!" Sol nodded to Evren's still bleeding arm. "You all right? Need a healing potion?"

Evren shrugged. She barely felt her arm now. "Maybe later."

Sol climbed down from the ice-slick tree nimbly as Abraxas started to tie down the wraith. It snapped at his hands and feet, but the elf was quicker than the beast. His scowl showed more annoyance than anything.

"If we don't quiet this one down, it'll bring it's brother." Evren looked at the darkened trees. "Who's got the potion Professor Elend gave us?"

Sol shrugged her shoulders and gave Abraxas a questioning

look. His frown deepened, and he put his foot on the rope to pull out a large bottle of glowing blue liquid. "Evren's got butterfingers, and you would lose your head if it wasn't attached. Honestly, did you think I would let anyone else carry it?"

Sol started to argue but stopped herself before she could. It was no use when he was right.

Abraxas let himself smile. "Now, let's keep the net on this one while I put him to sleep."

Evren and Sol shuffled into position and kept the net and rope tight so the wraith couldn't move, beyond some mild thrashing. Sol wrinkled her nose at the blood on its mouth but said nothing as Abraxas carefully pried the wraith's maw open and got the potion down its throat. No easy task, but the potion was highly potent. Even a splash would've been enough. Eventually, the beast stopped struggling and they were able to loosen the rope.

"Is it snoring?" Sol whispered.

Evren grinned and watched the shimmering outline of the wraith's stomach rise and fall. "Sounds like it. Maybe we should take some of that potion tonight?"

Abraxas tucked the half-empty bottle into his cloak pocket. "It's made for beasts, not us."

"Yeah but . . ." Sol looked back at the wraith and then him. "Just a small drop? It's so damn cold up here I can't sleep. My toes ache!"

"You have your toes still attached?" Evren laughed.

"Not for long."

Three months in the mountains of the Reino Terminan, and none of the Wandering Sols were getting used to the cold, except Gyda. The part-giant woman could walk out in the snow wearing little more than her small clothes and complain that it was too warm. Evren knew cold, but so far north where the nights were far longer than the days and the ice never melted was more than she bargained for. Of course, it was their own fault for braving the mountains in the dead of winter. Not that they had much of a choice since no one else wanted their help elsewhere. Tropical vacations would have to wait.

They gathered up the ice wraith by tying its four feet together and securing a soft but strong muzzle over its mouth. Their last one had woken up halfway back to the outpost, and the result had almost been ugly. Professor Elend, a short and balding human, liked the wraiths alive and had only paid them half for the dead one. Evren still considered the job well done.

"Fifth one," Evren grunted as she tied off the last of the rope. "Think he's got enough for his work?"

"I don't care if he does, no amount of coin is worth it at this point." Abraxas rolled the wraith onto a tarp and gave them each a rope. Dragging the two-hundred-pound beast through the Wilds wasn't fun, but it was easier than carrying it.

They pulled forward, following Evren's highly visible tracks and blood trail back the way they came, with only small grunts of excretion between the three of them.

"How do you think the others did?" Sol panted. Her feet dug into the slippery ground with every passing step.

"They're fine," Abraxas said. "If the wraith followed Evren over Sorin, then they'll just be bored."

Large groups terrified the quiet wraiths. They were mostly scavengers but would pick off lone hunters and wanderers if they had the chance. And they loved singing. It was a strategy they'd been using for the past few months in the Wilds. Split up into threes, one plays bait to get the wraith interested and then leads them to the other two. Sorin, Arke and Gyda had less muscle between the three of them, but they'd had the most luck catching the creatures. A part of Evren was just giddy she'd gotten the wraith this time.

They moved through the forest, Evren leading them back to the spot where the wraith had jumped her. The signs of a fight were obvious. The churned-up snow and earth, drizzled with Evren's blood, was hard to miss. She could see the wraith's claw marks on the tree she'd leaned against and shivered again. She'd beat these creatures time and time again, but that didn't make them any less dangerous.

"Hold a moment, I dropped by bow."

Evren dropped her rope and Sol sighed in relief. She was a talented fighter and a hell of a diplomat, but the ex-noble was not used to menial labor.

Evren crossed the battlefield to the spot where she remembered her bow being left. She could see the prints where the wraith paced and kept her cut off. Beyond that, the snow was empty.

She slowed to a halt and knelt down. No other tracks besides hers and the wraith's. The imprint of the bow was still visible in the snow. But it was nowhere to be seen.

She looked up, but the tree branches were empty. She circled the battlefield, past the trees she recognized, before coming back empty handed.

Abraxas frowned for her. "Where is it?"

She shook her head. "I don't know. There's no tracks, but maybe one of the others got it and is holding it for me."

Things went missing in the Wilds all the time. Just because Evren wanted to spend the rest of the night combing the woods for her bow didn't mean it was a good idea. People could go missing too.

She picked up the rope again and, without another word, they headed to where they'd left Gyda and Arke.

The terrain of the Wilds wasn't easy, but this part of the Terminan was a shallow valley that didn't get deep snow like the rest of the mountains because of the way it was sheltered. Evren would take steep trails and jagged rocks over deep snow any day. She kept her breathing slow and even as the cold air made her lungs ache and she started to feel numb. Beside her, even Sol couldn't keep up her useless chatter. Abraxas was always quiet during a job.

They worked like that for a while, until a familiar battle cry broke the silence and made them all freeze.

"That's Gyda," Evren said, worry knotting in her stomach.

"Could they be dealing with the wraith's twin?" Sol's voice was barely above a whisper.

"It shouldn't be following them at all. Even if it heard our wraith's capture, it makes no sense for it to travel away from us and attack others."

Wraith behavior was simple. It was something Evren had memorized at this point. No wraith would bother with potential prey if their twin was in danger.

Abraxas let go of his rope without a word and drew his sword. "Something else then. We'll come back for the wraith."

He took off in the direction of Gyda's battle cry. Sol shrugged and did the same. Evren winced and followed at as fast of a jog as she dared. The ground was slippery now, and she'd be little help wounded and weaponless. But she couldn't ignore the cold pit in her stomach. Something was very wrong.

She raced after her companions, dodging past trees and leaping over boulders. The sounds of battle grew closer.

They ran into a clearing eerily similar to the one they'd left. Only this one held the stench of decay and death. Gyda stood between a wounded Sorin and what looked to be two men, one already dead at her feet. But they weren't armed, and their skin was grey and peeling off in places. With a sickening feeling, Evren realized she could see frost-covered bones peeking through their dead skin. Ice coated their matted hair. She couldn't see their faces.

On the other side of the clearing, Arke stood on top of a boulder and held his spellbook in the air. The goblin bared his teeth at two additional figures clambering at his feet. He tore a piece of paper from his book, and as he crumbled it into his hand, fiery runes sprung up in the air. They swirled around his fist until they formed a flaming sphere in his palm. He hurled it down at one figure, who soundlessly stumbled back. The fire didn't catch on their clothes, but the smell of burnt flesh filled the clearing.

"Took your damn time!" Arke shouted as he noticed them.

Abraxas wasted no time descending on the figures. He slashed at the one Arke had burned and chopped its arm clean off. The figure didn't even flinch. It turned to Abraxas with frightening speed, its slack-jawed face and empty eyes brimming with a strange, ethereal light. Abraxas took a shocked step back. Evren wasn't sure if she imagined the fear in his voice.

"Undead!" he cried. "Aim for the hearts!"

Undead.

The air suddenly felt much colder than before.

Abraxas drove his sword through the undead's chest. The same bluish-green light poured from its wound. He twisted his sword in further, reached in and pulled something out of the creature's chest. Its heart. He tossed it to the ground and smashed it under his heel. The undead fell to the ground. The strange light left the corpse and took to the sky, leaving the body hollow and lifeless.

Arke and Abraxas took the next undead together. The same light whispered free of the body despite Arke's attempts to catch it. Evren turned to the ones who had Gyda on the defensive. Her shoulder was bleeding, but her greatsword was steady. It wasn't something Evren was used to seeing, but while Gyda's face was focused and furious, her eyes betrayed her fear. Anything that made Gyda afraid was enough to turn Evren's stomach.

Anything that made Gyda bleed normally just pissed her off.

Sol drew her daggers with a swift elegance. Before Evren could blink, she was across the clearing and had struck one of Gyda's undead three times. The creature turned its attention towards her, its glowing eyes somehow following her quick movements. It reached out to grab her, and Evren saw claws of ice at the tips of each finger. A swift cut from Gyda took both the head and the arm off. Sol drove her daggers into the undead's chest and stabbed until the light left the corpse and it fell to the ground.

Gyda's blade tore into the last undead as Evren raced across the clearing to Sorin. The human was curled up at the base of the tree, his brown eyes wide with fear as he stared at the corpses in the snow. She settled down beside him, checking through his many layers for wounds but finding none. His heart was beating so fast she almost couldn't feel the beats at all.

"I thought it was a wraith . . ." Sorin's voice was unsteady and far too soft. "I led them right to us, I thought . . ." He broke off, covering his mouth in horror.

"Sorin, look at me." She took his face in her hands and ignored how cold his cheeks were. "Look at me."

His eyes finally broke away from the corpses and looked to her.

"You're okay," she promised him. "We all are. Take a breath with me." She took a deep breath of cold air and let it out slowly. Sorin nodded and started to do the same. It took him a couple of tries to calm down his erratic breathing, but after a while they were in sync and his heartbeat had calmed.

She dropped her hands from his face. "Better now?"

He nodded. "Yeah, just . . . I didn't know, Evren."

"It's okay, you couldn't have."

She looked back at the rest of the party. Some wounded, all shaken. Undead weren't something they'd expected. That was something Melkarth and Vernes dealt with. It was why everyone in Etherak burned their dead. They hadn't had an issue in several centuries. And there hadn't been any reports of walking corpses in the Wilds ever. If there had been, no one would willingly go.

Evren turned her gaze to Gyda, who was holding her slug-gishly bleeding shoulder. "Are you all right?"

She turned to look down at Evren, and while her expression didn't change, she could've sworn her eyes softened. "It's just a scratch. Corpse got lucky."

"I'm sorry Gyda." Sorin struggled to get to his feet. Even with his lanky legs he was a good foot shorter than her. "I didn't mean to get you hurt."

She looked at him quizzically. "You did not hurt me,"

"But—"

"You did not," she repeated firmly. She tapped the edge of her sword against the corpse. "It did. Stop blaming yourself."

It was the same conversation after every battle, just with a different person. Evren eyed Sorin carefully. She watched him nod and burrow further into his heavy cloak. His eyes were distant. He wasn't even looking at the corpse anymore.

Something happened every battle now, where Sorin would freeze up, or stumble and almost get hurt. One of them would have to step between him and danger. Evren had done it, as had Arke and Abraxas. And now Gyda. Each time, Sorin apologized. She wondered what he was sorry for. Most of their injuries, if they had any at all, were minor. None of them had the heart to hold a grudge either. In their darkest moments in Serevadia, Sorin had been the glue. He'd changed after Heliodar had killed him, but who wouldn't be changed after that? There were nights Evren wondered if Abraxas's magic had brought him back whole, though. Tonight, as shame melted off of him in waves, she found herself wondering again.

"What happened?" Sol asked, turning to Arke as he jumped off the boulder. The three-foot-tall goblin was nearly swamped by his fur layers and waddled as he came up to Sorin.

"Fuck if I know." He shrugged. "Thought we were layin' down a trap for another wraith. Got five deadies instead."

Abraxas toed one over and used his sword to dig into the dried rib cage. "These undead are . . . different."

"How?" Evren asked.

"For one, they shouldn't be so nimble in this weather. Undead bodies move better in heat. And that light . . ." He shook his head and looked north where the light had disappeared. "I've never seen that before. The undead in Vernes didn't hold light like that. This is new magic."

"Great!" Sorin's tone was cheerful, but his voice was hollow. "Some crazy mage hiding in the mountains sending corpses after us. Just great."

"But they burn their dead up here," Evren said. "Everyone in Etherak does, for this reason. Where are they getting the bodies?"

No one had an answer for that. Not until Gyda knelt beside the closest corpse. She stuck her sword into the ground and let her hands hover over the body for a moment. Her face was unreadable. With a tenderness someone might not expect from the warrior, she pulled a tattered scarf off the body. The air was still, but the scarf was so threadbare it fluttered in her hand anyway.

"A clan weave." Gyda's voice was barely a murmur. "These . . . these are my people."

Evren sucked in a breath. Her eyes found the other bodies. Each had the same type of scarf. One had it around their head, like Gyda wore. There was little hair for it to cover, and Evren could barely tell that it was female.

Abraxas stepped forward and knelt opposite her. Even without his plate armor, he still held himself like a soldier. In the soft moonlight, he looked older than his five hundred years. "Are you sure?"

She nodded, her fingers tightening around the scarf.

"What do your people do to the dead?"

"It varies from clan to clan, but we've never had to burn them. No one desecrates the fallen like this. It's wrong." She looked back at the other corpses. "They are not laid to rest. They cannot join their families now. It is . . ." She took a breath and closed her eyes to compose herself. When she opened them again, all softness was gone. "Barbaric. Whoever is doing this is stealing people from their families. We have to find out who."

"I agree," Abraxas nodded. "But not right now. We'll return to the outpost and get some rest. Maybe some more information. Then, we'll go from there. So long as everyone is agreed."

No one spoke against it, but Evren could feel the unease radiating off her friends. Monsters and beasts were one thing. The undead was another. There was a reason Vernes was so widely hated by Etherak, and its use of necromancy was a major reason. In Melkarth, powerful and intelligent undead were rumored to rule. It was because of them that Eldridge was never able to conquer the kingdom. Undead were simple to take down in theory, but in swarms they were impossible. And every necromancer was different. They'd be walking in blind.

Evren looked at Gyda. The warrior never met her gaze, but she knew she was being watched. Her head bowed a little, and she tucked the scarf into her belt. The hollow look in her eyes wasn't one Evren enjoyed seeing. She'd wipe it away now if she could.

But only what laid beyond the Wilds could do that. And Evren knew Gyda would go, with or without them by her side.

2

Professor Elend Vaughn was a human with zero magical skills that willingly lived and worked in the Reino Terminan. To say the man was far from sane was easy, but it was best said out of his earshot. Be it the chemicals he worked with, or the unending cold of the Terminan, the professor was one to be cautious around.

Of course, that was just a suggestion. One the Wandering Sol's had thrown out the window only three days after meeting him.

"Too small." He sniffed and pushed his spectacles up his crooked nose. He looked at them over the rims with a frown. "Do you purposefully only get the runts?"

"You asked for another wraith, you never specified how big," Evren reminded him. "Besides, it's not like we could tell."

"I figured someone of your background *would* be able to tell, Hanali." Elend bent back over the table where the wraith lay, still sleeping. The room had far too many lanterns crowded in every corner, to make up for the lack of windows. The glass used was Terevasan made, which made the flames so bright that Evren had to squint to see properly. Still, it was rare to have a conversation with the professor without him complaining of the lack of light.

He poked at the bloody muzzle and his frown deepened as he compared it to Evren's arm. He said nothing. No doubt he was more upset about her getting blood on the wraith than her being hurt.

"No, no." He pushed away from the table. "I cannot possibly work with this specimen."

"You said that about the last two," Sol reminded him. "What's wrong with them?"

"They're not big enough."

"I was under the assumption that ice wraiths got no bigger than a normal mountain lion." Sorin raised an eyebrow at Evren. "What does he want? A dragon sized one?"

There was nothing quiet about Sorin's tone. He was meant to be heard. Elend scowled at him, and the deep wrinkles in his forehead deepened even further.

"The quills along their back are what I need. That is where I extract their unique invisibility from. However, ones of this size only have a handful of spines that I can use without harming the creature. Therefore, it is mostly useless to me."

Beside the fireplace Gyda mumbled something under her breath. It sounded a little like a growl, and Elend took a step back from the wraith just in case. When he turned to her, his spray of blond hair almost glowed from the firelight.

"I beg your pardon?"

"Mostly useless." She drew her eyes from the fire and over to him. "So, you can still use it."

"It would be pointless to—"

She pushed off the wall and stepped towards him. "It has use, so use it. Pay us and do your work. We have better things to do."

Without another word, Gyda walked out of the room and closed the door behind her. Evren watched as she did, her nails already digging into the soft flesh around her fingers. Gyda hadn't technically stormed out, but the energy was there. It crackled like bottled lightning, barely contained and eager to lash out. Elend was lucky he was just a nuisance between them and coin, and not a real threat.

Evren turned back to the professor, who was still blinking owlishly at the door where Gyda had left. "She's right, Vaughn. We did the work, and you have your wraith. Fair is fair."

His eyes flitted back to her, and then bounced along to every other member of the party. "What happened with this wraith? This sounds like the end of our partnership."

"It could be," Abraxas nodded.

It should be. Evren thought.

"Why?"

"We saw some undead during the hunt," Abraxas explained. "Gyda believes that they were Ikedree clans-people and wants to investigate."

"Ah, because they're her people, correct?" He pushed his falling glasses up his nose again. "So, she's prickly because it's personal?"

Below them, Arke's muffled voice sounded. "Couldn't be because of walkin' corpses, huh?"

Elend blinked. "Well, I assumed you were mistaken. There are no undead in Etherak. Nor are they in the Terminan."

"We were not mistaken." Abraxas said firmly. "Five undead, all carrying a strange light that fled north when they were destroyed. I know what I saw."

"Of course." Elend licked his chapped lips. "Of course . . ."

Abraxas took a step closer, and though his voice never raised, his tone was dark. "Don't be a fool, Elend. You know what I've seen. If I say they're here, they are here."

The professor stared him down, his resolve wavering. "But this weather . . . it's no good for necromancy. A corpse raiser would need warmth to keep the bodies fluid and malleable. These corpses would've been too stiff to do anything."

Sorin cleared his throat weakly. "They were fast. And quiet too. We—I thought they were a wraith."

Elend absentmindedly patted the wraith's side before turning to his desk. It was stuffed in the corner and useless for anything other than stacking more books, maps, and charts precariously, one on top of the other. The current highest stack wavered with every step and tottered right next to Elend's head. He stooped down and dug through a smaller pile, oblivious to the danger.

"If there are undead here, the Collective will want to know."

And there it was.

Evren groaned internally. The Collective was what got them this job. It was in charge of every adventuring party that was sent out to help people and kingdoms legally. In theory, the Collective was a very good thing made up of like-minded individuals looking to help keep order where kings, armies, and politicians couldn't. In reality, getting anything done through them took about as much time as crossing the Boreal Sea. They handed out adventures to the "right" parties, they decided who did what.

And they weren't big fans of the Wandering Sol's.

"Do we have to?" Sorin leaned against the desk and then shuffled back when the tower of books threatened to topple over. "I mean, that'll take so long! We're right here, Elend. Buddy. Pal. Friend." Sorin waggled his eyebrows at Elend, who just continued looking through the papers.

"Mister Trinity, please stop blocking my light."

"Right." Sorin snapped his fingers and wandered back to Evren.

"You know he's right, Vaughn. It takes weeks to get through the mountains to this outpost, and it'll take longer still to travel to the source of all this. By then it could be too late. We're right here and have the resources, prior experience, and someone who knows the land. We can—what in the hells are you looking for?" Evren asked, exasperated as he continued digging through his papers and ignored her.

As if to prove a point, he continued to rifle through papers and threaten to topple his book towers for a little while longer before finally snatching a paper into the air. With a sharp flourish, he turned back to her.

"This." He waved it in the air as if she could read erratically moving text.

"Dare I ask?"

"Outpost check in. It was delivered earlier this morning to my desk while you were still hunting."

"Fascinatin'," Arke grumbled.

"Indeed, my little green friend." He grinned. It was never a good thing when Elend smiled. "It says that you are not the only adventuring party in the outpost now. And that these people are far more qualified."

"Trollshit," Sol blurted. "Give me that!" She snatched it out of his hands. As she read, Evren shook her head.

"This is ridiculous. We've got a veteran who knows the undead," she gestured to Abraxas. "We've got Gyda, who knows the land and the Ikedree people. We've got a wizard as well. We are more than qualified for this job."

"Perhaps." Elend shrugged. "But that's up to me, being the highest-ranking Collective representative here."

There was something very punchable about his smug face. Evren was seriously considering making his nose a little more crooked when Sol handed the paper back to him.

"Who is it?"

Elend tucked the paper into his sleeve. "The Ashen Bond."

A moment of tense silence passed before Arke broke it. "Who?"

"A group of adventurers."

"Never heard of 'em."

"You wouldn't have." Elend said smugly. "They do their work quietly, with no need for their deeds to be shouted at the heavens. They also leave peace and order in their wake. Unlike you all, who left Dirn-Darahl in a state of panic and chaos."

"Ouch," Sorin grumbled.

"We're not going to argue about this again." Evren shook her head. "It's done, it happened. Let's move on."

"And if it had been done through the Collective's channels, it would've been done properly. But yes," he grinned, "let's move on."

A very punchable face indeed.

It wasn't technically illegal to adventure without the Collective. In reality, it was just safer. The Collective supplied regular potions and equipment. They had places all over Eith, like Keld's Outpost, that acted as hubs where parties could get new quests and rest up. But there were rules, and a hierarchy. Certain parties did things differently and got better results. Some were just monster hunters; others were political ambassadors with weapons. Evren and her friends joined because it was the best way to get new jobs. They carried with them a rather impressive story of narrowly prevented wars, political backstabbing, assassinations, and a very large worm. The surface reactions of Dirn-Darahl's stumble to stability after General Heliodar's failed coup, and the death of the King, were less than pleasant. The Collective didn't want problems solved if it left a mess for them to clean up. Which was why the Sols were in the far north hunting invisible monsters for a picky professor.

"Who are these adventurers?" she asked. "What have they done?"

"The Ashen Bond is a group of four. They come highly praised by their previous employers, which includes the Terevasan monarchy. From what I've gathered, they're the ones responsible for preventing Queen Marjorie's assassination last year. Before that, they were in Gratey and managed to keep a sleeping fire giant from awakening and destroying a whole city. Most recently, however, they've been rooting out strange new cults in Etherak. It seems like something in the north has caught their eye." He grinned. "I doubt it was my ice wraiths."

Abraxas came up beside the sleeping wraith. It rumbled a bit as he got close, but he never flinched. Instead, he looked over the table at Elend.

"You invited them." It wasn't a question, but Elend, in true fashion, answered anyway,

"Of course not! They are far too expensive for the work up here. But the threat of undead could be linked to their cults farther south." Elend shrugged, his bony shoulders visible even under the thick robes he wore. "As a member of the Collective, I decide who gets what quest. As far as I'm concerned, they will have it should they want it. You all have more hunting to do."

He tossed a bag of gold in the air, and Sol snatched it up quickly. She started counting while Evren kept her eyes on Elend.

"If we can convince them to give the job to us?" She raised an eyebrow.

"Then, theoretically, I can't stop you." He sighed. "But these are professionals. They won't turn down this job."

"Let us hope then that your judgement of character is as lacking as your manners." She gave him a thin smile. "Come on, let's go find Gyda and fill her in. She'll want to hear about this new group."

One by one, everyone filed out of Elend's bright laboratory. Evren was the last one to leave, as usual. Just as she was closing the door, Elend caught her eye.

"Be careful with your ambition." He tapped his nose. "It could be detrimental."

"I'm helping a friend. Gyda will go north regardless, and we will follow her."

"Just as you followed Solri Amet into the Deep, I'm aware." He pursed his lips. "Whatever the case, you're not the type of hero to solve this problem. You will leave it to the Ashen Bond if you know what's good for you."

"Do I look like I know what's good for me?"

"Fair enough." He waved her away. "Get yourself lost, eaten, or killed. Haunt someone else later."

"Thanks for the advice, Vaughn."

"Always a displeasure, Hanali."

She shut the door behind her and jogged to catch up with the others. The hallway was achingly dim after the searing light of the laboratory. It was only large enough for them to walk single file, while Arke darted back and forth between their legs. Evren was suddenly struck by how similar it felt to walking the tunnels of the Yawning Deep.

"So, what's the plan?" she asked as the wooden staircase came into view and they started climbing up.

"Sleep first, right?" Sorin asked. "I doubt these new guys are awake now anyway."

Almost as soon as the words left his mouth, she could feel the exhaustion tugging at her bones. The kind that came with the late nights, the hunting, and the arguing. But there was something more behind it. The near numbness on her arm was worrying and seemed to fuel the need for sleep. It had nothing to do with poison because ice wraiths had none, but it was concerning all the same. All she wanted to do was curl up and sleep for twelve hours.

Abraxas nodded; his eyes fixed on the steps above him. "Sleep first, and tend to our wounds. Someone will need to find Gyda so we can patch up that shoulder."

"I will," Evren said. "I'll have to redo my arm anyway." It kept her away from her bed a little longer, but she could manage.

"And in the morning?" Sol asked.

"We find these Bond assholes and get our job back," Arke grumbled.

She helped him up a steeper step. "It was never our job to begin with. What if they won't let it go?"

"Then we hope they're here for something else," Abraxas said. A faint hope, a fragile one. But that was usually all they had.

FINDING GYDA whenever she didn't want to be found was always a small adventure. For someone so large, she had the unerring ability to disappear. It didn't happen often. But when it did, it was always Evren that found her. She still wasn't sure if it was because she was good at finding things, or if Gyda wanted to be found whenever she passed by.

Regardless, it was the same quiet hunt, just a different location. Evren crept through the mostly empty outpost in the dark. The biggest part was the wide, ugly tower in the middle. It was the first thing built, and the tents and hovels around it were temporary and always changed. Elend's rooms took up the basement, and the other five floors were for anyone willing to pay to get out of the cold. Most were.

The floorboards creaked and cracked under her boots as she took to each level. There was a good chance Gyda went outside, but she wanted to enjoy the relative warmth of the tower as much as she could. The first four floors were quiet and dark. The only sources of light were the large fireplaces in the middle of each level. Even with them, the chill still crept in.

The top floor was the coldest, and Evren could feel her nose beginning to ache as she reached it. It wasn't for a lack of fire. It was still crackling merrily. The walls were mostly windows, all rimmed with frost. All with a breathtaking view of the Enrial Wilds, and the towering mountains beyond. The stars were hidden behind the blanket of clouds, but even so, the ice and snow made everything shimmer.

Evren rubbed her arms as she weaved in between the long mess tables to get closer to the fire. Someone had left their tea out. She tapped the rough ceramic with the tip of her finger. The mug was cold, and the tea lukewarm. Whoever had left it liked it bitter. Not Gyda then.

There was a soft sigh behind her, and Evren turned away from the tea. Gyda sat near one of the windows, watching her intently. Evren felt her ears burn. How had she not noticed her sitting there?

"I thought I'd have to go trudging through the snow to find you," she said, walking over to Gyda's table and sitting down. Next to the window, it was achingly cold. She tried not to shiver.

Gyda shrugged, looking out the window towards the mountains. "Would that have stopped you?"

"I might've been a little grumpy when I caught up to you."

She smiled but didn't take her eyes away from the view. Despite the chill emanating from the glass, she looked far from bothered. In her hands she clutched the clan weave from the corpse.

Evren tried not to stare at it. Even in its decrepit state, she could see the detail and care that had gone into it. The once vibrant colors were faded. She remembered how Gyda's had once been like that. Before the Yawning Deep and their first disastrous meeting with the Serevadian elves. Before Evren had nearly died and Gyda had given up her clean weave to try and stop her bleeding. She still felt guilty about that. She still hadn't paid her back.

"You know, if we go north we could always get you a new scarf," she offered. "I still owe you one."

"Perhaps."

That was far from the answer Evren had hoped for, but she swallowed down her disappointment.

"There's a chance we might not go."

That got her attention. Her eyes held the intensity of ice when they snapped back to Evren. This time, she did shiver.

"Why?"

Evren clasped her hands together. "There's another party here now. They have bigger pull with the Collective. We're hoping they're here for something else, or that we can convince them to let us have the job. Maybe, at the very least, we could tag along? Join forces?"

"Doubtful."

"True." She nodded. "But, hey, between Sol and Sorin, they can turn shit into silver. Maybe they can work this out for us."

It didn't matter, though, and they both knew it. Sol was a good talker, but she didn't have Sorin's gift. A gift even he wasn't sure he had anymore. They didn't have the coin for bribery, or the popularity to pull strings. Things had been simpler below ground, ironically.

"You'll go anyway, won't you?" Evren's voice was soft enough to be drowned out by the fire, but Gyda nodded.

"I don't want to."

"Why?"

She paused, her face unreadable again. "Many reasons. It will be difficult to get there this time of year."

"Midwinter won't be easy, no."

Gyda shook her head. "No, winter is fine. It is the way of the mountains. The real danger comes in two weeks. The Long Night is coming."

"Tell me that's not as bad as it sounds."

"It is exactly how it sounds." she murmured. "The sun sets and does not rise again for twelve full days. It is when we lose the most of our people. Sometimes to animals, sometimes to their own madness. There are clans that refuse to open their doors until the sun rises again, in fear of what the night will do to them."

Evren blew out a breath clutched in her tight lungs. "You make it sound like it's a living thing."

"Perhaps it is. It stole my clan the last time I saw it."

The breath caught in Evren's throat again. Across from her, Gyda looked the same. As if casually mentioning that losing everything had little effect on her. But deeper, under those glacier eyes, grief swam in the depths. She never talked about her clan to any of them, or what happened to have her wander so far from home. She only said she'd lost them before. Now, at the edge of her home and the reality of reliving it, she managed to utter the words.

"I won't ask how," Evren finally said. "If you want to tell me, you can on your own terms. But, Gyda, are you sure you want to do this?"

A long, sullen silence enveloped them. Outside, it had started to snow. The heavy white flakes drifted lazily against the blackness of the night. In the morning, everything would look new and fresh. Like covering up a scar with a clean bandage.

"No," Gyda said finally. "But it is something I have to do. It has been nearly a year since I've gone home. I need to set things right."

"You know we've got your back. Every one of us."

She smiled, but it didn't reach her eyes. "That is what I'm afraid of."

"Hey, we survived the Yawning Deep, prevented two wars, and befriended a giant worm. I think we can handle a really long, really cold night together. Especially with you to guide us."

The words were hollow, they both knew it. There were some wounds too deep to cover. There were times when going home was not a victory, but a step backwards. That held true for both of them. The only difference was Gyda was brave enough to actually face her past.

Evren decided to change the subject. "Let me check your shoulder. You can't brood in pain."

She frowned. "I do not brood."

"Oh, you brood, and you do it so well." She laughed. "Now, give me your shoulder."

Bandaging wounds was simple for them. It was a routine. Talking came easily, but nothing was truly said. The silence was calm. Beneath it all was the dread and fear of what was to come, but for a moment it was just the two of them. Beyond the windows, snow fell in soft sheets. Bandages passed between their fingers, and murmurs of thanks between their lips.

It was all Evren could offer Gyda in comfort. Long after she left for bed, she wished she could've stayed there a little while longer.

3

Fresh morning snow had a habit of remaking the world each day. It was the only part of the far north Evren truly enjoyed. The feeling of rebirth was a temporary bandage, of course. The wounds of the past still lay beneath the sheets of ice, waiting for a warm enough day to allow them to resurface.

When the sun broke over the horizon, all weak and watery in its daylight, it looked like the sky had tried to bury Keld's Outpost. There was more snow now than there had been in the three months Evren had stayed there. It came up to her knees, bitingly cold and already trying to slip through her many layers. She let the cold wake her up, rather than fight it. Breathing in lungfuls of mountain air, letting the wind chill her cheeks and the tips of her pointed ears, she let out a soft sigh.

"You almost look like you're enjoying the weather." Beside her, Sol was a four-foot-tall bundle of scowls and furs. Her nose was a particularly bright shade of red. She sniffled and glared at the weak sun in the sky. "Can't it do more?"

"We can't control the sun, Sol," Evren said with a chuckle.

"Pity that." She buried herself further in her coat. Ever since leaving the safety of Dirn-Darahl, it had been a struggle to get the dwarf used to the surface world. She'd never left home before, and the wide-open skies frightened her more than she let on in the first few days. Now that she was past the fear of falling into the sky, Sol had taken to grumbling about the weather. Climate in Dirn-Darahl was almost completely controlled. Dry and warm at all times. The surface had yet to bend to her will so far, much to her annoyance.

The two trudged through the heavy snow side by side. Around them, travelers dusted their tents off and dug out their belongings. Most were well accustomed to the climate. A few, judging by the chorus of curses, were not. They made their way through the camps towards the livestock pen.

A few stocky mules with thick winter coats were shaking off the snow that had gathered in their manes. Evren patted the soft nose of a particular one and let herself smile.

Sol sighed. "Found the Ashen Brand's mounts." She nodded to a group of four well-bred mountain steeds. Their coats were just as thick and coarse as the mules' but were covered by wool blankets. They dozed contently in the morning light, snorting softly when one leaned too far into another. "Even their horses are fancier."

Evren shrugged. "Can't take the horses past the Wilds. The trails get too small. Besides, good mounts don't make a good team."

"Makes for better tempered adventurers, though."

She chuckled. "And sore asses." She let the mule go trudging back to the others and scanned the pen hopefully. "Too much to hope that the goat is dead?"

Sol's blue eyes, almost direct mirrors of the clear sky above, brightened as she joined Evren's search. All the animals were huddled together, and for a moment, there was nothing to see except mules, horses, and the occasional wandering chicken. But in the corner a large mound of snow shuddered and shook. A potbellied, woolly goat tottered out. He huffed and shook more snow from his horns. His eyes were an unnerving shade of yellow and far too intelligent for a simple goat. He scanned the pen, and when he saw Evren and Sol, screamed loudly at them.

"Demon goat," Evren hissed. "It has to be."

Whether Keld the Goat heard her or not, he turned around and kicked a bunch of snow in her direction. She and Sol backed away from the fence.

"Definitely," Sol agreed with a grim nod.

Keld turned his attention to the poor mules trapped in there with him, and there was nothing they could do to save them from the screaming wrath of the demon goat. It brought the entire outpost out of its lazy morning routine. Soon everyone was glaring at Keld and muttering under their breath. She wondered which one of them would snap and try to cook him up for dinner first. Whoever it was would have to deal with Elend's meltdown.

The idea brought a smile back to Evren as she walked away, content to go warm herself back in the outpost proper. Before she went more than a dozen steps, something caught her eye.

Leaning against the ten-foot-tall, spiked fence that circled the entire outpost was a familiar bow, devoid of fallen snow and as clean as the sky above. Evren picked it up gingerly, noting the little marks in the handle she'd put there herself, and the particular way the bowstring was tied off. Orenlion's way of tying bowstrings, and the only way she knew how. There was no doubt about it—this was her bow.

"Hey, look at that!" Sol said cheerfully as she walked up. "Looks like a hunter found it."

"Yes, but who?"

Her eyes scanned the area, trying to pick out anyone new or suspicious. But this close to Keld's little prison was normally devoid of traffic. The closest person was walking away from them.

"Hey!" Evren slung her bow over her shoulder and jogged through the snow to catch up. "Hold a moment, would you?"

The figure didn't stop but didn't pick up its pace either.

Evren caught up to them, only to realize they were just as tall as Gyda, if not a bit taller. She grabbed onto their arm to stop them, and they resisted before sighing heavily and turning to face her.

Evren had to force herself not to take a step backwards. The man in front of her *was* taller than Gyda. His skin was a deep greyish-green, and two small tusks pointed out of his bottom lip. A jagged scar ran down one side of his face. Whatever had caused it had also taken a piece of his tusk as well, leaving them slightly uneven. Long dark hair fell in his face like a curtain, and he regarded her warily.

"May I help you?" The orc asked lowly.

"Um . . ." Evren fought for her words but found them slipping right out of her grasp. It shouldn't be so hard, but she'd never seen an orc before. They primarily kept to the western side of the Boreal Sea, far from Etherak and Terevas. Still, she felt her embarrassment creeping up on her.

She tried again. "Sorry, I was just wondering if you happened to be the hunter that found my bow?" She shrugged her shoulder and his eyes darted to it before coming back to her.

"I'm not a hunter."

"But you did find it?"

"No."

"Oh." Evren felt herself deflate and tried not to let it show.

The orc cleared his throat. "My arm, please?"

"Ah! Right." She tried to laugh her nerves away and let go of the arm she hadn't realized she'd still been holding onto. She'd gripped his sleeve so tightly it had started to ride up and leave his forearm to the winter wind. Wrapped around his wrist, and barely visible against his grey-green skin, a thick band of grey was tattooed. He pulled his sleeve back down, unbothered as Evren tried again for her words.

"You're part of the Ashen Bond!"

He nodded to her. "Yes."

"Well, that's great!" She pushed some of her fallen hair out of her face and walked around to the front of him. "I need to talk to you, actually."

"No, you don't."

She blinked at him. "What?"

"You need to talk to Sahar if you need to talk to anyone."

He brushed past her, his hulking form blocking out the sunlight for a moment as he moved away. Evren stayed rooted to the spot until Sol came waddling back up, her eyes still on the retreating adventurer.

"Well, I've seen better introductions," she said, "But I've also seen worse."

Evren winced. "I'm not good at the talking bit. That's what you and Sorin are for."

"You talked to Viggo just fine." She waggled her eyebrows and Evren considered pushing her into the pen with Keld. It was a joke, and even she smiled at it. Sol meant no harm, but thinking of Viggo was a painful endeavor that often left her feeling confused and hurt all over again. Despite everything he'd done, and would've done, she couldn't deny that she still missed him. Deep beneath the earth under her feet, Serevadia churned. And at the center was always Viggo. Serevadia's protector, her voice and shield. For however long he managed to stay alive against her coming enemies.

"Come on," she huffed. "Let's get inside and find something warm to eat."

"Finally!" Sol cackled and waddled as fast as the snow and her many layers would allow her.

The wide, ugly tower of Keld's Outpost beckoned them inside. The warmth never seemed to be enough when she was trying to sleep, but walking in from the cold Evren practically wept when the fire-heated air hit her cheeks. She and Sol shook off the snow and took off their heavier layers to let them hang dry. Already, the air smelled like breakfast.

The climb all the way up to the top floor was an odd mirror of the same one Evren made the night before. The only difference was the room was far from quiet, and light pooled in abundance through the many windows.

It was still noticeably colder here, and many people huddled their tables around the roaring fire in the middle of the room. Steaming cups of tea and coffee were in everyone's hands, more for warmth than for taste. Breakfast wasn't much, but the porridge was warm and hearty, and Evren found her mouthwatering for it despite having nothing but that for breakfast the past few months.

Sol wrinkled her nose and took her bowl with little complaint. Her eyes snapped to the corner of the room, where three people sat, two of them complete strangers.

"Sorin's making friends," she noted.

Evren shoveled a mouthful of porridge in her mouth and followed her gaze. Sorin was sitting at a new table in the corner with a jaw-dropping view of the mountains behind him. He was smiling and chatting animatedly to two women, although one wasn't paying attention.

Everything about the human he was speaking with radiated warmth. Her skin was the color of sun-warmed bronze, and her long black hair was tied back into a strangely intricate bun. She'd kept her coat on, but the make and cut of it was far from frumpy. The color was a rich purple, and the fox-fur lining probably cost more than the outpost itself.

The elven woman wasn't paying attention to Sorin, which was a remarkable feat in itself. She had skin as pale as porcelain, and her white-blonde hair was a mess that kept falling in her face as she tried to read from her book. She flipped through the pages; her eyebrows furrowed. She picked up a piece of charcoal in her still gloved hand and went to fix something on the page.

"I haven't seen them around," Evren noted. "More Ashen Bond?"

"I'm willing to bet that pretty one is Sahar." Sol nodded. "Sounds like a Vernesian name, and she looks like it."

"Those are not Vernesian clothes," Evren pointed out, but

she had to agree with her. "Well, let's introduce ourselves, shall we?"

They made their way through the maze of tables towards Sorin. He saw them approach and beamed.

"There they are!" He waved them over to his side of the table. "I was telling you about them. Evren, Sol, these ladies are part of the Ashen Bond. The wonderful bookworm after Arke's own heart is Nerezza Quill. And this lovely lady is Sahar Al-Fasil."

Sahar stood up from the table, her deep black eyes friendly and welcoming as she extended her hand. "Short and to the point, I do love such introductions, Sorin. It is a pleasure to meet you both."

Terevasan accent, Evren noted as she shook her hand. A good thing for the inevitable moment she and Abraxas met. Hopefully the veteran could keep to his manners.

Nerezza didn't bother to look up from her book as they settled down around the table. Sahar patted the elf's shoulder to get her attention, but she just waved her away.

She sighed and turned back to them. "Forgive Nezza, she's not much of a people person. Unlike myself. I love meeting new faces. Is this your whole party, Sorin?"

"Oh no!" He grinned. "Divines know where Abraxas and Gyda are, but Arke is impossible to get out of bed at this hour. He'll crawl out when the hunger hits."

Evren could see the heavy bags under Sorin's eyes. He hadn't slept last night, which wasn't uncommon, yet he was glowing. Whether it was from the sunlight streaming through the windows or the presence of good company, she wasn't sure. Sitting across from Sahar, he looked more himself than he had in months.

"We've heard a lot about you and your team," Sol said.

Sahar's smile was blinding. "Really? I was just about to say the same about you."

Evren didn't know whether to be flattered or defensive.

Despite what they'd done, not everyone viewed their accomplishments in Serevadia as a good thing. Probably because they had kept the part about Serevadia and the strange elves that lived there a secret. It made their story incredibly odd and one sided, no matter how much flair Sorin put behind it. But it kept the surface from losing their minds over a new race of people below their feet and gave Viggo more time to stabilize Serevadia for the future.

"Flattery will get you everywhere," Sorin didn't miss a beat. "If it's flattery you're going with."

"Oh, I'm aware that not many are happy with what you did in Dirn-Darahl." She kept her eyes away from Sol as she spoke. "But I'm also aware that there are things stories leave out. The important part is you were duped into a dangerous mission and came back in time to keep a culture from collapsing in on itself. Perhaps people are angry over the chaos left in your wake, but a rock always leaves waves in a pond. Sometimes, disturbing the water is a good thing."

She blinked and turned to Nerezza. "I should coin that. Are you writing that down?"

The elf didn't look up. "Do you want me to?"

"If you have space."

She didn't say anything, but a tiny smile curled on her lips. Evren saw her turn the pages to a blank one and start to scribble something when Sahar turned away.

"Sorin's right." Evren nodded. "Flattery will get you everywhere."

"Oh, I know, darling."

"If you don't mind us asking, why are you so far north?" She raised an eyebrow.

Sahar sighed and swirled her coffee in her mug thoughtfully. "I must say, it wasn't my idea. As charmingly rustic as Etherak is, I prefer warmer climates. And these mountains are far from forgiving. But our esteemed leader has rightfully followed our quest here. Well, not here exactly. Further north. This is just a pitstop."

"This wouldn't happen to have anything to do with undead?" Sorin whispered.

Nerezza's head snapped up. "Why? Have you seen any?"

Evren hesitated before nodding. "Last night. Some of our party was ambushed while we were hunting in the surrounding woods."

"How many?"

"Five."

"Interesting . . ." Nerezza went back to her book. Beside her, Sahar's troubled look was enough to diminish the warmth at the table. Her deep eyes found Evren's again.

"We've been dealing with a cult that's had strange undead in their ranks throughout the continent," she explained. "They're mostly in Terevas, but our trail has led us up here. We're hoping to put an end to it."

"These aren't normal undead," Sol warned. "They have a strange light in them. One of our party has dealt with living corpses before and hasn't seen anything like it."

"And the ones we fought are natives from the nearby Ikedree clans," Evren added. "Another of our party was raised in those clans."

"Ah, a personal quest then." Sahar smiled sadly. "This must be difficult for them. I can't imagine." She shifted in her seat a little, glancing behind her as if waiting for someone to come upstairs. When no one came, she turned back to them. "I suppose this means you wish to join us?"

"The two issues are related," Sol offered. "Besides, we've been up here longer. We know the terrain. And there's strength in numbers."

Hope flitted like a baby bird in Evren's chest. She hadn't even asked. And while Sahar hadn't offered, merely guessed at their intentions, she was warm and reasonable. It seemed like a way in was actually possible. A way for Gyda to help her people was on the horizon, just within their grasp.

Sahar opened her mouth to speak, but before she could, a deeper voice interrupted her.

"What strength you find in numbers we find in ourselves. We have no need for anyone else on this quest."

They all turned to see the owner of the voice lurking a few feet away. He was a shadow of a man, and all harsh edges. The line of his jaw was square and sharp. His hair was cut short and kept out of his face. It was a common brown color, except for a streak of white near his temple. Two battle-axes sat at his hips.

Sahar, unlike everyone else at the table, seemed to relax. "Drystan! What have we talked about? Announce your presence before you ruin everyone's mood."

He stared at her a moment before nodding and turning back to them. "Apologies. My name is Drystan. And we're still not looking for extra members on this quest."

The little baby bird was smashed by the rock that was Drystan. Evren tried not to let it show.

"If it's the matter of sharing gold, I assure you we're not interested," Evren said. "This is personal for one of our members."

"It has little to do with gold."

"Then what?"

"Maybe we prefer to work on our own." He turned back to Sahar. "Vox has our supplies ready. The professor said the snow in the pass should be gone by the time we reach it."

"Wonderful." She sighed. "Here I was hoping for another snowstorm so we could stay warm a little while longer. I do hate camping."

Evren thought she imagined the small twitch of a smile at the corner of Drystan's mouth. She chose to ignore it anyway. Her porridge was cold in its bowl, but her hands were hot and shaking as she pushed herself to her feet.

"I'm trying to say this with more respect than you've given

us," she said, and drew Drystan's stony gaze to her. "I'm hoping you'll listen. I have no doubt that your team is equipped to handle this threat. We're offering to lend some assistance. Not only does one of our own know the area and the natives that live here, but we have another who knows how to deal with undead. We have a mage with us as well, and enough supplies to see us all comfortably through the Terminan and back. This is not us in any way saying you're incapable, or that we want the glory for ourselves. We just want to help."

"Your friend," Drystan added. "You want to help them, not us. In my experience, when a quest is personal, it ends badly. I don't know you, nor do I trust you, so I will not be endangering the lives of my crew by trying to do so. You have a mage? So do we." He gestured at Nerezza, who blinked up from her book. Her spell book, Evren realized too late. "I myself have worked closely with the undead, and so has another of our group. As for the terrain, we have a guide already. And the natives? That's what Lady Al-Fasil is for. We don't need, nor do we want, your help." He turned back to Sahar and Nerezza. "We're leaving in half an hour, don't be too long."

Drystan turned and walked out. Many of the people in the mess hall watched him go before quietly returning to their meals. Evren's face was hot with embarrassment as she sat back down. She forced herself to eat more porridge, despite the now terrible taste and texture.

Across the table, Sahar bit her lip. "I'm so sorry for that. Drystan . . . he means well, truly. But he's stubborn. I've found most from Melkarth are like that."

"Oh, he's from Melkarth?" Sorin asked. "Well, that explains the mood. And the pole up his ass."

"I wish I could help you," she went on. "But I'm afraid he's rather set on this. If it's any consolation, you'll be the first to know what we find in the north. We'll bring your friend some peace."

With that, the two adventurers gathered up their bowls and

left the table. As soon as they disappeared down the stairs, Sorin let his head thump loudly on the table.

"I hate making new friends," he muttered to the wood. "Why is everyone so difficult?"

"The only difficult one was Drystan." Evren took a drink of her tea and tried to think of things other than throwing it in his face. "It was like talking to a brick wall."

"Gyda won't be happy." Sorin sighed.

"Sure she will." Sol popped her chin on her hands. "We're going to follow them, right?"

"That's a terrible idea."

One that was going to happen anyway. Evren chewed her bottom lip a bit. Nothing was going to keep Gyda from returning home, and they were going to follow her regardless.

"We just have to stay hidden until the last possible minute," she told Sorin, who was peeking up through his dreads at her. "Maybe Gyda knows a way that's quicker than the one they know. We could go around them."

Sorin frowned at them both. "Never mind that we'll be caught by these new guys because, let's face it, we will. We'd be going against the Collective. Breaking the rules, doing even more damage to our reputation. No one will hire us for adventures anymore if we do this."

"It's not like we're being hired now. And it's for Gyda," Sol reminded him. "She'd do the same for us. And so would you, so don't act like you are a rule follower."

He scowled back at the table. He didn't look happy, or entirely convinced. But it was an argument he'd started knowing he wasn't going to win.

"Fine," he said, and then with a small smile added, "For Gyda. But we have to get Abraxas and Arke in on this too."

Sol whooped and stood to her feet so fast her chair turned over. "As if they'd say no!"

Evren grinned as she stood up. Sorin might be digging his heels in now, but once they were off he'd be better. And she'd see his smile again. "All right, let's go find our other halves. Sorin, you drag Arke out of bed."

He nodded and stood up, stretching. "On it. I'm fast enough he'll miss my fingers."

"Sol, can you get Abraxas?"

She nodded. "I'll talk some sense into him. Although I'm sure he's ready to kill undead regardless of the situation."

"Good. I'll try to find Gyda and get our stuff ready."

They broke away from their sunny breakfast nook and took to the stairs. From there, they split up. Evren took her time gathering up her bags first. Once she talked to Gyda, she knew she'd want to leave as soon as possible. She tucked in all her extra rations and arrows. The healing potions Elend handed out were tucked safely at the bottom, along with some extra bandages. Her bedroll and tent were rolled up as tightly as she could get them. She took the time to pack Sol's things as well, since they shared a room, but left her bag on her cot. There was a strange, budding excitement curling in her stomach as she put on her outside layers. Her fingers were buzzing so much that she could barely fasten on her cloak.

She tore outside, the pack bouncing on her back and looked around for Gyda. A day like this, Evren knew she would be outside. She liked the quiet, especially near the fence. But as she scanned the rows of tents, she didn't see her there. The livestock pen was empty, save for the horses, mules, and Keld the Demon Goat, who screamed at her from across the yard. She gave him a rude gesture with her finger and turned to look at the fences. They were all empty, except for the occasional hunter going to the bathroom.

Finally, she turned to where most of the commotion was. Where Gyda never would be willingly. The Ashen Bond was leaving, and everyone was watching them go. Drystan, Sahar, Nerezza, and the orc, which she could only guess was Vox, were all bundled up and ready to go. Beside them stood a familiar tall figure.

Evren's breath hitched in her chest. The Ashen Bond quieted the talking to silence and stepped back as she approached.

"Gyda?"

She didn't look at Evren and had a death grip on the strap of her pack. She wasn't wearing gloves, and Evren could see her knuckles were white.

"What are you doing?" Evren asked, hoping that she was wrong. Hoping that the hurt in her chest wasn't carrying in her voice.

"Going home," was all she said in reply.

"It seems like you know our guide," Drystan interjected. "She's kindly offered to take us through the Black Pass."

"You said you didn't do things that were personal," she shot back at him.

"Is this personal for you, Gyda?" He turned to her. Evren did as well, her eyes bright and pleading.

Trust me, she was trying to say without words. *Trust me as you've done before. I can get you home.*

Gyda finally met her eyes, but Evren couldn't tell what she was thinking. Her breath fogged in front of her face, and for a moment she couldn't see her at all. When it cleared, she'd turned back to Drystan.

"No, it's not."

"Well then, I trust her." He nodded to Evren's bag. "Don't do anything stupid. We'll be back."

One by one, the Ashen Bond turned and walked away. The heavy wooden gates of the outpost lifted for them, and the Reino Terminal rose to greet them. Gyda was last. She stayed rooted to the spot, staring at the ground.

Evren took a shaking step forward. Her chest was tight and uncomfortably hot. "You don't have to do this Gyda," she whispered. "We can do this on our own. Stay."

She held her hand out to her. It was shaking. From the cold or her own emotions, she wasn't sure. Gyda stared at it, and took a deep, shuddering breath.

"Don't follow me, Evren." She pulled away. "Stay here, if you care."

Evren watched her turn and walk away. Long after the gates closed behind her and she couldn't see Gyda anymore, her hand was outstretched, still waiting for her to take it.

4

Evren wanted to know why, but every possibility hurt a little more than the previous one. She swallowed down the hurt, along with the racing thoughts. How long had she stood in the snow before she let her hand drop? How long did she stare at the wooden gate, silently begging it to open, before she gave up on that too? Her feet were numb and her throat burned. She turned back to the tower just as the rest of her friends burst through the door and into the cold.

"All right! Who's ready for an adventure . . ." Sorin stopped short when he saw her face. He looked ridiculous in his heavy furs and goggles. He pulled them down to his chin, his brown eyes bright with concern. "What's with the long face, Evvie?"

Evren glanced behind him, at the rest of her friends. Sol's hopeful smile was slipping, and her eyes were scanning the yard for someone she wouldn't find. Arke was stuck like glue to Sorin's side, the new bag specifically made to hold his bulky spell book clutched tightly in his clawed hands. At the back of the group stood Abraxas. He was as still and serious as ever. Right then, Evren wished for the gentle healer rather than the stern soldier. At least his understanding was soft. She didn't say a word, so he spoke for her.

"Gyda left with them," he said. "Didn't she?"

Evren nodded.

"Wh-why?" Sorin stuttered. "What for? They're not her friends, we are!"

"She's acting as their guide," she said softly, to the snow more than him.

"Well, that's ridiculous!" His laugh had an odd edge to it. "She's our guide, right? Abraxas, back me up here."

Evren met Abraxas's eyes. They were unreadable. "It's not like we know much about her," he said gently. "She was always tightlipped, even to me. And we worked together in Dirn-Darahl before we met the rest of you. She's been different ever since she got here. Quiet, reserved. She has her reasons."

Sorin threw his hands in the air. "That doesn't mean that running off with a bunch of strangers makes any sense!"

"I did."

Sol's voice was soft enough to get drowned out by Sorin's pacing, but they all froze to look at her. Her eyes were squeezed shut, and her hand was gripping the hilt of one of her twin daggers. The same one she used to kill her King back in Dirn-Darahl. The same one that made her *krevas*, an outcast of her people, for good.

"I went with all of you into the Yawning Deep." She opened her eyes, and there was an intensity that made Evren almost take a step back. "I didn't know who you were, or what you could do beyond the idea of maybe clearing my name. I trusted all of you with more than my life. With my name and my family's legacy. Despite everything we faced, you never gave up on me, even in the end."

Sorin hesitated for a brief moment before laying his hand on Sol's shoulder. "Sol, you know we'd do it all over again for you."

"All of it?"

He flinched and took a step back. His hand went to the scar on his chest, where Heliodar had plunged a dagger into his heart. Where she'd ended him before Abraxas's miracle brought him back. The light in his eyes was gone again.

She turned to the rest of them. "If I'd known how it would end for us, I don't know if I would've gone through with it."

"Don't say that, Sol," Evren said. "We knew the dangers."

"Did we?" she shot back. "We knew nothing of Serevadia and the Mora. We knew nothing about how twisted they were, or how desperate my own people were for war. Just as we have no idea what's beyond those mountains."

She pointed north, her shaking finger showing a path through jagged peaks of black stone and thick snow. Even now, on a clear day, they were wreathed in fog and clouds that snagged on their sharp peaks. Evren always thought they looked like teeth.

"The only person who does is Gyda," she went on, dropping her hand. "There must be a reason she left us here. We're not prepared for what's in the north."

Like an unwelcome house guest, the memory of the night before sat front and center in Evren's mind. She would've liked to remember the good things about the memory, like Gyda's soft smile and how secure the bandages felt when she tied them off. The crackle of the fire and the calm serenity of the falling snow beyond the windows, like they were cut off from the harshness of the Wilds but still able to glimpse its beauty. Instead, all she could see was the pain in Gyda's eyes, and the stubborn clenching of her jaw. She heard how thick her words were with guilt, as if she was still standing next to her.

You know we've got your back. Every one of us.

That is what I'm afraid of.

"I think she's afraid," Evren breathed shakily. One by one, they all turned back to her with a mix of disbelief and shock. If there was one thing they were all sure of, it was that Gyda wasn't afraid of anything.

"Last night, she told me something," she began to explain. "About her clan, and why she hasn't been back to them. There's a time of the year, farther north, when the sun doesn't rise. It's coming soon."

"She lost her clan to it." Abraxas finally spoke, and she nodded. He sighed, shaking his head. "She's protecting us."

"Well, that ain't her choice," Arke growled. His yellow eyes were wide and bright as his pupils narrowed down to slits against the bright snow. Earmuffs covered his large, pointed ears, and made him look far less dangerous than he actually was. "You really think she's better off with a group of assholes like that?"

"Arke, you didn't meet them. They're capable people."

"They ain't us," he said firmly. "She don't need them, she needs *us*. Why the hells are we standin' around here arguing about this when we should be chasin' after her?"

Abraxas raised an eyebrow at him. "Strong words from you. And here I was thinking you didn't like to get attached to us."

The goblin scowled and shifted from foot to foot. His eyes found Evren's again, and he nodded subtly. She returned it. "Bah, you've grown on me. Like fungus."

The goblin looked over to Sol. "In or out, dwarf? You can't stay on the fence for this."

She pursed her lips into a thin line, looking for all the world like she'd say no just to spite him. But Evren knew her mind was filled with memories of the Yawning Deep and how many times Gyda put herself in harm's way to save them, to bring her home with her honor intact. It hadn't worked, but she'd fought without complaint anyway. The least Sol could do was the same.

"I'm in," she said quietly. Her sky-blue eyes flashed to Sorin. "You don't have to go. Endless nights and undead are far from your experience on the seas."

Something akin to hurt flashed on Sorin's face, but it was gone in an instant. He plastered on a wide smile—a fake one. "Neither were giant worms and underground tunnels, but I stayed with you anyway. The least I can do is the same for Gyda. So long as I'm in the back of the group when we find her. I'm not risking that temper."

In the back, Abraxas looked like a statue of black stone, but his eyes were alight with a fierce passion. When he'd made his decision, when one of the group had won him over, Evren wasn't sure. Perhaps he'd convinced himself. "To the north, then, if our tracker can find her way?"

Evren's breath caught in her throat. "I can find her," she said. *I can always find her.*

"Be that as it may, you will not be finding anything, Hanali."

Professor Elend looked entirely out of place in the sunlight. Despite it all, the scrawny human managed to make his oversized robes and threadbare blanket tossed over his shoulders look almost regal as he stalked through the snow over to them. He regarded their packed bags and readied weapons with disdain.

"I thought I made myself clear," he said. "You talked to the Ashen Bond and they said no. It's their quest, not yours."

Abraxas stood close to him, and to give Elend credit he didn't flinch. "Gyda is with them. We go where she goes."

"Gyda is with the Ashen Bond as a guide, one that I recommended," he said stiffly.

"You did what?" Sol exclaimed.

"Bastard," Arke grumbled under his breath. Evren followed that up with a few colorful curses of her own.

"I don't see the issue." Elend pushed his glasses up his nose again. "This way your friend gets what she wants, the Ashen Bond gets what they earned, and the rest of us stay where we rightfully belong." He fixed them all with a pointed stare. "I understand you want to help your friend, but she has made her choice. She went willingly and without complaint. Your presence will only complicate matters for both her and yourselves. So, you'll stay here and wait for her to return. Once she does, you'll have your merry band of misfits back together, and, until that time, I can continue my research. I trust you don't need her to hunt the wraiths."

Evren took a step forward. "You can't keep us here, Elend. We're not prisoners, and the outpost is a poor cage."

"No," he agreed. "But should you leave on this mission, I'll make sure you have no place in the Collective. Your career as adventurers will be very short-lived and you can crawl back to your homes with your meager gold and let the professionals do the work. Or . . ." he folded his arms in his blanket, a once beautiful weave from Gratey that had faded with time and age. "You can stay here and wait for her inevitable return. Only then will I grant you your leave, and my glowing recommendation will pull you from Etherak and beyond. To the colorful coasts of Gratey, and the golden deserts of Vernes, to the Fey-rich wilds of Terevas. There is a future beyond this, and I urge you all to think clearly before making a rash decision."

"You're bribing us," Evren scoffed. "Seriously? After months of sending us to fetch animals that are 'less than useful' to you, you're standing here and telling us that we can do great things with your recommendation? But only if we sit here on our hands and do nothing!"

"Oh, not nothing. I still need another wraith."

A low growl of frustration crept through Evren's throat. Her hand, once outstretched and soft to another, curled into a hard fist as she went to close the distance between her and Elend. Abraxas grabbed her shoulder and pulled her back.

"Don't," he whispered in her ear. "It's not worth it."

She shoved him away, veins boiling with fire-hot rage. "Gyda's worth it, and you know it," she hissed.

Elend had taken a step backwards and made a good show of trying not to look afraid. Under Abraxas's cold stare, he almost managed it.

"We'll talk it out," the elf said. "If you know what's best for your health, leave us alone for the day."

"Very well." Elend sniffed. "I hope you can track some common sense, Hanali."

"Hells take you, Vaughn."

"Indeed." He turned and walked back into the outpost, the door shutting firmly behind him.

Abraxas turned back to Evren, who was still seething in the snow. She imagined her anger was hot enough to melt it away, but if anything, her toes were even colder than before.

"What's there to talk out?" she snapped at him. "We'd already agreed."

"We did." He nodded. "But he raises some fine points."

"You're not serious."

"He better not be," Arke muttered.

The elf flashed him a dark look before returning to Evren. "I'm not saying I agree with Elend, but I understand what he's trying to do. We'd be interfering on another quest. Imagine how we'd feel if someone else did that to us. And then there is the matter of walking in blind. We have no idea what waits for us. I won't have another quest like Serevadia."

He stepped closer to Evren, and the snow crunched under his boots. He was close enough that his breath clouded her vision. She swallowed nervously as he lowered his voice to a whisper. "We're not doing this now. Let us wait for the cover of night."

She nearly melted in relief. Almost immediately, she felt the anger drain out from her, and all it left was her feeling cold and hollow. But, once again, there was hope. If Abraxas, the oldest and most seasoned of them, was behind this idea, how bad could it be?

"All right." She nodded. "We'll leave in style then."

He nodded and stepped back. Sorin scowled as his eyes darted between the two of them.

"So, we have a plan?"

Abraxas's grin was that of a predator. "Of course. We wait."

~

WAITING until nightfall nearly drove Evren's mind over the edge. Luckily for her, and every poor soul in Keld's Outpost, the days were very short so far north in the middle of winter. By the time the sun had set and the shadows had taken hold of the Wilds once more, the remaining Wandering Sols were discretely packed up and ready to go.

And Evren had caused a scene.

She, Sol, and Arke stumbled down the staircase away from the mess hall quickly. Behind them there was a mixed roar of confusion and laughter, interrupted every now and then by Abraxas's muffled words of apology.

"Was the food fight really necessary?" Sol whispered as she pulled a chunk of stew meat from her hair. Arke snatched it from her fingers and plopped it in his mouth, ignoring her sound of disgust as they spiraled down to the basement.

Evren shook food from her hand. "Had to sell it. And you know how much of a neat freak Elend is. He'll spend most of his night trying to clean up the mess we left."

"Lettin' us get his goodies." Arke snickered.

Sol sighed. "I regret ever telling you I learned to pick locks as a child."

"That's what happens when you decide to compare childhoods over drinks, Sol."

Above them, the din of the mess hall faded away. Abraxas would stall as long as he could, playing the apologetic leader Elend liked to imagine he was. If things calmed down too much, Sorin was there to stir shit up again. All that was left was to get into Elend's locked office and commit a crime.

Once they reached the basement level, Sol's nimble fingers made quick work of Elend's basic lock. The door swung open easily, and no magical traps went off as they stepped over the threshold. It was irritatingly bright, as usual. The heady warmth in the still air was tinged with the smell of damp fur and alchemical ingredients. Evren's nose hairs singed a little, adding a nice smokey undertone.

Evren eyed the sagging table off to the side, where the wraith's snores could be heard softly whistling through its teeth. She nodded to Arke that it was safe, and he quickly crept around to the back shelf, where a number of colorful potion bottles were stashed. The bright red of the health potions were appealing, as were the noxious green of the hydra venom Elend was so proud of. But Arke's eyes were only for the bright white ones near the end. He grabbed the lone bottle and waddled over to them.

"Time to cash in on all those hunts, eh?" he rasped, a wicked gleam in his eye.

"Let's hope Elend is as good of an alchemist as he says," Evren muttered and picked the bottle up. The white liquid was warm and seemed to hum against the glass under her fingertips. "All right, Sol and I will get us set up outside. Arke, you get the boys and meet us outside when you have the chance."

He nodded and scampered off. Evren and Sol followed him until they got to the door that led outside. Their bags and weapons were exactly where they stashed them earlier. They hurriedly put on their coats and furs, while eyeing the potion.

"Think it'll work?" Sol whispered.

"It better," was all Evren said. She uncorked the bottle and tipped it back before she could change her mind. Half the potion slid down her throat, thick as syrup and tasting like pine and frost. She held it out to Sol, who finished off the rest of the bottle, and put it in her bag.

Before their eyes, they started to disappear. The air wavered around them, like heat shimmering in the desert. When it stilled, Evren couldn't see a bit of Sol in front of her.

"Sol?" she whispered.

"Yeah?"

"It works."

Not for too long, with just one bottle between the two of them, but it would be enough for some mayhem. And *that* would be enough distraction to get everyone out in style.

Sol giggled. "Yeah. Let's go!"

Outside, the outpost was still and calm. The air was cold and biting, but the few tents set up were filled with soft breaths and sleeping noises. A group of guards shuffled back and forth to warm themselves near the gate, plums of white fog coming from their mouths. They didn't notice Evren and Sol, despite them still leaving tracks in the snow and vapor clouds trailing in their wake.

They crept across the outpost silently. In the pale white openness between the gate and the livestock pen, she felt entirely exposed. The back of her neck prickled like she was being watched, but none of the guards looked in her direction. They laughed at one another and traded a flask of something back and forth. None gave her shadowed form a second glance.

She got to the pen and let out a shaky breath. It was a vastly different place than it had been that morning. The animals were all huddled together under the small awning that sheltered them from falling snow and wind. Most of the snow had been cleared, but one thing remained the same. All the animals were as far away as possible from a particular goat.

Keld the Demon Goat snoozed on the opposite side of the pen in the open moonlight. His beard was crusted with ice crystals.

"There you are," she whispered, her grin back in place.

She reached for the latch to get into the pen with him when the same prickling sensation of being watched washed over her. She drew back, her eyes darting over to the guards. But they were still laughing over their drinks and trading the same bad joke about vampires that had been circling the outpost for weeks. She wrinkled her nose and turned to look behind her.

The figure that stood silently behind her wanted to be seen. She barely bit back a yelp of surprise as she scrambled backwards. The fence groaned beneath her as she leaned against it, chest heaving. The fear didn't last long, however. It was quickly replaced with annoyance and apprehension.

"You again," she hissed under her breath.

Sol squeaked in response and pressed closer to Evren. The cloaked figure bowed its head in response. It looked the same as it had when she saw it for the first time in Dirn-Darahl. It had saved her life then, only to urge her to dive deeper into the Yawning Deep.

It's one gold eye was the only thing she could make out from under the hood. The tattered cloak looked like it did little against the mountains' chill, but it didn't look bothered.

"Evren," Sol shuddered beside her. "Is that . . ."

"Yes," she bit out, then turned to face the figure. "What do you want?" she asked. "If you're here to keep me from going after Gyda, too, then you're in for a rude awakening."

"Of course not," it rasped, its voice low and hoarse, as if it had been screaming for years and had shredded its throat. "I'm only here to warn. And to help."

"Well, I don't have anyone for you to turn to ash tonight. Sorry."

It cocked its hooded head to the side. "You blame me for what happened in Serevadia."

"You knew what would happen, didn't you?"

"Yes."

"And you didn't warn me!" she could barely keep her voice down.

"I did."

"Vague omens of danger don't count." She poked a finger at it. "So spill your useless bullshit and leave."

Something that might've been a laugh rumbled in its chest. "Useless? Such as an empty bow in the snow."

Evren froze. "That was you?"

"Of course,"

Sol muttered a Dwarvish curse, drowned out by Evren's own voice.

"You've been watching me."

"All of you. But I don't need to clean up after the others."

She narrowed her eyes at the figure, sure that was an insult, but less sure how to respond. Instead, she felt for her bow slung over her back. Familiar, reliable, and a taste of home. She felt a hollow ache in her heart at the thought.

"What's in the north?" she asked. "I swear, if you say ice, I will take out your last shiny eye."

The figure seemed to muse on the question for a bit, as if weighing how vague and riddle-like it could talk without losing an appendage. Finally, its cloaked shoulders shrugged.

"The Long Night awaits you there. The Expanse on which you will make your final stand will be far from dark, however. You'll have all the tools you need, should you keep your friends and the Bond together."

She wrinkled her nose. "We have to work with them?"

"If you are to succeed, yes."

"Fine." But she wasn't finished yet. "In Serevadia, I had two people tell me my blood was magic. What did they mean?"

"That I cannot elaborate on." It sighed. "All I can say is that they were correct, and such magic comes at a price. As does all power."

"I don't know how to use it." Evren bit her lip. "Bleeding does something to me, but it has to be more than that."

"Look to other forms of magic to help. They are all connected."

She took a breath. Sol spoke before she could, her voice strong despite the shaking Evren could feel. "All right. Is that all? Cryptic messages and vague answers?"

She swore she could hear its smile in its voice. "Beware of the night, but fear the lights that thrive in it more."

With a cloud of smoke, the figure suddenly vanished and left them alone in the snow. She bit back another curse as she looked down at her hands. The edges of her fingers were shimmering back into sight. The potion was wearing off. They didn't have much time left.

She could feel Sol's burning gaze, but they both knew they didn't have time to talk. If anything, the sight of the figure that heralded dangers and mystery seemed to drive home even more the need to get to Gyda.

Evren turned back to the pen and this time found Keld's

demonic eyes staring right at her. Without breaking eye contact, she lifted the latch and the gate swung open.

He flicked his ears back in confusion, and she stepped in. She fully expected him to start screaming, as he always did, but he kept silent for once. She crept around him towards the horses and mules, who were all fast asleep. She untied their harnesses if they had any, and otherwise freed them from sleep and rope both.

She scratched between one of the mule's ears. "Ready to cause some trouble?"

It just blinked sleepily at her.

She ducked around the groggy, but now awake group of animals, and pulled out a singular arrow. Keld the Demon Goat regarded her warily before deciding that she wasn't worth his time more than sleep was and turned his back to her. Nothing bad ever happened to Keld. Elend didn't allow it. So why would the goat fear anything?

Evren flipped the arrow over in her palm until the fletching was pointed out. Then she drew her arm back and whacked it across the goat's ass as hard as she could.

Keld's demonic scream could've been heard all across Etherak. It was bloodcurdling, and much more demonic than goat-like. Even better? It did exactly what she thought it would do.

The horses and mules, and one very confused chicken, all ran out of the pen in a panic. Keld caught the first sign of movement and bolted after it. The unlucky chicken was the last one out of the pen, and the first Keld set his sights on. He screamed bloody murder as it ran after the squeaking chicken. Feathers and snow went flying. Horses and mules scattered through the yard, dodging tents as the chicken and Keld ran along the fence line screaming at each other.

"Perfect." Evren laughed as she put her arrow back in her quiver and hunkered down in the pen. Sol, becoming more visible by the second, joined her. Her smile was showing through the potion.

The chicken did some work, but Keld was the real chaos worker. All the guards were scrambling after the goat, who was running after the chicken, who was trying very hard to follow the horses but kept getting confused so it just ran in zig zags through the yard. From horse to mule, back to another terrified horse, it was a glorious mess.

And the perfect cover.

As everyone from the outpost case outside to help, the rest of the Wandering Sols snuck into the empty animal pen. Arke was covered in feathers, and Sorin could barely keep his laughter at bay. Abraxas nodded to them both in turn.

"I see the theft worked in our favor," he said, distaste only slightly dampening his words.

Sol pulled some rope out of her bag and dug around for her grappling hook. "It's not stealing if we did all the heavy lifting. We just took a little compensation, that's all." She tossed the hook over the fence and pulled to make sure it was secure. Before Abraxas could say another word, she scrambled up the rope and over the edge. Sorin and Arke followed quickly.

Abraxas held the rope out to Evren, and she took it gratefully. Sounds of Keld's battle with the chicken were winding down. They'd be discovered soon. She climbed up the rope with some difficulty. Her hands didn't grip well in her gloves and the fence was painfully slick, so she had to rely on nothing but her arms. But soon she made it over the top. She narrowly avoided the spikes at the edge and dropped down on the other side beside her friends.

Her feet tingled painfully for a moment, but she breathed in the crisp night air in glee. It smelled like freedom.

Minutes later, Abraxas was over the edge. He pulled the rope and hook down with him. They all stood at the fence panting a bit. Sweat gleamed on their foreheads, and the thrill of escaping hummed like lightning in their veins.

Sol gathered up her rope and hook in her bag while the others looked at her. She smiled giddily.

"Right," Evren breathed, sharing her grin. "We won't have much of a head start, so let's put as much distance between us and the outpost as possible. I doubt Elend will send anyone after us, but I'd rather be safe than sorry. I assume the Ashen Bond aren't worried about being followed, so I'll track them easily. Ready?"

They all nodded, and from his spot at Sorin's side, Arke bared all his pointed teeth in a goblin-like smile. "Let's go get our girl back."

5

They traveled as far as they could and as long as they dared before setting up camp. Maybe it was a little foolish to light a fire, but Evren wouldn't go the night without it. The Reino Terminan could sneak its way into their furs in the night and end their adventure before it even began. If a fire drew predators, they'd deal with them. If Elend and the outpost came for them, they'd deal with them, too. She wasn't going to freeze to death.

Taking watch was easy. They'd gotten into a routine in Serevadia, and that hadn't broken during their travels. Abraxas always took the first watch, no matter what. He had a habit of not waking anyone for the next watch but was slowly breaking out of it. If only because Sol took watch with him and made sure he did.

Watching in pairs kept Abraxas from overextending himself, and two pairs of eyes were better than one. Abraxas and Sol, Arke and Sorin, and Evren and Gyda. Only now they were uneven, and the absence was weighing more than she thought it would.

The early hours where the sun had yet to break were still and quiet. The fire had settled down to cooling embers, and Evren wrapped herself tightly in her furs. Frost had encrusted the forest around them. It would be a beautiful sight when the sun rose.

Her eyes combed the surrounding trees, but nothing stirred. She kept as still as possible, a sentinel in the gathering dawn, but her mind was not the same. Thoughts and unbidden fears swirled like a hurricane behind her narrowed eyes. They were always there, of course. She only *acted* reckless and without fear. But that was easy with people she trusted, and who trusted her in return. Evren could do things with the Wandering Sols that she could never do on her own, and facing her fears was one of them.

But a figure spouting words of caution and of the dark future never helped. She'd seen it before and took it as a sign that she didn't have a choice but to go forward. Now, it was pushing her out as she was racing towards the unknown on her own. The fear was there, as always, curled like a viper in her chest waiting to strike. Sol seeing it too only made it more real.

Fear was good. It was useful, and always there for a reason. Fear had been the only thing that kept her alive when she was on her own. But now? When she had a group of people that watched her back and relied on her? What was better suited, fear or courage?

Like pain, fear was useful to an extent. She had yet to find the end of it.

Almost instinctively, Evren pulled her hand out from her furs. The glove slipped off easily and the biting winter air immediately stinging her exposed skin. She fought the urge to curl her fingers into a fist and fight for warmth. All she could see was the jagged scar that ran across the length of her palm. Not a clean line like a blade would leave. Looking at it, she could almost feel the rock breaking the skin open. She could taste the desperation on her tongue and hear the ground start to break under her feet.

She shivered and put her glove back on. Alkimos would never leave her. She could almost feel him now, at the edge of her mind. Whatever she'd done, because she still wasn't sure, had yet to fully break.

Such was the price of power. Or whatever she'd managed to get herself into.

Behind her, Evren heard some shuffling and low grumbling curses as someone rose from their sleep. She didn't turn around but was surprised to see Arke waddle up beside her and plop down on the cold ground. His white hair was a massive, spiked mess sticking up in all directions. It would've been comical, had the goblin not been known for being nearly murderous in the early morning.

"You're up early," she said softly.

He grunted.

"Couldn't sleep?"

Arke shrugged. He only looked at her as she tucked her arm back into her furs. Those large yellow eyes weren't as good at Evren's, but they caught enough.

"You all right?"

She blinked at him in surprise, and he scowled at her. "Don't get the wrong idea, you've just got that look."

Evren couldn't shake her smile. "Are you worried about me?"

"You're fuckin' weird and I'm askin' if you're okay is all." He sunk further into his cloak.

"I'm weird?"

"Lookin' at your hand again."

Almost as if the mere mention of it was enough to draw some sort of reaction, her scar started to prickle underneath her glove. She winced and tried not to fiddle with it.

"It's fine."

"Didn't ask that."

"Ass," she muttered, and he gave a little chuckle. After a minute of silence, she let out a weighty, cloud-spun breath into the air. "I don't know, Arke. I feel weird."

"You are weird."

"Thanks."

"You never did tell us how you got Alkimos to work with you."

A piece of black hair fell in Evren's eyes, and she brushed it away. She could feel the heavy, cold weight of the winter air on her cheeks. "I wish I knew myself," she admitted. "I think . . . I think there's something wrong with my blood."

"What, like a disease?"

"No! Like . . ." she struggled for the words. "There's things that happened down in Serevadia I can't explain. And they all happened when I was bleeding."

Arke gave her a weird look. "We did almost die a lot."

"I know that. But Ainthe and Viggo mentioned it several times. There's something about my blood they thought was powerful. Ainthe feared it, and Viggo was fascinated. It kept me from dying when Ainthe's shadows nearly killed me in Alkimos' nest. Apparently it also made me immune to the poison on their blades. And I can't explain it, but the pain and the bleeding it . . ." She paused, and the quiet grey of the world descended like a blanket over her. She didn't understand what she was saying and, judging by Arke's furrowed brow, he didn't either. But it had been nagging at her from the moment Ainthe mentioned it. Saying it out loud couldn't be any worse than locking it up in her head.

"I like the pain," she said finally. "It makes things clearer for me, like I can suddenly see better, and move faster. Like there's this moment of clarity where everything is simpler and easier. Like the act of drawing blood gives me . . . something, I don't know! Help me out here."

Arke stared at her for a while, his face unreadable. A soft breeze ruffled his hair and made him squint his eyes to look at her. Worry, twin viper to fear, reared her ugly head back, and Evren suddenly wanted to snatch every word from the air and swallow them back.

"I still think you're fuckin' weird," he said finally. "I ain't met someone who enjoys pain."

"Small amounts," she countered. "Everything still hurts and eventually it gets to the point where it's too much. I can't focus."

"Like a regular wound,"

She rolled her eyes. "Yes."

"I ain't ever heard of blood magic," he said slowly. "But, then again, I'm still learnin' myself. Could be you got somethin' weird. Somethin' new."

"Maybe." Evren wanted to tear at her fingers again, but remembered the gloves so she started chewing on her bottom lip. "I think that's how I got Alkimos to help. There was a moment when one of his spikes broke, and I grabbed it to keep from falling off. With my hurt hand. It was like when our blood mixed, I could see through his eyes, and he could see through mine. We were each other but still separate."

"Right . . ." he drew out. "I'll say again, fuckin' *weird.*"

Evren allowed herself a small laugh because it was. It was ridiculous and strange, and she'd been bottling it up for months, because who could understand it if she didn't? She sounded insane. But Arke didn't look at her like she'd lost her mind. He just looked thoughtful and a little bewildered.

"Look, I don't know what to say," he said. "But, hells, if I can help you figure out what this is, I will."

"You will?" She tried to keep the shock from her voice.

"You have a habit of comin' back from every fight covered in blood." He eyed her knowingly. "One day, you might spill too much. I don't know much about magic, but I do know one thing."

"What?"

"Shit's dangerous if you don't know the limits. If you start messin' with it and have no clue how far you can go, one day you'll go too far. For me, that could mean a lot of things, from turnin' myself into a plant to rippin' a hole in a mountain. For you? I think that could be a whole lot more painful, and personal. Let's try not to do that."

The figure's words about magic and exploring other branches

to figure out more of her own suddenly came to mind, and she couldn't help but smile. She suddenly opened her arms and enveloped him in a hug. Arke hissed and went completely stiff, as he did every time. But eventually he started to soften and patted her arm awkwardly.

"Thanks," she murmured. "For not calling me crazy."

"Oh, you're crazy," he huffed. "But I like your crazy."

Dawn broke lazily. The dark skies lightened to a dull grey, heavy with clouds that pressed down oppressively. All around, the frost crystals glistened in the low light, and for a moment, the world felt like a still and dazzling portrait. She almost didn't want it to end.

But no matter the talk of blood and magic, one thing remained the same—they had to find Gyda.

THE CHANGE in their surroundings as they stepped out of the Wilds and into the bare mountains was drastic. The trees gave way to grey, frosty rock. The wind whipped through their hair, and the sudden feeling of being incredibly small in the shadow of the mountains overwhelmed Evren. The Enrial Wilds had acted as a shield to the true harshness of the Reino Terminan. As hard as life was in Keld's Outpost, it was livable. That was far behind them now.

Evren wanted to cover as much ground as possible before the sky inevitably covered them in snow. The further they traveled from the outpost, the worse the weather was getting, and the still grey of the morning had long since been replaced by howling winds and piercing cold. Despite their winter gear, Evren feared it wouldn't be enough.

She buried her nose into her scarf, fighting the numbness as she marched forward. Their trail had turned very narrow, and they could only walk single file. Patches of slick ice clung stubbornly, and the trail had a bad habit of dropping off into sudden, sheer drops out of nowhere.

And it was getting harder to track the Ashen Bond and Gyda by the hour.

By midday, Evren had made them stop in a small alcove. It was a tight fit, but it was out of the wind and cold. Everyone's breaths were bouncing off the walls, and outside the wind lurked like a stalking predator waiting to throw them off the mountain side. It could very well get its wish if they weren't careful.

"How far is the Black Pass?" Abraxas asked. He had ice encrusted on his eyebrows and eyelashes.

"Not too much farther," she admitted. "But we'll be lucky to get there before the weather kicks in."

"And the Bond?"

"Had a head start. They traveled lighter than us as well. The wind isn't helping their tracks either."

"But you haven't lost them?"

"No." *Not yet.* "But if they didn't get through the Black Pass before the weather hit, they'd have to wait out the storm. And by then they'd be truly lost."

"So, uh, quick question." Sorin raised his hand. "What are we doing after the pass?"

Sol nudged him. "Getting Gyda back of course."

"Yeah, well, her temper might say otherwise. And we don't know where we're going, do we?"

"Gyda will," Evren said. "And the Ashen Bond."

"Again, once they find us they're not going to be happy. Who's to say they'll even work with us?"

Abraxas laid a hand on his shoulder. "We'll convince them."

Arke cackled and sounded more like a wind spirit than a goblin. "Or we don't give them a choice!"

Sorin sighed and shook his head. "Why did I expect anything less?"

Evren frowned. "You can always go back, Sorin."

"Oh no, I'm fine. I'm just cold and miserable and can't feel my nose. I'll get over it once it falls off."

Sorin did not, in fact, get over it. But his groans of complaint and discomfort were easily drowned out by the wind. Once they picked up their pace through the mountains, the wind tried to tear them off the rocks and toss them over the Black Pass. If Evren thought they'd land all right, she was tempted to let it. But she kept her feet firmly on the ground and one hand on the rocks beside her. Slick shards of ice and snow flew through the air and tried to worm their way through her layers. And that was just the snow the weather was picking up. Abraxas's banished gods had better help them if they were caught in the brunt of the storm.

Leading the group slowly through the mountain trails, Evren rounded a sharp corner. Her hands fumbled with the other side, tentatively seeking a grip should the trail suddenly fall out beneath their feet. As she pulled herself around, she let herself look up from the ground. And her breath caught in her sore throat.

The Black Pass was not easily missed.

The dull grey rock that made up the Reino Terminal suddenly fell away into sharp, glossy black stone that stood out starkly from the white snow. The stone itself was smooth and arched in an elegant curve to the sky on either side of the pass. Pieces of the stone looked as sharp as swords, their edges gleaming as they pointed towards the heavens. The Black Pass looked like something had carved the mountain in two, and the resulting blast had created a cruel, beautiful work of art only the desperate could see. Like a beacon drawing them closer, Evren let out a sigh of relief.

It was short-lived.

"We can't walk through it." She turned back, her voice loud enough to contend with the wind whipping at her hair.

"Why not?" Abraxas called.

She pointed back to the pass, but along the bottom of it.

What should've been a somewhat smooth and easy trail along the bottom was covered in giant, jagged spikes of black. It looked like a graveyard of broken spears and swords—if all the weapons were much larger than themselves. There was no room to get through them, and the idea of crawling through them in some vain hope of a path sent Evren's skin prickling with fear. No one was meant to walk that path.

"So, what now?" Sol asked.

Abraxas shook his head. "People use this path all the time. Travelers and natives alike."

"We can't walk that!" she argued. "The wind coming through there could rip us to shreds along those stones. We'd be as good as dead."

"So how do the Ashen Bond expect to get through it?" he pressed. "There has to be another path, another trail."

"Over." Arke grunted. "Along the sides."

Sorin laughed nervously. "Surely not! There's no way to hold on."

But even as he protested it, Evren knew Arke was right. She couldn't see the path from her vantage point, but what other choice was there? Her stomach felt like an unending pool of dread, and she tried to shake the feeling off.

"Arke's right." She nodded to the goblin. "It'll be a trail with one side open to the air. Sheer drop, so we'll have to be careful."

"Again, I say we will have no grip!" Sorin countered. "The wind will snatch us right off."

"We have each other," Abraxas said, with an attempt at a comforting smile. Sorin didn't look comforted. "Have faith."

The Vasa bristled at that and took a step back. He looked at Evren and she raised an eyebrow at him. She wouldn't force him to go, and his fears were valid. She just didn't know where they ended and his courage began.

He nodded to her curtly, his jaw set. "Fine. But if we survive this, I demand a nice vacation in a warm area with flat land, all right?"

"I second that!" Sol said.

It was something they could all agree on. That, and tying a rope between all of them. Evren didn't know if it would actually help or if it would send them all to their deaths if one of them fell, but she felt better tying it around her waist anyway.

The climb to the Black Pass was easier than she expected. The wind seemed to be dying down to let them get there, just to throw them off the side. She tried not to think about that when the grey rocks turned to black under her feet, and she could see her reflection staring back at her. She tried not to think about how long the fall would be if she did lose her footing, and which of the strange rocks would impale her. She looked up instead, and her stomach dropped. The pass's unusual design nearly blocked out the sun entirely. Her neck hurt from looking up. She felt as small and insignificant as possible in its shadow, and some childish part of her wanted to curl up in a ball and hide.

Whatever had made the Black Pass had been monstrous, and she was glad it was long gone.

Arke was right though. The path cut into the side was marked with a faded red flag that hung limply against the rocks. The path behind it was cut out by hand, and narrow. There was very little, if anything, to hold onto.

Evren was still in the lead, and she felt Sol nudge her from behind. She didn't look back, and hesitantly put her foot on the trail. It was a step up, and she could feel her boot slide against the slick surface as she hauled herself up. Her left hand found the side of the pass that soared high above them, and the right gripped the rope between her and Sol.

I wish Gyda were here.

The thought came out of nowhere, but it wasn't surprising. Gyda would be good to anchor them against the wind. She was incredibly strong and could easily pull a few of them up if they fell. Evren would feel better if she was with them. Now, she just felt far too weightless against the shrieking wind.

It tore through the pass like a banshee, and Evren couldn't

help but feel like it had a mind of its own as it slithered between the blades of jagged rocks and tugged at her clothes. She inched along, foot by shaking foot, and tried not to look down. That never helped.

A quarter of the way through the pass, and Evren was as tense as a drawn bowstring. She was grinding her teeth but couldn't force herself to stop. Her jaw ached and her legs cramped. But she kept going. One foot at a time. That was all she could do.

Something out of the corner of her eye moved. Far below, like the stones themselves had shifted. Evren froze.

Sol bumped into her, and she gripped the stone to keep from falling.

"What's wrong?" Sol asked.

Evren's eyes scanned the bottom of the Black Pass. There was so much empty air between her and the rocks she felt sick just looking down. But as she stared, she willed something to move. The alternative being her mind was playing tricks on her, and she didn't need that as a problem. But as she stared, nothing moved. She didn't relax.

"I thought I saw something," she said, and tried to swallow her unease. It didn't work.

"Look!"

Sorin pointed ahead of them. Squinting against the wind, Evren could make out a couple of shifting figures moving slowly along the path ahead of them. For a jarring moment, she thought they were moving towards them, and her hand immediately went for her bow. But she forced herself to relax when she realized they were moving away.

The Ashen Bond.

Evren took a hopeful step forward. No matter how much shit she was bound to get for finding them, they were a welcome sight. But as she did, movement at the bottom of the pass caught her eye again. Quick as lightning and hurtling up the side of the pass like a galloping spider.

And headed straight for the Ashen Bond.

"Gyda!" Evren's cry of alarm was snatched away by the cruel wind. She watched as the figure leapt over the side of the trail and launched itself at them. It was met with a singular axe to the face, another swiftly through the chest, and was tossed back into the depths.

"We've got company!" Abraxas drew his sword, and the ring of metal drew her attention away from the Ashen Bond.

She watched in horror as more of the creatures crawled up the wall, their eyes glowing with a strange bluish-green light, and their frozen faces staring at her in horror.

Undead.

Evren drew her bow and yelped as her elbow smarted against the wall at her back. She didn't have much room to work with.

She fired an arrow instinctively into the eye of an undead coming over the side. It didn't even flinch, and she fired another arrow into its chest. The light in its dead eyes fluttered out, and it fell back into the pass.

She nocked another arrow as Arke sent a wave of fire down the side of the pass, scorching the stone and air. An unholy shriek tore through the air and several of them fell, the light in their eyes burning with hate.

Abraxas stood at the back, his shield raised and the only barrier that kept the wave of undead from overwhelming them. They clawed at his shield and tried to push him back, but he never wavered. His sword, blackened from fires of ages past, tore through the air and through the chests of two separate undead. Four more took their place.

And more were coming.

They were piled on top of each other, crawling up the wall with a fervor unknown to the living. They were scrambling to cut the Sols' way forward, long, icy limbs sneaking up the lip of the path. She could hear the cracking of bones and the smacking of dead flesh even over the wind and shouting. It was like they'd been lying in wait.

Sol turned to Evren, her eyes wide with fear and the edges of her dagger gleaming in the light. "We've got to get out of the pass! There's no way we can hold out here."

But they couldn't move as one. Not with Abraxas holding the back. Evren and Sol knew that immediately.

The dwarf took her dagger and sliced through the rope tying the two of them together. "Get to them! We'll be right behind you."

Evren didn't wait to see if Sol would keep her word, she took off down the trail.

She ran, weightless, her feet barely touching the glassy surface of the pass. She was also fearless, and that was much more dangerous. She tore down the narrow path, could see the Ashen Bond ahead of her. They were stuck, just like she'd been, fighting with their backs to the wall.

An undead leapt into the path ahead of her, it's gaping mouth wide and black. Her arrow sunk deep into its heart, and she leapt over its body long before it fell off the side. Another arrow fell into her bow, and she let it sing through the air and hit an undead clawing at the tall figure in the back.

Their head snapped up. She couldn't tell if it was Vox or Gyda, all she could see was their height and more undead. Just as they turned around, something ice-cold slammed into Evren from the side.

Evren hit the ground hard, and panic seized her as her legs dangled over the open edge of the cliff. The undead on top of her smelled of rot as it clawed at her. She took her arrow and with a cry jammed it into its heart. Its light flickered, and it stilled. It started to slide off of her, but it's frigid fingers wouldn't let go. It was falling, and it was taking her with it.

The corpse fell, and Evren joined it. Her fingers scrambled to find some purchase but found nothing but smooth stone. The air fell out from under her as she slipped down the side, the wind tearing the scream straight from her lungs.

A hand grasped hers and pulled her up sharply. The weight

lifted from her legs as the corpse shook free. She grasped her savior's arm and hauled herself up and over the edge. They gripped her shoulders tightly and kept her close to the wall as she heaved and struggled for breath.

She found Gyda staring down at her.

Evren struggled for words, and they all slipped through her fingers like sand. There was so much to say, but she could still feel herself falling and hear the screams of the undead and fighting.

"Don't be mad," she said instead, her voice an octave too high.

Gyda said nothing. She turned behind her as the rest of their party fell back. Arke was slinging fire left and right, and Abraxas was the only thing keeping them from being overwhelmed.

Behind her, a sharp, commanding voice broke through the fighting. "Nerezza!"

Evren turned to see Drystan kick another undead into the chasm below. The two axes in his hands were coated with dark blood, and his face was grim. Beside him, Sahar somehow managed to look frightfully polished in the middle of the battle. The wind swept her long black hair from her bun, and she looked wild as it flew free. She tossed a bottle of something down at the climbing pile of undead, and it exploded in a cloud of eerie white fire.

"Nerezza!" Drystan called again.

The elf in question looked like the calm in the middle of the storm as she flicked through her spell book. She was far from bothered by the chaos around her, but when she looked up there was a cold fury in her eyes. She tore two pages from her book, which hovered in the air in front of her. She crumbled them into her fists, her mouth moving soundlessly as arcane glyphs sparked to life where the papers had been. They swirled around her arms until she brought her hands together.

A wave of fire tore through the Black Pass. It was hot enough to turn winter into summer for a few glorious seconds. The stench of burnt flesh and hair filled Evren's nostrils and she tried not to gag. Fire was all she could see as it swept over the pass and then further down. It caught the fleeing undead and enveloped them in a fiery embrace. Evren was glad the wind drowned out their screams.

Nerezza let her hands fall and grasped her book from the air, breathing hard. Drystan turned to see Evren and her party behind them. He scowled.

"To the end of the pass," he barked. "Quickly!"

There were no complaints. Drystan held the back of the Ashen Bond as Sahar led them through. The path was slippery, and the wind was still trying to knock them off, but her feet were sure and steady. Behind them, the crackling of flames had subsided, and Evren could hear the undead pick back up the chase.

They flew through the Black Pass as fast as they dared, the wind and the dead at their heels. The end of the black stone was abrupt. They stumbled through the edge of the Black Pass, one after the other. The spine of the next mountain was sharp and unforgiving, but Evren welcomed it.

They ran until the Black Pass was a dark stain on the landscape, until the sharp mountain air felt like it was stabbing their lungs. One by one, they all slowed down, then collapsed on the ground.

Evren felt snow seep into her clothes, but she didn't care. She could barely catch her breath, and her grip on her bow was so tight she didn't think she could ever will her fingers to let go. All she could see were glowing eyes and black stones waiting for her fall. She squeezed her eyes shut and willed the images away. Anything but that. She'd seen death before, and she was not eager to see it again.

When she opened her eyes, she saw Gyda above her. Her icy eyes were cold with the fury of a thousand blizzards. Her sword was still in her hand, and the rage that flowed off her in waves should've scared Evren. It didn't.

"I told you not to follow me," she hissed under her breath. "I asked you not to."

"Gyda—"

"You didn't listen!" She pointed at her with the tip of her sword. Too far away to do any damage, but the message was clear.

Evren pulled herself to her feet and tried to keep her hands from shaking. "We came to help you."

"I asked you not to."

"Yes, well, turns out we value you a lot more than common sense."

"We are not even into the thick of this and you nearly died!" This time the sword pointed at the Black Pass behind them. "Why couldn't you just listen to me?"

Evren started to protest, but Sahar cleared her throat behind them. Both of them, still shaking with anger and a riot of other emotions, turned to look at her.

"Not to break up this lovely little feud, but we have bigger problems." She pointed to the horizon where a blur of white and whipping snow was hurtling towards them. The storm was on them at last.

6

T he only good thing about imminent death was how it forced people who would rather strangle each other into working together. No matter how much the Wandering Sols and the Ashen Bond would rather argue until they were blue in the face, they'd all prefer to be alive to do it later. And there were few things in the Reino Terminan that would kill them quicker than a blizzard.

Evren couldn't tell if she was relieved or disappointed, however. Things needed to be said, but the mountains were having none of it.

Think, Hanali, she urged herself. They needed shelter first. Not much to go on so high up on the mountains.

"We need cover. We'll be corpses in minutes out here."

Sahar gathered her hair out of her face, her dark eyes scanning the mountain but always straying towards the coming storm. "A cave, perhaps?"

"Any cave will be occupied." Gyda sheathed her sword and moved away from Evren. She felt herself deflate a bit. The confrontation was over, for now.

"Hells, even some trees or a particularly large rock would do," Evren said. "We have to get out of the wind before it hits."

"Survive many blizzards, have you?" Drystan asked drily.

She bristled at that. Mostly because she hadn't. Evren was a hunter, a tracker, and had lived the majority of her life in the wilderness. She knew nothing of the north, however, and only a little of blizzards, based on what she'd learned at Keld's Outpost. But the basis of survival was always the same, blizzard or not. "I know how to make a shelter that'll keep you alive. You're welcome to stay out here, however."

Drystan opened his mouth to argue and took a step forward. Everything about the man was menacing, as if he was cut from the same stone as the Black Pass; sharp and cruel and cold. But just as he got closer, Sahar laid her hand on his arm. He stopped and looked down at the finely made glove and then back at her. She shook her head.

"We don't have time to argue," she urged, then nodded back at Evren and her party. "We work with them to survive the storm, and then we'll deal with the consequences."

He frowned, and for a moment she thought he'd brush her off entirely. But a whisper of a sigh left his lips and he nodded. When he turned back to Evren, his mouth was set in a firm line, almost as if he was in pain at the mere idea of working with her.

"Fine. What do we need to do?"

"Cover, first and foremost," Evren said again. "Our tents won't last on the mountain face. Gyda, do you know any place close by?"

As one, they all turned to where Gyda stood away from them. Her face was stony and unreadable, her eyes narrowed against the biting wind. Evren followed her gaze down the slope of the mountain. A thick swath of trees stood out sharply in a ravine cut into the mountain's side. Not a forest by any means, but a chance, if they could make it in time.

Evren moved past everyone to stand beside Gyda. At the edge of the mountain path, the wind was colder, and she shivered in her furs. Beside her, Gyda was as immovable as the mountain itself.

"Can you get us there?" she asked quietly.

All that replied for a while was the wind, and Evren thought she'd ignore her. When she looked up, Gyda had her eyes closed.

"Yes," she murmured, so softly that the word almost didn't make it to her, as if it weighed the world.

Evren turned back to the two adventuring parties, a plan in her head, a storm at her back, and something stirring in her chest.

~

THE RACE to the trees was no easy thing, even with Gyda showing them the hidden trails to follow. The mountain slope was slick and steep, and hidden patches of ice lay in wait with every other foothold. But they made it down in time, wind nipping at their heels and snow kicking up a trail behind them.

The trees were nearly bare. Evren chose to ignore how much the branches looked like grasping finger bones and set to work on the shelter.

Individual shelters would take too long, and with no hope for a fire, they'd need each other's body heat. Evren got everyone to take out their tents, and with some struggling that only ended when Sahar figured out what she was trying to do, they started scrambling together one large tent. Detaching poles from one tent, taking the canvas and pinning it to another. Evren muttered incomplete ideas, and Sahar's mind managed to put them together into something coherent. Before long, both parties were working in tandem. Passing out supplies, shoveling out snow, cutting down extra tree limbs. Desperation tinged the quickly whipping air. Evren could taste it on the back of her throat.

Evren looked up long enough to see it. Abraxas had set his shield aside to hammer down the posts with Drystan and Vox. Nerezza and Arke melted snow the best they could while Gyda and Sorin shoveled the rest out of the way. Sahar, Sol, and Evren were nailing down and securing the canvases that would keep the snow out. No easy task, but it was all they had. For a moment, in the grim quiet, they looked like one big team.

The snow was cleared, the poles were set, and the canvas was pieced together large enough to cover it all. A patchwork of greys, browns, and threadbare greens, but it was enough.

Just barely.

The last knot was tied as the world suddenly went white.

The wind hit her like a bull, and Evren barely kept on her feet. She clung tightly to the side of the tent, gasping as snow clung to every inch of her. The white was both blinding in its brightness and suffocating in the sheer volume of it. She could feel the snow dragging her eyelashes down, the ice coating them so thick that they would stick to her face when she squeezed her eyes shut. What the lashes didn't catch flew right into her eyes. The tiny pieces of snow felt like daggers, and she hissed in pain. The snow worked its way through her layers, down to her skin, where it stayed there, chilling her to her very bones.

But it was better than the mountain. She had to keep reminding herself that, even as her body revolted at the strange numbing pain.

The wind suddenly changed directions, and Evren stumbled forward. Her hand still stayed on the tent, and she forced her eyes open, shielding them as best she could with her other hand. It did little to help.

She needed to find the others. Who all was still caught outside the tent with her? Desperation suddenly wasn't just an aftertaste; she was drowning in it.

Evren stumbled forward, always keeping her hand on the tent even if she couldn't see it. She willed her eyes to see some-thing, anything, besides white.

Let me find them.

As she forced herself forward, the haze of white parted for a shadow in the snow. She lunged forward and grabbed their arm as they started to walk away from both her and the tent and pulled them back. They fought only for a moment, before the wind changed direction again, and sent them tottering back into her. She grabbed their forearm, their shoulders were much too tall for her, and made them face her.

Vox wiped the snow from his face as best he could, his eyes hazy and unfocused as he swayed in her hand.

"You all right?" she called over the storm. Snow flew in her mouth and made her choke on any other words. Vox gripped her hand tightly to right himself and nodded.

"Where is everyone else?" she asked.

He shook his head, snow flying from his long hair. He leaned forward so the wind wouldn't snatch his voice away. Even still, she had to strain to hear him.

"Nerezza wasn't in the tent. I went to find her."

Evren's stomach plummeted at the thought of the spindly elf being caught in the snowstorm. However powerful her magic was, she was more likely to be blown away than last long out here.

"Anyone else?" she shouted. Her throat was going to pay later if they survived.

Again, Vox shook his head, and Evren felt a surge of both guilt and relief. Her people were safe in the tent. All that was left was her and half of the Ashen Bond.

The survivor in her told her to leave Nerezza. Surely a mage of such power had a spell to find her way back. She and Vox had little to help them survive, and if they left the safety of the tent, they had no way of getting back.

But Nerezza had saved her life in the Black Pass, and everyone else's as well. Besides Gyda, Evren was the best suited to find her. And Evren wasn't going to call Gyda out when she was already in the thick of it.

"Got any rope left?" she asked Vox.

"Not much." He pulled out a coil of rope. Evren guessed it to be only twenty feet long. Not a lot of room. She took it anyway and fumbled with the knot work as she tied it to one of the posts. She took the other end and tied it to her waist, all the while swaying with the wind and trying not to lose her footing.

She tightened the knot. "Get back in the tent. Follow the canvas until you find the opening, it should be easy to open so long as someone is there to help you."

"No."

"What?"

Vox looked uncomfortable, but she couldn't tell if that was from the storm stinging their skin, or the weight of Evren's gaze.

"I swore to protect all of them," Vox said. "Nerezza included. I'm going with you."

No time for arguing, especially with an orc that weighed twice as much as she did. "Right, hold my hand then. And don't let go. I'm your tether back to the tent."

He nodded and took her outstretched hand. She couldn't feel any warmth between their thick gloves, but he was something solid to hold on to as the wind and ice tore at her from every direction. Together they stepped away from the tent, and the blizzard swallowed them whole.

Even with the rope, Evren felt like she was going to fly away. Around her, all she could see was white. Occasionally the dark sentinel of a tree would pop into view, but almost always when she was only inches away from running into it. Fear clawed at her throat. Fear that she'd never find her way back, fear that she was doing something incredibly stupid for a woman she didn't even know.

Now, more than ever, she longed for the towering giant trees of the Deep Wood. For the leaf-filtered sunlight and warm breeze. This forest was a bare corpse of that memory, small and cold and harsh. The ice that clung to her skin tore the memory away even as she grasped for it and left her hollow.

It was one thing to say she'd never go home; it was another to fear she'd never see it again without a choice in the matter.

The only thing that grounded her was Vox's hand in hers. He stumbled and swayed, and occasionally tripped over the quickly tightening rope that trailed behind her. But he was there, and he was living. He was all she had in a world of ice and skeletal trees that rose and fell in her vision.

The rope suddenly tightened and pulled Evren to a halt. Vox took a few more faltering steps before he too stopped. The end of the line.

"Do you see her?" she cried over the storm.

Vox's strangely bright eyes were desperate as he combed through what little he could see. Frustration turned the corners of his mouth into a sharp frown, which was almost comical around his tusks.

She heard him growl in frustration and call out to Nerezza. But the wind cruelly took his voice and tossed it away. Evren knew it wasn't any use, but she peered into the white too. All her life she'd been praised for her eyesight, but she felt like it was against her now. She couldn't focus, and every time she tried, ice and snow flung themselves in her face. She was struggling to breathe with the flying snow, much less see through it.

So, she closed her eyes.

What could she do if she couldn't see? How many hunts did she rely on sound alone? So many in the past months. The wraiths were invisible, but not silent. And neither was Nerezza.

Let me hear her.

She strained against the howling wind and the creaking trees. She strained against the muffling of the snow, and Vox's desperate shouts. They could very well be hers, if the roles were reversed. If it had been Arke, or Sol, or Sorin lost in the storm and not a stranger. She focused on what she remembered of Nerezza, of the soft-spoken mage who never seemed to fear anything in her path. As calm as the still pools in a temple. But who would be calm in the face of death?

Not even the most powerful mage could withstand the might of nature trying to smother them, and Nerezza was at its mercy. She would not be calm and quiet.

Evren tilted her head slightly. A piece of a voice not her own or Vox's hurtled through the wind and barely snatched on her ears.

Nerezza was alive, and close, but terrified.

Evren's eyes flashed open, and she tugged on Vox's hand. He cut off his shouting to look at her.

"I hear her!" she shouted and pointed in the direction she heard Nerezza's voice. They both stared into the empty white as another fragment of her voice echoed back.

"We can't get to her!" Vox was breathing hard. "Not unless I let go."

Evren chewed on her lip, a bad plan forming in her mind. Normally the only type of plan she ever had. Risky, and almost certain to fail. But it was either that or turn back and leave Nerezza. And they were so close.

Evren placed Vox's hand on her shoulder to free her own hand. "Don't let go," he looked confused but didn't argue as she untied the rope around her waist. She clutched the very end of it in one hand and took his other hand in hers.

"This'll give us a few more feet," she told him. "If we can't reach her with this, we're as good as dead. We can't let go, understand?"

He stared down at her, the scar on his face caked in ice and twisting painfully as he grimaced and nodded. "I'll get her. Don't let go."

"That's the plan."

He tightened his grip on her hand so much she felt her finger bones creak under the pressure. But he slowly walked forward, stretching out as far as he was able. Evren did the same, one hand as tight as she dared around the rope, the other caught in Vox's grip. They stretched out until her shoulder popped, and the wind rushed between her arms and torso. Until they were as taut as the rope and had nowhere else to go.

Evren could still hear Nerezza, fear clogging her voice. She couldn't tell if they were any closer. Ahead of her, Vox reached out into the white abyss, hand grasping at hissing air.

"Nerezza!" he called. "Nerezza, we're here! Walk to my voice!"

Evren shivered as he continued to call. She felt utterly exposed, as if she would freeze to death in the same spot and never move again. If she thought too hard, she could imagine the ice creeping up her legs, melding her boots with the earth as, inch by inch, it overcame her entirely. The ice bit at her cheeks, and she closed her eyes. To think of warmer things, of sunlight on her eyelids and warm syrup on her tongue. A hand in hers that wasn't clutching her in a life-or-death grip but was soft and loving. A tether of choice, not necessity. Someone warm to lean into, but because she wanted to, not for survival.

Evren hadn't found herself longing for anyone in a long time. That thought scared her more than it should've. Perhaps she was dying for a second time. This was worse than bleeding out in Gyda's arms.

Evren suddenly felt Vox's grip loosen until all she had was his fingertips in her grasp.

"Vox!" she cried out in warning.

He ignored her and lunged forward. When he pulled back, he had someone with him. Nerezza, frightened and nearly blue from the cold, but alive.

Evren pulled him towards her with the last bit of strength the cold hadn't sapped from her. She put the rope in his hands and urged him forward.

"I'm right behind you!" She nodded.

His eyes swam with gratitude as he hooked his arm around Nerezza and took the rope in his free hand. Inch by inch he crawled towards the tent, towards safety. She grabbed the rope he left and followed after him. One hand after another, even as her feet sank into the growing snow. Even as her feet grew numb and her steps slowed. Once again, Vox was nothing but a shadow in front of her, Nerezza at his side with her white-blonde hair whipping in the wind and blending in with the snow. But she had the rope in her hands and felt herself start to relax. She imagined what it would feel like to get into the tent and out of the wind. She imagined how thick the atmosphere would be with unspoken works, and the grumbles of complaints as everyone packed into one another to get as warm as possible. She felt herself start to laugh and choked back the snow that wormed its way into her mouth. By the time she'd stopped coughing, she was ready for all of it, the good and the bad.

But she was also empty handed, and alone in the white.

The panic wasn't like pain. It didn't clear anything for her. Panic was the thickest volume of fear, and she was powerless against it. She felt herself faltering in the snow, a dark scream of desperation clawing at her throat. If it ever did find its way out, she couldn't tell. All that she knew was the wind and the ice, and the surety of death if she didn't think of something.

The wind would kill her faster than the snow, she knew that. She forced her panic down, even as it clung to her bones like the cold. There were two rules for surviving a blizzard, and they'd been drilled into her since she arrived in the Reino Terminan.

One, don't move. With the wind and the poor visibility, she was just as likely to walk off the mountain than find the tent. What she thought was a straight line was more than likely a full circle.

Two, get out of the wind however she could.

Her body, drunk on fear and adrenaline, worked where her mind couldn't. She took her bow from her shoulders and fell to her knees. And she began to dig. Inch by inch, she dug into the snow. The hole just had to fit her, a trench to keep her alive, a grave to keep her buried if it didn't. She tossed the snow against the brunt end of the wind, and watched the pile grow higher even without her help. Inch by panicked inch. Her knees were numb, and every breath was so sharp and cold she felt like she was taking a dagger to the chest each time she gasped.

She dug until her body screamed to stop. Until the trench was just big enough for her, and the makeshift wall on one side was breaking the wind in a way to allow for some small level of comfort.

Evren laid down in her hole and tucked her hands and legs as close to her as she could. Her bow never left her grip. This time, she was sure she wouldn't be able to let go of it. The snow seeped into her clothes and she shivered. Above her, the blizzard spit ice and screaming winds but couldn't quite reach her.

She closed her eyes, her breath coming out in ragged puffs as the storm tried to wipe her from the mountain completely. Sleep came far easier than it should've.

7

Evren was dreaming in her frosted tomb.

In her dreams, she was far from where the mountains touched the sky, and the air was harsh and thin. In her dreams, she was cradled by soft shadows in the dark depths of the underground. The serenity she'd come to expect from the vast stillness of the Yawning Deep filled her to her very fingertips. The air was warm and smelled of damp earth, and she could taste the moisture on the tip of her tongue. Somewhere in the shadows, she knew someone waited. Someone who could've been important to her, who might've been everything had the twisted hands of fate and duty not dragged them away.

In her hand, the silver moth broach fluttered to life. Its metallic wings shone with an inner light, illuminating the darkness gently.

In her dream, Evren opened her fingers to release the moth. The cage of her hand was laid open and bare. There was nothing to hold it back. Still, it refused to fly. Its gilded wings sank low to brush her palm, and the light inside it flickered ever so slightly.

A part of Evren was glad it stayed. She'd come to love that little moth. It was something to remind her that despite all the horrors she'd faced in Serevadia, there were those who shone a light in the dark. A guide for the lost.

But it would need to fly eventually. Maybe not now, not in this dream. But maybe another one.

Normally in dreams like this, Evren would stay until the moth flickered out and the shadows overtook her. She'd fall back into a restless sleep and wake up grasping for the pin that was tucked safely in her bag. She'd find it cold and a little worn; nothing more than a pretty pin, far too extravagant in her dirty, callused hands.

This time, it was light that overtook her. Not from the moth itself, but from everywhere. Bit by bit, it took away the warm comfort of her shadows. It was cold and far too bright. She felt the chill settle back on her even in her dreams, until the light was so bright she couldn't remember where the dream ended and the real world began.

Evren woke to the bright white of a world reborn and didn't know whether to laugh or cry.

Her trench was far from comfortable, but the high wall of packed snow to her right side had saved her life. It looked like a frozen wave, crested, and curling over her but too frozen to collapse. Bright, snow-filtered sunlight streamed into her trench, nearly blinding in its intensity.

Bit by bit, she worked herself free. She shook out her arm and grimaced at the tingles of sharp pain that spiked up her cramped muscles. Ice caked her clothes, and in the cracking of it she felt like she was emerging from a cocoon. The side of her cheek was almost frozen to her bow, and she hissed as she felt the skin pull and peel when she separated the two. Her legs came next, and she tried not to think about how she couldn't feel her toes anymore, not even pain. And then she set to digging her way out.

The snow didn't want to give. Evren's body didn't want to move. With every chunk of snow moved, fresh and bitterly cold air swooped in and she felt herself retreating back. There was no warmth in the trench, but it was better than the outside.

Only, she'd freeze easier if she stayed still, and if she didn't freeze, she'd surely starve. There was no way she'd let herself die from something as simple as starvation when she'd faced monsters and stopped wars.

Gritting her teeth, she forced her frozen limbs to work. It was slow and sluggish work, but it got her blood pumping. Soon, she was out into the open air, gasping for breath. She wriggled on the snow for a while, working her legs free. Then she forced one knee up, and then the other.

Pushing herself to her feet, she realized she was laughing. The stuttering bubbles of joy were bursting in her chest and never fully making it up her throat. She wheezed more than she truly laughed, and her torn-up throat hated every minute of it. But as she stood in the crisp new snow, swaying on her unsteady feet with the bright blue of an unending sky above her, she laughed. Her head was tossed back, her tender skin soaking up the weak rays of sunlight, and her lungs taking in one painful breath of air after another.

Such was the cost of living for Evren Hanali, and she could laugh at it.

She didn't know when she stopped laughing and started realizing just how royally fucked she was, but it was just enough time for her to realize that all she had was the snow and the sky. There was not a single tree in sight.

Her stomach twisted itself into its usual knots as she did a full circle. The mountain rose up behind her, but she couldn't see the Black Pass anymore. The circle of trees where she'd left her friends was nowhere to be seen, and while the fresh snow was deep, it was nowhere deep enough to bury trees. If that had been the case, she wouldn't have made it out of her trench.

Evren tried to warm up her cheeks with her gloved hands and set to worrying her bottom lip until she tasted blood again. A bad habit, and the sharp cracks in her lips were far too easily broken. The taste of her own blood did little to help her, aside from reminding her that there was a color aside from blue and white in the world.

"Well, shit," she muttered, and the urge to laugh again was coming back. She swallowed it down.

Surely she hadn't wandered so far during the blizzard. How could she have walked until there were no trees and not noticed?

"Idiot." She pulled her sodden furs tighter around her. "You don't even remember when you let go of the rope."

Evren was lost, cold, hungry, and utterly alone in a wilderness she knew next to nothing about. With no map, and very few supplies.

And so, her survival checklist began.

She slung off her pack, which was wet but in decent condition despite it all. Besides her tent, which she'd used to make the larger one for all of her friends, everything was pretty much the same.

Air? Fresh and clear.

Food? A few more rations.

Water? Less than she'd like. She'd have to boil some snow soon. If she could even get a fire going.

Shelter? Absolute negative.

Medicine? One potion of healing.

Evren focused on the small first. She counted her supplies, and then cleared out a hefty square of snow to settle down. She wanted the health potion, for her limbs and her throat, but it was always a bad idea to take a potion on an empty stomach. She took one of her rations and ate most of it, then drank the water as sparingly as she dared.

She only drank half the potion. Of course, she wanted more, but she didn't want to waste it. The metallic taste on her tongue made her grimace and she tried to take it down without tasting it at all. A subtle warmth filled her from the inside out. She felt her fingers and toes again, and the light pain and soreness that came with them was welcome. Her throat knitted itself together, and she stopped shivering, if only for a moment.

Evren let out a shaky breath, and slowly corked the bottle and put it back in her bag. She licked the last drops of potion from her lips, savoring the small beads of warmth even as the air tried to snatch them away. Her body was awakening. It wasn't even close to a good day for her, and she could already feel a headache forming at the base of her skull. But, again, she had to remind herself that she was alive, and that was no small feat.

It was the silence that reminded her how alone she was.

Evren put her face in her gloved hands, relishing the bit of warmth and the darkness that came with it. She could feel the tears start to prick her eyes and stubbornly tried to blink them away. A few months ago, she wouldn't have teared up over being alone. She might've even preferred it. But if the gaping hole in her chest was any clue, she'd spent far too long with the Sols to be that woman anymore.

It hadn't been so long ago that she'd been on her own. She didn't need to lean on anyone for help. But she missed it all the same. The familiar comfort that came with trusted companions left a gaping hole when it was absent, and she wasn't sure how to fill it.

Evren sat back and looked up at the sky. Spilled tears cooled against her skin, and the wide expanse of sky made her stomach flip. Suddenly Sol's fear of falling off the earth didn't seem so ridiculous.

But no matter where on the map she was, she knew how to center herself. The sky was constant, no matter the seasons. And the sky pointed out north as easily as a compass would've.

From there, she had an idea of where to go. She had no clue where she was exactly, but south would eventually bring her to the Black Pass. Not a viable option, no matter how much she wished for warm winds and safety. And north would keep her going in the same general direction they'd been heading. Further towards the source of the undead, further towards hostile lands, and further toward civilization.

Maybe, even closer to her friends.

They'll look for me, she told herself as she gathered all her belongings and stood up. The mountain below her feet was steady and sure, despite the fresh snow. *They'll look for me and find nothing. Until the Ashen Bond pulls them away, until the threat of dwindling supplies makes them turn back to the quest. I know they'll look. But I'll find them first.*

She had to believe all trails led to the same destination in the Reino Terminan. True or not, it was the only thing that kept her spirit hopeful as she started her descent down the mountain and farther north.

8

I t took of two days of slow travel for Evren's positive attitude to plummet straight to the hells. Despite how infuriatingly short those days were, they still stretched on forever. The mindless hours trudging through the snow and trying not to slip on ice were filled with nothing but what her mind could conjure and the steady stream of obscenities that flew from her mouth. The long nights where the temperature plummeted and she had little for shelter other than more damned trenches did not help her mood. She was always cold, and was starting to believe that warmth was a myth she'd never be able to touch again. Wood was sparse where she was on the mountain, and always icy or soaking wet. Fire was something she could rarely afford, and only to melt snow for drinking water, not for warmth. Any creatures that strayed across her path were pathetically small and no good for eating, or wise enough to keep away from the foul hunter.

By the third day, Evren knew she was being stalked.

She was picking her way down what barely resembled a trail when she felt the familiar sensation of eyes on her. The prickle at the back of her neck made her stop; it made her hopeful. She turned around, half hoping to see the hooded figure. She might kick it off the mountain, but it would give her something to talk to for a bit.

But all she saw was nothing. Just an empty, ice-slick trail.

The feeling didn't go away. She scowled at the crevices in the mountain, searching for whatever had the gall to hunt her and make her day even harder.

"Whatever you are, I wouldn't try it." Her voice bounced off the rocks and echoed back at her. "I'm in a foul mood, and if you test me enough I'll gladly throw us both off the mountain and see who survives the fall."

Nothing answered her, although Evren hadn't expected it too. No chance she'd get a conversation on top of her life-threatening event for the day. She narrowed her eyes at the mountainside but saw nothing. If she stared any longer, she might start seeing things in the rocks that weren't there.

Still scowling, she took her bow in hand for good measure. The familiar weight made her feel better, even as the heavy feeling of being watched pressed down on her.

She turned back to the trail, muttering what Elvish curses she could remember as she made her way down. She got maybe two or three steps before she heard rocks clattering behind her.

She swiveled around quickly, already nocking an arrow as her eyes caught . . .

Nothing.

Pebbles rolled to a stop on the trail where she'd been moments before, but there was nothing else for her to see. She stared nonetheless. Being alone for so long made the presence of something else extremely noticeable, malicious or not. Either that, or she was losing her mind.

"Can't rule that thought out," she muttered, and put the arrow back in her quiver. She squinted at the rocks again as the wind tugged at her hair and urged her back.

"Whatever you are," she called up the mountain, "if you're going to kill me, at least make it a fair fight. I'd like some fun before I'm made something's dinner."

With that, she turned and continued her hike, the feeling of being watched and the telltale signs of being stalked continuing to show themselves. Evren made it down the mountain, and pointedly ignored whatever was watching her with a little flicker of glee in her chest. With the added danger, the days got a little shorter.

~

Who would've thought Evren would cry at the sight of trees? Certainly not her. And she would adamantly deny it should anyone accuse her of doing so.

But there was no mistaking the wet gleam of her eyes as, nearly two days later, the ground started to level out and thick, tall pines crowded the trail. She took a deep breath, loving the rich earthy scent, even as it was muddled with ice and cold. The shadows the trees cast didn't help with the chill, but Evren's face was starting to burn from the unrelenting sunlight and she was grateful not to squint her eyes anymore.

With trees came shelter, and eventually food. She was still hopelessly lost, but she was far less prone to bad Elvish cursing than she was before. She didn't dare let hope flicker to more than a spark. But there was a bounce to her step as she found a suitable spot to camp, mostly clear of snow.

She cleared out the rest of the snow and went to work on making a shelter. She took down small branches she could reach and picked up fallen ones. The process of cleaning off the wood, getting the pieces straight, and lining them all up was time consuming, but she loved it. She was so ready for a roof over her head and something to keep the wind back, her fingers were shaking as she put it all together. She chopped and tied and bound everything together until she made something small but suitable, and leaned it against a large tree. It was far from her best work, but to her it was a palace.

With the rest of her wood, she made a fire. It was small, and the wood was still damp enough to hinder her efforts, but the sparks soon turned to flames and she was huddled as close to the warmth as she could get.

When her shivering subsided enough, she ran through her checklist again. All but food was decent. Her rations were spent. But a forest meant hunting, and that was one thing she was sure she could do.

Hunting was where her mind quieted. The work of tracking and creeping as silently as possible through unknown woods kept her body alert but her mind relaxed. The hunger in her belly drove her further than her tired muscles would normally allow. She marked passing trees so she wouldn't get lost. It was all routine and familiar, despite the strange forest.

A part of her wanted to get lost. The part of her that loved the quiet and stillness of the wilderness where nothing was expected of her. No need for conversation or smiles or to answer pointless questions and help others set up their tents.

But it was lonely and she was tired of it. She didn't want to slip back into the Evren she had been before Serevadia. She had to make sure to find that sacred balance and keep it locked up in her mind.

Dusk came infuriatingly early and plunged the shadowed forest into a deep, hazy grey. She pressed on, though. She found pawprints in the snow, and the idea of a fox for dinner sounded like a feast. She crept along steadily, taking the time to find quicker paths than what the fox chose, and close the distance.

By the time she found it, shuffling around the underbrush with its pure-white fur coat, night was quickly descending. She nocked an arrow, quietly, as an all too familiar feeling of being watched washed over her.

She gritted her teeth. If whatever was hunting her was waiting for her to starve to death before it ate her, it was about to be sadly mistaken. Divines knew what or where the damn thing was, or she might've eaten it already. But she had her dinner, and she wasn't going to let it go.

The fox paused its foraging and lifted its pointed nose to the wind. Its ears flipped back, and Evren's stomach sank. It could smell whatever was hunting her. The telltale signs of fear shone in its eyes as it started to dart away, but she let loose the arrow anyway. It caught the hind leg, and the fox screamed in pain.

The peaceful serenity of the forest was broken. Evren shivered as the fox screamed, still pinned to the ground unable to move. She hated how human it sounded when it cried.

"Sorry, bud," she whispered to it, and quickly put it out of its misery.

She stood with the fox limp in her hands. The surrounding woods were thick with nighttime shadows, and she could still feel her predator at the edge of her senses.

"If you let me go, you can have half of this." She shook the fox in the air. "But I'm going to camp regardless. You know where to find me."

Talking to a predator should be a sign of madness, Evren thought as she started to walk back to her camp. She could still feel its eyes on her, but it let her pass. She walked all the way back to her homely little fire and shelter with no more trouble than tripping over some roots.

Evren relit the fire, and the orange glow drove back the gloom as she started to skin the fox. Out of the corner of her eye, she saw a flash of glowing eyes in the darkness. Far too large and predatory for it to be any intelligent creature, but it was smart enough to circle around the camp.

She pulled off the pelt cleanly and took to carving up half of the fox as much as her knife could manage. The eyes vanished as she stood up and walked over to the edge of the camp. She lifted the meat in the air and let it hang. She could feel the full attention of the beast now.

"Like I promised, half."

She tossed it into the trees. There was a pause of stretched silence before the sound of ripping meat filled the air. Evren smiled as it carried it farther away from her. As if she'd go through the trouble to take it back from whatever creature was out there.

She settled back next to the fire and cooked her own meat. She devoured it when it was done. Stringy, but after nothing but cold rations, the flavor of the hot, juicy meat was enough to overwhelm her. She ate everything and gnawed on the bones a little to scrape away every last bit of meat. She licked the juices from her fingers, her stomach growling for more, but more content now than it had been in days.

In the shadows, she imagined the beast contently licking the blood off its mouth and settling down for the night as she did the same.

"Keep this up and maybe I can make it out of this," she said to no one in particular. Sighing, she looked to where she imagined the beast sat in the darkness. "Don't eat me, all right? I can get you better food than me."

The beast didn't answer, and Evren took its silence as a hopeful compromise as she settled to sleep feeling a little more hopeful.

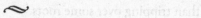

SHE WOKE up the next morning alive and with a pile of cleaned bones at her feet. The next two mornings went very similarly. At all times of the day, Evren could feel the beast right at the edge of her vision. She never saw it, but she talked to it often. More than once, she wished it would talk back. But it kept to itself, even during mealtimes. Her life had become a very odd routine of survival, hunting, and feeding the beast whatever she'd found in hopes that it didn't try to kill her.

The long trail north was a little less lonely now.

As the sun started to set on the third day, it turned the world was red. The sky was a deep ruby, and the rays caught on every passing ice crystal. It set the forest on fire through the ice. Evren had to take the time to just watch it.

She leaned against the tree, breathing steadily as the now crimson crystals glinted in the quickly fading sunlight. She thought she heard the impatient huff of the beast behind her and smiled.

"Enjoy the view," she tossed over her shoulder. "It'll only last a few minutes."

The beauty was short-lived. As fast as the blood-red sun had appeared, it sank beneath the horizon. The sky remained red and purple for a time afterwards, like the clouds were desperate to cling to what little color there was in this frozen corner of the world.

Evren pushed off the tree with a sigh. She still had to catch dinner and set up camp, but she could do both in the twilight easily by now. As she started scanning the ground for a sign of her next meal, she found some tracks far too clean and clear in the snow.

She stopped dead and knelt down. Her fingers barely brushed the outlines in the snow, but it was unmistakable. No matter how many times she blinked to try and get the image to clear and show itself to be animal tracks, it was always the same.

Boot prints. Humanoid tracks. And they were heading north.

9

Evren had to force herself to set up camp and hunt dinner that night. Every bone in her sang to follow the tracks, even in the sucking black of night. Her usual routine of hunting, feeding her beast, and staring at the fire before she went to sleep felt like it took years. But she trudged through anyway, eating her half of a scrawny arctic hare as the beast in the shadows did the same. She crawled into her shelter feeling almost excited. It was only the danger of tracking at night that kept her by the fire. Once the sun set, it felt like the cold became a life of its own. It was a silent killer, and she would not survive the night wandering blindly in it.

Sleep did not come easily.

The next morning, she was quick to move on and follow her strange footprints.

Whoever she was tracking made no attempt to try and hide from her. In many ways, it felt like she was meant to find them. The snow never brushed over the tracks; the underbrush never hid them. Evren could always easily pick them up, no matter where they went. Considering that everything after the blizzard had been as challenging as pulling teeth from a live dragon, she should've been concerned. But the thought of another face, even a stranger's, set a fire in her chest she couldn't ignore.

She was so tired of being alone and afraid. Just a little rest, and maybe some decent conversation, would breathe new life into her.

Her beast remained out of sight. Throughout the day, she spent all her energy on the footprints and very little time talking to it. By midday, she was sure she could feel it pouting just outside her vision. She tried not to laugh; her frosted lungs couldn't take it.

"I suppose you're worried you won't have any easy meals from now on, huh?" she asked as she moved forward. The snow crunched musically under her boots, and her teeth chattered in a similar rhythm. "Don't worry! Maybe if you stick around, we can work something out. So long as my friends agree. After all, you have been my only tether to sanity for . . ." she counted the days under her breath. "Nine days! Almost ten now. Stick around as long as you want. The same rules apply, don't eat me and I won't kill you."

The same bargain, struck time and time again with each sunrise. And yet, the beast was always silent in its answer. But if it wanted her dead, there were easier times to do it. She slept with this creature prowling around her camp. By all accounts, she *should* be dead.

Whatever it was either preferred her hunting or was just lazy. Either way, Evren couldn't fault it.

The trees started to thin out, and she suddenly felt exposed. As if with each growing gap she was giving up a piece of clothing to the snow. The tracks led ever forward, and soon she was stumbling to a halt by the last of the trees.

The white expanse in front of her stretched on for what seemed like forever. There was little more than snow and ice for as far as she could see. The mountains curled around the land on each side, like two massive, grey shields. Or two walls of a very large cage. Black water glinted against the sunlight at the very north, barely visible from where she was at. And, buried beneath the ice and halfheartedly scraped away, was a thin trail winding its way further from the trees. Following it with her eyes, she could see it continued north and branched off to the east. If she squinted, she could almost see the dark smudge of a village there.

Tracks or no, a road meant people to travel it. She just had to get to that village before nightfall.

Evren took a step into the vast, exposed expanse. As she took a breath, she swore that the air tasted different. Saltier, like she was near the sea. It was a welcome change.

She walked forward a few more steps, ignoring how much more pronounced her faltering feet were now. The sun was in her eyes and though it blinded her by bouncing off the snow, she couldn't help but smile. Her feet tried to go faster, to keep up with the frantic hope thrumming through her veins. She wheezed a laugh when she almost tripped over her feet.

Her cheeks ached, either from the wind or her ridiculously wild smile, she wasn't sure. And she didn't care. She didn't care how her body protested when she started to jog instead of walk. She didn't care that her left leg spiked in a dull pain each time she used it and she started to veer off to the left.

It was the dark shape in the middle of the road that made her stumble to a halt, breathing hard as the playful but bone-chilling breeze whipped at her hair. She squinted against the sun-bright snow, trying in vain to make out any more details. They were tall, unmoving, and unbothered by the cold. The curved hilt of a sword poked out from the cloak thrown over their shoulder. Evren felt her throat close up with nerves. It felt like too much to hope for, and yet . . .

"Gyda?"

Her voice was barely a hoarse whisper in the wind, but the figure stopped anyway as if they'd heard her. They turned around to face her, and Evren felt the breath leave her body in an aching shudder. She knew that face, those eyes. She'd know them anywhere.

This time she was laughing and running at the same time. The wind blew back her cloak and tore her hair away from her face. She could feel her tears freezing on her smiling cheeks. The ground seemed to propel her forward as she ran. It suddenly didn't feel like a struggle with her goal so close.

Gyda ran too. Her face was frozen in shock until she put one foot in front of the other. Slow, hesitant steps turned into a sprint as she desperately tried to close the gap between them.

When there was only five feet between them, Evren suddenly stopped. Fear clawed at her bones. Not because she was in danger but because the last time she'd seen Gyda she'd been angry, and rightfully so. And then Evren had disappeared for over a week. What would she say? What *could* she say, as she came ever closer?

The gap closed quickly, and Gyda blocked out the sun as she slowed down to a walk. Evren struggled for her words again, her eyes wide as she stared up at her.

"I'm so sorry," she choked out, feeling shame burn her raw cheeks. "Gyda, I never meant—"

Evren was cut off as Gyda wrapped her arms around her and pulled her close. The hug was fierce, which was fitting for a woman like her. But Evren was still shocked enough to be frozen solid for a few seconds before she hesitantly wrapped her arms around her as well. She buried face in her furs and clung to her. The body heat, the familiar smell of leather and sword polish that always clung to her. It felt like coming home, and Evren savored every second of it.

Gyda had never been one for physical contact. Even after they brought Sorin back from the dead, she'd been the first to break away from the group hug. But holding her now, Evren didn't want to let go.

The moment ended too soon when Gyda pulled away, but her hands were still firmly set on her shoulders as she looked her up and down. She took in the ice-encrusted furs and the red, raw skin of her face. Her chapped lips, her hopeful eyes. When she finally spoke, her voice was hoarse.

"You're alive."

"Just barely." Evren felt her lip split at how wide her smile was turning. She watched a wet sheen gather on Gyda's eyes and tried to swallow down her shock. "Are you crying?"

She blinked and shook her head. "No."

"You are!" Evren laughed. "You really thought I didn't make it."

She scowled and pulled away from her. Her stance was back to its normally defensive and rigid posture. But her eyes betrayed everything. Evren wasn't used to seeing so much raw emotion from her.

"I was not worried," she muttered. "You've been extremely difficult to find is all."

Evren bit back a gasp of surprise as she stared up at her. "You were looking for me?"

She scoffed. "Of course I was looking for you. After the storm cleared, we all did. But you left no trace. So, I left a trail for you to follow."

"The boot prints were yours." Even as she said it, Evren felt stupid for not noticing earlier. How many times had she tracked those very footsteps in the past? Gyda always walked with more pressure on her heel. It left a distinctive print she should've instantly recognized.

Even so, Gyda didn't seem to notice her shame. Instead, she offered a small smile, her full lips curling up in a rare sight few had the pleasure of seeing. "I knew you'd find me."

"I always do," she couldn't help but finish. "Even without trying."

As quickly as it had come, Gyda's smile vanished and was replaced with a familiar frown. She picked up the frayed edge of Evren's cloak, her nose wrinkling ever so slightly as she once again raked her eyes over her, from the top of her head down to her boots.

"You look terrible."

Evren batted her hand away and the cloak fell limply back down. "That's what happens when I'm left to my own devices in a strange wilderness."

"Are you hurt?"

Evren started to answer and then frowned. Was she? She truly had no idea. She was lucky to keep track of the day, much less everything wrong with her body. "I don't know," she said truthfully. She hadn't dared to pull off her boots or gloves to check for frostbite. She'd rather not know.

Gyda nodded, looking both concerned and furious. Evren was content to know she was mad at the situation and not her, but she still felt guilty.

"Come, we should check you over." Gyda jerked her head to the east road. Evren hadn't even realized they were near the fork.

"We?" She couldn't keep the hopeful tone from her voice. Gyda started to walk that direction, and Evren struggled to keep up with her long legs and fast pace. She seemed to notice and slowed her steps down, giving her a look that somewhat resembled pity.

"The Ashen Bond is in Lostwater," she explained.

"And our people?"

"North, to the other settlement," she said. Before Evren could argue she put her hand up. It wasn't gloved. "Direwall will take too long to get to. We'll see them again once we get you back to normal."

Evren closed her protesting mouth and turned to the road ahead. The town of Lostwater was still little more than a black smudge on the white. "Why'd they split up?"

"They couldn't agree on the best way to find you." Gyda shrugged. "I left during the arguing, but they are all fine. Do not worry."

It was too late for that, but Evren nodded anyway. She'd see her friends again, just not yet. She couldn't wait to hear Abraxas's scolding and Sol's laugh. She wanted Sorin's lanky hugs filled with all the energy of the warm sea, and Arke's grumpy but relieved smile. It wasn't that she hadn't realized she missed them —she'd been acutely aware of the gaping hole in her chest every day. But now that they were so close and she was still so far, she was antsy again. She'd been alone for far too long.

Evren stopped suddenly and turned back to the tree line. Behind her she heard Gyda stop and mutter a question, but she wasn't listening. Her eyes scanned the wilderness for some sign of her beast. There was nothing but ice until the tree line, black and thick as it stretched far into the mountains further south. Evren's stomach twisted at the thought of her climb down and out, and how much it had taken out of her. But she hadn't been entirely alone.

There was no creature in sight, however. All she could see was the wind sweeping snow into tiny dunes, and the shadows of the mountains obscuring any light from getting to the forest.

"What is it?" Gyda asked again.

Evren shook her head and tore her eyes away. "Nothing. Sorry, let's get out of here."

～

LOSTWATER WAS a corpse of a village at the edge of a frozen lake, and it did little to calm Evren's nerves.

She didn't expect a town like in Etherak, where the homes were small but the roads were bustling with people, and mangy dogs running around with mud-covered children. But she didn't think the dark homes would be so empty and quiet either.

They were all on stilts, and their roofs were sharply peaked to keep the snow from piling up. There was a strange beauty in the little carvings along the doorways and rooflines, but everything else was built to be practical. The wood was nearly black and covered in clinging frost and ice. Some of the steps leading up to the houses were rotted and broken. And not a single sole wandered through.

"Where is everyone?" Evren asked as she and Gyda walked. She couldn't raise her voice above a whisper. Everything was so silent she could hear the dull creaking and groaning of the ice from the lake.

"Dead," Gyda said simply. When Evren gave her a startled look, she shrugged. "Lostwater has been for a while now. It is nothing to worry about."

Evren shivered. There was an edge to Gyda's words that she couldn't quite place, but her face was as impassive as ever. "If you say so."

They walked to the center of the village where one house had smoke coming from its chimney. Gyda took the steps up two at a time, but Evren was much more careful as she followed. However, once she opened the door and felt a rush of warm air, she nearly sprinted inside.

The interior wasn't much more impressive than the exterior. Everything was dusty and looked like it had been abandoned for a while. But a roaring fire took up the massive fireplace in the middle of the room, and Evren was so relieved she could've cried. Her little campfires were nothing compared to this.

Around the fire, the four members of the Ashen Bond sat and ate something that steamed in their bowls. Their heads snapped up when Evren and Gyda walked in, and once the door shut, no one said anything for a while. Everything was silent, and thick with the kind of awkwardness Evren hated. She squirmed in her boots until, finally, Drystan nodded to her.

"Look who's finally back from the dead." He sounded almost impressed, but she was sure she imagined it.

"Considering your quest, that's a poor joke to make," Evren said with a nervous laugh.

Sahar abruptly stood up from her spot by the fire and ushered her forward. "Well, don't just stand there! Come here and get warm. Vox, tell me we have some more of that spicy porridge to share."

Sahar herded her next to the fire and sat her in a chair that creaked so much she was afraid she'd fall through. The heat was almost too intense, but she started to feel her fingers tingle again at the warmth. She took her gloves off with shaking fingers. She swallowed back her sob of relief. They were red, and a little swollen, but thankfully no closer to falling off than she expected. When a warm bowl of porridge found its way into her palms, she was nearly overwhelmed by heat. She stuck her nose in the steam, relishing the slightly painful tingle as the steam brushed her nose and cheeks. A wave of spices also hit her nostrils, far more than she was used to, but she didn't care. She was finally warming up.

She let herself savor that warmth before her hunger got the better of her and she started shoveling the food in her mouth. It burned her throat, both spice and temperature, but she was so hungry she barely tasted it. She didn't even notice when Gyda threw a fur pelt over her shoulders and settled down next to her.

By the time she was finished scraping the bowl clean, everyone was watching her. She wiped her mouth with the back of her hand and set it down on the stone hearth.

"Thanks," she said softly.

Vox picked the bowl up and nodded. Beside him, Nerezza stared at her intently, as if she was trying to pick Evren apart and figure out why and how she'd survived. The mage looked a little rougher than she remembered, her pale hair tied back from her face. Her lips were pulled into what looked like a permanent frown as she looked Evren up and down. She blinked and softened a little before bowing her head.

"I don't remember much from the storm," she admitted. "But Vox told me how you risked your life to save me. You have my gratitude."

A nervous giggle left Evren's mouth, interrupted by a burp.

She winced before waving her off. "Oh, it's fine. You saved my life in the pass. Let's call it even, shall we?"

The elf blinked slowly before nodding, looking confused. When she settled back in her chair, Evren was drawn back to Drystan, who was staring her down with no emotion whatsoever. After a few minutes of it, she raised an eyebrow.

"Is there something on my face?"

He frowned. It seemed like all he did was frown. "No. I'm just trying to figure out why."

"Why what?"

"Why you'd risk your life for two strangers."

Beside him, Sahar rolled her eyes and muttered something under her breath. Evren tried not to bristle at the tone of his voice and leaned forward to stare at him over the fire. The heat made his face shimmer and wave, and his eyes reflected the glowing flames.

"I did what any decent person would've done," she said. "I had no other motive."

"So you say." He nodded. "But I know Etherakians are fond of their life debts."

"I'm not from Etherak," she shot back. "I'm from Orenlion. I couldn't give two shits about life debts. I stayed outside to keep your people alive because that's what decent people do. I thought that was something taught universally, but I'm guessing you wouldn't have done the same."

He pursed his lips into a thin line. "No. Not out of personal dislike, but out of general practicality."

"If it had been me, I'd believe you," she said. "But if you had been out there with Vox and Nerezza, you would've gone after them the same way I did."

"They're my people, of course I would have."

"So why doesn't it make sense that I would do the same for people I didn't know?" she asked. "You're looking at the same woman who blatantly ignored orders to follow you and her friend into certain danger, after being told not to multiple times.

Is it so hard for you to believe that I don't have any other motive except to see everyone through this?"

"Yes." His tone was heavy, heavy enough to send her back against her seat. But after a while he sighed and ran his hand through his closely cropped hair. "Although, to be fair, it's hard for me to believe that of anyone."

"That's the closest to a 'thank you' I'll get from you, but I'll take it."

Sahar scowled at him and smacked his shoulder as she stood up. He rubbed the spot she'd hit frowning up at her. "What?"

"You and your manners." She shook her head and took the bowls from Vox. "What did they teach you over in Melkarth? How to be bitter and stubborn?"

"That, and more unpleasantness," he said dryly.

"Well, you and I have been working together long enough for you to know at least how to say thank you." She turned to Evren, her deep brown eyes as warm as the fire itself. "He won't say it and Vox will trip over his own feet trying to get the words out, so I will. Thank you, Evren, for saving the lives of our dear friends and finding your way back to us. I promise we normally have better manners than this."

Evren felt her smile returning. "It's okay, really. I understand the mistrust. We didn't really get off on the right foot."

She snorted in the most ladylike way possible. "I don't know what you're talking about. I found you simply delightful. It just so happens that our illustrious leader has a tongue sharper than his brain."

Sahar took the bowls and walked to an adjoining room. Evren watched Drystan as he watched her. He looked thoroughly ashamed but hid it as soon as he realized others were watching him.

Evren felt a heavy hand on her shoulder and turned to see Vox standing over her.

"You let go," he grumbled, looking at the ground.

She patted his arm reassuringly. "I like a challenge, what can I say?"

"Thank you," he bit out each word, as if it was painful. "I'll make it up to you one day."

Evren shook her head. "No, I don't work in debts—"

"Vox does," Drystan said curtly and stood up. "Lucky you."

The human walked out after Sahar, and Vox let go of her shoulder.

"My debts with Drystan come first, but I won't forget yours," he said. She could tell by the tone of his voice that there was no convincing him otherwise. Still, she hesitated before nodding. She didn't like the idea of someone risking their life for hers. No doubt Vox must have felt the same way.

He took her acceptance and walked off. Looking at the fire, she noticed that Nerezza had slipped away silently sometime when she wasn't paying attention. As Vox left the house to brave the bright cold of the lakeside, Evren realized she was left alone with Gyda.

Gyda stood up and ushered her to her feet. "Come, let's get you out of those clothes."

As she was herded through another door into a dim, but warm, back bedroom, Evren couldn't help but scoff. "I had no idea you wanted to undress me so bad."

Gyda looked at her blankly. "Your layers need to dry for you to be truly warm. And I need to check for injuries"

"Ah." Evren's ears were burning again. "I can check myself. You don't have to."

"I've already seen you naked." Gyda raised her eyebrow. "Remember?"

The memory of the bathhouse in Andovine hit her like a wave, but it was a good memory despite its awkward beginnings. She could hear Sol's snorting laughter and feel the warm water of the bath.

"I remember," she said slowly. "This is still different."

It's just the two of us now.

Evren refused to say it out loud, and Gyda didn't seem to understand anyway. It was easy to forget how differently they'd been raised until moments like this.

She sighed and threw the pelt on the bed. "All right, give me a moment."

Gyda shrugged and turned around.

Evren swallowed down her ridiculous nerves and tried to chant the same thing over and over in her head. *It's just a body. It's just a body, Hanali. You've gleefully broken nearly every rule in Orenlion but can't get past this prudishness so she can make sure you're not going to die? Idiot.*

With each word in her head, she stripped out of her layers. As she did, she began to notice how damp they really were. She remembered after the blizzard, of course, but had she really ignored them all nine days? She shivered and tossed her soaked boots in the corner. She was lucky she didn't freeze to death on that mountain top.

Her bare skin prickled uncomfortably as the air hit it. Warm, but it still made goosebumps dance across her arms and shoulders. She laid out every dirty, soaked-through layer until she was completely bare. Then she snatched the furs she'd put on the bed and covered herself up as she started to shiver again.

"Done," she muttered.

Gyda turned back to her, and a hint of a smile curled up her lips again. "You covered up."

"It's cold!" Evren protested. "Besides, I'm fine where I am covered. I checked."

"Your leg?"

"Bad bruise," she admitted, lifted the fur a bit so she could see the massive webbing of purples and blues across her hip and thigh. "I think I remember hitting it on my way down. Nothing a potion can't fix."

In truth, she probably fractured her hip bone as well, but again, a potion could fix that. She was more worried about how she forgot that during her trek.

Gyda hummed in agreement and looked down to her feet. Evren winced as she did the same, noting how bad they looked. The tips of her toes were starting to blacken. It at least explained why she couldn't feel them anymore.

"Frostbite on my toes . . ." She sighed. "At least another potion."

"And your nose."

"My nose!" She covered it up, tentatively feeling the tip. "How bad?"

Gyda's laugh was like a rumble of thunder. "I've seen worse. You'll be fine."

Evren scowled and continued to cover her nose. She didn't want to think about how it looked. If it was anything like her toes, she was glad she didn't have any mirrors on hand.

Gyda started gathering up her clothes. "I will ask Sahar for the potions and work on drying your clothes. You rest."

"Here?" She looked at the dusty bed. By all accounts it wasn't the worst place she'd slept, but it still felt wrong. Like sleeping in a grave.

"You will be fine." Gyda promised. As she took all the clothes and headed towards the door, she paused and looked over her shoulder. "I'm glad you found your way back to me."

Evren's smile was warmer than any fire. "I'm glad you were out there looking for me."

She didn't need to say that she'd always find Gyda. That part went unsaid.

10

"They were worried about you."

Evren blinked out of her warm daze, staring at the fire, to look at Sahar. Even in an abandoned shack after trekking through the wilderness, she still somehow managed to look put together. Her fine coat was dusted with snow and mud caked the edges, but she wore it like a cloak of jewels. Evren got the feeling that she could wear a pile of leaves and still manage to make it look presentable.

Sahar sat next to the fire, stirring strange ingredients into a steaming pot of even stranger liquid. Evren had never watched a potion being made, and made a point not to look at the ingredients Sahar flicked into the pot with her long fingers.

"Who?" Evren finally asked, but she knew the answer.

"The Wandering Sols." Sahar cut her a small smile. "It took a lot of effort to keep them from scouring every mountain top to find you once the storm cleared. It was the goblin that kept everyone in line, surprisingly."

"Arke." Evren pulled her now dry cloak tighter around her shoulders and tried not to smile. "He's the most practical out of all of us."

"I thought that would've been the black knight."

There was an edge to her words, just the slightest bite of hurt in an otherwise honey-sweet voice. Her face betrayed nothing as the pot began to glow a dull red. It was like she'd captured the ruby color of the sunset and concentrated it.

"Abraxas," Evren said slowly. "He's the oldest of us. There was a time I would've agreed with you. He did start that way. But he's changed, and he's a lot more heart-driven than he gives himself credit for."

Sahar tsked and added what looked like a knuckle bone into the pot with a loud plop. "I thought men like him stayed tucked away in their silent temples."

Evren sucked in a breath. She knew Abraxas as well as she could, given their time together, and she trusted him with her life. He was a fierce warrior and a steady friend. But she couldn't deny that there was a shadow that clung to him the same way the ash clung to his armor.

"Did he say something to hurt you?" she asked softly, already dreading the words as Sahar started to take the pot off the fire.

But Sahar just shrugged and poured the steadily steaming red liquid into a cup. "Nothing I didn't expect. He wouldn't be the first to look at me and get the wrong impression."

She slid the cup over to Evren, who took it in her numbed fingers gladly. The rest she poured into empty glass vials, slowly and methodically. Never a drop spilled, nor a bottle broken. Five glasses were filled to the brim and corked, and then she set the pot aside. She wiped her brow, sighing as she slumped into the chair next to Evren. Even with her boots propped up on the hearth, she still managed to make herself look poised.

"The funny thing is, I grew up in Terevas." She smiled and gestured to her coat. "My family left Vernes not long after the occupation ended. I've never owned a slave or talked to the corpse of a family member. I am more Terevasan than I ever was Vernesian, and yet that's all most people see when they look at me. The echo of a people who banished gods in order to save themselves." She furrowed her brows and looked at Evren again, as if trying to read her bones. "I know your knight still believes in the Divines. He wouldn't stop praying during the storm. But what about you? Do you see the threads of divinity in our world?"

Evren hesitated, the rim of the cup hovering just at the edge of her still chapped lips. She licked them nervously before taking a drink. Somehow, a fresh potion managed to taste better. Or maybe it was the heady warmth of the fire that seeped into her very bones as she drained the whole cup that distracted her from the aftertaste. When she set the cup down, she still didn't have an answer.

"I don't know," she admitted. "I didn't grow up with the Banished Faith, but my father's people worshipped dead beings just the same. There are times where I look at the world and I can see such beauty that I can't imagine it being made without a guiding hand. But . . . they've all left us, haven't they? The Divines were pushed out, the Elders died off, and the giants are few and far between. I think to worship one of them is to find comfort in the fact that the skies aren't empty, and there's a purpose to why we're here. But, for me personally, I've never felt the presence of a god. Any of them."

"And yet I'm told you keep coming back from the brink of death."

This time Evren grinned, and it didn't hurt when she did. She could feel the tip of her nose again, and her toes started to tingle. She propped her feet up by the fire and wiggled them in her boots.

"I think I'm just lucky." She shrugged. "Or very stupid."

"Most would call that bravery," Sahar said gently. "Sorin talked about your time in the Yawning Deep, and how you almost died there."

Evren shook her head. "I wasn't thinking clearly. If I had been more careful, I could've come out a lot better than I left."

"And the blizzard?"

"I'd do it again."

Sahar leaned forward, and the fire reflected in her eyes made them dance. She might not have grown up in the sea of sands, but Vernes's fire lived in her all the same.

"Why?" she asked. "Not that I'm not grateful, but surely you grow tired of throwing yourself at deadly situations to save others."

"Wouldn't it be worse if I was doing it without the need to save anyone?" Evren asked. "If some good comes out of it and I keep bouncing back, what's the harm?"

Sahar frowned and nodded to her face. Evren's hand involuntarily went to her nose. It was healed, but she could feel a puckering scar there, running along the ridge and down to the very tip. "That's the harm."

Evren shrugged and let her hand fall back down. "I've always had scars. I've had worse than this." The one on her chest prickled in response.

"Potions aren't supposed to leave scars, Evren." Sahar pressed. She looked back at the line of red bottles still glowing on the hearth before coming back to her. "You don't believe in gods, yet you throw yourself into danger and crawl back from the brink of death for others, as if you know something will bring you back. You bleed more than anyone, from what I hear, and never fully heal. And for what?"

"Because I have to." *Because if I don't, who will?*

Sahar stared back at the fire, her eyes continuing to dart between it and the potions she made. With every passing second, her brow furrowed further.

"I tried to justify your self-sacrificing as a devotion similar to your knight's," she said, "But you say you don't turn to the gods, that it's just luck bringing you back. Is that what you believe in? Luck?"

"I don't know," Evren said, as honestly as she dared without feeling like she was bleeding her truth all over the hut. "I don't think about that really in those situations. I just think of what I did to get there and how I need to get out."

"How practical," Sahar muttered to the fire.

"Why do you care?" Evren didn't mean the words to be harsh, and she was sure Sahar didn't take them that way. But it still felt like she was spitting blades with her words. Why did it matter what she believed in or why she risked herself for others? Isn't that what heroes were supposed to do for those they cared about? How else would Sahar have her fight for them?

She sighed and straightened in her chair. Her inky black hair fell in her face like a curtain, and for a moment, Evren saw a very young girl just trying to put the pieces of the world together so they made sense. Evren was just a very difficult piece.

"I can't fight the way Drystan can," Sahar finally said. "I can't learn magic like Nerezza. I can't swear off weapons and still be useful like Vox. All I can do is this." She nodded to the potions. "I can heal, I can hurt, I can get information. I can make a fire that never goes out or ice that never melts. I keep my friends alive, and I speak for them when their voices fail. That's my role in my party." Her eyes flicked back to Evren. "What's yours?"

Evren started to speak. She was many things. A hunter, a tracker, and a survivor most of all. But as she tried to speak her words died in her throat. She was an archer who found herself far too close to her enemies during battle. She was a leader who couldn't speak for her team, and a half-elf caught between two worlds, belonging to neither.

She thought of her final battle with Ainthe, and the shadows that consumed her before her blood somehow repelled them back. She thought of her own gentle smile when Viggo showed her the wonders of Andovine. She remembered the burning rage when she found his lies and the map of Eith with all the red. She thought back to the humming energy of Alkimos beneath her palm, of his cry mixed with hers once Sorin fell.

She'd been a warrior in the battle, running without a hope of making it to her target. She'd been an ambassador for the surface with Viggo, and their voice when she exposed his lies at the Convocation. And she'd been part monster in the battle with

Alkimos, rage and power flowing through her veins in equal measure.

She hadn't been the same since.

What was Evren Hanali? Shield or arrow? Monster or hunter?

Now, she wasn't sure.

"I'm just a hunter," she said with a rueful smile. The same words she told Viggo over and over again. Oh, how soft and fragile they felt on her tongue now.

Sahar nodded, although Evren wasn't sure she believed her answer or not. Hells, she wasn't sure if *she* believed it.

"Adventures make heroes," Sahar said. "They take the simple and make something new. I sometimes wonder if all they make are heroes though."

"That's always what the stories tell."

Sahar's smile didn't reach her eyes, it was as sharp as a knife. "Only the stories we hear."

Lostwater was frighteningly silent in the dwindling sunlight.

Twilight was clinging to the world and painting the village in a barely illuminated grey. The air was still and quiet, as if it too didn't dare make a noise in the dead village.

It was still bitingly cold as Evren trudged outside. Icy mud slipped dangerously under her boots, but she managed to keep steady. Her breath was white in the air around her, the little clouds floating up into the grey sky with every passing breath.

Her cheeks were already stinging and her aching body longed for more time around the fire. But her clothes and furs were dry and warm again. Her body was as whole as it could be after more than a week half dead. With her bow slung over one shoulder and her quiver full again, she felt more like herself than she had in days.

Drystan and Gyda were talking in hushed tones at the edge of the frozen lake. Gyda had called it Loch Lorn, the lonely lake. As she stared out over the frozen blue where nothing stirred, Evren couldn't help but think that the name was disturbingly accurate. If loneliness had a taste, the air was tinged with it.

The air was even colder near the water's edge, and snow had gathered in small drifts that crunched under her boots. Vox stood near a rotted wooden pier and nodded to her as she approached. Nerezza still had her nose in her spellbook, and was flexing her left hand stiffly as she murmured and paced.

"So, what do you suggest?" Drystan asked Gyda as she got closer. "Should we wait another night or move onto Direwall?"

"We won't find your necromancer in Direwall," Gyda said, crossing her arms. "But it'll be the safest place to be when the Long Night comes."

"How long do we have?" Evren asked, and both of them snapped their heads over to her. Drystan scowled but had lost most of his steel since she'd arrived. Gyda was as unreadable as she usually was.

"A couple of days, at the most." Gyda frowned. "We will not want to be outside of Direwall when that happens."

"The Long Night will be the perfect opportunity for whoever is behind this to take the undead and march them past the Black Pass in greater numbers." Drystan argued. "We need to stop this now."

"Why will it be easier?" Evren asked.

Nerezza shut her book, looking up at the sky with narrowed eyes as she spoke. "These undead are made with strange magic. Those in Vernes can't operate in extreme cold. These are different. They're stronger because of the ice. Without the sun to warm them, they'll be even harder to kill."

"But you found undead in Terevas," Evren pressed. "Most parts down there don't even get frost in the winter."

"They were easier to deal with then." Drystan scowled and

thumbed the handles of his axes. "There was significant frost magic around them, but they weren't hard to kill."

"They weren't as fast either," Vox grumbled and kicked a stone across the ice. It skittered across the slick surface, resting against the deep blue as he went on. "There were far more undead in the Black Pass than we anticipated."

"Many fall there," Gyda said. "The bottom is a graveyard."

"It felt like it." Nerezza nodded.

"That still doesn't mean we can get to your necromancer before the Long Night," Gyda said. "Once the sun falls, the cold will be the least of your worries."

"Why?" Evren asked. "What happens?"

She wouldn't have dared ask before, but now, with imminent darkness closing in, she needed to know. Gyda looked pained when she turned to her, and there was something unnerving flashing in her glacier eyes—fear.

"The first Long Night bred stories of monsters in the dark," she said, her voice soft, but the still air amplified it regardless. "Monsters that came from the glacier to the northeast, we call the White Cairn. We were taught to never leave our homes during that time. They used to say that even Mortova, the great sea monster that plagued our waters, would hide until the sun came up again. Every Long Night we would lose people. Children, and even whole families. Their doors were locked and frozen over, their houses as cold as the ice itself."

"Is that what happened here?"

She looked over the frozen town, achingly quiet and untouched until now. Compared to the rest of them, piled up with furs and nearly waddling with their massive layers, Gyda looked ill-prepared for the weather. She didn't look cold, but she shivered anyway, and turned from the buildings with her back hunched.

"Yes," Gyda murmured. "The Long Night took Lostwater last year."

Twilight was deepening and all Evren wanted to do was take

Gyda's hand and tell her it was going to be all right. How had she not seen what Lostwater was? Or the pain now so clearly etched on her face? This grave of a village had been her home, and Evren hadn't even noticed.

Shame welled up inside her, hot and uncomfortable. For not realizing, and for not knowing what to do. Her fingers twitched towards Gyda in the fading light, but she curled them back. She didn't know how to comfort her, or if that was even what she needed. And, as usual, her words were not enough. So, she swallowed them down, wishing she could do more.

It was Nerezza who broke the silence. She looked blissfully oblivious to the sudden discomfort that settled over them as the shadows grew. Her pale skin almost glowed in the twilight.

"There's a power here," she told Drystan. He turned away from Gyda and tucked the understanding on his face away to look at his mage.

"Like before?"

She nodded. "Yes. It's strong, like in the pass. Remnants of what happened last year, perhaps?"

Vox raised an eyebrow, and the scars on his face twisted. "Are we in the same danger as the Black Pass?"

Gyda frowned and answered before Nerezza could. "The Long Night doesn't kill; it consumes. There are never any bodies left, no signs of struggle."

"But those people in the Enrial Wilds were Ikedree," Evren said softly. She watched Gyda's form stiffen at her words. "They had to come from somewhere."

"Not here," she growled. "They weren't from my clan."

"What about Direwall?" Drystan asked. "Is it possible it's like this?"

Evren felt sick, and the air felt like daggers again down her throat. Unbidden images of her friends as shambling corpses flashed in her mind, and she couldn't shake them off. Sol's sky-blue eyes replaced by the sick glow, Sorin's smile turned into a rotting grin. It was too much.

Evren's panicked eyes met Gyda's. She shook her head, but that did little to calm her even as she spoke the words.

"Direwall is home to many clans. It is large, and I doubt the city would've been lost as easily as here."

"That still doesn't determine where we need to go next," Evren bit out, her panic closing up her throat bit by bit. "Either we wait out the Long Night in Direwall, or we face it."

"No one has gone into the Night and come back out," Gyda argued. "No one will."

"Perhaps." Drystan shook his head and looked in between Nerezza and Vox. "Thoughts?"

Vox shifted from foot to foot, the wood of the pier creaking under his large form. One of his tusks worried his top lip as he considered. It continued to do so, even as he spoke.

"Wherever you go, I go," he nodded to Drystan. "You've never led us wrong."

Drystan looked like he wanted a different answer but expected nothing less. His mouth was a thin line as he nodded back, and Evren wondered how he'd look if he ever smiled. Wrong? Better? He looked at the world as if there was nothing but despair to be seen. Those sorts of eyes were earned; no one was born like that. When they fell on Nerezza, they didn't soften.

She straightened up, still flexing her left hand. "We have a day of light left. Let us see what comes of it. Perhaps we end this before the Long Night. And maybe with help?" She looked at Evren expectantly.

Evren frowned. "I go with my party. Once I'm with them, we'll do what we can to help. So long as we're wanted."

Drystan shrugged, and a cloud of frost came off his furs. "You're in this now, regardless. I'll speak to Sahar and get her opinion. Whatever we choose, we'll leave at sunrise."

He trudged back to the warm hut as darkness finally settled over Lostwater. The silence was deafening, only the crunching of snow under boots breaking it. Evren turned to Gyda, a million words at the tip of her tongue, and so many questions that needed to be answered.

Gyda looked like a vision in the dark snow, a silhouette of grief and strength as the cool light that emanated from the lake framed her from behind. Evren took a step forward, that comforting hand reaching for her, as the light grew brighter.

The bluish-green was breathtaking. Like the auroras she'd read about in books trapped beneath the ice. The light was dim because of the ice, but still managed to glow in the air around it. It made Nerezza's hair glow almost white, and it deepened the scars on Vox's face. Gyda's silver eyes almost took on the same hue as she stared at her quizzically.

"Does the lake always do that?" Evren asked. It was beautiful, but a familiar feeling of dread was pooling in her stomach.

Gyda whirled around, her hands already reaching for her sword as Vox leaned closer to the ice. His long hair fell in his face as an almost childlike sense of wonder overtook him.

"Vox . . ." Evren called out as a warning. Nerezza had stepped away, falling back with her. But Vox was rooted to the spot.

"I think . . ." he whispered, inches from the ice now. "I think there's something in here."

Gyda unsheathed her sword fluidly. The bone handle glowed a bright blue with its runes, and the air hummed with arcane energy. She lunged for Vox, grabbing him by the collar to yank him away from the ice.

As soon as she did, a hand pressed against the ice right where Vox had been.

"Get inside! NOW!"

Gyda's voice rang through the fear-thickened air
like a knife. She tossed Vox back, and he stumbled
into Evren. He was shaking, his eyes still staring at the lake and
the handprints. The hundreds more that were joining it and
eclipsing the light. This light she suddenly recognized.

She pulled Vox back and shook his shoulders until he looked
at her.

"I heard them," he whispered, the horror clear on his pale
face. "What they were saying . . ."

"I SAID GO!" Gyda roared.

Evren took his arm and grasped for Nerezza. Until she realized she had Vox's other arm. She nodded firmly, her mouth set
in a determined line as she started to pull her friend away from
the lake. Evren did the same, but it was no easy task. Vox was
bigger than both of them, and stronger too. He dug his heels in
the icy ground, craning his neck backward for another glance.

Evren gritted her teeth and jerked his arm hard until both he
and Nerezza stumbled around the corner of a building. He
slumped against the side, pressing his hands to his ears as
Nerezza looked at her with round, frightened eyes.

"Get to Drystan and Sahar," Evren ordered, and forced a harshness she wasn't used to into her voice as she pulled out her bow.

"But Gyda—"

"I'm not leaving her." Evren whipped out an arrow so forcibly she could feel the arrowhead cut into the leather of the quiver. She tried to hide her shaking hands. "We'll meet you in Direwall."

Vox gasped as if he'd been struggling to breathe. His eyes were so wide she could see the whites glowing in the growing light. She turned to walk away, but he snatched her arm back, holding her with an iron grip.

"I'm with you," he wheezed.

"No." She shook him off, her arm throbbing where he had held her. "Get to Drystan before it's too late."

"You can't do this on your own."

"Neither can Gyda. Now go!"

She shoved Vox away, even as he tried to follow her. Nerezza caught him again and drew him back. Her pale eyes were dark as they met hers. Before she left, she reached her hand out and grasped Evren's free palm. Her grip was surprisingly strong and stiff as she forced a wad of paper into her gloved fingers.

Survive this, she seemed to say without words and let her go.

If only it were that simple.

Evren turned and didn't watch to see if the two of them actually listened to her. In her mind, all she could hear was Sahar's voice questioning her all over again.

. . . surely you grow tired of throwing yourself at deadly situations to save others?

The bow was heavy in her grip, as was the paper. Evren didn't dare look at it as she tore around the building and back to the lake. Her blood was hot in her veins, but her skin was ice-cold. She had the unyielding certainty as she took the steps back to the lake that fear wasn't going to be an ally this time.

It was like a blue sun was trapped under the ice. Gyda stood before it all, her sword drawn and her hands steady. Evren couldn't see her face, but she imagined it stony and hard, without fear. She refused to believe she was afraid.

"Gyda!" she cried out and stumbled to a halt a few feet from her.

Gyda whirled around, her eyes catching sight of her and freezing with exactly what Evren didn't want to see, just as the ice cracked.

The sound was like a clash of thunder. It rolled over the quiet town as the ice buckled and bowed under the strength of so many hands. Evren watched in horror as the middle of the lake split like an egg, the ice several feet thick but tossed aside as if it weighed nothing. Wet, bony hands clawed at the edges and hauled themselves up. The light from their eyes was still beautiful, but paired with the chilling grin of their waxy, melting faces, it made her want to curl up into a ball and hide.

They tore across the ice frighteningly fast. Without thinking, Evren let loose an arrow. It landed square in the heart of one and sent it tumbling back into the frozen depths below. She felt the warmth of pride flicker inside her, until one of the undead locked its eyes on her.

She froze.

There was nothing but that blue-green light. It swam in her vision, enveloping her in an icy embrace. Unseen hands seemed to dig into her face, caressing her cheeks softly and urging her forward. Towards the ice. Towards them.

Come, come, a thousand voices whispered in her head. *There is warmth to be had here. There is family and belonging. You will never be alone again. Come, come, little child of the Deep Wood.*

Evren could feel the cold, but below it was something more. The smell of home, of food and damp earth and endless stars reeling above her head. She could feel the spider-silk covers beneath her fingers, the comforting warmth of someone with their arms around her.

She took another step forward.

Yessss, the voices cooed. *Come home with us, little child of blood and sacrifice.*

There was the ring on her finger again. She couldn't see it, but she could feel its weight. The coolness of the silver shone in her mind, even without the light. She felt her father's hands on her shoulders, along with a wave of guilt. Even as the hands disappeared, and the scar on her chest ached, she was choking on guilt and grief. On the wrongness of *something* her mind refused to reveal.

Little lost child, follow us . . .

Evren took another step.

The moth pin fluttered in her mind too. This was harsh and sharp in her vision. Nothing like the images she was seeing, the ones that were guiding her closer to the lake's edge. The moth hummed in its pocket close to her chest, its wings beating fruitlessly as it tried to escape.

Evren stumbled backward as another voice found her ear. This one was deeper, and it stood alone, echoing above the many as they hissed and screamed for dominance. This voice was soothing, familiar, and sad.

Evren Hanali of Eith, you are not alone. This light is not your guide.

Evren gasped as clarity hit her. The lake. She was standing on the ice. The dead were racing towards her, and the ice was wavering under her boots. She could hear Gyda's voice screaming her name behind her, even as Viggo's faded from her mind.

Under her hand, something crackled. She opened her palm to see the paper Nerezza had stuffed in there. The page was littered with arcane glyphs and elven words. Strange words, but she knew them. She could read them clearly.

Wall of Fire.

Evren's stomach was in knots as she turned away from the undead and ran back to shore. How had she ended up so far from it? How had so many undead slipped past her? She'd thought that they would've grabbed her, but all their focus was on Gyda. Gyda, who was being swarmed by them. She swung her sword in a shimmering arc of blue light and its keen edge and took down four at once. Immediately, four more took their place. She was stumbling back, her eyes wide. She'd stopped yelling for Evren, but her mouth was still moving.

She was talking to the dead.

Evren's feet were slippery as she flew across the ice. Her bow in one hand, hope in the other. Not for the first time, she wished she had Arke with her.

"Gyda!"

Her friend's eyes snapped towards hers, wet with tears and relief. When she saw what Evren was waving in her hand, she understood. She let out a cry of rage as she took the length of her sword and pushed the group of undead back. They stumbled on the ice and over each other. Most toppled like felled trees but were back on their feet in seconds. Some were still crawling through the tangle of legs and arms to get back up.

Gyda broke away, meeting Evren at the lake shore and pulling her onto land.

"Come on!" Evren panted as she ran away from the lake. She could hear the snarling and scraping as the creatures chased after them. Gyda was hot on her heels.

"Can you make this work?" Gyda asked. Doubt was an ugly thing to hear in anyone's voice, but Evren held the same doubt close in her chest.

She skidded to a halt where the town truly began and the buildings were thickest and turned back to face the undead. A good choke point. She tossed her bow to Gyda, who caught it easily, and took her glove off of her free hand. In her other, the spell shook with adrenaline and fear.

"I don't know," she held her hand out to Gyda, "but I need you to cut me."

The warrior took a step back. "What?"

"I'll explain later, if we survive." She could hear the clambering footsteps on the solid ground now. "Just do it."

Gyda gritted her teeth and looked like she would say no. But she took her sword and neatly sliced Evren's palm open with ease and a fair amount of pain. Evren hissed and drew back. Blood welled up in her palm quickly, and the bright splash of red against the white was refreshing to see. She felt her vision clear, and her adrenaline sharpened each and every breath. Time seemed to slow down for a bit, and she could see the plan in front of her. The paper held all the instructions, yet looked so mundane.

There was power in the Written word, just as there was power in her blood. She needed to unlock both.

Evren took the paper in her bleeding palm. She watched the parchment greedily soak up the crimson liquid. She could feel a strange warmth in her fingertips.

The undead swung around the corner, their sucking breaths echoing through Lostwater.

Evren shivered as she felt a familiar power course through her veins and into the paper. She closed her eyes and muttered the words. Words not her own, words she didn't fully understand. But as she spoke, everything in her hand got hotter. She could feel the flames licking at the paper and the glyphs springing to life with each word. She tightened her fist, finished the incantation, and opened her eyes.

The glyphs around her weren't fire orange. They were crimson.

She slammed her hand on the ground with a cry, and a wall of crimson flame leapt up in front of her.

The undead fell back, fear in their glowing eyes. The fire wall spread across the choke point, hot and blazing. The flames turned from red to their normal orange, and the sudden heat was intense enough to sear her eyebrows.

She stumbled back, her hand still bleeding and now coated in ash. She stared at the wall of fire as the undead on the other side wailed. The power was still thrumming inside her, but was dying down. She could feel it start to leave her.

Evren was shaking. With awe and fear. One question circled around her head as she watched the flames burn.

What am I?

Gyda's hand latched onto her upper arm and pulled her away from the flames. Their reflection in her eyes were bright, and almost hellish. Evren tore her eyes away from the fire, from Gyda's strange gaze, and back to reality; Lostwater was swarming with undead, and its buildings were catching on fire. There was only one other option.

Run.

She gathered her discarded bow and glove, and even with her fingers slick with blood and ash she somehow managed to keep a good grip as Gyda pulled her away. The fire roared at her back. The crackling of flames licking up dead wood filled the eerie silence of the night and drowned out the cries of the undead.

Her feet churned up ice and mud as she tore through the village. Rounding another corner, she saw the hut that had been a safe haven only minutes ago. Framed in the orange glow of the fire, it looked completely different. The undead crawling up its walls made it look like a corpse covered in maggots.

A burst of searing white flame tore through the undead blocking the door. They hurtled back, clawing at the strange fire that stuck to their melting skin, and leaving just enough room to squeeze through. Evren started to go in, the stench of burning flesh and acid clogging her nostrils, but stopped short when she saw Sahar and Drystan charging through.

Drystan hurled one of his axes at a recovering corpse, picking it up with ease as he ran past. Sahar was hot on his heels, her feet fast and sure but her eyes wide even as she caught sight of Evren and Gyda. She took another vial of white liquid and threw it over her shoulder as the undead closed in. The burst of flame was enough to catch the hut in its entirety.

"Nerezza and Vox?" There was no edge in Drystan's voice as

he came up to them, panting. His left shoulder was bleeding sluggishly, his blood joining Evren's on the snow below.

Evren shook her head. "They ran ahead of us."

Something akin to terror sparked in Sahar's otherwise calm face. Her eyes turned up to the black heavens. Was she searching for a god in this situation? What god could possibly survive in a place as harsh as this?

"We don't have time for this, the town will be in flames soon," Gyda's voice was calm, but Evren could see her sword arm shaking. Darkness had taken her home first, and now fire.

Evren felt like she was going to be sick.

"We're not leaving without them." Sahar put herself between Gyda and Drystan. She turned to him, her back straight and her chin up but there were tears in her eyes. Longing coated her pleading words like a deadly poison. "We're not leaving them, Drystan . . ."

For the first time, Evren saw him break. As if her words were a hammer to his glass walls. He shattered and took a faltering step back. "Sahar, they could be gone already."

"Better we die with them than carry on without!" She took his hand, the one that was coated in his blood, and he flinched. But he didn't pull away from her touch. "Please, Drystan. Let me do this."

He swallowed. "I promised I wouldn't let you."

She pulled away. "You've broken such promises before."

Evren looked behind her. Not that the undead were a welcome sight, but she felt like she was watching something private. She could see the light from her fire she'd made. Shadows the shape of men were clawing their way through. Their time was up.

She whipped back around. "They can't be far now, but we need to go. They're smart people, they probably headed away from the lake when they saw the hut being overrun. Gyda, what's the quickest way out of town?"

But Gyda wasn't looking at her. Her eyes were on the pile of undead burning in Sahar's strange fire. Their faces were twisted in anguish, their gaping mouths screaming silently. Could the dead feel pain? One reached a flame-wreathed hand out, almost like it was pleading for Gyda to save it.

"Gyda!"

Evren grabbed her arm and pulled her away from the corpse. She snatched herself out of Evren's touch, her eyes on the ground now. Evren's gut twisted further when she realized she was refusing to look at her.

"We need another way out," Evren said. "We need you to get us out."

Gyda said nothing. She clenched her jaw and tightened her grip on her sword. The runes wasn't glowing anymore. She turned and walked briskly away. Evren, Sahar, and Drystan had no choice but to follow.

The paths through Lostwater were a maze of undead and fire-ravaged huts. Evren's wall of fire had caught most of the town in the blaze, and now that was all she could see. The air was thick with smoke and ash that clouded her vision like twisted snow. The only advantage was that the undead shied away from the fire and barely touched them as they ran past. But every corner they turned there were more waiting. Each time Gyda turned around and ran in another direction, a little more of Evren's ever dwindling luck slipped away like ash in the frozen air.

Even with the growing inferno, the air was still bitingly cold. The extremes of intense heat and bitter ice flashed back and forth across her exhausted body. Her palm pulsed in pain, her grip on her bow waning as she followed Gyda down another path. Her footsteps were faltering, a sudden, lulling wave of fatigue washing over her with every passing second. The only things that kept her going were the chilling eyes watching her from every corner, and the two humans following behind her.

Gyda stopped so suddenly that Evren barely avoided running into her. The heat from the fire next to her was enough to make her squirm, but Gyda didn't change course. She simply stayed rooted to the spot. Behind her, she could hear Drystan curse under his breath.

"Why have we stopped?"

Gyda gave no answer.

Evren swung around her to stand by her side, and whatever explanation she would've had died in her throat.

The white expanse stretched before her, glittering and glowing in the dim light shed from the town. The path forward, the way to freedom, blocked.

The crowd of undead that stood between them and the ice were still and silent. The flames crackled around them, but their eyes were fixed forward. Dozens of them, nearly a hundred, stood between them and their path out.

Evren tensed, her hand going for an arrow. She expected them to lunge, to start their mad scramble and overrun them. She wondered what death would feel like under their cold, clammy hands.

But as she notched an arrow with sticky, shaking fingers, they didn't move. None so much as twitched in their general direction, even as one of their pant legs caught fire and they began to smolder.

"What is this?" Drystan hissed as he came up beside her. He was holding his injured arm now, and Sahar was glued to his side. There were no careful words coming from her now.

Evren looked behind her, sharp eyes scanning for an alternate route if Gyda couldn't find one. Her vision swam as black dots kept her from completely focusing. But she didn't need to see clearly to know that the rest of the undead had surrounded them and were now standing perfectly still as the town burned around them.

"Why aren't they attacking?" Sahar whispered.

"They're waiting." The answer came unbidden to Evren before she even realized it had left her lips. Sahar looked at her confused and terrified in equal amounts.

"For what?"

That, she didn't have an answer for. But slowly, the undead started to answer for her. One by one, the ones blocking their path parted. Evren couldn't help but think of the Black Pass and the way it dissected a whole mountain as they moved in tandem. Drystan moved Sahar behind him, his axe bloody and gleaming in his hands as he stared forward with a killer's intensity. Evren readied her bow but faltered again when she saw two familiar figures being pushed between the dead.

Vox and Nerezza were each held by undead. There were three on Vox, and he looked beaten and dazed. His eyes fluttered around as if he couldn't quite focus on anything. His fists were soaked with black blood and dangled uselessly at his side.

Nerezza didn't look much better. Her pale hair was soaked red and it was sticking to her face on one side. Her spellbook was nowhere to be seen, and she looked as frail as a wisp of smoke in the hands of the corpse that pushed her forward. But there was a murderous glint in her eyes that made Evren shiver despite herself.

Sahar sucked in a hopeful breath and tried to take a step forward. Drystan kept her back.

"Don't," he whispered firmly.

Tears spilled over Sahar's soot-caked face. She didn't move, just as he said. But she leaned against his grip anyway towards the army in front of her.

"What do you want?" she cried.

"WHAT DO WE WANT?" The undead spoke as one. A hundred voices joining like some kind of twisted choir. Their frozen vocal cords snapped and cracked under the pressure, but they continued to talk anyway. Each word seemed to draw Gyda further towards the dead..

"WE ARE THE LOST AND THE WAITING. WE ARE THE FORGOTTEN AND SACRIFICED THAT THE NIGHT CONSUMED. WE ARE FLESH AND ICE MADE ONE. AND WE WANT THE DAUGHTER BACK."

All eyes, living and undead, snapped to Gyda. She was frozen, her mouth parted as if she was trying to speak, but no words came out.

Rage overtook fear. Evren stepped between Gyda and the reaching undead. She was not much of a shield, but she drew herself up anyway.

"Gyda belongs to the living," she bit out with as much strength as her weary body could muster. "You can't have her."

"ALL BELONG TO THE DEAD, CHILD OF BLOOD. ALL BELONG TO THE PRIME AND HIS FAMILY."

"Prime?" Drystan scoffed. "Are they the one behind you all? The mage who sends corpses to do their dirty work?"

"THE PRIME WAS THE FIRST. HE IS THE LIGHT IN THE NIGHT THAT GAVE US LIFE AGAIN. HE IS THE FATHER OF THE WHITE CAIRN, A GOD OF THE ICE AND THE NIGHT."

Sahar let out a sob. "There are no gods!" she screamed as she strained against Drystan's grip. "Do you hear me? They're dead and gone. We don't need them! Just let them go, *please!*"

Drystan pulled her back and let his axe fall to the ground with a soft thud. He held her with both arms, even as she struggled against him. He angled his body ever so slightly to shield her, his cold gaze fixed on the undead. He bounced from one to another, until he finally landed on Evren. He shook his head the tiniest amount, and she understood. There was no way out, none that he could see.

She turned back to the undead holding Vox and Nerezza. "What do you want from us? You can't have Gyda. But why stop us when you could easily overrun us now and take her?"

All in unison, they cocked their heads to the side in confusion. The cracking of bone and splintering of ice-clogged skin filled the air.

"WE FOLLOW THE PRIME IN ALL THINGS, AS YOU WILL EVENTUALLY. HE IS NOT UNKIND. HE OFFERS A TRADE. A CHOICE. THE LOST ONE AND THE BROKEN ONE, IN EXCHANGE FOR THE DAUGHTER. A FAIR DEAL."

"That's not happening," she said, but her voice and her will were weak. And the undead weren't looking at her anymore, they were looking at Drystan.

"MAN OF IRON AND ROT, YOU HAVE LOST MUCH. HOW MUCH CAN YOU SAVE YOURSELF FROM LOSING AGAIN?"

Drystan bared his teeth. "I will not bow to the threats of the dead again."

"Drystan . . ." Sahar whimpered.

"I swore I wouldn't." But as he said the words, he looked at Evren "This is not a choice I can make."

"TWO LIVING SOULS FOR THE PRICE OF ONE ALREADY DEAD, AND STILL YOU REFUSE." Their heads snapped upright quickly, and then they all smiled. Most were but skeletons, so the grin was there anyway. But those that had skin made it stretch far too wide for a normal smile. "PERHAPS A DEMON-STRATION THEN? IF YOU DO NOT WANT BOTH, WE WILL TAKE ONE."

"No." Drystan sounded far away.

"THE LOST OR THE BROKEN?"

"Don't," Sahar begged between sobs. "Please don't. Drystan tell them!"

His eyes were wide. Darting between Vox and Nerezza, and then to Gyda. Evren's hand curled around her bow. She wouldn't let him trade Gyda to those monsters. But just how much would she do to keep her friend out of their cold hands? She glanced at Vox and Nerezza. She'd saved them once. Was that only to throw them to the wolves now?

"I won't make deals with the dead," Drystan said, bringing her back to him. There was steel in his spine but dread in his eyes. "I'm sorry. I can't."

"VERY WELL THEN." The undead turned to Nerezza and she struggled in their icy grip with no avail. There was more strength in her now than Evren had seen before. They turned to Vox and he bowed his head. His eyes found Drystan's, and the smile on his lips was sad, the echo of something greater. A shuddering breath left Drystan's chest.

"It's okay, my friend," Vox said. "My debt is paid in full."

"THE BROKEN IT IS."

There was no time between their declaration and Vox's death to even take a breath. An undead plunged their hand into his chest with a sickening crunch. Sahar's cries of anguish didn't disguise Vox's last sucking breaths, nor the sound of his still body hitting the ground. His heart lay in the creature's hands, dripping and steaming in the cold. For a while it continued to beat, until it finally stilled and was tossed in the snow and ash next to his body.

Vox's eyes never closed and stared sightlessly at the sky above him.

"Monsters!" Nerezza kicked and thrashed in her captor's arms. Her hair was wild and her teeth bared into a snarl but they held her in place even as she struggled to get to him. "I'll kill you all! I swear I'll drag you to the hells myself!"

They ignored her, and their collective voices drowned out her pained threats as they turned once more to the rest of the living. "THE LOST REMAINS. GIVE US THE DAUGHTER AND SHE CAN RETURN TO YOU. ONE LIFE FOR A SOUL ALREADY DEAD IS A FAIR TRADE."

"Gyda isn't dead," Evren said weakly. It took everything in her to keep her eyes away from Vox's lifeless body. "She's living, and she doesn't belong to you."

Behind her, Gyda's rumbling voice sounded far away. "Evren . . ."

Gyda's heavy hand on her shoulder felt like an anchor back to reality. She could feel again all the things she hadn't realized were starting to numb inside her. The pain in her hand, the cold on her cheeks, the panic creeping up her throat. And the hopelessness threatening to overwhelm her entirely.

It was like a wave she couldn't escape. It pulled at her legs and feet, its shadow crested over her as Gyda pulled her back and stepped forward.

"No!" She fought her and the wave. She grabbed Gyda's hand and tugged back desperately. But for all the clawing pain and desperation she was little more than a breeze against the mountain that was Gyda. Unmoving, unflinching, and steadfast.

She didn't look at Evren when she spoke, but her voice was cold. "You wouldn't damn a life you already saved for me. Let go."

"Don't tell me what I would and wouldn't do!" She fought back the hot tears blurring her vision. "There's another way out of this! Just like in Serevadia and Dirn-Darahl. You don't have to sacrifice yourself for this."

"The way out of Dirn-Darahl ended in Sorin's death. Tell me, who else would you kill for me?"

Evren's fingers felt numb as she let go. The wave was crashing. She couldn't control her feet as she staggered backwards, the shock and the hurt of her words reverberating in her chest in such a painful way that she struggled to breathe. She couldn't help but think it would've been kinder to cut her with her sword again.

When Gyda spoke again, there was no anguish in her voice. Not like what Evren felt. "I asked you to stay behind. I told you that if you cared at all, you would not follow me."

"I do care—"

"Not enough to let me go."

Evren struggled to breathe. The ash and smoke and ice-cold air were all too much for her struggling lungs. "You wanted this?"

There was a heavy pause, as everyone, living and dead, waited for the answer.

"Yes." Gyda closed her eyes and breathed in deeply. When she opened them again, they almost reflected the same bluish-green light that the corpses' held. She stared at them. With fear?

Hope? These people she knew, all reaching out with boney hands. All saying the same thing without words.

Come back to us.

"I'm going home."

Gyda didn't look back as she stepped forward.

Something grew in the gaping hole in Evren's chest. Her scar burned and she struggled to breathe. She wanted to reach out, to take a step and get her to stay. But her legs couldn't move. She watched her friend, her ally and companion, turn her back completely and walk to the dead.

Nerezza was shoved back to them, alive and mostly whole. She turned back as if to lunge at the undead with her bare hands, but Sahar ran to her and grabbed her before she could. She held her, and while the elven mage relaxed, her eyes never left the corpses. The cold fury in her pale eyes was matched by something else Evren couldn't place and didn't have the strength to wonder about.

Gyda walked into the ranks of the dead. As she did, her grey skin and faded scarf blended in entirely. For one, sick and horrifying moment, Evren could see her as the dead did. Skeletal and ashen, a woman of both living and dying. As she stood in the crowd, they seemed to swallow her. She was taller than all of them, but she disappeared entirely. There was no way to pick her out from the rest.

The ash fell, the dead parted, and Gyda was gone for good.

The path the dead left for them to walk through led straight into the cold, unforgiving tundra beyond. They didn't move a frozen muscle as the remaining three of the Ashen Bond walked hesitantly through. Sahar stumbled in front of Vox's body and tried to pick him up, but Drystan pulled her away.

"We can't," he whispered in her ear. "Let him go."

He pushed Sahar and Nerezza ahead, then turned back to Evren. Something in him was as broken as Evren was, and there was a strange mirroring between the two of them that made her recoil. The fire of the town at her back, Vox's dead body at her

feet, and a sea of parted corpses leading the way into an unforgiving abyss in front of her. She felt trapped. This was not a cage
she had ever prepared for, and she didn't know the right way out.

Drystan clutched her shoulder and shook her none too
gently. His face was grim, firm, and entirely human in its pain.
He didn't try to hide it. "We walk together, as we grieve
together."

She nodded. There was no use for words anymore. She let
him guide her through the undead. Her eyes scanned their faces,
searching for one she recognized. For a face wrought of stone
and eyes like ice, but a smile that could melt the snow like the
summer sun if brought out. She found nothing but cold, grinning faces staring back at her, and hate curling in the space
where her heart should've been.

She and Drystan walked into the free space of the expanse
untouched. Nerezza and Sahar waited for them, looking as lost
and broken as the undead. Ahead, the warm lights of Direwall
could barely be seen flickering in the north.

"I'm sorry," Evren muttered. To whom, she wasn't sure. But
it was Drystan who replied as the black sky suddenly bloomed
with a gorgeous aurora of dazzling blues and greens.

"As am I." He let go of her shoulder and faced the trail
ahead.

12

The only saving grace they had that night was that the sky was never truly dark. It was a mass of swirling, twisting colors so beautiful it stole Evren's breath. Every ice crystal glimmered the colors back, until the whole white expanse shone with colors and light.

She didn't take the time to crane her neck up at the sky and watch. If she did, she could almost still see the orange haze of fire from Lostwater behind her. It took hours for the smell of smoke to leave her nose. The ash refused to leave her, and she covered her throbbing hand back up with her glove to hide the wound. She didn't care that every time she flexed or clenched her fist, she felt the fragile scab break and more blood ooze into her glove. By the time they reached the massive ice canyon bisecting their path, she could catch whiffs of her own blood as she walked.

The bridge that crossed the canyon was made of rope and wood. A thin sheen of ice encased it, and beyond it the road to Direwall was clearer. It was obvious that the bridge was well used and sturdy, and in little danger of breaking underneath them. But they all paused just before the first step.

Evren took a deep breath. The smell of salt was stronger now.

She buried her scarred nose in her scarf to try and keep it warm as Nerezza turned on them.

"What was that?" she hissed.

"Nezza . . ." Sahar reached out to comfort her, but the elf sidestepped out of the way.

"Don't 'Nezza' me," she spat. "Why didn't you fight? Any of you?"

"We did," Drystan said wearily. He looked as tired as Evren felt, and he slumped against the wooden post that held up part of the bridge. It didn't so much as creak under his weight.

"And you." Nerezza turned to him, eyes flaring with that cold anger again. "You could've saved Vox. But you didn't. What the fuck was that about?"

Even Evren flinched back at her words. Sahar took a physical step back, but Drystan didn't blink.

"Vox knew," he said. "It wasn't my choice to make, and he realized that."

"So, what about her?" She pointed to Evren. Under her gaze Evren felt small and insignificant. She was almost too tired to care. "You risk your life in a blizzard, but can't let your friend go to save mine again?"

"That's not fair, Nezza," Sahar said softly.

"Isn't it? What, you'll sacrifice everything to save someone you barely know, until it comes down to choosing who lives and dies? You heard what they said. She was already dead anyway! She came here to be with them. For all you know, she could've been working with them all along."

Evren couldn't really feel her racing heartbeat, but the flood of rushing blood quickened anyway. It was something her exhausted mind could barely wrap her mind around as something equally cold and furious snapped inside her.

"Watch yourself," Evren said coldly. "Gyda was a friend. Regardless of what happened, you'll watch what you say about her in front of me."

"Will I?" Nerezza's nose wrinkled in disgust. "I'm sure you're glad it's an even trade then. A life for a life. It wouldn't have been fair if two of us got to live while you lost one."

"I didn't want Vox to die," Evren gritted out.

"Then why did you hesitate?"

"Because I'd seen one friend die and I didn't want to see it again!" Her voice, harsh and brittle, echoed across the cavern in painful waves. Nerezza closed her mouth, but her furious expression remained, even as Evren went on. Softer this time, so as not to wake the memories of Sorin's death.

"There was a battle we had no hope of winning," she started, her voice cracking as she did. "If we lost, we doomed two peoples to a war that would destroy them both. We didn't know the cost of winning, only that we had to. You met Sorin back at the outpost, but not the true him. What you saw, what I've been living with, is a shell of the man I knew. The man who used to sing and laugh and joke at every opportunity. The man who was the one who kept us together when we fell apart." She pressed her hand to her chest. "I was the reason the one who killed him stood down. I forced her hand and when she lost, she took Sorin down with her. I will *never* be able to give him back what was stolen. He refuses to even talk about it. Like it never happened. If he told the story to you, there would be no death. Because that's what heroic stories leave out, right? They don't talk about the deaths unless it's final."

She took a deep breath. The cold air wasn't enough to satisfy her lungs. "I clung to Gyda because I saw her slipping away the moment we first found the undead. I didn't want to lose her like Sorin, but now . . ." She looked at the sky with blurry eyes. It was a blaze of colors so bright they hurt her eyes. "Now I know that it's worse. Sorin fought to stay. He wouldn't have died if he had a choice. Gyda would've left eventually. She'd been trying to tell me since the beginning. I just didn't listen."

The wind started to pick up, a playful little thing that carried shards of snow and a not so carefree bite to it. It came from the south, smelling of pine and something burning and rotten. Evren turned her face away.

"I don't know how to beat this," Drystan said, his voice thick, as if he had a hard time speaking. "I didn't think it would end like this. A friend gone, and a mage who thinks himself a god and who knows us."

"He thinks he does." Nerezza kicked some snow down the canyon, her eyes narrowed. "He's about to see who we really are."

"This is a lot more than a disorganized cult," Sahar muttered. "We didn't prepare to take down a would-be god."

Drystan looked at her sadly. "But we can't leave."

Evren shuddered. Across the canyon, Direwall gleamed warmly. It was a beacon of warmth and safety. Behind its walls her friends would be waiting. Four more people she'd disappoint when she showed up alone. But they deserved to know. And she needed them.

She needed Sol's quick mind and Arke's blunt words. She needed Abraxas's quiet rage and Sorin's warmth. More than anything, she needed them together so they could get Gyda back or kill the bastard that took her.

"I happen to know a few people that can help you with your problem," Evren muttered, her eyes still on Direwall.

Drystan followed her gaze, and something of a rueful smile found its way onto his lips. "Are you sure they can help?"

She snorted. "They'll butt in whether you want them to or not."

"Their rates?"

"Nothing," she said truthfully. "Just a chance at some payback."

"To kill a god of the undead?" Drystan looked at Sahar and Nerezza. Slowly they nodded. It wasn't hope that filled their eyes, but something a lot more manageable—determination. He turned back to Evren. "I think we can manage that."

~

DIREWALL WAS a stack of icy wooden buildings all clinging to the dark waters at the edge of Myrefall Bay. Four tall towers rose above the rest of the city. Lighthouses, Evren guessed. They were cold and empty.

In the early dawn, Direwall shared a passing resemblance to Lostwater, with its steep roofs and stilted houses, but there was no silence to be found behind its massive wooden walls. Frost gripped the packed earth of the city streets, which were pock-marked with holes and ruts gathering pools of ice and muck. The buildings were larger, some were even painted dark colors of reds, oranges and deep purples at their doors. Market stalls were crowded with large, spiny fish on slabs of ice. Fishermen called out deals in stilted Core, their hands red and raw from the cold. Children ran with their brightly colored scarves streaming in the frigid air behind them, laughing as a litter of pups nipped at their heels.

The sound of the lapping shore, the smell of food, and the chatter of so many people was overwhelming. Evren felt herself shying away from the crowds and avoiding eye contact all together. There was something in the sudden cramped nature of Direwall that sent her skin crawling. She'd been alone in the wild for too long if she flinched away when a mother barked at her children to stay out of the street.

"We're not well received." Drystan's low tone was less of a warning than Evren needed, but she hummed a reply anyway. It was all her tight throat could manage.

But he wasn't wrong. Despite all the commotion, everyone in Direwall avoided the four adventurers like they had a plague. Merchants scowled behind their stalls, vendors kept their gazes down and away, even when Sahar offered up a charming smile. The common folk that walked the streets with furs and timber kept well out of their way. They didn't bother to disguise their distrustful expressions, or the whispers that bounced in the air as the group had their backs to them.

All at once, Evren was aching for Gyda to be at her side. It would be easier to meet the stern gazes of the hunters at the street corners with her as their stoic shadow. She could tell them what her people were saying, and why they looked at them with such disdain. But the spot at Evren's side where Gyda should've been was cold and empty. She put her hand in her pocket to keep it from reaching out for someone that wasn't there.

"If they don't like us, that should make my friends easy to find." Evren nodded to a woman passing by with a stack of laundry. She was bundled up tightly, almost comically so. Her head scarf of woven blues and purples covered her face as well as her hair, and she scurried away quickly.

"Mostly humans here," Sahar said. "Finding an armored elf, a goblin, and a dwarf shouldn't be too difficult."

"Assuming they're still here." Nerezza's first and only words in Direwall so far were as dark as all the others said before the gates.

Before Drystan could even bother asking her, Evren was already hunting for her party. It shouldn't have been hard since, as Sahar mentioned, they would stick out drastically from everyone in the city. She searched the sea of faces for someone familiar. Abraxas's stoic walk, a flash of Sol's pale gold hair, or even a wisp of Sorin's hearty laughter. All she could see were the distrustful eyes of the Ikedree people. Their faces covered in furs and colorful scarves; their shoulders hunched against the wind. She saw Gyda in all of them, no matter how short they were, or how dark their skin was.

But she saw no sign of the Wandering Sols.

She ground her teeth in frustration, taking another street that went nowhere as far as she knew. Direwall made no sense to her. Not many cities did. She didn't know where taverns would be, or other places for visitors to rest and gather information. She didn't know where leadership would reside in the city, or if it would be a good idea to find them. Everything looked infuriatingly similar and confusing. Nothing made sense, and none of the locals reached out to help her.

This is why she avoided cities. The constant chatter, the confusing layouts, the press of buildings on all sides. It was enough to keep her chest tight and her breaths short.

Andovine had been the only city besides Orenlion that Evren had found beauty in. But that was because she had Viggo to show it to her. Orenlion had grown on her as she aged, so she didn't have a choice but to know its winding paths and buildings. Even then, Orenlion was more forest than city. Direwall was stubbornly not the wilderness, which was a blessing in many ways.

Evren just wanted it to make sense.

There was a slight slope to the streets. Peering over the heads of so many she could just make out the scattered docks cresting above the water's edge. They were already empty, their boats gone to the strangely ice-free waters of the bay.

"Shouldn't the water be frozen?" Sahar whispered behind her. She heard Drystan shrug in all his furs, and her sigh. "Well, it's certainly cold enough to be frozen. At least that's what my toes are telling me."

"These people . . ." Nerezza looked at them all carefully, not bothered with acting civilized as she stared. "I didn't expect there to be so many of them. So many in one city."

"In preparation for the Long Night, probably." Evren nodded to a group of workers fortifying a rooftop as they passed. "Strength and warmth in numbers. It's easier to survive."

Drystan snorted. "It's also easier to get massacred. If everyone is here, then that makes this city a massive target."

If it was possible, everyone grew even more solemn at his words. But no one could deny their truth. Instead, Sahar huffed a big cloud of air and rolled her eyes.

"Ever a ray of positivity, Drystan." Sahar cut him a glare. It had a hint of her usual playfulness behind her naked grief.

To her shock, Drystan actually smiled. It wasn't much of one; just a bare twitch at the corners of his mouth. But for a man who spent most of his time scowling, it was a drastic change to his face.

They turned another corner, which opened into a wide square with a sweeping view of Myrefall Bay. The dark waters were choppy and whitecapped, and a low-hanging mist kept all but the barest shadows of the mountains across the bay shrouded from view. A wide, steep road led directly down to the docks and looked treacherously slick for anyone deciding to take a trip down.

No one was risking it. By the looks of it, anyone needed at the docks was already there. Daylight was precious and no one in Direwall was wasting it.

But someone was coming up from the docks.

It was slow work. Whoever they were slipped more than once and cursed twice as much. They stayed huddled in their dark cloak, their pace slow but as steady as they could be as they crested over the street and into the square. They were close enough now that Evren could hear the unmistakable sounds of Elvish curses. She wasn't as fluent as she should be, but she knew foul words when she heard them. And she knew the voice that spoke them even better.

Grinning, she quickened her pace and left the Ashen Bond trailing behind her. As she neared the figure, she didn't know whether to laugh or cry. Either way she was shaking.

"Do all holy men say such foul words, or are you the exception?" Her voice, unlike the rest of her, was steady and clear.

Abraxas's head snapped up from glaring at his boots. He looked wind-torn and his cheeks and nose were red from the cold. But as the hood fell back his hair tumbled free, and a wide smile lit up his shadowed face.

It was laughter that tore through Evren's throat as he scooped her up into a big hug. Desperate, stuttering laughter that made her fingertips tingle as she hugged him back fiercely.

She could feel the hard shell of his armor beneath his furs as he set her back down on her feet.

"Can we have one adventure without you risking death?" he asked breathlessly.

"How else am I supposed to keep you on your toes?" She raised her eyebrow and he snorted.

"Try lizards in my bedroll next time. It'll be kinder."

While a ghost of a relieved smile remained, his eyes went darkly serious as he looked her over. The new scars, the bloody glove and missing arrows. He took in the smudges of ash and soot, and the dark circles under her eyes. Evren felt her own smile wane as his gaze flickered behind her to the trio of familiar faces stopping just behind her.

He nodded over her shoulder to Drystan, who did the same. "Thank you for finding her."

"It wasn't us." Nerezza barely looked invested in the conversation. Evren could see the gears in her head turning. A new plan to deal with the impossible odds stacked against them. Or maybe a hundred plans.

"There are fewer of you . . ." Abraxas noted, his frown deepening as he did.

Evren winced. "We lost Vox on the way here. A lot has happened."

Abraxas swallowed hard. His throat bobbed underneath his layers, and she could see him shifting his hand to the hilt of his sword. Whether out of comfort or wariness, she wasn't sure.

"Evren, Gyda left with them to find you." He scanned the square behind her, trying to pick out the tall, unmistakable figure of their friend. "Where is she?"

It was like she was being stabbed again. Or maybe the knife had never truly left. She could still feel its edge digging into her flesh, the blade twisting with every hopeful glance and soft word from her friend. She took a shuddering breath, and she swore she could taste ash and rot on her tongue as she did.

"Gyda was taken," she said slowly. "The dead in the village

not far from here had us surrounded. They killed Vox and took Gyda. Then let us go."

"What?" The word hissed out of his teeth as he took a step back. In an instant, all remnants of the soft Abraxas were gone. An invisible armor slammed over him as pain clouded his eyes. "She was taken. Why?"

"We didn't really know her, Abraxas," Evren said, thinking of how she'd bristled at those very words before. Abraxas took them as well as she had. She willed him to quiet down with her eyes. People were already glaring at them, and in a city already wound up tight, they didn't need to set off a full panic. "I hate it too. I tried to get her to stay. But I think . . . I think she wanted to go."

Another flurry of Elvish curses fell from his lips and into the thick air. His grip on the hilt of his sword tightened. If it wasn't for the gloves, Evren would've seen his knuckles turn bone white. His feet twitched, and his aggressive energy fell off him in waves. He wanted to pace, to scream and shout. But one sidelong glance at a group of locals kept him in place.

His mouth was a thin, tight line as he turned back to Evren. "How bad?"

Images of the undead in Lostwater swam in her vision. Their gaping maws, too wide smiles, and the cold light in their eyes. She blinked them away and ignored the fear hardening in her veins.

"Bad," she muttered. "Bad, and much bigger than we expected. We have a lot to talk about."

He nodded firmly. "Follow me."

Abraxas didn't wait for them. He turned sharply on his heel and walked purposely across the square. Evren and the Ashen Bond stayed hot on his heels.

If the people of Direwall turned their noses up at them before, they went out of their way to avoid Abraxas. Maybe it was his dark clothes, or the stormy look of rage in his eyes. Either way, they had no trouble making their way through the streets to a squat little building overlooking the water. It wasn't much to look at. The only thing out of the ordinary about it was that it was attached to a crumbling tower which had long since lost its upper half. They took the stairs up to the door two at a time. The faded sign above the door simply said *The Lighthouse.* It clattered against the door as it swung open.

The Lighthouse wasn't impressive inside either. The small tavern only had a few open booths, and while the windows faced the water, everything in the room was shadowed and dingy. Few people were inside. A few locals were still eating breakfast and muttering to themselves over steaming bowls of chowder. A surly looking bartender missing an eye glared at them over the bar, her arms crossed and her lips pulled back into a sneer. But the room was far from quiet.

In the far corner, crouched over a freshly drawn map and with stacks of mugs littered precariously at the edge of the table, three figures sat. A tall, lanky human with deep brown skin and long dreads pooled over his shoulder as he pointed out spots on the map. A dwarf with cunning eyes the color of the sky and a single copper nose ring glittering in the low light. And a goblin, crouched on the table top itself with his feet digging into the wood and his ears twitching in their direction.

Evren practically threw herself at the table. They were all on her at once. With hugs and squeals of joy and some grumbles of "Don't do that again, kid." Their joy was so infectious, Evren forgot about what brought her there in the first place. She took her seat wedged between Sol and Sorin, her grin wide and her eyes wet as they chartered endlessly. The Ashen Bond and Abraxas sat down around the booth with less fanfare, and Sorin loudly called for drinks and food.

The Ashen Bond ate quickly. Abraxas didn't touch anything. His eyes were on Evren, and the underlying need of what they needed to talk about was there. But neither of them were ready to break their spirits yet.

Arke licked his bowl, his third bowl, clean and shoved Evren's closer to her with a grunt. She smiled and wedged off her gloves slowly. Her injured hand ached sharply in the open air, but the scab was holding better than it had before. Her whole hand was brown with dried blood. It was crusted around her fingernails and was still tacky in some areas.

Sol sucked in a breath and wiggled a couple inches away with her food. "What the hells happened to you?"

Evren looked across the table at the trio of people she'd dragged with her. They were all ready, willing and eager. They didn't have the daylight to waste anymore.

"Things have gotten a lot more complicated," Abraxas started, and the rest of the Wandering Sols went silent.

Evren told them everything she knew. Her trek through the mountains, how she survived the blizzard. She left out the creature that followed her. It wasn't important, and she was fairly sure it was just a figment of her imagination. But from there she told them the barest truth. Finding Gyda, and then meeting the Ashen Bond in Lostwater. She explained their hesitant plan before the attack, and how the lake lit up, and the town went up in flames. How they barely made it out alive and did so only by sacrificing two others.

Vox's death meant little to them, but when Evren told them about Gyda, they nearly rioted. Sorin stood up so fast his chair toppled to the ground behind him. His chest was heaving.

"You let her go?" he cried. "Why?"

"I tried to get her to stay, Sorin," she insisted. Her throat was burning with tears just from the memory. "She wouldn't let me."

"She didn't just leave us!" He swung his arm out to the group. "I mean, after all we've been through, she wouldn't just leave. Would she?"

Arke nudged his chair back up and pulled him down to sit in it by his coat's edge. Sorin thumped back in his chair without a word of argument.

"We don't know why." He patted the human's shoulder. "Maybe she had a reason."

"She tried to leave without us," Sol said wearily. She trailed the lines of the map on the table, connecting Lostwater to Dire-wall with a wandering fingertip. "Maybe they're right and she meant to do this all along."

"But that doesn't matter, right?" Sorin looked between them all. "We're going to get her back."

It wasn't a question, but it hung in the air as if it needed confirmation. Evren bit her lip, trying to taste something other than blood. The chowder did little to overpower the flavor.

"Your friend is a part of this," Drystan said slowly. His hands were on the table, and he looked like he was trying to be gentle with them. There was a hint of irritation in the tightness of his jaw, but he hid it well as he talked. "Perhaps a key. Whoever this Prime is, we need to get to him to stop the undead. His plans could destroy what's left of civilization out here."

"This Prime seeks to make himself a god." Abraxas scowled at the wood of the table. "Is there nothing sacred in Eith anymore?"

"We can stop him," Evren said. She forced more confidence in her voice than she felt.

"How?" Sorin asked. "What's strong enough to beat back the dead?"

Abraxas's breath was quiet but forceful when he spoke. "You know what is, Sorin."

Anger, true anger, flashed across Sorin's face. "Don't," he hissed. "Don't you start with your Divine shit again."

The elf didn't flinch. "You know the power of the Divines," he said gently. "You've felt it yourself."

"I don't know what I felt," he spat.

"Yes, you do. Haphion brought you back—"

"The fuck he did!" Sorin bolted to his feet again, his chest heaving and his fingers twitching the way they always did when he was angry. "There are no gods, Abraxas. And that's a good thing."

Hurt flickered in the elf's eyes. "How can you say that?"

"Because of this!" He pointed to his chest, where his fatal

scar was. "Because of what we're doing. Some weirdo with magic thinks he can become a god and we've lost a friend, and you want me to say that beings with unbridled power are *good*? Were they good when they let you march into Vernes and destroy their culture and lives? Were they good when they told you killing somebody different than you was justified?"

"They saved your life," Abraxas said hotly.

"I didn't ask you to!" Sorin yelled. Then quieter, his voice shaking. "You didn't think, Abraxas. You brought me back, but you didn't do it right. I'm not the same. I'm not whole. And you should be scared. Because I hear you pray every damn night, and no one answers you. So how did you do it, huh? How did you shove me back into this body while leaving pieces of me behind, while your Divine buddy sits in time out?"

Abraxas was quiet, his lips white with pressure.

And Sorin laughed a humorless laugh. "That's what I thought. You don't know. So don't tell me I should know how to defeat this Prime asshole. I don't. All I know is that he took my friend, and he'll probably kill the rest of us before this is done. He wants to become a god? *That* is evil. And that's all I know."

Sorin picked up his coat and wormed his arms into it as he marched outside into the snow. Evren started to go after him, but Arke pulled her back down and shook his head.

"Give him some time," the goblin whispered.

Sol looked at the door, guilt lingering on her face, before turning back to the table. "How does someone even become a god? Isn't that impossible anyway?"

"With the right amount of power, anyone can call themselves a god." Nerezza sniffed. "What truly defines divinity? Immortality? Unchecked power? Worship? These are things a talented and dedicated mage could accomplish with the right deals and time."

"Such power over the undead is unheard of." Abraxas shook his head. He'd seemed to put Sorin out of his mind. "Even in Vernes, their dead were different."

"These die the same, however." Sahar finally spoke up. Her elbows were on the table, and she was staring at the map. "They're quicker and have more numbers. But these undead don't have freewill. They're little more than mouthpieces for this Prime fellow."

"How does that help us?" Arke asked.

"Perhaps they can lead us to him." There was a sparkle in her eye. "I believe he's told us enough already. We just have to put the pieces together."

Evren made herself smile. "I do love a puzzle."

13

They were losing their last remnants of daylight, but none of the Sols would let Evren do anything but sleep. The Ashen Bond was no better off, but they didn't have a grouchy goblin shoving them off to bed.

"You can't expect me to take a nap when there's so much to do!" she protested as his little goblin hands shoved her closer to the bed. It was little more than a pile of straw covered in furs. It smelled of fish even before she laid down.

"You ain't any use to us half dead." Arke nudged her further.

"I am not half dead." She scowled.

"Then why do you look it?"

Evren started to protest but found no words coming to her. She shut her mouth but continued to scowl anyway. It felt appropriate, even if she'd lost to against Arke again.

"Eh, that's what I thought." He snickered. "Take a nap. We'll getcha when we've got a good lead."

Evren licked her dry lips. Whatever she felt, the bed did look inviting. That aching tug at the back of her eyes had turned to a whole headache, and she was finding it hard to focus. She wanted to fight Arke, but her body was having none of it.

"Fine," she grumbled and shook off her bow, quiver, and

outer layers. She tossed them in a heap unceremoniously in the corner of the room and flopped down on the pile of fishy smelling furs. Her words were muffled when she spoke again, her eyelids already closing. "But when I wake up, we've got to talk."

His large yellow eyes flicked down to her bloody hand. "Wouldn't miss it, kid. Now, fuckin' sleep already."

The door clicked shut, and she was already snoring by the time his feet padded down the stairs.

EVREN WOKE an eternity later to Sorin vigorously shaking her shoulder. She groaned and batted his hand away. Her limbs still felt heavy and sluggish. She wiped away the grit from her eyes as she slowly sat up. The ache behind her eyes was still there, but was now just a dull, annoying throb. She blinked to try and focus, finding it was easier now, but she still felt like shit.

"How long?" she murmured against her palm as she tried to rub some life into her face.

Sorin smirked. "Four hours."

She groaned and felt every urge to throw herself back into the furs and sleep another forty if she could. Instead, she pulled herself on wobbly feet.

"Why do I feel worse?" She yawned as she gathered her discarded things from their pile and put them back on.

"You look just as bad if that makes you feel any better."

"Thanks," she said dryly.

The bow and quiver were heavy and cold across her shoulders, but they helped bring her back to reality. She pulled on her gloves and flattened her hair as the last bits of sleep tried to cling to her. When she was done, Sorin was staring at her, his expression unreadable.

"I'm sorry," he said finally. "About my outburst down there."

Evren shook her head. "You needed to let it out. Abraxas can take it. Have you apologized to him yet?"

"No." Sorin scowled. "I don't . . . hate him. But I do resent him."

"For bringing you back?"

"Yes." He sighed. "And not doing it properly."

"Sorin." She touched his shoulder gently. "No one comes back from the dead whole."

"No one comes back, period," he said firmly. "But you don't get it. Evvie, I lost my magic."

She blinked in surprise.

"I lost what made me useful, don't you see? Back before Heliodar . . . I could say things and people would listen. I could do something no other Vasa could do! But now I can't. I've tried. I've been trying. On Professor Vaughn, on the Ashen Bond, on anyone with ears. But it's gone and I'm afraid."

His eyes started welling up with tears.

"Of what?" she whispered slowly.

"Without my magic I'm just a passable swordsman," he choked out. "I'm not worth having in the Wandering Sols. I'll just drag you down."

"That's not true."

"Isn't it?" He shook out of her grasp, tears flowing down his cheeks. "Evvie, what have I done recently that's helped? All I've done is be in the way. You all have hurt yourselves keeping me alive in battle. That's—"

"Normal," she said firmly. "It's normal to be afraid after you've been hurt, Sorin. You're not a 'passable swordsman.' You're quick as lightning when you don't think about it. But because you fell in battle, every time you draw your sword it's all you can think about, right?"

He nodded numbly.

"It takes time to pick it back up. But you don't have to if you don't want to. I see your hesitation, and your fear. You want to charge into danger like you used to, but you hold yourself back. And that's okay."

"I want to be who I was before," he said.

"You can't," she said, and he shuddered at her words. "You'll always be different. But if you want, you can make yourself stronger. We're always here for you, Sorin. Without question or judgement. But it's all up to you where you go next."

Sorin took a shaking breath. His tears hadn't stopped, but he finally looked her in the eyes. "These adventures . . . I know they're dangerous, but we seem to always get stuck with the kind chock full of death. We're always . . . dying. What if we all die trying to get Gyda back? I don't want to die, Evren. I can't do that again."

If there was any part of Evren left unbruised and unbroken, it shattered at his soft words. Her own breaths hitched as she tried to steady herself under his fearful gaze.

"I can make promises." Her voice broke against her will, and she saw him flinch. "I can swear to be the one that stands between you and death, that Abraxas would never let you fall again, and Arke would tear the world apart to keep you alive. But, for me, there's no power in words. Not like you."

She forced him to look her in the eyes, black meeting warm, tearful amber. She set her jaw and forced a smile. She didn't even realize she was crying until she tasted salt. "Whatever happens, I have your back. We all do. Without you, we would've fallen apart long before now. But I can't force you to go further than this. I won't. If this is too much, you can stay back. We'll all understand."

"I'm so scared," he whispered through gritted teeth. "Is it normal to be so afraid?"

Without hesitation, she replied, "Yes."

"Then why don't you ever act like it?" He wiped his wet cheeks, even as more tears fell. "You almost died in Serevadia, and then in the blizzard. But you never seem afraid."

"I'm always afraid, Sorin," she said. "But I have been for a long time. Fear is . . . useful, in a sense. I want it, I need it. It keeps me alive. And occasionally, it allows me to do good things." She squeezed his shoulder again, trying to push some reassurance into him. "Fear is a hurdle, a wall. Without it, we're exposed. With it, we can be blind. Use fear, let it fill you up. Listen to what it says, because it's normally right. But never, *never* let it consume you."

He let out a shaky laugh. "It can't be that simple."

She smiled ruefully. "It isn't. But that's because it's different for everyone. You'll learn what's right for you on your own terms. No matter what you choose," she added gently.

He nodded and pulled away from her. Her hand fell to her side, colder now. His tears had stopped, but his eyes were red and puffy, and he sniffled in the cool air.

"I'm so ready to be over this," he murmured, and patted his cheeks dry. He glowered at the window and the steadily falling snow outside. "Losing people, and not being able to save them." He turned back to Evren, and through the drying tears and shaking lips, she saw the barest glimmer of her old friend. It was like a ray of golden light slipping through the crack of a closed door. Through the keyhole even. He was there. "I'm not backing down from this. I won't sit here while you all run after Gyda. I'm going and I'll be better, I promise."

"Sorin, you don't have to promise me anything."

He shrugged. "But I am. I was raised to be better than this, Evren. And I will be. Just . . . just give me some time to figure out how."

"Take what you need," she nodded. "We're all learning."

"Thank you."

Simple words. And yet they felt bare and exposed in their naked truth. They meant more than a thousand beautiful words strung together in elegant sentences. Evren knew he was capable of both.

"Of course." She cocked her head to the side, seeing the brilliant oranges coloring the sky. "Tell me you woke me up for good news and not just the end of the sunlight?"

That brought his usual shit-eating grin to his face, and her chest felt warm again seeing it.

"Even better. We have an audience with the Jarl of Direwall."

"I take it that's much more helpful than it sounds."

"Only one way to find out, right? Come on! Let's not keep her waiting."

Sorin turned on his heel and darted out of the room. Evren had no choice but to follow him. Down the stairs, through the warm, musty tavern, and into the streets of Direwall. He slowed down only to keep from slipping as they walked side by side through the winding, icy roads of the city.

They darted up through the crowds, weaving through passersby under the blood-orange sky, until they made it to the steps of a rather impressive, well-built wooden home. It sported many colors around its doorway and roof, and as she climbed the steps, she could make out the faint pattern on the trim. Different colors and patterns, all of which she'd seen in the scarves each native of Direwall wore.

The door was guarded by two heavy men armed with large axes and bristling with armor under their furs. But they nodded to Sorin and pushed the double doors open for them to enter.

The doors opened into a large hall with high, vaulted ceilings. Scarves of every color hung from the rafters, fluttering in the wind that followed them in. The length of the hall was dominated by a firepit that stretched to either side of the room. It was almost uncomfortably hot as they skirted around it and followed the flames down the grand hall.

The walls were carved wood. Each one showed battles and victories as they passed. Evren saw the building of Direwall, and then a massive serpent writhing beneath the waves of the bay, destroying all boats who got close. She saw the battles between feuding clans, and the many wars won by the clans living in the city. She saw Jarls crowned and how they fell. Beheading, overthrown by the people, dying in battle, drowning in the bay in an attempt to wrestle the serpent. It was all carved and solid in the wood. Not as glimmering and jaw-dropping as the Serevadians, but every bit as awe inspiring.

At the end of the hall, a dais raised up on a few steps held a simple carved throne and the rest of her team, as well as the Ashen Bond. They gathered around the dais, never above the last step, and talked with echoing voices to the woman who sat on the throne.

The woman, who Evren could only assume was the Jarl of Direwall, looked like she might've been carved from wood herself. Her skin was the color of honey and glowed in the firelight. Her hair the color of burnished bronze, streaked with silver and gathered back in a thick braid. No scarf hid it from the world, only a simple iron circlet sat upon her head. That was the only difference between her and the people she'd seen on the streets. Her furs were the same, and she sat slouched in the throne as if she was in a tavern chair instead.

Her deep blue eyes narrowed as Evren and Sorin came to a halt just before the first step. Evren squirmed in her boots, unsure whether she should bow or kneel or do anything at all. She stole a glance at Sorin, who did neither of those things and instead smiled at the Jarl warmly.

"Jarl Eirunn, you look just as radiant as I left you."

Eirunn scowled down at him, but her eyes twinkled with warmth. Her voice carried a thick accent, even thicker than Gyda's. "You were not gone long, child of the waters."

"You can still call me Sorin, even with company,"

She snorted and waved away his comment. Her eyes landed on Evren again. "This is the hunter you spoke of?"

"Yes." He nodded quickly. "This is Evren Hanali of Orenlion."

He gestured to her to take a step up, and Evren winced as she did. The Jarl's gaze was heavy, and she felt like she was being judged simply by how she stood. She tried to remember how

Gyda held herself. Relaxed, but firm. A spine of steel, but soft shoulders. Head held high, even when talking to anyone below her. That wasn't an issue for Evren, but she tried to set her jaw in a way that gave her some semblance of strength.

"Sorin speaks correctly," she said. "I am Evren Hanali."

"The Worm Rider."

Evren blanched. Behind her, she heard Sorin cough and the subtle murmuring of her party from afar as the Jarl watched her with an amused expression.

"I . . ." she cleared her throat. "Yes, I did ride a worm. It was less of a ride and more of a death grip so I didn't fall, though. Lots of screaming involved."

"From both parties." She heard Sol's snicker bounce through the empty room.

"Impressive." Eirunn didn't look like a woman who wasted her time by lying. "And honest. That is rare to find from a warrior."

"Well, I do my best." She grimaced at her own words, but the Jarl didn't seem to mind.

"Tell me, Evren Worm-Rider, your companions speak of imminent death and decay. Do you confirm this?"

She blinked in surprise. "Of course I do. I saw it with my own eyes. And even if I didn't, I trust my party."

Eirunn shrugged. "The Long Night is deadly. You say now a god wishes to make it even worse. Tell me how a god has made it to my lands, when I have heard nothing of them returning."

"Whoever he is, he's not a god," Evren said firmly. "He's just a necromancer with too much power."

"True." Eirunn mused between her fingertips. "But how did he come upon my land?"

Evren looked at her friends for help. She felt like she was failing some kind of test she didn't have the answers for. But they all shook their heads and shrugged. Nerezza just stared at her, as if challenging her the same way the Jarl did. Evren turned back and tried not to sound defeated when she answered truthfully.

"I don't know."

"Fair honesty. Most refreshing." She stood from her throne, her belt of many metal links jingling merrily. All the scarves for the different clans were woven into the links, the only bright spot of color on her otherwise dark furs.

She stepped down to Evren's level, and still was able to look down.

"How much do you know of the Ikedree people, Worm-Rider?"

Evren followed her as she stepped off the dais and moved across the room to the other wall where more wooden carvings gleamed.

"Not much," she said. "I know you live in the Reino Terminan. You separate yourselves into clans, you're not a fan of southerners coming into your land. You normally wear scarves to cover your hair, to show your clan."

"I do not." As if to make a point, Eirunn flicked a lock of hair over her shoulder. "I am a Jarl to all clans; I belong to none."

"I was wondering about that," Evren admitted.

"My city holds fourteen clans in total. We used to have nearly seventeen. The Long Night has taken many from us, which is why we all gather here now. The Night makes it dark enough that all clan colors look the same."

"So, you put away your rivalries to survive."

"Yes."

"That's practical. But why are you telling me this?"

Eirunn waved her hand at the closest wood carving. It was older, and the dancing shadows from the fire made it difficult to pick out. But she could see a highly detailed map of the land Eirunn ruled. Everything the mountains curved around, and the sea of shifting ice held in place. The map included Direwall, Lostwater, as well as two other major settlements to the north.

"This valley is ours," she stated. "But we have lost touch with the land in the past decades. These two towns were lost to the

Long Night many years ago. And last year we lost this one." She pointed to Lostwater. "You have seen this."

"Yes." Evren nodded. "The being that works during the Long Night takes people. Whole villages it seems."

"Clans," Eirunn corrected. "Outside these walls, there are few Ikedree who settle. Most roam the expanse. Only Direwall and these three clans kept themselves to one place."

"That would've made them an easier target then." Evren winced as she sounded like Drystan

"Look at this map, Worm-Rider. What do you see?"

Another test. Evren huffed and focused again. Her fingers grazed the smooth wood, following the ridge of the mountains, the dip of Loch Lorn and the canyon, all the way to the northern sea and the jagged icebergs that rimmed it like a toothy maw.

"I see mountains," she said. "A dangerous sea. A canyon separating the land, a forest at the foothills of the mountains. A large bay." She shrugged and pulled back. "Why?"

The Jarl narrowed her eyes down at her. "This expanse is not kind. It is not easy to leave, and even harder to get into. The Black Pass to the south is the safest route out."

"Yeah, not safe."

"Yes, we know." She tapped the sea of ice. "Those who sail find nothing but death in these waters. The ice keeps them at bay. No ship has survived. "

"So . . ."

"So how did your mage get in?" She raised a thick eyebrow. "We have had no visitors in over seventy years. Through the pass or through the sea. You are all the first."

"Couldn't someone come through the land without you knowing?"

"No."

"Right." Evren blew out an exasperated breath. Geography felt like a waste of time when she knew the sun was inching closer to the horizon with every passing minute. She was itching with frustration. "So, either the mage has been here a very long time, or it's one of your people?"

"The Ikedree do not dabble in such magics."

"So, someone who has been here a long time without going to you for help or supplies." She frowned. "Who was the last person to travel here?"

The Jarl grinned as if she'd finally asked the right question. She turned to Sorin, who was poking the fire with a long iron stick. His hand was bare, and the Vasa tattoo stood out starkly against his skin.

"Children of the waters traveled here, seventy years ago." She shrugged. "Give or take a few years."

Sorin perked up and put the poker back down on the hearth. "Vasa were here? We don't normally come this far north."

"And you said no ship survives the ice," Sol pointed out. She sat on the steps, cleaning under her fingernails with the point of her dagger.

"They did not survive," the Jarl said. "Their ship was broken by the ice and has been trapped ever since. Here." She pointed far to the north, near the seashore. "It has been many, many years since their landing. The story we have been told was that the ship brought many treasures. All cursed from a far-off land. It also brought Mortova."

"Mortova?"

"A great sea beast. He never left the waters after the shipwreck, and lives in Myrefall Bay to this day. The serpent has taken many of my people through the years."

Sorin's eyes suddenly lit up. "Oh! That makes sense, actually."

"It does?" Evren and Abraxas said in unison.

"Yes!" He was grinning from ear to ear. "Everyone knows Vasa can be born with the power to manipulate the storms and the sea, right?"

"Of course." Sahar nodded. "That's why they live there instead of on land."

"Ehh," Sorin wobbled his hand, "kind of. But you get the idea. Not all Vasa have that power. Some are normal sailors, but every now and then a Vasa is born with a Sea Bond."

"Normal speak, please," Arke said.

"Sea Bonds are when a Vasa and a sea creature have a powerful bond. They can call on each other, even work together. It's incredibly rare, and the more powerful the Vasa, the more powerful the creature. Mortova must've been Bonded to one of the Vasa on the ship. Probably the captain, if he's as bad as you say."

"Will he not leave?" Eirunn asked.

Sorin shrugged. "It's hard to say. Most Sea Bonds aren't fun for either creature or Vasa. The stronger and more intelligent the creature, the more they normally fight against the Bond. But if Mortova had a good relationship with his Vasa, then it's safe to assume he's waiting for them to come back. He doesn't believe they're dead."

"That's very tragic, but what does this have to do with the undead?" Drystan stepped down to be level with Eirunn. "Unless the sea serpent is the Prime?"

"No monster can do necromancy." Abraxas shook his head. "That is a sin reserved only for mortals."

"Or those looking to make themselves a god," Evren said. She rounded to face Eirunn. "You think the Prime is a survivor of the shipwreck."

She nodded. "It is where I would, as you southerners say, place my bets."

"So, a Vasa shipwrecks." Evren turned to Sorin. "The crew dies, except for one. Why doesn't he go for help? Why turn to necromancy?"

He opened his mouth and then shut it, looking confused. "I don't know. We don't practice that magic. I mean, every ship is different, but it's still frowned upon. If a Vasa was strong enough to have Bonded with a serpent, then the ship itself would've been seen as strong. They wouldn't have needed to resort to that."

Finally, Nerezza spoke up. "It could've been something on the ship. Something they were transporting." She looked at Sorin for confirmation.

"That could've been anything." He shrugged.

"Seventy years ago?" Abraxas cocked his head to the side. "Etherak was still occupying Vernes at that time. Many Vasa ships were used to transport cargo to and from that country."

"And many Vasa did not return the artifacts they stole." Sahar nodded. "Vernesian or not, there could be something on that ship that gave our survivor new power."

"A shipwrecked Vasa with no way home, carrying potentially dangerous cargo, and all alone." Evren sighed. "That doesn't sound good. It's been seventy years, give or take. They're past the point of survival."

"There must be a point to making an army of the undead," Abraxas insisted. "This Prime has said very little about marching that army farther south."

"And yet their undead were found as far south as Rheinwall," Drystan said.

"What were they doing?" Sol asked. "What got you to take them out?"

"Undead aren't normal in Terevas," Sahar explained. "But people still know what they look like. Livestock went missing a lot, farmers disappeared trying to find them. We went looking and found these undead, and a strange following of people with them. Normally the lost farmers. It was some sort of mind control, we thought. They swore allegiance to this Prime even then. Now, I'm starting to think it wasn't a cult. They were just the newest undead."

Nerezza started pacing, her cream hair catching the firelight as she did. "But why were they so far south? What were they doing if not taking over towns like in Lostwater?"

"They were looking for Gyda."

All eyes turned back to Evren. She felt sick even saying it. By uttering her name, all she could see was her. She could smell her leather, hear her low rumbling laugh. She shook the memory away.

"They wanted Gyda in Lostwater, right?" Everyone hesitantly nodded, except the Jarl who watched her curiously. "The undead we met in the Enrial Wilds went for Gyda's team, not Abraxas, Sol and I. After that, Gyda was pressed to get back here, but wanted us to stay away. If she was the last survivor of Lostwater, she knew what happened. She knew they'd come looking for her. She was in Dirn-Darahl most of the year though, they couldn't find her, so they kept going further south, until they got even your attention."

Evren turned to the remaining Ashen Bond. "It wasn't a cult at all, it was a search party."

The pieces of this particular puzzle fit. It was like everything was clicking into place neatly after she'd been trying to shove them together for so long. But there were still some pieces that didn't fit. The picture wasn't complete.

The Jarl hummed in agreement, watching them all with hawk-like eyes. "So, they wanted Gyda Soul-Dust. Now they have her. What is next?"

Evren didn't have time to ask about the name. Drystan was already talking, and with more force and strength than she'd seen since Lostwater.

"Direwall. The Prime has been going and taking the smaller towns. If he wants anyone else, Direwall is the next target. You've got all the other clans here. One big hit, and that's a massive pool of people to join his undead."

"That still doesn't solve the 'why' behind this." Sol pointed at him with the tip of her dagger. "And I don't think we'll figure that out if we stay here. The answers are on that ship."

Sorin nodded eagerly. "Yes! Definitely! So, we go to the shipwreck."

"Yeah, but here's a giant pile of shit in your plan." Arke waddled between them. "We're out of time."

Evren's hope plummeted like a stone. Their daylight was officially running out. "Arke's right. With the Long Night coming now, we're playing on the Prime's turf."

"And there are the people of Direwall to consider." Abraxas eyed Eirunn.

She scoffed and puffed her chest out. "You think we will just cover behind these walls? We are a warrior people. Many will fight."

"The undead have massive numbers," Sahar warned.

Drystan nodded. "These aren't simple foes to fight. Your people will need help."

"Direwall is not without its defenses." Jarl Eirunn cocked her head to the side, and for a brief moment the iron circlet shone like the brightest gold. "But I would appreciate the help. We have time yet. What do these creatures fear?"

"Fire," Nerezza said immediately.

"We have much whale oil."

Sol whistled lowly. "That could work. Make a ring around the city?"

"It buys us time, at least." Evren shrugged and remembered the way the undead piled on top of each other to get over the wall of fire. "The people fighting should know to go for the heart. That's the only way to kill them."

"And that these aren't monsters," Drystan said quietly. "Your men and women might see faces they recognize. Are you sure they can handle that?"

Eirunn walked the few steps it took to close the distance between them. They were close in height, but there was something in her that appeared to make her tower over him.

"We know the living from the dead, little man. We will fight for the living and lay our dead to rest. But you have also lost to the Prime. If you face him in battle, are you sure your aim will be true?"

Evren watched doubt flicker wild and hot across Drystan's face. And for a split second, fear as well. He swallowed hard and raised his chin to meet Eirunn's harsh gaze.

"To lay our dead to rest, my aim will be as true as the north wind."

14

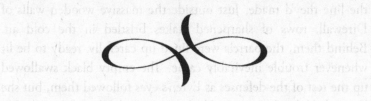

The sun's last red glimmers disappeared in a matter of minutes. Even so, those colorful rays painted Direwall crimson. Myrefall Bay glittered like blood, and for a brief second, Evren could've sworn she saw a jagged fin breaching the waters, right before everything went black.

She'd seen sunsets before. The elves of Orenlion loved the night sky, so she was no stranger to the deep darkness. In many ways, she preferred it over the scorching rays of daylight. There was something unmistakably simple about the night. The creatures that thrived in it did so for a reason. Those people who didn't clung to their lights and slept soundly in their walls. The night was meant for the hunters and the survivors. Those who carved out a spot in the earth with blunted claws and bared teeth. To hunt in the dark was to court those creatures with the claim that she was one of them. To creep in the shadowed underbrush, to use the pin-prick stars as the only source of light, to hunt the beings who refused the bright light of day until the pale glimpses of dawn broke through the horizon—that was the night Evren knew and loved.

The Long Night didn't feel like that.

The moment the sun slipped below the horizon and plunged

Direwall into darkness, it felt like the very air itself stilled. A shiver ran down the length of her spine, tapping each of the bones with soft, icy fingers. She struggled to ignore it as she rolled another barrel to a stop near the southern gate.

It thumped softly against a pile of snow, and she heaved it up with a grunt of effort. It fit perfectly against the other ten they had lined up, and she stepped back to admire the length of the line they'd made. Just outside the massive wooden walls of Direwall, rows of sharpened stakes bristled in the cold air. Behind them, the barrels were lined up carefully, ready to be lit whenever trouble inevitably came. The empty black swallowed up the rest of the defenses as Evren's eyes followed them, but she knew she'd see the same at all three exposed sides of the city. Jarl Eirunn was convinced the bay held no threat and believed the rough waters and resident sea serpent would keep the undead from attacking there. After Loch Lorn, Evren was less sure, but there was no arguing with the Jarl.

She panted slightly in the painfully cold night air. The sound of crunching snow and a barrel rolling into place drew her eyes to the side, where Drystan pushed up the last of the barrels in the south.

"If I never smell whale oil again, it'll be too soon," he growled, and wiped his hands off on his pants. He'd replaced his lost ax with another he'd bought in the markets. The metal looked black and dull compared to his remaining silver one, still gleaming on his hip.

"Sorin says it'll stink up the whole mountain range when it lights up."

If possible, he scowled even further. "Lovely."

Evren turned to walk back into the city. Direwall had already lit its lamps and braziers. Sparingly, since they had to last the whole Long Night, but the city was still a beacon of warmth and light. Her skin crawled as she turned her back on the black abyss stretched out behind her. But that wasn't what made her pause and turn around.

"Drystan, are you coming?"

He stood like a sentinel at the edge of the night. There was no wind, and he was so still he might've been made of stone. His face was blank, but his eyes weren't. She knew that look well.

"Stupid question," she said as she shuffled up next to him.

"It's always a good idea to announce stupid things," he muttered.

"Well, that's going to make everything I say longer. But, back to the original question. Are you okay?"

His laugh came abruptly and seemed to shock them both. There was no humor in it, but he looked less like a lifeless statue when he turned to stare at her with astonishment.

"That is a stupid question," he said finally.

She shrugged. "I did warn you."

"You did." He turned back to the black abyss swirling around the sharpened edges of the stakes. It was all impressive considering how little time the people of Direwall had to put it up. But it still didn't feel like enough. Evren had a feeling that no wall or trench would be.

"It's not enough," Drystan echoed her thoughts.

"Obvious statement,"

He snorted. "Fair."

She took a deep lungful of air. It even tasted different. Sour almost, on the tip of her tongue. "It's all we can do for now. And it's more than we had back in Lostwater."

"I should've seen that coming," He narrowed his eyes at the dark, as if trying to pick out the waiting threat.

"How could you have? No one had a clue."

"Gyda did."

Evren frowned. "She didn't know they were in the lake. You weren't there to see her face."

"I wasn't," he admitted. "Still, a little warning about her past would've saved us a lot of pain. This is why I don't like making things personal."

An echo of the Drystan she'd met in Keld's Outpost shimmered behind him like a wispy shadow. She saw his hard jaw and closed-off eyes, the way he set his shoulders back and stood firm in all his decisions. He blew away in an invisible wind, and the Drystan that remained was a poor copy. Tired, with slumped shoulders and a cold look in his eyes.

"It's personal for all of us now," Evren whispered into the void. "How does that make you feel?"

His jaw clenched and unclenched. When he spoke, his words hissed through gritted teeth. "Like I'm right back where I started."

"Before the Ashen Bond?"

He nodded stiffly.

"Back in Lostwater, you said you wouldn't make a deal with the undead again," she started slowly, watching him stiffen with every word. "What did you mean by that?"

The still silence that hung over graves descended on the two of them as soon as the words left her. It was nothing new. Evren had begun to realize that he carried this feeling with him wherever he went. But now it blanketed her like a thick, cold shroud. She tried not to shiver.

"What kept me from saving Vox, you mean?" he asked coldly.

"Yes."

He sighed and, bit by bit, she saw his stiffness drain out of him. The feeling of graves never left, but it clung more to him than her. He gripped the handle of his silver ax, and he cracked. Just the slight slant of his eyebrows and the tremor in his voice gave him away.

"I served undead back in Melkarth," he said, as if each word were poison he needed to spit out in order to survive. "Vampires, to be precise. Cruel, cunning, intelligent. They run most of Melkarth. And I served them willingly for most of my life."

Evren stared at him, unsure how to respond. But he refused to look at her.

"I was given to the Freys as a gift, you know. A sort of

penance from the locals. 'Here, have a baby! Please don't eat us the next time you get peckish.'" He laughed bitterly. "They raised me like one of their own. Didn't bother to hide their horrors from a child like myself."

"That sounds awful."

"Obvious statement."

She shrugged. He huffed and went on. It was as if a dam had opened and he couldn't keep back the flood of words now.

"I knew it was wrong, even as a child. Still, where else could I go? My only world was Melkarth. My only home was the Black Hall, not the humans that had left me to the wolves in order to save their own skins. I did what all their good human pets did. I behaved, and I fought, and I killed for them. They had a good system to keep them fed. One could almost call it efficient. But not humane. And, when I was old enough, I helmed it for a time."

"And no one in Melkarth does anything about this?" Evren asked. She couldn't keep the horror out of her voice.

Again, Drystan laughed. She didn't like the sound of it.

"Do anything?" He shook his head. "The Freys are part royalty. They practically run the kingdom—the whole twisted family. Power corrupts, but when old age isn't there to keep it in check, you get a hellhole that even the great armies of Etherak wanted nothing to do with. Ask you knight, and he'll tell you that no one attempted to conquer Melkarth during King Eldridge's mad war. There's a reason for that."

"So how did you get out?" The chilling fingers playing along her spine seemed to tighten their grip now and hold her in place.

Drystan closed his eyes, as if he was seeing something in the dark snow he'd rather forget. "There was one vampire who wasn't like the others. A daughter. She was . . . kind, I suppose. No spine at all. But she was still young when I was there. Still new to the mess she'd inherited with her bloody immortality. I didn't even think about leaving because I knew nothing else. But she did, and she left a door open for me."

"She let you escape."

"In part. She couldn't help me escape her family. They sent her older brother after me because I knew too much. If she was kind, he was pure unbridled evil. Matthias was a hunter and took no time to track me down to kill me."

She cocked her head to the side. "No offense, but you're pretty alive right now." She paused, looking him up and down as doubt gnawed at her bones. She didn't know what a vampire looked like. "Right?"

He finally looked at her, and even had the gall to roll his eyes. "Stupid question. Yes, I'm alive."

"Then fucking lead with that instead of leaving off all dramatic and shit." She kicked some snow up at him.

Drystan shook off the snow. "To conclude my sad tale, I was cornered and had to make my stand. Better death than a lifetime of servitude to monsters. Even if that death was in the hands of someone who liked to play with his food." His lip curled up into a sneer. "But Matthias wasn't that simple. He liked to play games to draw me out. And innocents were involved in that. I'm ashamed to say I let dozens die before I found the courage to stop him. And his final victim was a wandering orc from Gratey, who got lost too close to the Black Hall."

"Vox." Evren breathed. His name felt heavy in the air.

Drystan nodded again. "I didn't know him at the time, but he was the one I finally stood up for."

"Did you kill Matthias?"

"Hardly. Vox and I barely escaped with our lives by falling into the ocean. That's normally a death sentence that far north where the Freys operate, and I knew Matthias wouldn't follow. Still . . . I was more surprised than anyone to find us crawling onto Gratey's shores, half drowned and looking like death. After that, Vox swore I'd saved his life and he wouldn't leave my side. A life debt amongst his people was a serious matter. But I have a feeling he was just lonely."

"Or maybe he knew you were," Evren offered. He looked

back at her, startled, and she took a breath. "You said it yourself, you had no one to call friend growing up. No one to trust. Maybe he saw that."

Drystan blinked quickly and looked away. Underneath his furs, his chest heaved, as if there was a war inside him that his ribcage couldn't contain. She ignored the wet gleam in his eyes, for his sake more than hers.

"What a good friend I was," he spat. "I let him die. And not in an honorable way. They didn't even . . ." His voice fractured and he didn't bother to try to pick the words back up.

"Drystan," Evren said softly, as if to try and soothe the sharp pain rolling off of him. "He didn't blame you. He knew you couldn't take the deal."

"I didn't even try!"

"You protected your team," she insisted. "Sahar needed you. Nerezza needed you. They both *still* need you. Vox knew what was going to happen. I think he took it as an end to your debt. I could see it in his eyes. And judging from how much death you've seen, I know you saw it too."

Drystan let out a ragged breath. He looked like he wanted to scream. Like his throat was straining against the voice clawing to break free. She could hear the leather wrappings around his ax creak and twist under the pressure, but for the first time since she'd met him, none of that anger was aimed at her.

"He was my first friend." He hung his head. "Without him, I would never have given Sahar and Nerezza a second glance. I can't . . . I can't lose them, Hanali."

He looked up and his eyes grabbed Evren's in a fierce, invisible grip. The desperation in them was enough to make her own stomach churn. She knew that feeling, but seeing it in someone else was different.

"I can't lose them," he said fiercely. "I'll do anything to bring down the bastard that took Vox from us, but if I can't protect them along the way—"

"They're strong people, Drystan. And they want this as badly as you do. Watch each other's backs, and you'll all make it out of this to see daylight again."

"You sound so confident."

"It's ignorance." She shrugged her heavy shoulders and let herself pretend to smile. He didn't return it.

"You're many things, but you're not stupid."

"And yet I somehow stumble my way into every bad thing that can possibly happen to me. I'm either incredibly stupid or very unlucky."

Evren looked out at the thick black abyss. It was dark enough to rival what she saw in Serevadia. Even the stars didn't shine as brightly in the sky, and the moon had yet to rise. She wondered if it ever would.

"Whatever happens, I'll do what I can to make this bastard pay for what he did." She let the cold of the air creep into her voice. If she stared long enough into the night, she could almost fool herself into actually seeing. "We all will."

"I think I might even believe you," Drystan said. The grave-yard-like silence settled down again. When he spoke next, his voice was soft enough to belong to another man. One who wasn't raised by vampires. "This is why I don't like personal. It's messy."

"Life is messy," she said. "We just have to take whatever is thrown at us."

Drystan grunted. Without a word, he put his stony mask back on. He was back to the irritating, cold man he always portrayed, but she could see through the cracks now. Cracks she knew she hadn't caused. She hadn't known him long enough for that. Someone else had been chipping away at him steadily.

She turned to follow him back to Direwall, to the Jarl's home, to hopefully get a better plan in motion, when a blood-curdling scream ripped through the still night air. Evren and Drystan shared one fearful look before their weapons were in their hands and they tore across the ground into the city.

The Long Night had just begun.

15

It took far too long to see what was truly going on behind Direwall's gate. Lit up it may be, it wasn't nearly light enough to see clearly in the swallowing darkness. Firelight flickered, shadows jumped, and at every turn Evren was sure she'd find a horde of undead waiting for her.

But the streets were empty.

Ice-cold panic seized an iron grip on her spine as she followed closely on Drystan's heels. The screams had stopped. What were they running towards?

"Wait!" she gasped as she skidded to a halt. A patch of ice nearly sent her tumbling to the ground, but she just managed to keep her footing.

"We don't have time to wait!" Drystan snarled. But he stopped anyway, pacing the length of the street.

"Where is everybody?" she asked.

"What?"

"Look around!" She gestured to the quiet, empty street. It wasn't a large one, but it was the stillest she'd seen Direwall since arriving. Nothing stirred. Only the sounds of the brazier crackling at the corner filled the air. "The Jarl said nearly everyone would be out on the streets to help prepare. We weren't finished yet. There's no way."

Drystan paled even further. His eyes darted to the jumping shadows, as if the undead were waiting to crawl out of the gutters themselves.

"Where is everybody?" he echoed her.

More importantly, who had screamed, and why? But that was a thought that didn't need to be said out loud. Evren tightened her grip on her bow and let out a shaky breath as her cut palm sent a spike of pain up her arm. She needed to see clearly, to focus. But all the buildings were in the way. The fire was playing tricks with her eyes. She swore under her breath.

"I need a good vantage point," she said. "Help me up on a roof."

Drystan didn't bother to argue with her. He put his axes away and, with a low grunt of effort, helped her up on the closest roof. Evren snatched a hold on the railing and pulled herself up and over. The roof was steep and slick with ice. But she kept her feet steady and one hand on the ridge as she stood up.

Direwall was finally opened up to her eyes. Thick, heavy flakes of snow began to fall leisurely from the sky. They didn't melt when they fell on her cheeks and hair. The wall that encircled the city stood tall and proud against the unending night. She could see the fire-lit streets, the sails of the fishermen's boats brisling along the edge of the bay. The four abandoned lighthouses sat cold and lonely in their watch, silhouetted against the raging bonfires and braziers that crowded the city streets. Below, the waters in Myrefall Bay were churning. The black water was turning white with foam. No wind tore across the water.

"Drystan," she called down. "They're coming from the water!"

"Of course they are." he growled.

Evren hopped off the roof. She didn't feel her muscles

smarting at the impact. "We've got everyone spread all around the city. There's no way we can get them to the bay in time."

"I know my people, they would've seen it." He pulled both axes out with a quick, decisive flourish. "Trust that yours will too."

Evren hoped. It felt like a useless emotion to cling to now; barely a sliver of warmth for the Long Night to snatch away. But it was all she had. She could only hope that her friends, separated in all corners of the city, saw what she did.

Meet me there, she silently willed. And then she nocked an arrow and took off.

The same scream broke the night air again. This time with her feet pounding in the same direction, Evren could feel the sound tugging her to the bay. It was high pitched and sounded female. She was suddenly reminded of the fox she killed in the forest, its white fur turning red with its blood. It felt like a lifetime ago.

When the scream fell to silence, it was just her and Drystan tearing through the streets towards the water. Direwall's maze of buildings rose up to suffocate her. Each brazier at the end of the streets felt like a beacon. Follow the fires, follow the screams, straight into the horde of undead.

The dangerous bubbles of maniacal giggling rising up from her tight, panicked chest. She wasn't unlucky. She had to be insane to run *towards* death. Casting a sideways glance at Drystan, who was easily keeping pace with her, she found an odd comfort in the fact that she wasn't alone.

Every adventurer was insane. It was the only way to look death in the eyes and thwart it time and time again. But how many more brushes with death did she have before she couldn't look away?

Tally the breaths, Hanali, she urged herself. *Until there's no more left to breathe. Make death work to get you.*

The air was thick with salt as they got closer to the docks. But something else hung in the air well. Rot, sickly sweet and sour just at the edges. The smell of decay, and death. The salt and smoke couldn't hope to cover the overwhelming stench.

Evren and Drystan rounded the corner into the small square they'd met Abraxas in. The night and creeping fires made the buildings look skeletal and hellish. It was like she'd stepped into a nightmare version of Direwall. Far below, nearer to the water's edge, she could hear fighting. She could smell the acidic burn of magical fire, and see it light up the sky.

In front of her, the sloping road to the docks awaited. And standing in perfect lines, dripping with salt water and staring sightlessly ahead, were hundreds of undead.

Drystan put an arm out to stop her. They both skidded to a halt, mere feet from the undead. Their glowing eyes snapped to them in unison. The two adventurers backed up as much as their shaking feet would allow, but the creatures didn't budge.

"They're blocking the way to the docks," he hissed under his breath.

"But why aren't they attacking?"

"SON OF DEATH, DAUGHTER OF BLOOD, WE HAVE BEEN WAITING FOR YOU."

A hundred voices at once, gargling with salt water and cracking with frozen vocal chords. And yet, even with a hundred different voices, she could only hear one lone voice. Lonely, cold, grasping for them.

"Enough with the vague titles," Drystan yelled.

"COME HOME TO US." The creaking of bones and smell of rotting flesh filled the air as they all reached their hands out. The smell of rot got stronger with every sharp move they made. Evren tried not to gag. "NO MORE FIGHTING. YOU DESERVE TO REST—"

The arrow was shot from her bow before she even had time to register she had reached for it. It whistled through the air and sank into the frozen chest of one undead. He fell to the ground face first, and another took his place without hesitation.

"AREN'T YOU LONELY?" They continued, their voices

droning in her ears and shaking her skull. "DON'T YOU WISH TO HAVE A FAMILY AGAIN? COME WITH US. BE ONE WITH THE PRIME. WE ARE ALL FAMILY UNDER THE PRIME."

"Thoughts?" Drystan asked.

"Only bad ones," Evren replied.

There was only one way forward. And an army of undead standing between them and their friends. The snow was falling heavier now, drifting lazily in the air and slowly covering the corpses.

Evren nocked another arrow. Beside her, Drystan shifted into a lower fighting stance. She didn't have to see him to feel the cold grin sweeping across his face.

"Bad plan it is then." His words hissed through the falling snow. The undead snapped to attention, their inviting hands turning into elongated, icy claws. Their expressions didn't change, but Evren felt their intent in the air.

Evren drew her bow. The arrow hovered against her finger, the bow string creaking with tension. All she could see was the army before her. Somehow, they all looked like Gyda.

She let loose the arrow just after Drystan charged, axes gleaming in the flickering firelight. The arrow hit home, just before he did. Three corpses fell, one for her, and two under his assault. A scream filled the air again, this time like sucking air and entirely inhuman. All at once the undead charged.

"NOW!" Jarl Eirunn's voice boomed, and the war cry that followed it mimicked the rumbling chaos of an avalanche.

The rooftops surrounding the undead and the square were bristling with spears and fire. Ikedree warriors rained down hell on the horde of corpses. Flaming arrows peppered them, burning through clothes and eye sockets, and filling the air with the smell of burning hair and flesh. Evren just managed to grab the back of Drystan's belt and pull him out of the way of the second volley of arrows.

Most didn't hit their mark in the heart, but the fire was spreading amongst the horde. Their attention snapped from

Evren and Drystan to the flaming, heavily armed threat from above. They scrambled to get to the walls, practically running over each other with a fury that burned hotter than any fire.

"DESCEND!"

Before they could make it to the walls of the buildings, the warriors dropped down. They leapt into the horde, swords and great axes cleaving through the bodies. Bones and limbs scattered in the air. They pushed them back from the buildings, keeping the flames away from the buildings. Crowding them, corralling them. The Ikedree were fewer in numbers, but if the mad laughter coming from the pits of the fighting was any indication, these were the odds they preferred.

"Keep them from our homes!" Eirunn's commanding voice was suddenly only a few feet away. Evren tried not to jump out of her skin.

The Jarl stepped on the skull of an undead as she came closer. She was a vision in her armor and furs, her iron circlet gone, and her face smudged with dark war paint. Her shield was covered in black blood, her war hammer shimmering with heavy heat. A dwarven rune burned at the hilt.

"Nice entrance." Evren nodded.

Eirunn ignored her. "They come from the bay."

Evren opened her mouth to say something along the lines of 'I told you so,' just a little more politely. She had no wish to piss off a woman who was in skull-crushing range. But Eirunn cut her off with a wave of her war hammer.

"I'm aware of my mistake, Worm-Rider. I thought Mortova would keep them from the bay. I was wrong."

Evren closed her mouth. The stench of death filled her head anyway. But it was refreshing to hear Eirunn admit her mistake anyway.

"What now?" she asked.

Eirunn raised a painted brow. "Now you get to the bay, and you stop anymore from coming. My people will keep as many of them from getting farther into the city as we can.

"There's no way we're getting through that," Drystan retorted.

The warriors let out a call and all suddenly hunkered down behind shields. The undead sprang to overwhelm them, but another volley of flaming arrows flew down from the rooftops. The warriors threw off their shields and pushed back at the undead again with renewed force.

"Not through," Evren said, watching the archers with a growing smile. "Above."

She turned towards Eirunn, who was grinning wickedly. "Any more whale oil at the docks?"

The Jarl shrugged. "Whatever is left, your little goblin and his human have gone after them."

Evren felt a wave of relief rush over her. "So Arke and Sorin are alive."

"And the others?" Drystan demanded.

"I did not see the dwarf and your woman, but the one who calls himself Abraxas is with your mage further down the way."

Drystan's face fell slightly. He could see the indecisiveness tugging at him. If Eirunn hadn't seen Sahar, where was she? If not at the docks, then where?

Evren put a hand on his shoulder, pulling him back to the present. "Trust your people, Drystan. She's the smartest of us, she'll make it."

He didn't look convinced, but there was no time for him to debate. Eirunn wasn't going to let him. With her shield and hammer, she herded them towards one of the nearby buildings. An undead managed to squeeze past her warriors and leapt at them. In midair it met the heated force of her war hammer. Its skull shattered and it fell to the ground, still crawling forward. Another swing passed so close to Evren she could feel the heat sizzling from the metal. It's rib cage cracked like an eggshell under the massive weight, and finally the corpse stilled.

They came up to the wall of the building. Evren could pick out the handholds against the woodwork, and quickly shouldered her bow so she could scramble up the side. She heard Drystan close behind her, and Eirunn calling after them.

"I do not care what you do, so long as you save my city."

Evren didn't get a chance to say anything else. She turned to look over her shoulder to see Eirunn charging back into the battle. Her shield was raised, and her hammer suddenly burst into bright flames as skulls and limbs flew in the wake of her path. The undead immediately turned their gaze on her; the biggest threat so far.

Evren tore her eyes away from the battle and swung over the side and onto the roof. It was still dangerously steep but there were wooden planks laid down to make the walking less treacherous. She scooted over and lowered her hand for Drystan. He took it firmly and she hauled him up to the top.

They got to their feet, standing on the wobbly boards with their weapons drawn. Ahead of them, archers stood at the very edge of the rooftop, raining fire down on the street with every command from Eirunn. Beyond them, the gauntlet to the docks laid open.

"Ready?" she asked Drystan, as if they had any choice.

"Stupid question," was all he replied.

She smiled. It really was.

Evren took off across the rooftop. Her light feet balanced on the boards, even as they rose and fell precariously under Drystan's heavier steps. Below her, the battle raged in fiery abandon. Smoke and snow clouded the air. Her fingers itched to let loose an arrow into the horde. As payback for Gyda and Vox, as a small way to help the people of Direwall fight for their city. But every time her footsteps faltered, she had Drystan at her back urging her forward.

"We can help by ending this!" he shouted over the fighting.

She tore herself away from the rooftop edge and continued to run.

The archers ended as the roof did. The decline steepened and the gap between roofs was approaching faster. "Gap!" she called behind her. She let her feet pick up speed, and gravity do its work. As she neared the edge, she felt her boots grip the edge and push her off. She sailed through the air, landing with a low grunt on the other side. She quickly got up as Drystan landed behind her unceremoniously with a string of curses.

In front of them, the boards continued, as did their path. She picked herself back up and took off. Drystan's heavy footfalls behind her eased her fear slightly. She took in quick, heavy lungfuls of icy air. Smoke curled in her lungs, but she ignored the itch. Snow blurred her vision, boards creaked under their feet. The writhing waters of Myrefall Bay were closer, but the heavy snow and smoke kept it obscured.

They leapt from building to building, barely keeping their footing in their mad dash to the water. Evren's ankles ached sharply with the unfamiliar pressure, and her breaths came out ragged. In the distance, she could see the snow and night sky light up in an orange glow from a burst of flame.

"Arke or Nerezza!" Evren pointed, and Drystan just grunted in response. He couldn't take his eyes off his feet and the boards in front of them.

Evren picked up the pace. Her feet were light, her chest was aching, and the fire seemed to grow brighter.

Icy cold hands suddenly wrapped around her ankle and yanked her down. Her cry of surprise was cut off as she hit the roof hard enough to knock the wind out from her. A corpse was pulling her down, hissing between its rotting teeth and spitting sea water in her face.

Another hand grabbed her wrist, this one warm and alive, and halted her fall. Drystan pulled against the undead, his face tight with concentration.

Evren gripped his wrist with that hand, clinging as hard as her gloved fingers would allow. She kicked at the corpse dangling off of her. It screeched again as its skull cracked under her heel, but it didn't let go. Underneath it were dozens more,

202 | GILLIAN GRANT

clawing at the wall. Their eyes glowed hungrily, their hands reaching ever upwards for her.

She kicked again, screaming in frustration. Her shoulder was tearing apart with the force of Drystan and the undead both tugging on her. She twisted in their grips to try and throw it off, but it clung to her stubbornly. She brought her free boot up high and smashed it down with as much force as she could muster.

Its skull caved beneath her book with a sickening crunch. She kept her foot there, bringing it up only so far just to slam it back down again.

Again and again, bones and gore covered her boot. The undead below her were getting closer, their sucking gasps echoing in her ears., If she listened close enough, she could almost imagine they were crying out in pain.

With a sharp cry of her own, she brought her boot down one final time. The corpse holding onto her collapsed as its spine cracked and crumbled under the pressure. Its boney fingers loosened just enough, and Evren yanked her ankle free.

Drystan hauled her up and onto her feet.

Her shoulder ached sharply, and her left foot was strangely colder than the rest of her. But she didn't have time to catch her breath. The undead clawed over the roof and surrounded them both.

Evren and Drystan stood back-to-back against the corpses. She nocked an arrow. He readied his axes. And the undead leapt at them.

Evren shot the first one that came at her, kicking it aside as it tumbled lifelessly to the street below. Another two took its place. She ducked under the swing of the first one and brought the bow up to smash the other in the skull. It staggered back, and she swung her leg around to catch the other one reaching for Drystan. It fell on its back, and she brought the pointed end of her bow's limb tip into its chest. The light in its eyes died, and she shoved it off the roof.

The one she'd hit in the face raced back after her. She shot another arrow into its chest and didn't bother to see where the corpse fell. Another four replaced it immediately.

"Switch!" Drystan called.

Evren felt his back against hers. He bent down into a crouch, and she rolled over his back smoothly, taking his spot to look up the incline.

Another three were tearing across the roof towards her, but at a good distance. Evren felt herself smile and she pulled back an arrow and lined the shot up carefully. She pulled the bowstring as taut as she could. Her muscles strained and screamed under the pressure, but her breaths were slow and even.

Time seemed to slow, if only for a minute. She saw every detail of their waxy flesh and cold eyes. She watched as the snow gathered in the decaying pockets of skin. Their hands were tipped with claws of ice, gleaming in the flickering flame in short flashes. Their gaping mouths seemed to suck the snow inside their lungs, all three, until the roof forced them behind each other. Until she saw only one.

Her grin was as sharp as a wolf's as she let the arrow, brimming with untapped energy, soar through the air.

It flew too quick to see, into the sucking chest of the first undead. Evren watched as that one swayed unsteadily, until the glow in its eyes flickered out and it fell. The one behind it crumbled to its feet, the gaping arrow wound in its chest little more than a small hole through its heart. The third stared at the arrow protruding through its ragged furs, almost as if it was confused.

"Get fucked," Evren hissed.

It fell to the streets as well, and the way behind it was clear.

"How're we looking?" she called as she looked back.

Drystan's axes flashed in the snow as he brought them both down in a heavy cross into the chest of a corpse. He kicked it back, and the three behind it fell like stones under its dead weight.

"I'd feel sorry for them if I wasn't so pissed," he gritted out.

One crawled over its friends and started to run forward. It met another of Evren's arrows. "You have the other two?"

He flipped the axes in the air. The remaining two tossed their allies' corpses to the side and got up, baring their black teeth in a threat, or a grin. They hadn't taken a full step forward when Drystan threw both axes at once. They somersaulted through the air, landing with twin thunks in each of the undead's chests and burying so deep she couldn't see their blades.

Drystan darted forward to get his weapons before they fell into the streets below. He shook the blood from them and kicked the undead still blocking the way off the roof. He sheathed the axes and breathed deeply before grimacing. He grabbed his side as blood started to seep through his heavy furs. Not a deadly flow, but enough to cause a spike of alarm to shoot through Evren.

"Are you all right?" she asked, stepping closer. He moved away before she could see the wound better and smiled through the pain. There was a fire in his eyes that eclipsed the pain entirely.

"Never better,"

"I think you enjoyed that," Evren said, straightening up.

"I think you did too."

"Gets the blood pumping. Come on, we still have a city to save."

Drystan led the way forward. His steps were surer now despite his wound. He didn't stumble or lose his speed. Evren couldn't deny that her blood was singing after the fight. Quick as it was, it felt good to fight rather than run away. Not only fight but *win*. If she ignored how vastly outnumbered they all were, she could pretend that their chances of surviving the night were better than they really were.

In front of her, Drystan slowed down as the decline leveled out. Her throbbing ankles practically wept in relief. The sound of churning water was loud in her ears now. She could see the masts of the small fishing ships swaying dangerously side to side from her spot on the roof.

"There!" Drystan pointed just as a bright plume of flame lit up the night to their right. A wave of heat washed over them, then disappeared as quickly as the fire.

They slid off the roof one at a time and landed on their feet in the muddy street. It was clear so far, and the gathering drifts of snow piled on the mud with nothing and no one to stop them.

Evren nocked another arrow, keeping it loose but ready as she ran alongside Drystan. The fresh snow crunched under her feet sounded like crushing bones. They darted into a side street, following the fire and the sounds of fighting. When they turned the corner into another street, the smell of sea air and rot hit them like a brick wall. Evren coughed and tried not to stumble back.

Myrefall Bay stretched out like a roiling sea in front of them. Waves crashed against the docks, spewing water on the surrounding buildings. From the frothing waves, corpses crawled out. Sodden with water, their bodies cracked and started to freeze in the snow, but they shook off the ice and threw themselves at the lone figure in front of the water.

Arke was standing between the dead and the rest of the city. His tiny form was surrounded by flaming arcane glyphs. They swirled around his body, lighting the street around him where the braziers had been soaked through and put out. The ground at his feet was a pool of melted snow, the air shimmered with heat. Each time an undead threw itself at him, a glyph would shift and catch it. The glyph would explode in a plume of fire that scorched groups at a time. When a glyph exploded, Arke tore out another page and made a new one. A pile of ashes was scattered at his feet, and his spellbook was noticeably emptier than before.

Sorin, on the other hand, had a mass of harpoons slung over

his shoulder and was rolling a barrel of whale oil across the street.

"What are you doing?" Evren asked, her voice strangely high pitched as another burst of flame lit up the night air and Arke's cackling could be heard over the clacking of teeth and bones.

Sorin's head snapped up, and the way the orange light caught his smile made him look like he was one of the corpses for a second. The flames died down and he looked normal again, but the smile remained.

"Oh, hey Evvie!" he said cheerfully. "We're all gonna die!"

"Probably," Drystan muttered.

Sorin laughed and continued to roll the barrel down the street.

"Sorin!" Evren called out.

"Right!" He didn't stop and continued to talk over his shoulder. "I've got an idea! Involves the lighthouses. Might still die, though."

"Mind letting us in on that plan?"

"Oh, yeah!" Something wicked gleamed in his eyes as he looked at her over his shoulder. She hadn't seen that crazy look in a long time. "I'm going to kill Mortova. Wanna help?"

A million thoughts ran through Evren's head at once. Her eyes darted to the churning waters, and the idea of something monstrous and seething lying beneath the waves. No, not lying. Mortova was kicking up a storm and lending the undead cover and help. If they could kill him . . .

"That's a tall order, Sorin," Evren said as another wave crashed into the docks and capsized boats under its force.

"How would we even get to it?" Drystan asked.

"He's close enough to cause all of this." Sorin waved a hand at the water. "We just can't see him. If we light up the water, we should get a good shot." At their hesitant faces, he sighed dramatically. "If Mortova is helping the undead, then the survivor *has* to be his Bond. He won't stop. Kill Mortova and we stop the undead from using the bay. It's our one shot."

"Four lighthouses," Drystan murmured.

"Four teams," Evren finished.

"Exactly!" Sorin threw his hands in the air. "I sent Abraxas and Nerezza to the northern ones. I haven't seen Sol and Sahar, but they were at the northernmost gate, so—"

"They're probably doing the same thing we were at the southern gate," Drystan finished for him. A renewed spike of energy seemed to jolt through him. He turned to Sorin with a glint in his eye. "You've got this side covered?"

Sorin scoffed and jerked a thumb over to Arke, who sounded more and more like a villain in some children's story with all his manic laughter. "He's having fun. The lighthouse isn't far, and I'll get mine lit."

Evren nodded, but worry was still gnawing at her. "When we get all of them lit, how do we kill it?"

Sorin shrugged and pointed to her bow. "You've got good aim, everyone else should have magic on their team. All it should take is a lucky shot. This is an old bastard, so let's put him out of his misery, eh?"

He turned his back on them and continued to roll his barrel to the next street. Despite the overwhelming odds and swarming corpses, his steps were light and quick. Evren could've sworn she heard him whistling.

She spared a glance at Arke, who was single-handedly keeping the dead back. He spared her a glance and winked. Sorin was right. He was having fun.

"Let's go." Drystan grabbed her arm and pulled her back. "We can check on Nerezza and Abraxas on our way up."

They took off in another sprint. This time with an actual goal in mind. She craned her neck up and could see the next lighthouse looming dark against the snowy sky. Closer than she realized, but farther away than she'd like. She urged her feet to move faster.

"Let's kill a sea monster," she said between puffed breaths. "That'll solve all our problems!"

Evren heard Drystan laugh through his running gasps. "You people really are insane."

"Don't act like you aren't," she shot over at him. They crossed back through the wide street they'd followed by rooftop, ducking into a small alleyway, and emerging into another road. "You're the crazy bastard that took this quest willingly."

"Fair point, Hanali."

There was no more energy or air for retorts now. They ducked their heads and ran. With every street they passed, every corner they ducked around, they saw battle. Every clan of the Ikedree people were working together. Banging their shields, shouting songs of blood and courage. Fire and steel clashed against bone and ice. If Evren didn't look closely, she could imagine the living were winning. She tore her eyes away from every final stand in the muddy streets, every bleeding body collapsing under the weight of a hundred undead.

The flickering light of the fires made the snow seem even thicker as they pushed further north. The lighthouse loomed ever closer, and sooner than she expected, they rounded another corner to find it rising to meet them.

The stonework was wind-torn and layered with years of salt. Icicles hung like waiting daggers eager to fall on whichever unlucky soul happened to be standing beneath them. At first all Evren could see was darkness, shadowed waves untouched by the infernos left behind them, and gnashing teeth, but none of it aimed at her. No braziers lit up the dark streets; it was slick and wet with blackness.

Light suddenly blossomed like a mini sun in the middle of the streets. Evren shielded her eyes as cries of pain erupted around her like an unholy choir. The smell of ash filled her nose. Something tickled the back of her throat and she coughed and waved away the snow in her face. Her gloves came back smudged grey.

True ash, not snow.

She looked back at the light. It had dimmed now, but a

shimmering bubble of radiant energy engulfed the base of the lighthouse and shielded the door. The undead around it were either turned to ash or getting back up, crying out in fury.

Inside, Abraxas was a figure in black armor. His furs were gone and his hair was undone. He knelt on one knee, his shield at his side and his head bowed at the pummel of his sword. His lips moved soundlessly and his eyes were squeezed shut.

Behind him, Nerezza stood at the steps of the lighthouse. Her brow was slick with sweat, but her eyes gleamed with arcane energy. One hand held her new spellbook, another was open in the air, palm up towards the crown of the bubble. She furrowed her brows as the undead threw themselves at the bubble again. It shimmered as their bodies piled on top it. She turned her open hand into a fist, and another wave of light flowed from the bubble and the closest dead were turned to piles of ash.

"Is he praying?" Drystan asked.

Evren couldn't even answer, but it didn't matter since he was already marching up to the bubble. A wandering undead caught sight of him and ran to intercept. He didn't even look at it as he cut it down.

"Are you praying?" he called through the bubble.

Evren's stomach sank. After all this time, Abraxas still clung so desperately to his Banished Divines. Sorin's revival had simply renewed that frenzy. But seeing him pray in the middle of battle while Nerezza kept the dead back didn't look good.

"Abraxas!" she called.

His head snapped up; his prayer cut off mid-sentence. He looked calm, far too serene in such chaos. She ignored how uneasy it made her feel.

"You need to light this up!" She pointed to the top. He followed her hand, but it was Nerezza who answered.

"Don't worry about us!" Her voice was strong, despite the strain Evren could see in her neck and jaw. A bead of sweat fell down her temple and to her chin. She wasn't smiling, but there was something akin to satisfaction gleaming in her eyes each time a corpse was turned to ash.

Abraxas stood up, his serene eyes taking in the bubble of light before falling back to Evren and nodding sharply. "We'll get this done. You move on."

Evren stole a glance at the new wave of undead headed towards the light. "But—"

"Go."

She swallowed back her protests and looked at Drystan. He was seething, but turned away from the bubble and nodded to the northern street. Neither one of them could argue with their friends, not with so much at stake.

They turned and put the searing light behind them. The screams of the undead never faded completely, but they eventually put enough distance between them that they could ignore it. Evren tried to bury her unease. She hated the undead and everything they'd done. But something in the way they screamed put her on edge. She couldn't shake the feeling, no matter how hard she ran.

The streets were dark and swirling with snow. She was hurting, her lungs and muscles were on fire, but she kept her feet still and sure, her breaths even. Drystan, for all his strength, was falling behind. His breathing was ragged, and his side was still bleeding. She had to slow down to make sure he kept up with her.

The braziers they passed were cold and filled with ice. Evren had a feeling that the snow hadn't snuffed the fires out. But they ran into nothing but still corpses as they ran. Most were undead finally at rest. But occasionally Evren spotted someone with pink still on their cheeks, eyes of green or brown instead of glowing blue. Weapons laid shattered and useless on the ground. The remnants of a battle they'd been too slow to see. The blood still smelled fresh.

The next lighthouse waited for them in the dark. Thick ice coated the path leading up to it, and the stairs looked like something out of a nightmare bristling with icicles. A barrel of oil was sitting next to the door. But there was no undead in sight, and the waves on this side of the bay were calm in comparison to what she'd seen before.

"We missed this wave," Drystan panted. "It's clear for now."

Evren looked back the way they came. The sky was lit up by the southernmost lighthouse, and she breathed a sigh of relief. Sorin and Arke had made it. Nerezza and Abraxas's was still dark, but she had faith in them. All that was left was the final two northern ones.

"You have flint?" she asked him.

He nodded wordlessly.

"All right, light this one up."

She turned to walk away, but he cut in front of her. "Where are you going?"

"The next lighthouse," she said, "We can't expect Sol and Sahar to know Sorin's plan if they're all the way across the city."

"We stick together," he insisted. "We light this one and then we go to the next one."

She shook her head. "We might not have that time. And someone needs to be at each lighthouse to keep it lit. I'm faster and you're hurt. I'll make better time on my own."

Drystan ground his teeth in frustration, the muscle in his jaw feathering out as he did. "We should go together. We have no idea what's up there."

"No," Evren agreed. "We don't."

"Then I'll go, and you light the damn tower."

"I'll send her back to you, Drystan."

Him and his anger stilled to a frozen stop. She couldn't read anything but barely bridled hope in his features, and a healthy amount of distrust. Every bone in him ached to argue with her, to toss her aside and go after Sahar on his own. And he had every right to do so. She had no real argument on why he should stay, and she should go, other than she was faster. And she wasn't bleeding.

That scream filled the air again and chilled her to the bone. She saw Drystan flinch, and knew he heard Sahar in it. He was torn between what he wanted and what was probably best for the city. There was no way he could have both, not unless Evren was fast enough.

"Get her back to me." His voice was little more than a whisper. "If you do nothing else, do that."

"Only on one condition."

He looked ready to punch her. Anything to let out all that pent-up rage and pain. "What?"

"Tell her how you feel."

There was no malice in his scowl. He nudged her toward the final lighthouse and used the momentum to take a few steps backward himself. "If we survive this. *Maybe*. Now go, before I change my mind."

He turned and started to slowly walk over the ice. Evren turned to the north, the last lighthouse dark and lonely and waiting for her. Hopefully two of the brightest women she knew were waiting for her as well. She willed her tired legs to work, just a little farther. She broke into a jog and didn't look back.

16

The farther north in Direwall she went, the darker it seemed to become. Her eyes strained against the shadows, barely able to pick out dangerous pockets of snow, much less waiting undead. Every time she saw a corner, she had to stop and listen. Was that chattering teeth she heard or just her own imagination? Did she see the glimmer of glowing blue eyes or had vision finally given up on her? Her blood pounded hot in her veins, but the chill of fear never left her.

She tried to remember what she'd told Sorin.

Use fear, let it fill you up.

Evren stopped at a corner and flattened herself against the cold wall. She tried to calm her breathing and quell the rising fear in her. And listen. What did she hear?

But never, never, let it consume you.

Her breathing hitched to a stop as her ears picked something up. Snarls of the undead, the sounds of battle. Voices, desperate and fearful. The sound of glass shattering overwhelmed it all, and the sudden smell of sulfur flooded her nose.

Evren coughed and wrinkled her nose. But there was her path, as clear as day, despite the lack of light.

She took off down the street and towards the chaos. She

moved her feet as fast as she could, but they were starting to feel heavier, like she was dragging bags of sand with her. It took no time at all for her breathing to turn rapid and labored. The scar on her chest itched with each heave of her chest. The first time she was running towards something and it reacted, rather than when she was running away.

Evren burst into a battlefield. It was little more than a small pocket of empty streets, but a mass of undead crowded it and clamored towards one corner. Huddled in the corner, back-to-back, Sol and Sahar stood. They were wide eyed, bloody, and terrified, but alive.

Sol found her across the sea of bodies. Her eyes were hopeful then and brimming with tears. She nudged Sahar, who whooped with joy when she laid eyes on her. As Sol slashed her knives in an arc and sent a curve of undead to the ground, Sahar pulled out a bright white bottle. She tossed it in the air, gave it a goodbye kiss and winked at Evren as she launched it in the air as far away from her and Sol as she could get.

Evren watched the bright bottle arc through the falling snow. Some of the undead even reached their decaying hands for it. She drew an arrow without thinking, nocked it, and let the arrowhead follow the falling bottle. Closer and closer it inched towards their heads. Out of the corner of her eyes, she saw Sol and Sahar hunker down. The thought to do the same didn't reach her until she let the arrow loose.

It shattered the bottle easily. The white liquid sprayed over the undead, following the arrow and coating nearly all of them. That was only the first second. The next, everything was on fire.

The sudden combustion sent a wave of white fire and heat through the undead. The force threw Evren back, and she slammed against the nearby wall, gasping for breath. Her bow nearly fell out of her hands, and as she fought to breathe again, she gripped it like a lifeline. She blinked her eyes, trying to see past the haze of green light. She saw nothing other than the undead writhing in pain and trying to put out the fire. It quickly ate at their flesh, burning even the bones to cinders. Her morning porridge started to make its way up her throat as the burning skeletons fought each other to tear the fire off their skin and clothes.

Through the ringing in her ears, Evren heard her name. She looked over to see Sol and Sahar running through the undead. They were covered in soot and ash, but the flames didn't touch them. They were both grinning from ear to ear as they came up to her.

Each hooked an arm under her and pulled her to her feet. Evren tried not to wheeze as she coughed up ash. She patted Sol's shoulder and leaned on her. She didn't realize how exhausted she was until she'd been forced on her ass.

"You enjoyed that far too much," Evren coughed, when she finally got her voice back.

Sahar dusted the ash off her coat as primly as she could, seeing as the coat itself was torn and covered in black blood. "I was saving it for a special occasion."

"You couldn't do it earlier?" Sol joked.

"The area of effect was far too large for that. I needed to make sure we wouldn't get hit." She turned to Evren; her normal smile strange to see on her battle-worn face. "Nice shot."

Evren waved her off. "That's what I do."

Evren forced herself to stand without Sol's help and dragged them back the way she came. The streets were still dark, but thankfully she saw no more undead prowling. Hopefully the ones Sahar had lit on fire were the last in the northern part of the city.

She turned to her and nudged her south. "See that lighthouse?"

"Yes?"

"Get there as quick as you can. Drystan is waiting and he's going to need some help."

Fear flashed in her eyes again. "Is he okay?"

"He's hurt and stubborn as a fucking mule." She tried to

smile and soothe her worry. "But he's fine. I promised him I'd send him your way."

Sahar took a hesitant step forward, her eyes bright with hope as the lighthouse lit up. All three she'd passed were lit now. She looked back at Sol and Evren. "But what about you two?"

"We're going to the last lighthouse."

"We are?" Sol asked.

Evren nodded. "Sorin's idea. If we can find Mortova and kill him, that should be enough for us to send the rest of the horde packing."

Sahar let out a weary sigh. "Kill a sea monster, why not?" She shrugged. "I'll check that off my bucket list."

"The streets between here and Drystan should be clear. Just be careful."

She nodded. "I will. Thank you both. Try to stay alive, yes? I owe you."

Sahar turned and looked back up at the lighthouse. She murmured something soft and hopeful under her breath, too quiet for even Evren to hear. If she was the religious sort, Evren would've thought it was a prayer, it was said with such reverence. But before she could ask her, Sahar had disappeared into the dark streets towards the light Drystan had lit for her.

"We really have to do something about those two," Sol said.

"I'm working on it." Evren turned north, hopefully for the final time. "Come on, let's kill a sea monster."

Sol tossed her head back and laughed. "That's a terrible idea. I love it!"

The two didn't run fast, but they made good enough time through the maze of streets and buildings. Again, that scream pierced Evren's ears. It was coming from where she was going. Had it been this whole time?

"I don't like the sound of that," Sol said, gripping her knives. They were closer to the docks again. Evren could taste the salt in the air, stronger than the leftover sulfur on Sol's clothes.

"I've been hearing it since this all started," Evren said, shaking her head. "I can't shake it. It sounds like a fox."

They turned the last corner. To their right, the lit-up bay was red. Evren could see fins and the wide, slick body of something massive writhing beneath the waves. Harpoons were sticking out of it, its pale scales gleamed red with blood. Scorch marks marred its body as well. It was close enough to shore that every thrash of its tail sent a wave of water crashing over the docks and into the streets.

Evren and Sol stepped back before the water could soak their boots. As she did, something moved out of the corner of her eye. She whirled around, bow drawn and arrow ready to fly. She froze, however, when she saw a lone hulking figure standing at the base of the last lighthouse.

Two glowing eyes peered out from the shadows, familiar and haunting. Its head cocked to the side, so unnatural it made Evren sick. Vox stood before her, his chest open and frozen, completely devoid of a heart. And he was smiling.

Sol squeaked beside her. "That's not possible . . . without the heart?"

Not-Vox tsked and shook his head. "Worry not, I'm not like the other bumbling idiots you've hacked through tonight. I'm here to help."

The voice was not Vox's. The strange accent and lilt to the words were muffled by the tusks, as if whatever it was wasn't used to speaking around them. There was a dark edge to the voice too; an intelligence sharpened by age she couldn't fathom.

"You . . ." Evren could barely speak, and she didn't lower her bow. "You were the beast that followed me through the woods."

The grin stretched so far, Evren was sure Vox would never have been able to do it around his tusks. His lip split open against one tusk, as if to prove her point.

"Yes, although I was in a different body then. And I enjoyed your meals. Took you long enough to follow my voice, though." Not-Vox sighed. "I made the fox sound just for you."

"What are you?" she hissed.

"*Who* am I would be more polite," it said and pushed off the wall. It trailed a cold finger on a barrel of oil, the snow showing its journey mirrored the creature's footsteps. "You can call me Keres, and for now let's just say I'm an invested third party."

"You're possessing Vox's body!" Sol cried. "It's wrong!"

"Why?" Keres asked, seeming genuinely curious. "He wasn't using it anymore."

"He was a friend."

"Oh, please, you didn't even know him." Keres waved her off. "Now, are you going to sit here and debate with me, or do you want to save this wretched town?"

Evren and Sol shared a look. Doubt swam between them. Everything they knew about the Prime's undead was completely opposite to Keres, whatever they were. They seemed to be fully in control of themselves, and Vox's body. Which was a problem. But Evren knew that stare. The familiar prickle on her skin of being watched. She lowered her bow and turned to meet Keres' gaze.

"Why didn't you kill me in the woods?" she asked.

Keres seemed to consider it, twisting Vox's face into a ridiculous copy of a frown. After a while, they shrugged. "I liked being fed. Or maybe I knew you and the little King slayer over here would need my help tonight."

Sol blanched and nearly dropped her knives. "How does it know that?" she asked, her voice shrill and high. "Evren, how does it know me?"

"I don't know." Evren felt frustration welling up inside her chest. "I've gotten used to weird assholes knowing more about me than I know about myself. It's starting to piss me off."

"Light the fire, kill the slippery bastard causing a fuss, and then I'll tell you." Keres extended Vox's hand. "Deal?"

Evren frowned at the hand. She could still shoot Keres, but she wasn't even sure what manner of undead they were if they didn't have a heart. She'd have to drag them back to Abraxas to be sure, and Drystan.

Oh, she wasn't looking forward to that conversation.

"I'm not shaking your hand," she said. "But you better have answers after this."

Keres shrugged and let the hand fall to their side. "I'll take what I can get. This way!"

Too cheerfully for the body of a dead man, Keres turned around and slung the barrel over their shoulders with the ease of a man picking up a toddler. It was strange and horrifying to watch. Something that stiff and dead should never move so easily. But even as she watched them take the stairs without complaint, there was telltale signs of strain. Keres wasn't as fast or fluid as the undead she'd seen, and she tried to ignore the sounds of creaking muscles and crackling cartilage as she followed them up the steps and into the lighthouse. Sol stayed behind her, and never put away her knives.

It was somehow colder inside the lighthouse. Like the stones amplified and trapped the cold air. But it was blissfully free of corpses and falling snow. She shook the snow from her wet hair and followed Keres up the tight, spiral staircase.

"Just why are you helping us?" Sol asked, and her voice bounced off the stone in multiple echoes of the question.

Keres waited until the echoes died down before answering. "I don't like the little shit that calls himself Prime. I don't like the cold. And I really, really, don't like Mortova. And since you're big heroes, I thought I'd lend my great assistance. You don't mind taking help from someone of questionable morals, right?"

"The fact that you're asking that isn't comforting," Evren said.

"Sorry! Did you want me to be all sweet and soft about it? Bounce around the topic with a lot of nice words and empty promises, like your Herald of Light? I'm afraid that tactic only works if you're pretty."

Evren gripped her bow tight enough she thought it would break. "How did you—"

"All in due time." Keres got to the top of the lighthouse and stepped aside so they could pass by. Sol nearly fell back down the stairs trying to stay as far away as possible. Evren made a point to put herself in between the two, but Keres didn't stay put for long.

The barrel was cracked like an egg over the massive tub in the center of the room, and golden, foul-smelling oil spilled into it. Once empty, Keres tossed the wooden shell aside.

Frosty, cracked windows encircled the whole room. The massive metal disk that was held in place above it had seen better days but was polished enough that it would shine where they needed it to.

Keres moved to the opposite side of the room, and without hesitation, smashed a window open. The wind and snow rushed in, but the view of the bay was unchallenged. She could see Mortova beneath the waves as clear as day, even with the snow and how high up she was.

Evren pulled out her tinderbox and carefully sparked a flame. She tossed it into the oil, and it took to it immediately. The whole room lit up as the fire grew large and hot. Evren and Sol backed up, shielding their eyes. The heat was intense but constant. A welcome change to the cold they'd had no break from all night.

"King slayer, you'll want to use that to direct the light." Keres flicked their hand towards a rope to the side.

Sol scowled. "Don't call me that."

"Why? It's such a good name. You should be proud!"

"And Evren should toss you into the bay," she grumbled and took up her spot near the rope. She had to stand on her tiptoes to reach it at first and struggled to line it up. The disk swung around wildly once, twice, then three times before she finally got control over it. Teeth gritted, she pulled the rope inch by inch, until the light was streaming through the window next to the one Keres broke.

"Very good!" They clapped. "Now, Evren, it's time to do what you do best. Don't miss this time. Remember that deer you almost had in the woods? And then we both went hungry that night!" They laughed. "Oh, I almost killed you out of spite then. But I didn't! So, don't miss it."

Evren sidled up to the window, the frosted stone cutting through her armor like a phantom knife. She pulled out an arrow, one of her last three, she noted grimly. She nocked it and eyed the monster below.

"Are you going to kill me if I miss?" she asked, never taking her eyes off Mortova. A stream of fire came from Nerezza's lighthouse and turned the white scales black.

"Now why would I do that?" She could hear Keres' grin in their voice. "You'll kill yourself in due time."

She shot them a dark look out of the corner of her eyes. They just shrugged their frost heavy shoulders. With Direwall under siege, they looked incredibly calm. Relaxed, even. Warning bells rang loudly in her head, but she pushed them back.

It was two on one if Keres decided to try and hurt them. She and Sol had taken on worse monsters.

"All in due time," Keres muttered, their eyes glinting in the darkness. "But first, Mortova."

Evren turned back to the window. Direwall was in chaos in the distance. She could see the fires raging and being put out. More than half the city was dark. Snow swept through as if to cover the death and destruction. In the bay, the water looked like it was starting to boil. Pieces of Mortova would break through the churning waves; a fin here, a length of powerful, corded muscles covered in glistening scales there. But never his head.

What would a sea serpent's head look like? she wondered as she drew back the arrow.

She watched as fire and magic flew from the lighthouses, all scorching the monster and causing him to writhe in pain, but doing little more than chipping away at his health. A harpoon flew through the darkness, aimed true but bouncing off the tough scales harmlessly.

Evren narrowed her eyes. Her bow didn't have the reach to power through the scales, not at this distance. If she had a longbow, perhaps. But even then, would her arrows, which were made for fur and skin, make a difference against natural armor like that?

"Stop thinking about it," Keres hissed in her ear, and she jumped. "Cut your finger if you have to."

"What?" Her words were steel as she snapped back to them. They took a step back but were still only inches from her. She could smell the death coming from them.

"You heard me. Cut your finger. It'll help."

Evren pursed her lips into a thin line as she stared them down. Behind Keres, Sol shook her head. Her eyes betrayed the same fear Evren had been harboring in her scarred chest for a long time.

"I'm sick of people telling me to hurt myself in order to make it through battles," she told them. "I'll do this my way, with no magical blood."

She turned back to the window and redrew her bow with greater focus. Although her eyes stayed pinned on Mortova, she could feel a ripple of laughter behind her tickle the hairs on the back of her neck.

Her cut palm pulsed uncomfortably against the grip of her bow. The scar on her chest itched. It was like they were all calling for her to use them. *Remember what we did. Remember what we helped you win.*

Nothing. She gritted her teeth until her jaw ached. Not a damn thing.

She didn't need magic to solve her problems.

Evren watched Mortova's lithe form sweep in and out of the

surface. She saw the new wounds, fresh and bleeding, but nothing more than surface wounds. She saw old scars, the tissue shining light against his pale scales. How long he must've lived to gather so many marks. It was almost a shame that he ended here.

Evren let out a breath and an arrow at the same time. It tore through the air and fell onto Mortova's side with barely a chip in his scales.

"You missed," Keres said.

Evren ignored them and drew another arrow. She waited, counting the breaths between the snowflakes. She watched the waves and the massive form of Mortova. The black water lapping against his great white form, tinged with red. She watched until she saw her chipped scale and let loose the arrow again.

Again, it sailed through the air. Its strength died feet from Mortova's side, but it still hit home. It bounced off his armor and disappeared into the water.

"Look, I know you're stubborn, but this is ridiculous," Keres said behind her. "Just prick your damn finger and get this over with."

"You almost sound afraid," Evren mused as she pulled out her last arrow. She didn't take off her gloves as she notched it.

"If you don't kill Mortova, then the city will be overrun."

Evren drew back the last arrow, never taking her eyes off the sea serpent. Her words whispered against the wood of her arrow as she focused.

"Funny thing about adventuring parties, Keres." She blinked away a snowflake from her eyelashes. "We work together. I don't need to kill Mortova. I just need to make sure someone else can."

As soon as she finished speaking, she saw her chipped scale come back to the surface. It was old, worn, already loose from decades of fighting. She smiled and released her last arrow.

True flying as the others, it found its way to Mortova's side. A glancing shot, not meant to pierce or wound. The arrowhead caught the loose edge of the scale, and as it flew over, lifted the scale clean off its body. The shining flesh underneath was as clear as day; a target open to the air and the aim of another.

Evren let her bow fall to her side, rolling her tight shoulders in a vain attempt to work the pain out. Her body was stubborn, and not having it. It served her right for stretching it to the limit.

"You'd trust someone else to make that shot?" Keres sneered.

She glared at them. "You wouldn't?"

"Anything worth doing can be done alone." They snapped their teeth and cut another piece of Vox's lip open. No blood oozed out. "Who will make that shot if not you? The little witch Abraxas is following? The injured Black Guard who should be dead a few times over? Or perhaps you're hoping little Sorin who's never killed anything in his life worth noting can?"

"It was his plan," she said carefully. "Take a seat and watch. Maybe you'll learn something."

Keres didn't move from their spot opposite Evren. Neither did she. But she made a point not to look at them. She turned back to the bay and ignored the cold stare raking up and down her face. Whatever they were, whatever they wanted, could wait. She was done with cryptic messengers and information worded in a way she couldn't understand until it was too late. Eith might be without gods, but there were plenty of beings that were acting like them. Or at least talking like how she imagined a god would.

For a long, cold moment, fear crept up her spine like the gathering frost. Mortova lashed out in the water, curling away from every spell or fiery grenade sent his way. She heard the hissing of a thousand snakes even from her spot so high up, and she could've sworn she heard laughter in the hissing. Again and again, the exposed skin crept into the open air before it was snatched back into the water, as if Mortova was taunting them. As if he knew what she planned and wanted them to make mistake after mistake before he destroyed them

Again, her many scars tingled. *You should've used us.*

Her elven, practical side agreed. Her father always taught her how to use everything she had to her advantage. But her mother hadn't been around to help her curb the recklessness of her human blood. The one that longed for chaos and playing games of chance. Nothing beat that thrill.

Out of the darkness, a harpoon flashed briefly in the light of the burning lighthouses. Its metal gleamed like the brightest silver, and it winked merrily in the firelight. Then it plunged back into the darkness, into the waters, and into the soft flesh of the sea serpent.

Mortova's scream shook the lighthouse to its foundations. Dust and mortar rained down from above. Sol yelped and let go of her rope as a piece of stone fell from the roof and almost on her. Evren gripped the side of the window, looking back out as the bay suddenly seemed to rip in half. The water tossed itself deep into the streets of Direwall. Boats were capsized or their hulls were shredded as they sank beneath the waves, never to be seen again. The force of the new current was so strong she could see pieces of the boats being pulled into a sucking whirlpool, which was desperately trying to make up for the vacuum left as Mortova rose from the water.

He rose like demons from the hells, dripping fury and water in equal measures. His mouth was massive, and cut into his angular face in a wide slit, as if someone had personally carved it but made it too wide for his face. Red eyes, burning with a hundred years' worth of hate, stood out sharply from the white and silver of his scales. Spines of quivering fins shone red with veins as light caught them. They shook in the night air as he reared his head back and bellowed into the snow thickened skies. He continued to rise from the water, his tail coiling beneath the waves to support him. He was eye level with the lighthouses now, and furious.

"Jalaa's arse," she heard Sol shudder. "We really are going to die."

There were only a few terrifying seconds between Mortova's scream and his next breath, but they seemed to stretch out like an eternity. He looked at each of the lighthouses in turn, a seething intelligence too great for a normal monster swimming in his red irises. His gaze landed on Evren, who was naively still standing in front of the broken window.

She froze, unable to move as one of the red eyes leveled her a death stare. A promise underneath those eyes gleamed like fresh blood. He knew what she'd done.

His jaw parted, and she could see every one of his bristling, black teeth. Pieces of bones and boats were still caught in there. She thought she saw the bright orange and red of a Ikedree scarf waving in his cavernous mouth before it flew down his throat, snatched away by his sucking breaths.

The jaw was open. She could see her path to death as clearly as if it was lit by daylight. But instead of snapping at her, his head whipped around faster than lightning. Towards the southern end, towards the lighthouse that had sent the harpoon into his flesh.

Towards Sorin and Arke.

His head reared back, his long body curving in a massive imitation of what she'd seen when vipers struck. His hateful gaze fixed on the ones who dared make him bleed.

"No!" Sol's voice cut through Evren's haze of panic. She turned back just in time to see the dwarf grasp the rope she'd abandoned earlier and turn the mirrored disk towards Mortova. The beam of bright light cut through the water and the docks swarming with undead, all the way up to the great sea serpent's face. It bore into his eyes with a glaring intensity, and he reared his head back from the strike, trying to shake off the sudden piercing light.

Evren watched as Sorin and Arke's light beam did the same. Their light hit him head on, blinding the beast as he cried out. Abraxas and Nerezza's light joined the fray. His jaw almost unhinged, looming larger than any cavern and reeking of death.

One second it was dark and dripping with saliva, the next a bright ball of fire was launched straight into it and down its throat. The screeches of pain were cut off as the fire sailed down his throat, ripping and burning skin as it went. Evren could see the ball of fire burning down the length of his twisting body as he writhed in anguish.

An arcing wave of water tore through the air as Mortova's body ripped itself from the bay. The tail lashed out, trailing a shower of sea water. It whipped past the lighthouse, mere feet from Evren's shocked face. She barely had time to register the smell of sea and blood before it slammed into the base of the tower.

She gripped the side of the window as the whole lighthouse shook violently. The cracking of stone mimicked thunder. She could feel the whole tower going to the side, inch by inch.

"We have to go!" She reached a hand out for Sol. She dropped the rope without hesitation and ran over to take it. Her warm hand clasped in Evren's was a little bit of security where surety of death was taking over. She barely spared a glance at Keres, who was staring down at the dying serpent with shock.

"We're leaving!" she shouted at them and took off down the stairs.

The steep stone steps were worn with age. But as the tower crashed down around them, Evren found her feet skipping over two or three steps at a time. Her throat was tight, her boots barely skimming the stones. Sol's hand had a death grip in her own.

A chunk of the ceiling fell, cracking the steps right before their feet. They stumbled, jumping over it the best they could and tumbling down the rest of the stairs.

Evren's ribs smarted and cracked under the impact, and she gasped in pain as she rolled to the bottom of the tower. Sol's hand was still gripping hers and the dwarf laid face first on the floor, her arm bent at an awkward angle.

The rumbling hadn't stopped. Looking up, Evren could see

the walls of the lighthouse splitting in half and toppling over. Her stomach gave way to dread. She tried to move, but she couldn't tear her eyes away from the toppling stones.

A grey hand lashed out and grabbed Sol by her collar. It hoisted her up on her feet just as Evren felt it do the same to her. Sol's nose was broken, spilling a fountain of bright red blood, and her eyes were unfocused. Behind her, Keres shoved them both towards the door.

"Move!" they barked.

Evren didn't need to be told twice. She pulled Sol through the waiting door, tumbling outside into the piling snow. The air was freezing, and thick with the stench of blood and salt. Keres quickly followed, slipping off the ice-encased steps just as the whole lighthouse collapsed on itself.

Keres pushed them roughly forward. They slipped on the ice, tangling on top of one another and yelping in pain. Sol let go of Evren and covered her head with her good arm. Evren did the same, squeezing her eyes shut. She felt the ground shake as bits of stone fell on the ground next to them. Pebbles bounced off their shoes and shoulders. Behind her, hunkering over her back, she heard Keres hiss in pain. Dust clogged her nose, ice-cold water peppered them, and the screams of the dying monster could barely be heard of the crumbling tower.

But then the earth was still. The rain of rocks stopped. All she could feel was the cold press of her cheek against the snow and Sol shivering with fear beside her.

Evren let out a shaky breath and let her head rise from the cage of her arms. Peering up into the sky, she blinked through the salt water and snow raining down on her. The haze of dust was still clearing, but far above it she could clearly see Mortova. Haloed by the lights of the remaining lighthouses, the gaping black scar where the fire had burned through his skin from the inside out reminded her sickeningly of the Black Pass. A mess of sharp, black wounds curving outwards against white scales. He still writhed back and forth, but he was slowing. His red eyes rolled to the back of his head, and then he stilled. Still in midair, for a moment she thought he would just freeze like that. Forever a statue to Direwall of the monster that lived beneath its waters.

But, like the tower before him, Mortova began to fall. Almost like time was slowing down, Evren watched the sea serpent fall to the city. It was almost graceful. The air turned his lulling head, almost like it was cradling him like a mother would a child. She saw the fins rip and split as they tore through the air. Water flung itself off his corpse and became icy sludge raining down on them.

All too soon it ended. He crashed into the docks close to Drystan's lighthouse with a massive boom that rattled her teeth. A wave of water crashed over the tower, coating it and everything nearby in a load of salt water. His last wave.

Evren held her breath, waiting for the tower to tip and fall like hers did. She only breathed again when it continued to stand, spilling light and water, but staying strong.

As the dust settled and the water fell back into the confines of the bay, Evren started to relax. The snow was coming down faster now, coating her and Sol in a fine layer of white. She had half a mind to stay there, dozing beside her. They'd killed Mortova, after all. Didn't that earn them a bit of rest?

The sound that broke the silence was the essence of grief. It was as if a thousand mouths opened and sucked in the remaining air into their wanting lungs. The sound of vacuous air leaving the sky was nothing compared to the cries of anguish that ripped through the streets. They pierced her ears painfully, and she clapped her hands over them to block the sounds out. The sobbing, the cries, and one profoundly loud voice above it all.

"MY BLOOD! MY BOND! MY FAMILY!"

The voice was a jumble of all the cries laced together. But the pain inside them was enough to make Evren gasp. She could feel their grief in her bones; it made tears well up in her eyes. She knew that feeling well, of one's heart being ripped in two. She hadn't been the cause of another's pain though.

Keres staggered to their feet as the wailing continued. For a brief moment, Evren saw fear glinting in their eyes. "We need to go."

She didn't argue. She got to her feet, bringing Sol's mostly limp form up as she did. She grasped her hand again. The dwarf squeezed back with only a fraction of her normal strength as she tucked her bad arm against her chest.

"Where do we go?" Evren asked.

Keres grabbed her shoulder and tugged her south. Her feet stumbled over each other as she followed them. "Gather your party and leave."

"Why?" Sol murmured through half parted lips.

"The Prime will want revenge, and replacements."

Evren's blood turned to ice, and she forced her steps to quicken. "What about the townspeople?"

"Did they kill Mortova?"

"No."

"There's your answer."

Evren gripped Sol's hand tight enough to crack her finger bones, but if she cared she didn't say. Keres led the way through the bloody, soaked streets while they trailed closely behind. Around every corner, she heard the snarling and wailing of the undead as they tore through the city, desperately trying to get to the water. That dreaded pit in her stomach only grew larger. She could retrace the steps she took all the way from Sorin's first tower to where she was now. But the idea of fighting through all the undead made her want to sob. She had no arrows left, and her limbs felt like they were filled with lead. Every breath was ragged. It took everything she had to keep herself standing and walking, much less able to fight.

She could taste blood again, and this time it didn't comfort her.

The only comfort was that the way forward was lit. Evren

could always see the shining beacon of Drystan's lighthouse above her. It was warm in its calling, in the faint hope it spread. She kept her eyes on it with every stumbling step. She watched as the light swung lazily around and around the glass windows too frosted to see anything inside. The beam cut through the darkness, calling her forward. She let herself breathe easier with every forward step.

One goal at a time. One lighthouse at a time, one team. One step.

One.

She ran into Keres as they stopped suddenly. Vox's massive form took up most of her vision and she stepped to the side to look around. Whatever shriveled hope had begun to bloom quickly turned to ash as she caught sight of the wall of undead ahead of her. An echo of Lostwater, they stood shoulder to shoulder; an impenetrable line between them and the lighthouse. They were closer now than Evren realized, she could see the stairs covered in thick ice between the feet of the corpses. The light swung lazily in circles overhead. The undead all stared at them with gaping mouths and wide eyes streaked with black tears.

"My family . . ." they moaned. "You took my family."

"No," Evren heard herself whisper. "You took ours first."

"My family!" An anguished cry ripped out of their mouths, and Evren cringed as she took a step backward.

Just over the sounds of the wailing, she heard a scream. A familiar scream.

Her eyes darted behind the line of undead. She watched in horror as the door to the lighthouse burst open. Five undead squeezed through the doorway, breaking bones and leaving scraps of skin where they couldn't all fit at once. After them tumbled a heavily bleeding body with a streak of white in his hair. They had their hands wrapped around him, and drug him carelessly through the streets. His head lulled to the side, bleeding from a wound at his temple. His eyes were closed.

The screaming became worse as another two pulled Sahar from the lighthouse. She kicked and screamed furiously, her black hair whipping around her and snagging on the boney hands clawing at her. She kicked the shin of one of the undead holding her, snapping the bone in half. It crumpled to the ground, and she tore her arm free, reaching towards Drystan as the undead started dragging them towards the bay.

"Drystan!" Her voice broke with the force of her desperation. She struggled against the other undead holding her. Her slender fingers reached towards him.

Drystan's eyes opened. Only slits, barely focused. But her voice brought him back as the undead slowly pulled him into the water. The cold reached his feet and his eyes widened. All he saw was Sahar, tears streaming down her face, still reaching for him.

Evren didn't see his hand move. She couldn't hear his voice, but she saw his mouth move. One word.

Run.

Something bright flashed in the light, and the one second later, the undead holding Sahar had an ax in its chest. It slumped to the ground, and Sahar tore the ax free. She ran the first few steps towards him but stopped when he was suddenly sucked under water.

Her cry of anguish mixed with the undead as they snapped into action. They surged towards Evren, Sol and Keres. Sahar was lost in the wave of bones and sea rotten flesh.

Evren could only watch as one lunged at her, mouth open wide in a pitiful imitation of Mortova. She was sure that mouth would latch onto her neck and rip her throat out, but Keres roughly snatched her away with so much force she felt her neck pop with whiplash.

And then they were running.

Keres was charging through the undead, dodging lashing hands and gnashing jaws. All Evren could do was follow as close as possible and hold on tight to Sol. Her eyes swam with Drystan's final expression—the small smile, blood trickling from the corner of his mouth. She could still hear Sahar. Was she still alive? Or was Evren's mind playing tricks on her?

She dodged under the hand of an undead, breathing hard and trying to keep up with Keres. Sol's hand was warm and tight in hers. A lifeline. If she had that, she could do anything. She couldn't let go. All she had was Sol right now.

Until she didn't.

Sol's hand ripped out of her grip. Evren whipped around, planting her feet in the ground and letting go of Keres. She saw Sol gripped by her neck by a large undead, her feet dangling in the air and kicking fruitlessly.

"Sol!" The scream tore through her throat and she lunged for her.

Sol's hand went to hers again, and their fingertips brushed. Evren grasped on to what little she had, trying to pull her friend back to her. Fresh tears shone in Sol's bright eyes.

"Please don't let go!" she sobbed, her arm straining as the undead pulled her away. Evren gripped her hand harder, refusing to let her slip away. "I don't want to die."

An arm encircled Evren's waist and pulled her away. Sol's fingers slipped away from her grip, and she kicked and screamed.

"NO!" She thrashed and reached out again. "Sol!"

Her friend's tear-streaked face was full of fear before it was swallowed by the horde of undead.

Something barely healed in Evren broke. She kicked and screamed against the cold body holding her, but it wasn't dragging her to the bay. It was pulling her away.

"Stop fighting!" Keres hissed in her ear.

"Let me go!" she screamed. "I have to get Sol!"

"She's already dead! Move on!"

But she didn't. Evren fought Keres every inch as they pulled her through the undead. She kicked and fought and even bit. The taste of cold flesh made her gag. Her throat was sore, and she could swear it was bleeding. She couldn't even see through all her tears. All she knew was she had to get to Sol. She couldn't lose anyone else.

Keres dropped her as quickly as they'd snatched her up. She fell to her knees, chest heaving before getting up and running back the way she came. Tears blurred her vision; she ran nearly blind. Until she realized she wasn't meeting any resistance.

Evren stumbled to a stop, trying to clear her eyes. She was feet from the water now, watching as the undead walked into the bay. Their glowing eyes never left her, and the water bubbled as their voices rose to the sky again.

"FAMILY FOR FAMILY. SOON WE WILL ALL BE BLOOD AND BONE UNDER THE MIDNIGHT SKY."

They disappeared into the water. Soon, there wasn't even a trace of bubbles to show where they went. Evren stared at the black water, willing for a miracle. For Sol's blonde head to pop up out of the water, near death and cursing. For her to come swimming to shore.

But all she was left with was a broken harbor, and the steadily falling snow.

17

Time had stopped.

Not in the sense that everyone stopped breathing or the snow stopped falling. The waves didn't freeze mid-crest, the lights of the lighthouses didn't stop their rays from swinging around in a circle. All of that went on. But for all Evren cared, they might as well have.

The dead had left Direwall and had taken any fresh or old corpses with them. The streets were thick with bloody snow, but there wasn't a single body left to bury. None to mourn over, none to cling to and cry.

Evren didn't remember being brought into the Jarl's hall. She didn't register the warmth of the fire or the prodding of the healer. She just stared blankly ahead while her wounds were bandaged and the blood was wiped away. The hushed whispers and choked sobs didn't even reach her still-ringing ears.

It was all painfully numb.

The only thing Evren was sure about was the fact that Keres was nowhere to be found. She knew they probably got her to the Jarl's hall, but since there was no screaming and all the hands she felt were warm and alive, she could only dimly assume they'd left.

If only they had left sooner, she thought bitterly. Fresh tears threatened to overcome her already exhausted eyes.

If she closed her eyes, she saw Sol. Her fearful face, her hopeful hand still reaching out for her. If she focused, she heard her screaming. Over and over again.

I don't want to die.

Evren buried her head in her knees, curling up into a ball as tight as she could. Here, in the confines of her legs, she could measure her breathing. Count the ragged breaths, think of the way the air enters, curls around her lungs, and then leaves. Picture it fanning against her face and thighs. Then do it all over again.

It was better than crying. It was better than replaying the scene over and over again.

First Gyda, and now Sol.

Her breath hitched, frozen in its spot in her chest.

She just kept losing them.

The breath tore out of her mouth in a heavy sob. She squeezed her eyes shut, trying to keep back the flood of tears. All she saw behind her eyelids was Gyda's back as she walked away from her for the second time. She saw Sol's glove hanging half-off her hand, nearly torn off by the force of Evren's grip. She watched Gyda pause at the sound of her pleading voice, before disappearing into the ranks of the undead. She saw Sol's mouth fill with water before she was dragged below.

None of her fighting and struggling had been enough then. Would it ever be? Or was she just doomed to lose people?

Someone warm sat beside her. They smelled of blood and smoke, like everyone else, but also the sharp tang of chemicals. Their own breaths were interrupted by hiccups. Too much crying, and the body just couldn't keep up.

Evren lifted her head. Her tears cooled instantly on her cheeks, but they just kept coming. She rested her head against the wall, not staring at anything in particular but knowing who sat beside her.

There was comfort in that, at least.

"I think I understand now," Sahar rasped, her voice far too low and broken to be her normal honey smooth.

"Understand what?" Evren managed to choke out.

"You. Why you throw yourself into danger to the point of risking death over and over again."

"And why's that?"

There was a slight, heavy pause. Not the silence of grave-yards, but of an empty, grieving mind. It felt familiar, the way home felt after being cold and empty for so long.

"The pain of death is much more preferable than the pain of grief," Sahar finally answered. "Death can be slow, yes, but at some point, it ends. Grief never truly leaves you. It's a pain that plagues you until you find death yourself. Until you can dump it onto some other soul who had the terrible misfortune of loving you . . ."

Her voice, which had started strong in the beginning, shattered like glass at the end. She put a hand over her mouth to cover her sobs, but they wracked her body so painfully her back heaved with the effort.

Evren tried to breathe through her own tears. With a shaking hand she reached out. She hovered just beside Sahar's leg, her palm up and open. A lifeline for them both.

Sahar grasped her hand tightly, her bare fingers soft and smooth.

They stayed that way for what felt like eternity. Until the tears dried up and their lungs were too sore to handle anymore. Until the hall filled up to the brim with the injured and grieving. They watched it all from their little corner on the floor while the wind whistled outside and the snow piled high. They sat, and waited, hand in hand, until they slept.

EVREN WOKE to a dozen voices in her ear at once.

She wanted to shove them all away and curl back up into her dark corner. Sleeping forever sounded like a nice alternative to facing what the Long Night had left to offer her. More ice? Another snowstorm? Oh! Maybe she'd lose another friend! The Expanse had proven to be nothing but consistent.

She shoved away a hand shaking her shoulder. Slapped it away. But it was persistent, so she forced her gritty eyes to open, swallowing hard to get rid of the harsh dryness in her throat. She rubbed her face, stealing a few more seconds of lonely darkness behind her hands before she dropped them in her lap and glared up.

"What?" she bit out, her voice croaky and completely different from her usual tone.

Abraxas took a step back, his eyebrows furrowed. He still hadn't gotten out of his armor, and his long hair fell in strings in front of his face. His jaw was set in a hard line as he looked her up and down. His eyes softened though, as they always did. They reminded her that there was a soft soul behind the tough iron soldier he put up. A healer locked in armor.

"I couldn't find you after the battle," was all he said.

He was worried. For some reason, that put a sour taste in Evren's mouth. She was far too raw to want or need his worry. Like salt purifying a wound, she'd rather fester than let herself hurt all over again.

"I've been here."

She looked beside her, where Sahar was slumped against her shoulder. Soot stained, coat torn, bloody. Nowhere near the smiling lady she'd met in the outpost. Evren made herself stay as still as possible. No need for her to wake up to the real world yet.

"How—"

"I don't know." She cut him off. She didn't even know what he was asking. She didn't care.

His lips pursed into a thin line. "Evren, I'm trying to help. I can't find everybody. Where's Sol and Drystan?"

She was lucky her lungs were too far gone, and her throat was too torn up to allow her to cry. Or laugh because something manic and terrible was bubbling in her chest. Instead, she sucked in a sharp breath, and looked him dead in the eyes. Soldier, healer, priest with no gods. Whatever he was, it was too late.

"Gone," she rasped, letting the word catch on every sharp edge of her throat.

Abraxas blinked. "Gone?"

"The dead took them. Because we killed Mortova. Surely you heard them screaming about family, right?"

"I . . ." His eyes flickered down. To the floor, to her pale bloody fingers still grasping Sahar's. "I didn't. Nerezza and I were stuck in our lighthouse for some time. The door had frozen over."

"Ah."

He didn't deserve the bitterness in her voice. A softer part of her knew that. That there had been nothing Abraxas could've done to prevent happened. But still, she was bitter and aching. And she was tired of it.

"Don't tell Sorin." The thought came to her like the quick snap of a whip.

Abraxas finally looked back at her; his head cocked to the side. "He'll notice Sol is missing."

She shook her head. "About the dead taking her because we killed Mortova. It was his idea. He'll blame himself."

"Evren . . ."

"That insane little mind of his saved Direwall, but if he finds out that it was at the expense of Sol's life he's going to crumble. He just started to put himself back together. I'm not going to take a sledgehammer to him."

"Evren." It was less his voice that stopped her rambling and more the cold gauntlet-clad hand resting on her knee. She shut her mouth with a snap, as if he'd pressed some secret button and turned off her voice. His hand was still on her knee. At one point it would've been reassuring. Now she struggled not to squirm away from his touch.

His eyes were pleading as he stared at her, willing her to meet them. She barely managed that.

"It's all right to grieve," he finally said. "But there's still a chance she might be alive, just like Gyda."

She snorted. "They drug her into the bay, Abraxas. The temperature alone would kill her if she didn't drown first. They have no use for the living."

"I have faith."

Faith.

Oh, how she hated that word. She chewed on it, trying to shred it with her teeth and finding nothing but empty air. Abraxas always had faith, and it was always enough for the whole party. If not faith, then hope. Evren could do hope. That was something she recognized and could sink her teeth in. But even that had failed her.

She wanted to tell him that his faith was no good. Scream at him that his faith led him to a war that slaughtered thousands of innocents because they didn't worship his Divines. And now it had led him here, with her. To a place she was sure his precious Divines wouldn't touch even if they weren't banished.

She didn't want faith, or hope. What she wanted was her friends back. And if she couldn't get that, she'd settle on something a little more tangible.

Blood.

"I think I've had enough of faith." she said carefully. She leashed all her frustration and tucked it away. It wasn't good for right now. "What's our next move?"

The hand disappeared from her knee and he stood up. His face was unreadable.

"We're discussing it with the Jarl soon. You should bring Sahar when you're ready." He hesitated before adding, "If you're ready?"

She brushed away his comment. "We'll be there soon."

Abraxas nodded stiffly, and with a jangle of armor and wounded concern, he walked deeper into the hall. She watched him for a while, just to make sure he didn't stop and watch her. He moved through the tangle of wounded and sleeping people, disappearing behind a group of healers as they brought steaming bowls of melted snow to clean the wounded. Once he was finally gone, she started to relax again.

"You shouldn't be angry with him," Sahar mumbled into her shoulder. Exhaustion clung to the edges of her voice, slurring her words. She kept her eyes closed, as if she was willing herself to drift back to sleep.

"I know," Evren said.

"Then why are you stiff as a rock?"

"Because I don't know who else to be angry at besides myself."

"There's always the Prime. That's what I'm focusing on."

That was something Evren couldn't deny. But the Prime was someone she hadn't met. His voice wasn't tangible; it was just a jumble of a thousand stolen throats. He seemed distant in his threat, and while Evren was still angry, she couldn't aim her anger at him. She didn't have that kind of range just yet.

"They're going over our next move," Evren said.

"I heard."

"Do you want to go?"

Sahar sighed and sat up. She blinked wearily at the fire and the people around her. She tore her eyes away from the group of children in the corner, dirty and sniffling and utterly alone.

"I look dreadful, don't I?" she asked, raising a well-groomed eyebrow caked in dried blood.

Evren couldn't help but smile a little. "I'm a bad judge. I tend to like my women a little rough around the edges."

Sahar laughed and, although it sounded hollow, it was nice to hear. She combed her fingers through her knotted hair and began to tie it up again. "Oh, I've noticed."

"You have?"

Sahar smiled knowingly. "You are far from subtle."

Whatever that was supposed to mean, Evren let it go. With Sahar off her shoulder, she forced herself slowly onto her knees and then to her feet. Her body ached fiercely, and her bones crackled like fire with every shift of her muscles. But she took it all and swallowed it down. Pain meant she was alive, at whatever cost she had to live with.

Evren wanted that pain. She needed it. The ache in her chest she could do without.

She held a hand out to Sahar, and helped her to her feet. Sahar winced and rubbed the base of her back. Then she smoothed her torn coat, tucked any loose strands behind her ears, and lifted her chin to walk away. With her straight back and steps even, she looked like an echo of a noble caught in the wrong body. But that had to be Sahar's armor. Not metal or stinging words, just the comfort of acting like she belonged no matter where she walked.

Evren didn't bother to clean herself as she followed. There was no point in pretending to feel better than she did; she felt like death warmed over, and she was sure she looked like it, too.

As they walked to the back of the hall, where Evren remembered the Jarl's throne being, the people began to thin out. The worst of the wounded were near the front. The closer to the throne, the less crowded it was. More warriors napped, some right on top of each other and some depressingly alone. Some stared blankly ahead, or at the wood carvings on the wall. But none met her eyes as they walked past.

Evren was glad. She didn't know how she would react if one of them did.

The long pit of fire ended, and then they were at the dais of the throne. The Jarl sat on the steps, still clad in her armor and scowling as a healer bandaged her left eye. The bandages smelled sharply of herbs; Evren could smell it from several feet away. They were already soaked with blood. The Jarl's one good eye snapped to them as they walked up.

"Ah good, you survived! And whole too."

Evren nodded. "That's more than I can say for you." She gestured to the bandaged eye, and Eirunn snorted. She waved the healer off once he secured the bandage and sent him scrambling down the steps.

"The corpses got a lucky shot." She shrugged. "But they got my bad eye, so the joke is on them, as you would say."

Beside her, Sahar let out a little cry and rushed across the room as Nerezza emerged. The mage had little time to breathe before she was yanked into a tight hug. Her eyes were dark, but she melted into the hug, whispering soft things into Sahar's ear as they held each other.

Behind them, Abraxas stepped around the embracing friends. Followed close behind him were Arke and Sorin. Arke's feet dragged along the ground and the tips of his ears drooped. Sorin's eyes were red and puffy, and he kept sniffling. So, they knew. A tiny bit of relief flooded in Evren. She didn't want to talk about Sol again.

But she found her feet moving towards them of her own accord, and before she realized it, she had one arm slung around Sorin's neck and the other grabbing for Arke. Sorin hugged her tightly, wrapping both of his lanky arms around her as if she would disappear. Arke fought. He always fought on things like this, but it was weak. Sorin snagged his cloak and dragged him to them, and before long he was sandwiched between them in an awkward, curse-filled hug. But there was no venom in his words. And she felt his arms wrap around her, too.

By the time they'd all let go of each other and separated, Evren's eyes were misty again and Eirunn was grinning.

"Family among battle fellows is common, but always a beautiful sight." she said, "Though where there is family, there is also loss. We grieve differently here. We take our pain and bleed it into our work. Weapons, armor, even the foundations of our buildings. We make something new with our grief. What is it that you southerners do?"

Wallow and try not to drown in it, Evren thought.

"It varies from culture to culture," Sahar said.

Eirunn nodded. "I can respect that. However, perhaps you take our ways into your own for the path ahead?"

"How so?" Evren asked.

The Jarl leaned forward, her elbows resting on her bloody knees as her eye gleamed. "Cut them in half with your anger, Worm-Rider. I find it is the best weapon against those who wronged you."

Evren felt something in her blood stir at her words. Something to use, to latch onto and push herself forward. But then Abraxas lifted his hand, almost physically cutting the two of them off in their fierce stare.

"That is something to keep in mind, thank you Jarl Eirunn," he said crisply. "But using anger as a motivation can lead to more tragedy."

Eirunn frowned and leaned back against the stairs. Her throne sat empty above her, but the stairs were more than fitting with the way she lounged on them. "Are you scared of vengeance?"

Abraxas shifted his weight. "More like I know where it comes from and want nothing to do with him."

Nomien, the God of wrath and fire, who had nudged King Eldridge's crusades in the first place. Evren shuddered underneath her leathers. More than ever, she was glad Vernes had banished the Divines. Maybe they weren't all like Nomien, but they hadn't stopped him. And she didn't want a world that he could influence.

A flick of her finger and the Jarl had Abraxas taking a step back. That part of the conversation was over. She wanted less to do with Abraxas's gods than Evren did.

"How many were lost?" Evren asked.

"We are still looking." The Jarl's shoulders drooped. "There is much devastation in the city. Many buildings destroyed and warriors missing. But my people tell me the numbers as they guess them. A little less than half."

Evren winced. There had been so many Ikedree warriors fighting on the streets, she assumed most would've made it out. Suddenly the hall felt a lot emptier.

"With the serpent dead, Myrefall Bay is starting to freeze over again." The Jarl shrugged. "This changes little. Mortova's meat will feed us for many seasons."

"So long as you survive this one," Arke growled.

"I do not intend to let the dead win, little one." It didn't feel like an insult to him when she said it, and Arke only burrowed himself further in his cloak. "But you bring up a good point. We will not survive another attack, although I suspect that the Prime will take his time before attempting to take Direwall again."

"It still doesn't make sense," Nerezza said. She was gripping Sahar's hand, and like Evren, hadn't bother to wipe the blood and grime from herself. She still looked like she was in the middle of the battle. "Why are they doing this?"

"Let's think of things we do know," Evren said, catching her eye. "One, these undead work like a hive. The Prime is the queen, so to speak. He speaks through them. These undead have no individual goals. They're mindless worker bees."

"Two," Sorin said hesitantly. "They're connected to the surviving Vasa in some way. That's why Mortova helped them. If they were an extension of the Prime, and the Prime was the one Mortova was Bonded to, then he was loyal to the cause. That's why they freaked when we killed him. It wasn't them; it was the Prime."

"Three." Sahar lifted her chin. "They took the bodies of the slain with them. So, whatever their plan is, they're still building it up."

Arke raked his clawed hand through his wild hair. "Four, we made it personal."

The Jarl blinked at him. "How so?"

He jabbed a thumb to Sorin. "Like he said, Mortova was

loyal to them. Seems like it was just the two of them for a long time. I'd be pissed if someone killed my pet monster."

"Arke's right." Nerezza's eyes brightened.

"Of fuckin' course I am."

She ignored him, a wave of energy coursing through her suddenly, like a spark of fire on a bowl of oil. "No, I mean, it's personal for the Prime now! All this time he's been working in the shadows. Taking villages and travelers and building up to the goal of taking Direwall. We don't know why, but up until this point it's just been a plan. Now we've pissed him off. We robbed him of his one connection to life before he got here. Now everything he knew is dead, and he's got nothing left to lose."

"Uh." Sorin laughed nervously. "How does that help us? Please tell me that's supposed to help us and not them, making it even more difficult for me to sleep at night."

"He's been incredibly cautious up until this point. Methodical even. And now," she turned to Evren with the same gleam in her eyes that Eirunn had, "now he's going to act irrationally. We killed Mortova. Now, we're a target."

"Still terrifying and not helpful," Sorin whimpered.

But Evren was smiling. This was good, this she could work with. Maybe it was just the acknowledgment that she had hurt the Prime, and in doing so maybe everything she'd lost wouldn't go to waste.

"We don't know his true motivations yet," Abraxas said carefully. "But we did have a plan to get to the shipwreck to find that out."

"Get information, and draw the Prime's attention away from Direwall?" Evren's grin was wicked sharp. "I can handle that."

"It's a start," Sahar said. "Although with the Long Night, I don't see how we'll move quick enough to stay ahead of them should they decide to give chase."

"You will not go on foot," the Jarl announced and stood up. The firelight winked against the bloodstained metal rivets on her armor. "We will lend you sleds and our fastest dogs."

"That's very generous," Sahar said. "Almost too generous."

"You killed a massive thorn in my side, and plan to kill another. My people cannot do this on their own, and I must stay to lead them. Why should I not lend adventurers who swear to free us from the dead a few sleds and dogs? Unless you prefer to walk."

"No!" Sorin said quickly. "Dogs are great. I love dogs. Really, I think we've always been dog people all around."

Jarl Eirunn chuckled. "That is what I thought. I will send for these and what supplies we can spare. They will await you at the northern gate." Her eyes were as piercing as any winter wind as she stared down at all of them. "The fate of my people rests in your hands. Do not be bumbling fools with it. I'd hate to rip your throats out, alive or undead."

Her almost mad laughter followed them out of the hall. Evren thought she could still feel it rattling in her skull.

She found her bow lying in the snow, still caked in ice and blood. She cleaned it off and restocked her quiver. They each used a health potion, mending any bruised flesh and cracked ribs before their journey. There wasn't much left, only about three bottles between the six of them, but they needed the wash of strength that came with it.

They washed the blood and grime off the best they could. They tied back their hair, secured their armor, and stuffed their bags with as much supplies as they dared. The map of the Expanse was clenched tightly in Evren's hands as she led the way towards the northern gate.

"How long of a journey?" Abraxas asked, pulling his furs taught across his armor. A low wind whipped up the snow and swirled it around their legs, lifting their hair, but Evren barely felt it now.

"Maybe a day." She frowned. "Or less. It's hard to tell; I've never traveled by sled. And it'll be hard to keep track of time anyway."

Above them, the pitch-black night sky was starting to clear

itself of clouds. It had dumped more snow on Direwall than Evren had seen in a lifetime. It was nothing the Ikedree people weren't used to, and they'd cleared most of it out of the streets. There was a good foot of it left, but it covered the scars of the battle. Evren didn't mind that too much.

Behind them, Sorin helped Arke through the snow the best he could. "What happens if we get to the ship and the undead are waiting for us?"

Abraxas looked back at him. "We fight."

Sorin rolled his eyes. "I shouldn't have expected any less."

Arke stumbled through a snow drift again, and Sorin pulled him up and sat him on his shoulders. The goblin scowled furiously and looked like he was going to launch himself off. But instead, he shook the snow off his boots.

"We're gonna make them pay, right?"

The answer came easily to Evren. "Of course. We're going to make them bleed."

He bared his sharp teeth. "Good."

The sound of barking signaled their arrival at the northern gate more so than the widening of the street. The gate itself was simple and wooden, made of thick cut timber and lashed together with iron laced rope, and was opened to the frozen plains beyond. The black sky above and the shimmering white below seemed to stretch on forever.

Before the gate were three sleds. Simple, nothing ornate but made of light wood and resting easily on the snow. Nerezza and Sahar were already done packing theirs, and their dogs were practically biting at the cold air for the chance to run.

Evren dumped her bag on the sled, and then went to the dogs. One by one she let her fingers run through their thick coats. Their wet noses bounced happily against her gloved hand, and their bright eyes were far more intelligent than those of the hounds she'd seen in her childhood.

A pack of eight for each sled. Each varying colors of black, silver, and warm taupe. They all nipped and bounced around in their harness playfully. Goading each other and working the playful energy up into something useful. She scratched one at the front behind her soft pointed ears.

"I have a feeling you know more than I do about where we're going," she said,

She barked, as if to confirm.

"Good. Let's get there fast."

She went back to the sled. Sorin and Arke had taken over their sled and were already bickering about where they were going to sit or stand. Evren turned to Abraxas, who was standing at the back of the last sled. His hands gripped the wood.

"Navigate or drive?" he asked.

She paused, as if the answer wasn't obvious. She was the one with the map, after all. And there really was no way to 'drive.' The dogs were leading. She hopped onto the back of the sled, getting her feet wedged firmly into the planks.

"Navigate."

Abraxas nodded, and then looked down at the sled. "I don't know how to drive this."

Evren smiled as the dogs howled into the night air and jumped in their harnesses. "They do. Trust the process."

Abraxas nodded, his brow furrowed. He wasn't looking at her, and his shoulders were sharp and tense. He took a breath, as if to speak, but Evren cut him off.

"I'm sorry," she blurted out.

He blinked over at her, his brow smoothing. "For what?"

"Snapping at you. You didn't deserve it, not after everything we did. Sol . . ." Evren struggled to breathe through her words. "She was your friend too."

Abraxas let go of the sled and put his hand over her's. The cold gauntlet didn't feel friendly, but the intent was there. She looked up at him, finding no smile of reassurance. Just naked understanding.

"I've lost people before to battles like this," he said softly. "I'd rather you angry, even if it's at me, than a husk I'd have to cut down. I hope Solri is alive, just as I hope Gyda is as well. But no matter their fates, the fight is the same, as is the journey forward. I follow you now, as I did before, as I will in the future."

Evren's chest tightened with a knot of complex emotions. She nodded once, sharply, not trusting her voice to be steady. Abraxas let go of her hand, and together they looked back at the Expanse.

A call to action went up. And all at once the dogs leapt forward. They churned the snow underneath their paws, and the sleds jolted into motion. Before she knew it, Evren was flying through the gates and into the wilderness.

One hand was holding tightly to the sled. With the other, she lifted her scarf to cover the bottom half of her face as the icy air rushed past her eyes. Ahead of her was the glittering unknown, and the key to everything.

She unfolded the map carefully, holding it firmly in the whipping wind. The dogs had gone silent the moment they'd taken off, and now all she could hear was the wind and their panting. She smiled underneath the scarf, her finger tracing up the map to the place Eirunn had marked as the shipwreck.

We're coming for you, she thought as her eyes shot up to the black horizon.

18

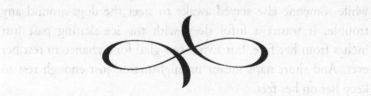

Out in the vast, seemingly endless plains of snow and night, time mattered less than it did back in Dire- wall. Overhead, the stars wheeled by, the moon turned the ice silver, and the wind whisked stretches of fog and ice through the air in a chaotic waltz. Whenever her face needed a break from the constant wind, Evren would crane her neck to look up at the sky. The constellations were distantly familiar, her mind too fuzzy to work on remembering their names. The moon seemed to bulge against the mountain peaks it hung low over.

Viggo would've loved the starlight and the way it reflected off the ice crystals. He would've loved the aurora even more. But he loved beautiful things, and light was, above all, beautiful. He'd take it in any form. Even if it was struggling to shine in the Long Night.

The landscape changed little once they stopped following the coastline and headed more inland. Evren didn't see how a ship could be so far from water but trusted the map Eirunn had given them. When there was nothing but ice, snow, and the occasional rock outcropping, it was hard to keep the mind occupied.

She and Abraxas said little, other than to go over the map and make sure they were headed in the right direction. All three sleds stopped every few hours to rest the dogs and stretch out the adventurers' cramping muscles. After so long of moving against the wind, Evren's cheeks stung as she stretched out her tight legs. Her feet were killing her, but from what she could tell they were making good time.

Most of the trip went similarly. They rested while the dogs did. Occasionally, they'd take turns napping between the bags while someone else stayed awake to steer the dogs around any trouble. It wasn't a fitful sleep with the ice skating past just inches from her face, but Evren was glad for a chance to rest her eyes. And short naps meant no nightmares, just enough rest to keep her on her feet.

It was during such a nap, when she was half sleeping and trying to remember what a warm bed felt like, when the sled suddenly jolted underneath her. Her eyes snapped open, meeting nothing but sky rushing above her. She heard a sharp yelp, and Abraxas cursing as the sled turned sharply. Too quickly.

Evren felt one side of the sled tilt up into the air. Far too late, she realized they were rolling. She barely had time to tuck her head into her arms before the whole sled flipped over and sent her, and all the supplies, tumbling into the snow.

She hit the cold ground hard, her many layers of furs barely softening the blow . She rolled along the snow, teeth clashing against each other with every bump, and kept her arms and legs tight. She was struggling to breath as she slowed to a stop, her cheek pressed against the snow.

She grunted as she pulled herself up, her shoulder and hip sending little jolts of pain up and down her right side. Looking around, she saw the overturned sled and their bags strewn across the snow. Thankfully not far from where she landed. Abraxas was also on the ground, shaking the snow out of his hair as he sat up.

"Are you all right?" she asked.

He nodded.

"What happened?"

Before he could respond, the other two sleds pulled up to a stop next to them. Sorin bounced off his and ran over to help them both up.

"That was a nasty fall," he said.

Abraxas scowled and shook more snow out of his armor. "Truly."

"What happened?" Evren asked again.

"I think one of the dogs ran into something." He winced. "I might have overcorrected."

"What in the hells is there to run into out here?" Sorin laughed lightly.

Evren moved past him and towards the dogs. They were a mess of tangled collars and harnesses, but most of them were standing and just plain confused. However, one of them, one of the smaller ones at the front, was laying down in the snow and whimpering. A few of the others were gathered around it, as much as the harnesses would permit. They strained and whined lowly, licking at their fallen friend's snow dusted fur.

Evren knelt beside them, shushing the worried ones with soft tones and little pats on their heads before she got to the injured one. She whined at Evren, lifting her head to look at her with pitiful amber eyes.

"Hey there, little love," she cooed and cupped her fluffy cheek. The dog melted into her touch, closing her eyes but still whining in the back of her throat. "Let's have a look at you."

It was hard to see anything against the dog's black fur with so little light. But eventually, Evren's gentle fingers found the source of the problem. She winced inwardly as she grabbed the paw, twisting a little to get a better look at the massive chunk of wood hanging out of her paw.

"Okay, this is going to hurt." She gave the dog a knowing look. She just blinked back, steady and calm despite the pain.

She grasped the dark wood tightly and took a deep breath. She wasn't sure if it was to prepare herself or the dog, but it helped, nonetheless. Before she could lose her nerve, she yanked the wood out quickly.

The dog gave a sharp yelp and jerked her foot asway. It immediately started leaking dark blood. Evren tossed the wood aside, turning around to ask for help and finding bandages right at eye level.

"These should help," Nerezza said, holding them out to her.

"Thanks." She took them from her. "The dog will thank you too."

"That's all right."

Nerezza walked away and left Evren with the injured sled dog. It took a little while to calm her down enough to wrap the paw. But after a little talking and more reassurance that the worst was over, she let Evren stop the bleeding and tie off the paw.

Evren unlatched her from the harnesses, and heaved the dog up into her arms. She stood up, her back aching, and could barely seem beyond all the fur. It was in her nose and her mouth. She struggled not to gag as she carried her over to Sorin's sled.

"Better move Arke," she wheezed around the fur.

"What the—ah, shit!"

Evren couldn't see him, but she heard the chaos that followed as he scrambled out of the way. She laid the dog down in the empty space and straightened back up to stretch her spine.

"All right, you can't work like that, so you get to ride, okay?"

The dogs huffed and seemed to grumble a reply in the back of her throat. The look in her eyes told Evren everything. She was *not* happy about having to lay down while everyone else got to run. Evren scratched behind her ears again, and that seemed to lessen her frustration.

"No use in you hurting yourself more, little love." She tapped her finger on the tip of her snout and laughed at the bewildered look the dog gave her. Then she turned around and headed back to her people.

Abraxas and Sorin had already righted the sled and were starting to put the discarded bags back in. Arke had been by busy untangling the dogs and trying to order them to sit still. It was going less than well since he was almost small enough to be their size, but Evren didn't have the heart to stop it.

Sahar, on the other hand, was focused on something in her hand. The massive, bloody splinter of wood Evren had taken out of the dog's paw.

"What is it?" Evren asked.

Sahar's eyes were wide and bright. "King's Ash!"

"Uh . . ."

"The wood!" she explained. "It's King's Ash. Normally found in Terevas."

"Uh huh."

Sorin bounced over, taking the wood from her. "Vasa ships use King's Ash! It's lightweight but extremely durable. Treated right, it can stand the test of time like no other wood."

"And!" Sahar added with a raised finger. "It's only found in southern countries. While the wood itself is extremely durable and adaptable, the tree is incredibly picky about the conditions it grows in. One hard freeze stunts its growth for several years."

"So, the Vasa ship should be somewhere nearby?" Evren asked.

"Yes!" they said in unison.

Evren instinctually began to scan the horizon. The moon had gone back to cowering behind the mountains, and that left them with little light except the stars. She saw nothing but the barren plain in front of them, and the low curve of the northern sea winking in the far distance. Her stomach plummeted at the thought of the ship being trapped under the ice. In these temperatures, melting the ice would take forever. Chipping away inch by inch wouldn't help either.

"Sorin, please tell me we can find this ship." She looked at him pleadingly.

"I killed Mortova and you're asking me to find one ship?" He laughed and tucked the wood splinter in his pocket. "I can find the ship."

"So, the harpoon was yours." Sahar looked impressed and Sorin's grin grew wider.

"Damn right!"

Nerezza walked up, looking like a ghost in the low starlight. Evren had a feeling the final fireball was hers, but she wouldn't say anything. "It's not a matter of simply looking for it. Have you noticed the ground is different?"

All of them gave each other curious glances before shaking their heads no. Nerezza sighed, looking almost disappointed as she stuffed her hands deep into her furs.

"Come on, Nezza." Sahar bumped her shoulder. "What's wrong with the dirt?"

"It's not dirt, it's just ice."

Sorin's giddy grin was wiped away. She thought she heard Arke actually squeak before jumping into the sled. Uneasiness settled in Evren's bones, but she bounced on the balls of her feet. There was no movement, no cracking. It felt like solid ground.

"What does that mean?" Abraxas walked up beside them, although Evren noted how carefully he was walking now.

Nerezza's lips quirked up into what might've been a smile had it been on anyone else. "This is sea ice we're standing on. Frozen incredibly thick and in no danger of cracking under the measly weight of one goblin." She shot Arke a knowing look and he gave her a rude gesture with one of his fingers. "In the summer, it's still incredibly cold, but the ice would move. Defrost, break up, shift, and then refreeze come winter."

"A sea of moving ice then?" Evren asked.

"Of a sort, yes. If the ship was here, it's likely that it moved with the ice, just like a normal ship would move with the currents."

"So, the ship was here." Sorin said. "But it's moved. Well, that's shit. It could be anywhere now."

"Don't ask me to track a ship." Evren groaned. "Unless it

leaves giant planks with its name on it every few feet, I can't do it."

"We don't need to." Nerezza held her hand out. "The map?"

Evren handed it over without hesitation. She took it and snapped it open with enough force that Evren thought the map would rip. Nerezza's greedy eyes drank in the details.

"As I thought." She turned the map so everyone could see and pointed to the marker that Eirunn had left for the ship. "This is where the ship was last seen. That was a few decades ago, since the Ikedree think it's haunted and refuse to go near it. But! That carving on the Jarl's wall was carved back when it was first found and had the ship over here."

She moved her finger to the left, stopping about an inch away from where the marker was. At least a couple miles, if Evren was reading the map correctly.

"All right, I think I understand. Stop me if I'm wrong." Evren raised an eyebrow. "So, instead of us continuing north, you want us to head more to the east because the ship has moved since then."

"Yes." Nerezza folded the map back up and handed it to Evren. She took it back gingerly, making a point to be careful with the soft parchment as if to apologize for Nerezza's rough grip and handling. She tucked it into her pocket, looking at the rest of her companions. She knew Sahar wouldn't have a problem, but she wanted to make sure her boys were okay with the new plan.

"Everyone on board?" she asked.

One by one, they all nodded.

"All right, let's find this ship." She turned to Arke, still huddled in the spot Evren had been napping in until the sled had flipped. "Since you're already there, stay there. Those dogs could use the break. I'll drive with Sorin."

It took a little while for everyone to get situated again, but before long they were turning their dogs northeast and flying across the ice again. The wind snatched Evren's breath away and went back to stinging her everywhere that wasn't covered up. She gripped the railing tightly, her eyes firmly on the ground below.

As they tore across the sea of ice, Evren was either checking for more hazards to the dogs or checking on the one she'd put on bedrest in the sled. Instead of laying down and napping, she had her pointed head against the wind, resting on top of one of the bags with her eyes half closed. Every now and then, her paws would twitch like she was running.

Evren couldn't help but smile. To love something so much that she had waking dreams about it was something she'd always strived for. She'd yet to find something to capture her whole heart that way. The closest would be traveling with the Wandering Sols, but now she wasn't sure if that was helping or hindering her. At one point, she'd feel breathless and weightless, flying under a star-riddled sky into the unknown. The next, the hole in her chest where Gyda and Sol lived reminded her of the cost of such freedoms.

So many times, Evren had raged against the idea of a collar or a cage. She was not an animal content to live in captivity at someone else's whim. More than once, she'd considered chewing off a limb to escape a trap, metaphorically. But cages, while boring, were safe. Collars, while stifling, meant you always had a home to belong to.

Did Evren even have a home? She had a house once, nestled high in the thick branches of the Deep Wood. A family too, she supposed. Although those were hazy memories driven off by years of harsh reality. Orenlion wasn't unkind to her, but even in her youth it felt like a cage. And when she had to slip that ring over her finger, forever binding herself, body and soul, to another, she'd panicked. She would've cut her finger off if it meant freedom.

There was more to the world than Orenlion. She remembered thinking that, over and over again, while she paced the vast golden halls. And there was. But Evren had yet to find a place to call home. Only darkness, and ugly hatred, and monsters. Would that be all her life was? Shying away from the idea of home because she couldn't stand a cage, but uncomfortably alone in the wild world? Was there anything other than those two extremes for someone like her?

If there was, she'd yet to find it. Maybe she never would.

Suddenly, Sorin was grabbing her arm and yanking her back into reality. "I think I see something!" he called out over the whipping wind.

He pointed ahead of them, and Evren squinted to follow his finger's direction. At first, she saw nothing but endless ice. The moon was starting to peek back up from the mountains, reminding her of how long they'd been traveling. But the closer they got, the more she looked past the haze of ice and snow, the more she was able to catch a glimpse of something.

Something dark and jagged against the soft dunes of snow. Something large and almost monstrous as they got closer. It started to loom ahead of them, one sharp tooth-like arm piercing the air. Another lay broken against it, pieces of wispy hair dangling from the skeleton. She could see a mouth cut into its side, forever grinning into the ice with rotted, missing teeth.

But as they slowed down, the monster faded away. Pulling into the shadow of the beast, Evren saw the corpse of a ship. Massive and grand, an aching echo of a past with greater glory. One of its masts was broken and leaning against the other, the shredded remnants of the sails still clinging to their ropes. A massive hole was torn into the ship near the front, and it looked like an open jaw. The back half of the ship was encased in ice, sunken after so many years adrift. But the rest was covered in snow and icicles. Along the side, barely legible, was chipped paint. In swirling letters that must've been elegant at some point was written the ship's name.

Mortova's Maw.

"Found it," Sorin's voice was weak as he stared up at the ship.

One by one, they piled off the sleds, all of them craning

their heads up to stare. It must've been a beautiful ship, once, although Evren had no prior knowledge to compare it to. There was still something incredibly elegant about it, even as it lay dead and half buried in ice.

Evren ran her gloved hands along the side of the ship. The hull was cracked and splintered; a shell of what it used to be. A thick layer of ice and snow covered it as well, but with each passing sweep of her fingers they crumbled away. Carved into the hull, now faded and mangled by time, was a near life size etching of Mortova. Even the blood-red of his eyes had survived the test of time and glared down at her accusingly. She shivered and let her hand fall away from the carved scales.

"This is an incredible ship," she breathed as Sorin came up alongside her. "Or, well, *was*."

Sorin nodded, his deep eyes drinking in the image of Mortova in front of him. A flash of pain, maybe even grief, streaked across his face like lightning. It lingered, even as he spoke.

"She would've been a sight to see on the waters," Sorin said. "With the actual Mortova at her side, no less. I suppose it's a good thing she was all the way up here and never had a chance to bother *Fortune's Trinity*."

Evren stared at him. "Who?"

"My mothership." He put a hand on the carving's neck, tracing the scales and frills as he spoke. "The ship I chose when I was only five, I think. Vasa don't keep blood relations on their ships; there's too many things that can go wrong. We like to put the bonds of crew and earned family over bloodlines, as it makes for a stronger ship. But Vasa children can pick what their homes are, where they learn and grow up, and who's to be their new family. *Fortune's Trinity* was mine."

"Is that how you got your last name?"

He nodded. "Vasa's last names are their ship's names. Unless that ship changes, a Vasa will keep their name until the end of their days."

Evren stared at him as he knocked a piece of ice off Morto-va's carved face. He looked like he was a world away, sailing on warm seas with the sun at his back and the wind in his hair. He also looked incredibly lost.

"You never talk about your family," Evren said.

"Neither do you."

"There's no one left to talk about."

His hand fell away from the hull, his body as taut as a threat-ened snake ready to strike. Evren couldn't tell if it was barely contained anger or grief locking his muscles up. But when he turned to her, his eyes were kind, and his smile was genuine.

"Looks like we have that in common then, Evvie."

Sorin walked away then. He stayed near the hull, but Evren thought that was more to find a safer way inside rather than lingering over the corpse of a ship. Still, she found herself rooted to the spot, staring at the chipped paint of Mortova's gleaming red eye.

Vasa ships were their homes, and the crew were family. No bloodlines to connect them, just the wide-open sea and the skies above. Vasa found a family where there was none. Maybe it was the nature of the Boreal Sea to drive them to do so, because she couldn't imagine anyone on land adopting that lifestyle. Family, blood family, was everything. Nobles relied on it to keep power; peasants needed family to stay alive. People supposedly had chil-dren for love, but she knew of more than one marriage that was bound to children simply for the sake of an heir. Had that not been the life Evren herself was headed towards before she ran away?

It was a simple way of life. Respected, no, *expected*. If the Vasa could throw that tradition out the window, why couldn't she do the same? Why did she have to feel so guilty?

"Hey!"

She snapped her head around to see Abraxas waving her over, further down the hull.

"We found a way in," he called and ushered her over. Evren

pulled herself away from Mortova's painted stare and walked
briskly across the ice to him. As always, his dark furs and hair
made him look more like a shadow than a living elf, but it was
comforting to have him waiting for her regardless. As she got
closer, she saw he was standing next to a smaller hole, and the
sounds of talking and bumping around were already filtering out
into the winter night.

"Started without me?" she asked.

"You looked busy." He stepped aside so he wasn't blocking
the way. "After you."

Evren didn't hesitate to climb inside the belly of the ship.
The moment her feet touched hard wood instead of ice, everything was pitch-black. What little light there had been outside
was gone. The inky blackness of the ship seemed to suck away all
light like a hungry beast. When Abraxas crawled in after her, his
tall form blocked out the entrance, leaving them in a pitch darkness that reminded her far too much of the Yawning Deep.

It was silent for a while, except for some muffled shuffling
around and heavy breathing. It took no time at all for Evren's
skin to start to crawl.

"I suppose it's too much to ask that we light a torch?" she
called into the dark.

"I have something better." Sorin's voice sounded far away,
but she started blindly walking towards it. Carefully placing each
foot on the ground, hands outstretched for anything to hold
on to.

All of a sudden, it was like the sun had risen in the dead of
night. Warm, golden light blossomed and coated the entire belly
of the ship. Evren blinked, suddenly realizing that she was inches
away from a massive wooden beam and turned away with hot
cheeks and burning ears.

Sorin was in the middle of the wrecked cargo hold. Most of
it was caked in thick sea ice, and the icicles were longer than
most of them were tall. Frost wreathed around their feet, almost
playful in the light of the Luminstone.

"You kept it?" Evren almost laughed. "I thought you tossed it after we left Dirn-Darahl."

"I almost did! But where else am I going to get a glowing shit stone?"

Little peals of laughter echoed in the hold. Even Sahar was shaking her head as she wore a small smile. Only Nerezza didn't look impressed. She just looked confused.

"Shit stone?" she asked.

"It's a long story." Sorin shrugged and then raised the stone high above his head. "Shall we?"

"Lead the way, master shit stone," Arke snickered.

With Sorin and his Luminstone guiding them forward, it was relatively easy to get through *Mortova's Maw*. But, to Evren, the ship was a maze of dark, frosty wood. A good portion of the ship was cut off, too frozen and dangerous for them to even attempt to go through. Sorin led them through the cargo hold, muttering little things under his breath as he did. He pointed out split barrels coated in ice as the ship's water barrels. Empty crates of rations, moldy and torn sails, and piles of rope that tripped her more than a live snake.

"Where are the artifacts?" Sahar asked as they moved up to the next level. "Shouldn't they be down there?"

Sorin didn't even look back at her. "Depends on the value. But this ship is missing a lot of what I expected."

"Such as?"

"Bodies."

A chill snaked down Evren's spine that she struggled to ignore. But Sorin was right. A ship this size would've had a decent sized crew. Where were they?

"Perhaps the Prime took them." Abraxas spoke up from the back. "His first group of undead."

No one answered him, but Evren agreed, and she was sure everyone else did as well. Considering that the only thing they knew about the Prime was his habit of building a horde of corpses, it seemed like the most obvious, if concerning, answer.

The further into the ruined ship they went, the more the mood soured. Sorin kept muttering words she didn't understand. Ship's terms, she guessed. But with every room and every new word, he seemed to get more and more disappointed. *Mortova's Maw* was a wreck, but in the same way a burned home was a wreck. There were echoes of memories leaking out of the very woodwork. Carved initials on the massive beams running through the ships, a deck of cards missing all of one suit for some reason, a roster of names in the galley to see who's in charge of cooking next. The crew's quarters were the worst. The hammocks were stiff and coated with a fine layer of frost. But there were still pairs of boots lying next to some. Trunks lay open to the elements, filled with useless trinkets and books full of bad poetry. One was stuffed with a dozen different letters from another ship called *The Iron's Storme*. The words were too smudged to read, and the paper was falling apart in her hands, but Evren could feel the light of life in the ship. She could almost smell the briny salt, mixing with the oil of the lamps and the sweet tang of rum in the air. She could practically hear the jovial laughter as the ship tilted with the waves, and the crew sang songs of storms and stars into the sky.

For many, a ship was just a ship. People on land, people like Evren, would look at it and see a way to get across the Boreal Sea. They would see a way to ship goods or smuggle people to safety. They didn't see the home the Vasa had built. The crew who'd had a monster riding the waves with them were more than just sailors getting from place to place. They were family.

Evren's chest was tight as they made it to another door. Sorin stopped in front of it, fingers tapping on the thick wood.

"What's wrong?" she asked.

"Nothing. Captain's quarters and all. We should get some answers here."

Hopefully.

That went unsaid. They were all quiet now, and eager to find some answers. So far, all the ship had given them was another reminder of how cruel Eith could be to its people.

Sorin had to shoulder the door open. It cracked with frost as he pushed all his body weight against it. Once he had a gap large enough to squeeze through, he went in and took the light with him. One by one, they filed in after him until they were all crowded in the captain's quarters.

The room was small, but spacious enough for one person. A cot was pushed up against the wall, its feet bolted to the floor to keep it from moving in the night. The same was done to a desk in the middle of the room, which was littered with broken bottles glinting against the light from Sorin's hand. Small crates were stacked in the corners, some opened and spilling moldy straw, others still sealed tight. But what caught everyone's eyes was what was on the walls.

There were no windows. No paintings or star charts to take up space. No, the walls were full of fresh carvings. At least, that's what Evren thought. As she moved closer, her stomach dropped. They weren't carvings at all, they were words. Evren's fingers traced the passage next to her. The letters were cartoonishly large and scribbled harshly.

Day 16,

It's quiet. Never liked the quiet. Never had it before. Akonda was always singing, or Bran was shouting. There was always the wind and the waves. And there was always Mortova. But even he's left. I don't feel him next to the ship. I don't hear him humming in my head. I only dream about him, and those are never good dreams. He hates the ice. So do I. But I'm alone. How can I even get to him?

EVREN LICKED HER LIPS, moving to the next passage. The marks in this one were harsher and deep with anger.

Day 20,

He's gone. They're all gone. He left me and I have no one.

It's useless to cry, I know that. Captain Von told me all the time that I never need tears when I have Mortova and the crew. But now there's no one left. I know tears won't help, but the salt reminds me of home. Before the ice. Before the cold.

I wish I had died with them.

"I THINK WE FOUND THE PRIME," Evren said, turning back to them. They were all staring at the messages on the walls. Some were like the one Evren had just read, a little hard to read but neat in the way they were organized. The further down the walls they read, things got worse. More like the scribbles of a madman instead of a survivor.

Across the room, Sahar knelt. "Day five. The quartermaster was put down, his body stored in the cargo hold. Captain says that the only good thing about the cold is that the bodies won't rot. I don't see that as a good thing. Then again, I don't see a lot. Including the Captain. But I hear him. That has to count for something."

"Day eleven." Arke cleared his throat. "Can't drink without warmin' up the water. Not a lot of food left. I never learned how to cook. We never had to hunt before neither. And there can't be anyone alive here in this wasteland. I don't understand. Why are we here? Why did Captain Von make us sail so far north when he knew Mortova and I didn't like the cold? This is worse than Etherak in the winter. Worse than the cliffs during a storm. But . . . I still wouldn't go back."

Nerezza was on her knees tracing the next one. "Day thirty. I'm so hungry. There's nothing left to eat here. Nothing I can do. The only meat left is . . ." Her words caught in her throat, and she pulled her hand back.

"What?" Abraxas asked.

"He ate the crew," she said, looking horrified. "It says it here."

Evren was instantly sick to her stomach and tore her eyes

away from the passage that Nerezza had been reading. She couldn't make out the words, but they were burned into her eyeballs regardless.

"Can someone find the end?" Abraxas asked. "Or the beginning? We need to know more."

Evren nodded and went back to her wall. Day 16, Day 36, Day 42, Day 49, she counted them all. As they got harder to read and understand, she had to reread them multiple times. Finally, she was at the end of the wall. There were a few feet of open, clear wood left. No more entries after this one.

"Day 74." She forced her voice to carry across the cabin and heard everyone still behind her. "I ate him. The voice in my head. Not Mortova, not Von. I ate the leech in the gem. It's not what he wanted. He screamed. I screamed. I think I even laughed. But I can feel it now, that promise. No more hunger, no more loneliness. I will make this land home. I will make its people family. I will never be alone again."

She cleared her throat, pulling away from the wall. "I can't make out the rest. It's all gibberish."

A heavy silence fell over the group, broken only by Sorin rummaging through the desk. The snap of drawers being pulled out only to be shoved back in. Glass splintered as he tossed things to the ground. Like he was trying to keep grief away with every erratic movement.

Finally, he swept everything off the desk in one long shove of his arms. Evren tried not to jump as it all clattered to the ground. A broken bottle rolled to her feet. It looked like it was caked in dried blood.

"Sorin?" Her voice was shaky. She didn't move from her spot. "What are you doing?"

"Looking."

"For?"

"Names!"

If the desk hadn't been bolted to the ground, he would've flipped it over. He was seething, pacing, his body tight with so much energy that could only leave in short, violent bursts. She'd never seen him like this. Angry? Yes. He was always angry at Viggo and the Serevadians. Spiteful? Frightened? Desperate?

Yes. But never all at once.

Arke moved carefully through the glass and strewn papers. At first, Evren thought he was going towards Sorin, like he always did. Instead, he knelt beside the desk.

"Hey, kid." He snapped his fingers at Sorin. "Found some names."

Sorin's body was rigid as the ice for a few seconds before he dove to Arke's side. Evren peered around, looking through their bent heads to see more carvings. These were names and titles. Who everyone was, their age, and what they did on the ship. They were all crossed out, except one.

"Gail." Sorin sounded like his throat was lined with the broken glass bottles. "His name was Gail. He was twelve years old when he wrote this."

All the air was sucked out of their lungs for a brief second. It was like merely speaking the name of a child who'd fallen so far was enough to draw him in. Evren wanted windows to peer out of and found none.

"A child?" Sahar's hand went over her mouth. "The Prime is a child?"

"Not anymore," Abraxas said.

Evren looked around the room again. She took in the devolving carvings, the carefully noted downward mental spiral. She didn't need to read them all to get the full picture, but it felt wrong not to.

"So, the ship wrecks," she started. "Most of the crew died within the first couple of days. One by one, until only Gail is left. He talks a lot about being alone, separate even from Mortova. So, who is he talking about at the end?"

"It could be a fiction of his imagination," Sahar offered.

Abraxas shook his head. "Gail might've been a powerful Vasa, but Sorin's already told us they have no power over the dead. Something else was here. Something that his notes don't mention, that gave him power."

"This ship went to Vernes." Arke held up a couple papers. "Just like you said. Maybe the necromancer was here with him?"

Sorin let out a low groan of frustration and sat down heavily behind the desk. He let the Luminstone roll to the edge, teetering but not quite falling as he rubbed his face.

"They went to Vernes during Abraxas's stupid war," he muttered into his hands and didn't see Abraxas flinch. "They get something valuable. Why?"

"Not someone?" Evren offered.

"No, Vasa don't do slave trading or smuggling. Lots of other questionable things but we don't deal in people, especially in a war. That's a good way to get killed. Okay. Okay, they get the cargo, they sail east. But why go so far north? Why avoid Etherak?"

Nerezza crossed her arms and leaned against the wall. "You assume these Vasa were working with Etherak. Perhaps it was the opposite."

Sorin's head snapped up, his eyes gleaming. "That's it! It must be! The ship was hired to smuggle important things out of Vernes, to keep them safe. But avoiding Etherak's navy at that time would've been nearly impossible since they were fucking everywhere in Eith. So, what do they do? They go so far north that even Etherak's ships can't follow them!"

"And they crash along the way and end up stranded here for the next seventy or so years," Evren finished.

Arke scrambled up the side of the desk to sit next to Sorin. He crossed his legs, his yellow eyes almost glowing. "So. What was so damn important to sail to this frozen hellhole?"

"A Xirstine." Sahar barely breathed the word.

Arke blinked. "Uh, bless you?"

This time, it was Abraxas's eyes that went wide. If possible, he paled even further, his skin turning the color of blank parchment as he locked eyes with Sahar.

270 | GILLIAN GRANT

"That is . . . entirely possible," he choked out. "As well as terrifying, if true."

"What the hells is a Xirstine?" Evren asked, breaking up the two with her words and forcing them to focus on the rest of the group.

"A Xirstine is a special prison," Sahar explained. "Vernes's culture is surrounded by undead and their paths after their deaths. Necromancers are supposed to watch them, guide them, and keep them from doing anything rash while in their new form. Occasionally, a necromancer is forced to seal a rowdy undead in a Xirstine. It would look like a dark gem to you, but it would contain a living spirit."

"So, the Vasa had one of these with them? A prison doesn't sound like a good thing."

Sahar shook her head. "I suppose under extreme measures someone not dead could put themselves in there, in the hopes of laying low until the fighting stopped. But it's also entirely possible that a very knowledgeable, powerful spirit was put in there and smuggled out to keep them out of enemy hands."

Behind them, the wood didn't creak. No footsteps sounded. But Evren's hairs on the back of her neck prickled and her blood went cold, just as a familiar, raspy voice came from the doorway.

"Very good," cooed Keres. "Here I was thinking I'd put my lot in with a bunch of idiots."

19

The mood in the room instantly snapped from cold depression to white-hot rage and confusion.

Sahar actually screamed. The sound that tore out of her throat was guttural and heart-wrenching as she stared at the broken, mangled body of her dead friend. The air in the room suddenly crackled with arcane energy as Nerezza's hands lit up with fire. Abraxas's sword was out and level with Keres' chest. Arke was hissing. Sorin had fallen backwards out of his chair.

Evren was pissed.

"And just where in the hells have you been?" she snapped at Keres.

"Following you, of course."

Suddenly, all eyes were on her. Some horrified, some confused. All were brimming with anger.

"Evren . . . ." Abraxas didn't lower his weapon, but his tone was clear. Explain, and do it quickly.

"This is Keres," she said, scowling. "Or so they say. I met them with . . . with Sol. During the battle. They claim to be a spirit who's, um, borrowing Vox's body."

That too wide grin stretched even wider. "Honestly, orcs

aren't my style. But since little Prime has taken every other corpse, I had to make do."

Abraxas didn't back down. His grip on his sword tightened, and Evren watched him shift his stance ever so slightly. She'd seen him do it a thousand times before. Always right before he was about to attack.

Before she could even fathom what she was doing, Evren found herself between Keres and the point of Abraxas's sword. It wavered only slightly, his eyes narrowing past her.

"Move, Evren," he hissed.

"Lower your weapon," she said.

Behind her Keres cackled. "Yes, do—"

"Shut up," she shot over her shoulder. Once nothing else came out of their mouth she turned back to Abraxas. "Listen, I know this looks terrible—"

"Terrible? *Terrible!*" Sahar shrieked. "That's Vox's body! It's possessing him. How is that supposed to look?"

Evren winced inwardly. She was grateful she only had to deal with Abraxas and not Drystan, but the mere thought of relief that Drystan wasn't there disgusted her. Still, she had to admit Keres had picked an awful vessel. It still made her skin crawl. She could feel the waves of cold radiating from them.

"Terrible, I know." She shook her head. "Look, I didn't ask for Keres' help. They stalked me when I was alone in the woods, and then they were in Direwall. Not entirely helpful, but they kept me alive. And they want to stop Gail as much as we do."

"Why?" Nerezza's face was frightening, framed by crackling flames. She looked far more sinister than Evren was used to.

Keres rolled their shoulders, the bones and muscles popping like thunderclaps in the small space. "Well, I should think it's obvious by now. I was what this ship was supposed to smuggle to safety."

"*You* were in the Xirstine?" Sorin poked his head up above the desk. "Why?"

"I used to be someone of extreme importance and power. Those in charge of my spirit thought it best to keep me out of enemy hands and put me in that stone to protect me." Keres' eyes gleamed dangerously when they fell back on Abraxas. "You are one of those Divine Knights, yes? You look like you've lost your touch."

A low growl rumbled deep in Abraxas's chest. His sword went past Evren, streaking towards Keres. Without hesitation, she brought her bow up. Steel and wood clashed against each other, but she held strong and twisted until the sword fell away. His eyes widened, his grip still tight on the hilt of his sword, but the tip didn't leave the floor.

"What are you doing?" he snarled. "You can't trust that thing!"

"When did I say that I did?" she shot back.

"Nothing, and I do mean *nothing*," he spat at Keres, "that parades around wearing the corpse of someone else is good!"

"Would you feel better if I went back in the Xirstine?" Keres asked.

"I'd feel better if I drove my blade through your skull."

"Oh!" Keres's eyes sparkled dangerously. "Say it again. That made me tingle."

Evren shoved them back against the wall just as Abraxas went to lift his sword again. She put her hands out at both of them, the familiar flickering flame of rage burning in her chest. She'd had *enough*.

"Knock it off! Both of you!"

Abraxas took a step back, his blade falling to his side. Somewhere in his dark mask of anger Evren thought she saw a little flash of hurt. But it was gone before she could truly confirm. On the other side, Keres was just grinning, although they'd done as Evren had asked and hadn't moved or said a word. She could see a million sharp words at the tip of their tongue. For their sake, she hoped they didn't use them. She wasn't in the mood to hear it.

"We don't have time for this." She let her arms down slowly. "If we want to stop Gail, we'll need Keres to help us."

Abraxas started to protest but Evren held her hand up and he closed his mouth again, glaring behind her.

"I don't like the idea of working with them either." This time speaking to the rest of the party. "But it's us against an army that thinks as one. We don't have the numbers, or the knowledge, to do this on our own. So, for right now, we take what Keres has to offer. So long as it's helpful and not demeaning." She shot them a knowing look, and the corpse had the gall to look offended. They even pressed their hand against the hole where Vox's heart used to be.

"I'm hurt, truly." They rolled their eyes. "But I'll behave. So long as your knight does."

Evren turned to Abraxas. He hadn't changed. He was still staring at Keres with unbridled disgust and hatred. For one, brief moment, Evren could almost see who he was before she knew him. A man in shining armor, fighting for a cause he was told was right and divine. But she also saw what Keres saw, what so many in Vernes and Gratey and Terevas saw. A shadow of a man wielding a sword meant to cut down all who didn't share his beliefs.

Evren blinked, and the image was gone. He was just her friend, who was desperate and reeling from the loss of two friends.

"Abraxas." She forced her voice to be soft. His eyes flicked down to her, barely softening at all. "I need your word you won't hurt Keres."

His lip curled in anger. "You want me to keep that *thing* alive?"

"Yes."

The hurt on his face smarted as if her words had physically slapped him.

"Why? It's not natural, Evren. You don't know what it's

capable of. It has no right to walk on this earth like this! It's sickening and goes against the cycle of nature itself."

"Maybe," she agreed. "But it's not our job to judge them right now. Right now, we need help, and Keres wants the same thing we do."

"So it says."

"Exactly. Abraxas, Keres has done nothing to personally harm us. I don't trust them, but I see no reason to kill them on the sole principle of what they are and where they come from. You wouldn't allow someone to kill Arke just because goblins raided their home once, would you?"

He scoffed. "Of course not."

"So, do the same for Keres." She took a step forward, pushing his blade aside and looking him dead in the eye. In the Wilds, eye contact was a challenge of dominance. Those who looked away first were admitting their submission. Abraxas had never broken eye contact before. "Trust me. Trust that I'll end Keres if they do anything to harm us in any way. You've followed me into the unknown multiple times. Through Alkimos's nest, through Serevadia's politics, through the battle to stop Heliodar. All I'm asking you to do is trust me again."

Abraxas took a step back, but he never broke eye contact. "Fine. But the moment, and I do mean the very *moment* it so much as breathes betrayal, I'm the one that puts it down."

If that's what it took. She nodded. "Okay." Then she turned to the rest of them, one by one. Arke and Sorin were still behind the desk, warily watching her and Abraxas. Nerezza and Sahar couldn't tear their eyes from Keres, who seemed to be pointedly ignoring them. As if feeling her gaze on them, her companions all turned to her, questioning, hurting, and confused.

"This is all of us," she said. "Nerezza, Sahar. I know you are your own party, but you're still working with us. And Keres isn't exactly . . . sensitive to their chosen body. Will you be all right?"

Nerezza narrowed her eyes at Keres. She curled her palms into fists and the fire vanished but seemed to appear in her eyes

276 | GILLIAN GRANT

instead. "I'm assuming you have more information than you've given us so far?"

Keres cocked their head. "Well, obviously. I have a lot more. So long as everyone agrees to let me talk without ripping my new throat out."

Nerezza looked at Sahar, but she'd already made her decision. Looking to her last friend was just a formality. Sahar herself still looked like she was going to be sick. She took a hesitant step towards Keres.

"Those that were taken," she started carefully, softly. "What happens to them?"

"Many things."

"And Drystan? What happened to him?"

For the first time, Evren saw a flicker of remorse in Keres' face. Their smile slipped, and their body let go of a bit of their nonchalant nature.

"The Prime can do many things to his new followers," they said. "Drystan was a fighter, I saw it. In Lostwater, and in Direwall. However, his survival would depend on Gyda keeping her mind."

All at once Evren's world seemed to crash in around her. Or maybe that was just Arke falling off the table and smashing more glass under his feet.

"You better not be playin' us for fools!" The goblin waved a clawed finger at them. Keres regarded it in an amused expression.

"Is Gyda alive?" Sorin sounded like he didn't want to get his hopes up, his voice wavering with every word. Evren didn't trust herself to speak for the same issue. All she could do was stare dumbfoundedly at Keres.

Who, infuriatingly, started to get their grin back. "The definition of life is so loose, but by your knight's terms, yes. Gyda is alive and whole. And should she be as strong as I remember her being as a child, she could have gotten to your other friends as well."

"Meaning Sol and Drystan could be alive." It was too much to hope for. That little flickering light in her chest was so warm to her cold bones that even the tiniest spark was heating her up. It was all too much, but she grasped the fire anyway.

"It's possible," Keres mused. "However, that requires Gyda to oppose the Prime's hive mind and keep the two other alive in secret. So, don't get all teary eyed yet. They could all be corpses."

Whatever bucket of ice-cold realism they were trying to toss over her, Evren evaded entirely. Her eyes met Sahar's across the room. There, glittering with a hundred unshed tears, was the same hope. Was it so wrong for her fingers to already be stretching for a new lifeline, and this time bring it in?

She forced herself to breathe the cold air. It felt like a dagger in her lungs, clearing away some of the warm tendrils of hope. Just enough to think clearly. It left plenty to dream with. She turned back to Sorin and Arke, a silent question in her eyes. They both nodded. Perhaps too eager, given the mouth the news came from, but they needed it. Like they desperately needed the sun, they all needed their friends back.

Evren turned back to Keres. For the first time, she felt like she had some semblance of control. "All right. We agree to work with you. Now, spill your damn story."

BY THE TIME Keres was finished dancing around their story, Evren was sick to her stomach. Whether that was because she was constantly having to shield them from everyone else and had the smell of rot stuck in her nose, or just the weight of their story, she couldn't tell. But she needed air afterwards, and so did the rest of the party. Once they found a way to the main deck, Keres was not so politely told to stay in the captain's quarters. To Evren's shock, they actually listened.

The deck of *Mortova's Maw* was a mess of damaged, curling boards and dangerously tilting masts. The wind whistled between the masts, and a thick layer of ice coated every inch of the railing. Nevertheless, Evren leaned against it and looked out to the south.

It was an incredible view. The moon had disappeared again, but now the aurora had finally made an appearance. The twisting ribbons of green and blue light danced across the sky. It lit everything in a glorious glow. She couldn't help but stare up at it, dazzled, even as she turned Keres' story over in her head.

In dark contrast to the sky, her mind was not a bright place. Keres had said that living in the Xirstine was painful, almost tortuous. They had no idea what happened in the outside world, aside from the voice of Captain Von, who'd been a young, successful elf aiding the Vernesians during Etherak's occupation. It was Von's first voyage as a captain, and the one where he changed the ship's name to honor Mortova. A symbol of strength against those that opposed them. Von was supposed to take Keres to an ally in the east, one that even Keres didn't know. But when the shipwreck happened, all they had was Gail.

Gail was, in every way, a boy with far too much power to be left alone. Even without Mortova at his side, he was stronger than the rest of the crew and survived far longer than them. And he refused to talk to Keres for weeks. When he finally broke down, Keres wanted him to break the Xirstine and release them. They had no idea the situation, but they could be of more help outside the gem rather than doing nothing but waiting in pain. But Gail refused. Again and again, week after week. Keres said they heard his mind start to crack under the pressure, as anyone's would. They felt their own fracture too.

What Keres was now is a fraction of what they used to be. At least, that's how they put it. That when Gail 'ate' them like he mentioned on the wall, he consumed a vast portion of Keres' soul and powers. Keres had been drifting as a formless spirit for decades, unable to leave and unwilling to do so without their full power.

And then there was the heavy question; should they give Keres their power back? Would they even have that choice?

Evren put her head in her hands and rubbed her tired eyes. She didn't trust Keres. She couldn't even pretend to like them. But she was sympathetic. They'd been powerful and respected in life, and precious to their people in death. Keres could be the key for modern Vernes to unlock all the history that had been erased in Etherak's occupation. Did her personal feelings really matter when a whole country of people deserved that second chance?

And then there was Abraxas. He hadn't said a word during Keres' story, and nothing since. If he had it his way, Keres would be very permanently dead. And Evren had a sinking feeling that he wouldn't let Keres return home.

She hated how she was starting to resent Abraxas for what he did, and what he was still trying to do. Vernes wasn't a good place by any means, but what Keres had said about the occupation, what Abraxas didn't even try to deny, had her skin crawling. It was the past, she knew that. He'd told her that much their first night in the Yawning Deep. She still didn't like to picture what he'd done under the banner of a just cause.

Evren sighed. She had no right to judge Abraxas, just as she had no right to judge Keres. The awful truth was that they were two sides of the same coin. Neither wholly good, but with a similar goal.

Hopefully, it would be enough.

The warm heat of a body settling in next to her made Evren look up from her hands. Nerezza stood rigid beside her, looking out over the sparkling sea of solid ice. Her mouth was twisted into a small frown; it had been for hours now. Her hair had come loose from its updo and hung free around her shoulders.

"You all right?" Evren couldn't help but ask after a few minutes of silence.

"What an odd question," the elf murmured. She looked at her sideways. "I'm not sure."

280 | GILLIAN GRANT

"I feel the same after that . . . well, 'story' doesn't feel adequate."

"Keres was honest about who and what they were, and their motivations. They didn't have to be."

"I doubt a lie would've sounded less crazy. Still," she shook her head, "eating souls? How does that transfer power?"

Nerezza shrugged, almost casually. Like they were discussing which flavor of cake was superior and not the fact that a little boy ate a thousand-year-old necromancer's soul. "Our souls are imprints of who we are. Our memories, our loves and hates. Power, or the lack thereof, is imprinted there as well. I can't imagine how he came by the idea of such magic, but taking Keres' soul did give him that power, albeit changed to new methods. From what I hear, necromancers in Vernes tend to want their undead to follow them willingly and of their own accord. Gail doesn't give his a chance."

"He was afraid they'd say no," Evren said. "He was scared and alone. And the Ikedree people aren't open minded like Vernes would be. So, he forced them all to do his bidding. It's a little sad."

"A boy with too much power to begin with gaining more through the devouring of a soul." Nerezza shuddered. "It's not sad. But it is enlightening."

Evren's skin prickled uncomfortably. "What do you mean?"

Nerezza's smile was as cold as the ice, but she did seem genuinely happy that Evren asked her. "I am a scholar, Evren. I scour the world for new magics every day. I'd found little. Things unattainable to mortals that shaped Eith anyway. But now, I've found two."

"Two?"

"Souls and Blood."

Evren's throat was suddenly dry. For no logical reason, she felt the urge to run away from Nerezza. There was nothing in her stature that was threatening, but she was still unsettled.

"You knew," Evren rasped.

"I guessed."

"How?" she demanded.

Nerezza turned to face her fully. She was only a few inches taller than Evren, but haloed with the light of the aurora, she had this gleam in her eye that made Evren feel small in comparison. She was still smiling.

"You never heal," she started, gesturing to her visible scars. "Not fully. Each time you bleed, you get stronger. That's not normal. And you used the spell I gave you."

"It was a test," she guessed.

"It was a precaution." She looked her up and down. "Blood magic seems to blur the lines of Written and Inherited magic, but at the cost of your own life. That's why you've felt perpetually sick for so long."

"I don't feel sick," Evren protested.

"But you don't feel well, either."

That shut her up.

Nerezza's eyes softened. "You're always tired, right? Always sore, always on the verge of breaking. Somehow, you keep pushing on. Maybe it's what gave you the magic to begin with."

"What gave me the power? I haven't—"

"From what I've learned, Blood magic can't be held without first being given a sacrifice." She narrowed her eyes, as if looking for the answer in all Evren's scars. "What did you give?"

"Nothing," Evren said, suddenly defensive. "I've sacrificed nothing for a power that's killing me."

"You don't know how to use it properly."

"Do you?"

Nerezza paused for what seemed like an eternity. Overhead, the sky blazed green and blue and back again. After a while, the elf shook her head.

"No." She looked guilty for simply admitting something she didn't know. "But, if this goes well, maybe I can teach you what I do know."

"What if I don't want to learn?" Evren asked. "It can't kill me if I don't use it."

"Maybe it can, maybe it can't. How can you give up that magic in your very veins?"

She tried not to laugh. "Nerezza, I didn't even realize I had it until a few months ago. I didn't even know what I could do with it until Lostwater. And it scares the shit out of me. A bow is a weapon, plain and simple. I know my bow, and my arrows. I know its limits. I don't know what my blood can do, other than somehow help me fight or cast walls of fire." She tore a hand through her hair, trying not to let the frustration seep out of her. Weapons were simple, magic was not. Evren just wanted something in her life to be simple again

"How do you know about Blood magic?" Evren asked, looking back at Nerezza. "Did you meet someone else like me?"

"Yes," she said softly.

"What happened to them?"

She swallowed hard, looking like she'd rather dive into the ice below than answer the question. When she did, her voice was as soft as the lights above.

"She was a little girl I grew up with in an orphanage in Terevas. Young, naive. She'd prick her finger and cause the lanterns to dance with green light. She'd cut her knee open while playing and suddenly the whole yard was covered in frost. And she was always sickly, and tired, unless she was bleeding."

Evren didn't want to know, but she needed to. "What happened to her?"

"She died." Nerezza blinked and focused back on Evren. "Little girls die all the time. Little girls with magic they can't control even more often."

"I'm so sorry, Nerezza," Evren whispered.

"You didn't know her." She waved her off. "But thank you. She was . . . well, I suppose she was the closest I had to family."

Evren groaned and leaned against the railing on her elbows. The ice was cold even through her many layers. "Family. Seems like that keeps coming up over and over. In the cabin, with Mortova's death. All Gail wanted was a family, and he chose the worst way to find it."

"Yes, but how long before his family should reach beyond the mountains?" Nerezza asked. Her hands gripped the railing hard enough to crack the ice. "We must stop him. Mercy killing or vengeance, I don't care."

"Except the one thing Keres doesn't know is where he is," Evren pointed out. "This place is huge, and the only lead we have is under Myrefall Bay. None of us are surviving that trip."

It was gnawing at Evren like a dog chewing on her bones. Having an explanation, a reason behind the hell that she was putting herself through, but no way to end it. There was so much she couldn't understand. Too many puzzle pieces that were not fitting where she needed them to. Her head was hurting. Her stomach was queasy again. And she had the sudden urge to nap, which didn't help after Nerezza's Blood magic talk.

"You don't look well," she said, eyeing Evren intently.

Evren huffed and tried to play it off. "I've felt worse. Maybe it's just the light."

She pointed to the aurora above her, and Nerezza seemed to notice it for the first time. She seemed almost impressed.

"Beautiful." Her breath whispered like a cloud in the air. "Amazing what light can live in such darkness, isn't it?"

Evren suddenly stood up straight, her spine rigid and her eyes glued to the sky. Beside her, Nerezza started like a wild deer hearing a twig snapped.

"What's wrong?" she prodded, but Evren wasn't listening.

"Beware of the night but fear the lights that flourish in it more." She almost laughed as the cloaked figure's words echoed from her lips. "You son of a bitch! You meant the aurora!"

Nerezza made a noise of confusion as Evren tore away from her and raced up the slick deck to the highest point of the ship. The back end was encased in ice, and the whole ship's forward deck rose towards the sky like it was frozen mid-sinking. She sidestepped Sorin, who was shifting through some ice-encrusted rope, and ran to the forward point of the ship.

The bowsprit was far too slick and damaged to climb onto, but like a skeletal finger it pointed across the sea of ice. Evren slid to a halt, panting and barely catching herself on one of the remaining ropes. She followed the finger as it trailed across the ice. She could see the distant glimmer of Myrefall Bay reflecting the aurora. Past that were soaring mountains that they looked like they were encased in white ice. A massive hunk of it, miles long, stretching between the mountains. A glacier, just at the edge of the Expanse.

Evren turned her eyes to the sky. Watching, waiting, even as her friends gathered behind her murmuring questions to themselves. None of them bothered to ask her directly. Either that, or she didn't hear them.

She let out a cry of joy as she watched a small, glowing piece of the aurora's light zip away from the sky and to the glacier. The ice lit up for a brief second before going dark again. But that was all she needed.

Evren turned back to her friends as they gathered around her. They were all confused. Abraxas even looked worried. Far behind them, Evren spied two glowing eyes peering out from the stairs that led to the lower deck.

She bounced on the balls of her feet, and for the first time since getting to the Expanse, she let hope run rampant. "I know where they are," she said, breathless. "I know exactly where the Prime is."

20

Keres called it the White Cairn, once everyone had calmed down and joined them below decks. Out of the wind and the suddenly chilling aurora lights, it was easier to think. And now that they had a destination, they needed a plan.

"Are you sure this glacier is the right spot?" Sahar asked as she passed out their rations. They steamed up the air, but Evren barely felt the warmth as she ate.

"That's where the light went." She swallowed some more and explained. "Correct me if I'm wrong, but aurora don't typically lose their light to giant rivers of ice."

She sniffed primly and sat down next to Nerezza. "No, they don't."

Abraxas picked at his food. "The aurora does look like the lights the undead held in their eyes. Each one we killed we saw the light go somewhere else."

"Too much to hope for that it would just go *away*, huh?" Sorin sighed. "Right, so the glacier. What do we know about it? Other than the very obvious name?"

They all looked at Keres. They were standing in the corner of the room, picking away at the ice encrusted on the walls. When they realized everyone was looking at them, they let out a low, soft groan of annoyance. "All I know is the name. And that's because I've been trapped here for so long. I got bored, heard people talking about it, and now it makes sense!"

"But it's solid ice," Evren protested. "How does Gail hide there?"

"Not necessarily solid." Nerezza waved her spoon in the air like a wand. "Glaciers can have pockets of air, even caves and tunnels."

"Great," Arke grumbled. "More caves."

She ignored the goblin and continued. "But the ice is constantly moving. Think of it like a massive sheet of ice traveling down from the mountains to the water. There's no beach to land on, no cave entrance that would be easy to see. Under normal circumstances, I'd suggest hiking around to take the mountain path and coming at it from above. There must be fissures that lead into the heart of the glacier."

"Under normal circumstances?" Evren pressed.

Nerezza scraped up a bit of her food but didn't eat it. It sat bouncing in her wooden spoon as her hand trembled. "That could take days. More than likely, it would be weeks. We just don't have that much time."

"And yet, crossing straight would require going through the bay." Abraxas shook his head and pushed his bowl away. "We don't have the means to get across. If we circled back to Direwall, we would lose more time. And the water near the city is shallow. We saw it freezing without Mortova."

"Meaning all boats would be frozen as well." Evren forced another spoonful into her mouth and swallowed it. She barely tasted it, whatever it was. Some kind of fish? "So that leaves us with Nerezza's plan of hiking around. At least the dogs will cut down some of the travel time, so long as we have the supplies to keep them fed."

Arke reached out silently and took Abraxas's bowl. He scraped it clean, with the help of no spoon. Keres went back to picking at the ice and muttering to themselves. Abraxas offered no more options. Nerezza looked like she was trying to conjure a spell that would take them across, and if her brow furrowed anymore Evren was sure her face would be stuck like that permanently. The only thing Sahar did was keep herself turned away from Keres.

Evren was steadily losing her appetite. Eating was better than useless words, and she was tired of talking. But she was tired of the silence too. Surely, they didn't come all this way just to be stopped now?

"Hang on a minute!" Sorin flew to his feet, his empty bowl clattering to the ground and Arke hissing when he nearly lost his as well.

"What is it?" Abraxas asked.

"People, look at where we are!" He grinned, spreading his arms wide to the room.

Evren raised her eyebrows, taking it in and hoping to see what he saw. "Uh . . . the mess hall?"

He let out an exasperated breath as his hands fell to his slides with dull slaps. "No! Well, yes. But beyond that. We're on a bloody ship already!"

Keres stopped their art experiment on the walls to look at him. It was as if they were finally noticing him for the first time. "Well, well. The Vasa has a brain after all."

"I didn't see you making the suggestion," he scoffed, but looked proud, nonetheless.

Evren, on the other hand, was developing another headache. She set her bowl aside and rubbed her temples. "Sorin, I love the idea, but this ship is stuck in the ice. We can't even get to most of it. Besides, it's wrecked! Holes everywhere. And we're nowhere near liquid water."

"No no, Evvie!" Sorin crouched beside her and gripped her knees. She could feel the warmth through her furs. Or maybe it was the hopeful grin that kept growing larger with every second. "Look at this ship! It's massive. We don't need all of it, just the good parts. Don't you see? It's just like the sleds, only bigger. And once we get to the water? It's a boat again!"

Evren swallowed down the lump in her throat, which was probably the fish again. She tried to picture what Sorin's mind was capturing. "You want to build a ship that could travel across the ice and the water?"

"Yes!" He launched to his feet so fast that he almost hit her nose. "For the love of the stars, *yes*! We have everything right here. This wood?" He knocked on the wall, and Keres ducked out of the way of his long arm. "It's not rotten. It's still good! We take the parts we need, and we build ourselves a smaller ship. Big enough for all of us, but light enough that the dogs can still pull. Until we get to the water where we cut them off, unfurl the sails, and then ride our way straight to the glacier."

Maybe it was just his enthusiasm seeping into the air, or maybe she was too exhausted to tell the difference between a good idea and an insane one. But he was starting to make sense to her. Far more reasonable an idea than she had when she decided to call Alkimos to the fight with Heliodar. At least this was a plan.

"That . . . is almost not terrible." Sahar spoke up. She rose to her feet, hesitantly. Her finger tapped her chin, and with every step across the room she grew more confident. "It would still take time. And there would be no testing it to see if it would actually float. Building it would have to be done quickly, and we'd only have one shot."

Sorin bounded over to her, his whole body practically humming with untapped energy. "But I'm right! It can be done. We've got two brilliant mages, some muscle, and I assume Keres has some benefits from Vox?"

Keres snorted. "You're asking me to do menial labor."

Sahar stepped forward and met their gaze for the first time. "He's asking you to help us get to Gail. But I'm not."

Keres blinked at her in surprise. It was like they were truly seeing each other. Sahar, with her commanding voice and straight back, and Keres being a mere echo of what they used to be. There was something like respect that kindled in their eyes. Sahar did not return that, even as Keres bowed their head.

"Whatever the lady requires." They looked up at her through Vox's matted, dull hair. "I have a feeling this vessel would've wanted the same. Call me what you like, but I'm not a monster. Above all, I respect the wishes of the dead, and those brave enough to command them. You, I think . . ." They looked her up and down. "Yes, you will do fine. Whatever you need, so long as it's not my permanent demise. We share a common goal, after all."

Sahar kept her face neutral, but Evren saw her fingers twitch in surprise. Apparently, a heritage that the living looked down upon was more than helpful in life-and-death situations.

"All right then." She turned back to Sorin, who was still gaping at the two of them. "You have Keres to help. Abraxas can keep an eye on them and help with the heavy lifting. I have few supplies left, but I'm sure I can find something to help this sled-boat thing into existence. Perhaps some blueprints?"

Sorin snapped back to her. "Oh, yeah, that would actually be super helpful."

Arke kicked at his shin and missed by a foot or so. But it caught Sorin's attention regardless.

He turned to the goblin with a smile that wasn't reflected back. "Arke! Buddy!"

He scowled. "What does your crazy ass want me to do?"

"Oh, simple spells, you know? Knock off some of the ice, help bend the wood to the right shape, keep things steady while we work. That sort of thing? You and Nezza are so creative, I'm sure you'll figure it out."

Arke looked over at Nerezza and shrugged. He'd never tell Sorin no, but that didn't mean she couldn't. She stood up slowly and put her bowl to the side as she leveled Sorin with a cold stare.

"If you call me that again, I'll turn you into a piece of wood and nail you to your own ship. Understood?"

Sorin laughed. "Is that a yes?"

She sighed. "Yes."

He whooped and jumped in the air. The floor trembled when he landed and Evren eyed some wobbling icicles dangling from the ceiling like deadly chandeliers. One moment her eyes were just on the ice, and the next all she could see was Sorin's face. She scooted back a few inches.

"What?" she asked.

"You need a job."

She rolled her eyes. "All right, Captain Sorin, what am I doing to add to this insane plan of yours?"

She shouldn't have asked. The look in his eyes made her want to snatch the words back. Was this what following her around in Serevadia had felt like?

"You, my friend." He gripped her shoulder. "Are my jack-of-all-trades."

~

JACK-OF-ALL-TRADES APPARENTLY MEANT BOUNCING AROUND from job to job as he saw fit. Which was not nearly as bad as Evren had imagined, but it was still hard work.

It all started with Sahar making the sketches of what the ship would look like, and then arguing with Sorin about what was needed until everyone was put to work. It was all menial work at first. Evren, Abraxas, and Keres spent most of their time finding good pieces of wood and ripping them out. Evren had to always stay between the two and ended more than six arguments over the span of a couple hours.

What wood they couldn't get out because of the ice was left to the mages. Fire in a wooden ship was dangerous, but the two kept their flames white-hot and controlled. The floors were slick with puddles when they were done, but the wood was undamaged and easily pulled free.

Of course, they lost track of time. Evren had no idea how many hours had passed when Sorin bounced down to her spot in the crew's quarters as she tore another plank free.

"Hey, that's a good piece!" he said cheerfully.

Evren just grunted and let it fall to the ground with the others. She rolled her shoulders. They were sore before she started taking the ship apart. Now they were on fire, and her headache had worsened.

"Actually, I think that's enough." Sorin huffed and looked over at Sahar's elegantly scribbled notes, and then back at the wood. "Yeah! That's perfect!"

"Great." Evren sighed. "Get Keres to take it where you need it. I'm taking a nap. Wake me in a couple hours."

She patted his shoulder, gave him an encouraging smile, and made her way to the spot in the mess hall they'd cleared out as a home base. Sahar was snoozing on one of the tables, her charcoal still held tight in her fingers. Evren found a spot piled high with their collective sleeping bags and crashed there. She was asleep before her head hit the furs.

Sorin didn't wake her like she'd asked. Instead, she woke up with the mess hall empty of people and filled with all of the sled dogs. The injured one was curled up beside her, snoozing peacefully, while the others were padding around the room and roughhousing with each other. Evren took the time to feed them all and make sure they all had water before slipping out to rejoin the building efforts.

The next job for her was scavenging. Quite literally finding whatever was on the ship that they could use. Evren spent hours finding undamaged rope and shaking it free of stubborn frost. She dug through yards and yards of sails before she found one that was only slightly less holy than the others. She took apart furniture and unhinged doors simply for the iron nails that weren't rusted. She even unbolted the captain's desk but made sure to keep her eyes away from Gail's markings.

Nails, sails, rope, and anything else that Sorin and Sahar said they needed was dumped into piles outside. A good portion of the ice next to *Mortova's Maw* was a mess of supplies and the slowly building body of their sled-ship. It made no sense to Evren. She couldn't see either a sled or a ship being formed as Abraxas and Keres pieced wood together section by section. All she saw was them bickering over a misshapen wooden skeleton while Arke ran underfoot tempting death by nail and wood every couple hours.

Nerezza kept the area lit so everyone could see. Little orbs of fire hovered around everyone's heads as they worked. Only Keres had an issue with it, but given their aversion to fire, Evren didn't blame them. Sorin lent them the Luminstone.

She might not have any idea what she was building, but she was elbow deep with the rest of them. Sahar called out instructions and shortcuts. How to make the skeleton of their ship so it was flexible and light but wouldn't break with a hard impact. Which pieces of wood would fit best together, and how to make them airtight so they wouldn't leak when they came to water. With every nail hammered in, every plank fit into place, it started to come together. Arke would come behind them and carve some sort of rune into each set plank.

"Just in case," he'd mutter and then scamper off.

Evren didn't know what the rune was supposed to be or what it would do 'just in case.' She decided she was better off not knowing.

They all took shifts. Sleeping while some worked, and then trading off. Evren spent most of her resting time making sure the sled dogs weren't tearing up *Mortova's Maw* with all their pent-up energy. When she wasn't doing that or helping build, she was fixing their harnesses or working on sewing the sail's holes shut with Sahar.

The Long Night stretched on. The darkness never lifted. The

aurora came and went, but the only true way to tell the passing of time was by watching the moon. Evren decided she liked to remain timeless. She could boast about finishing a boat from scratch in one night.

It was little thoughts like that that kept her moving. Small jokes from Sorin that got them all smiling, despite their exhaustion. Keres would sometimes tell weird stories about the desert to pass the time as they worked. They talked about how the Waking Sands were made from the crushed bones of a thousand dragons, and that there was supposedly a whole kingdom beyond the bottomless pool in a hidden oasis. They talked of the sun, and its endless heat most of all. Evren wasn't sure they'd see either one ever again, but she listened anyway, and ignored the pang of longing in her chest.

Those wistful stories that were so obviously from a different time, all the bad jokes, and the constantly mind-numbing work wasn't enough to keep Evren's mind totally occupied. There didn't have to be silence for her to think about the little boy who ate souls and became a monster. She didn't have to be trying to sleep to think of those she'd lost. They were always there, in the back of her thoughts.

Drystan, and his longing for Sahar. His guilt over his past and what happened to Vox. He had no hope of a better life, but he still fought. A man raised by monsters who gave himself to more to save the woman he loved. Did he tell her how he felt before the undead found them? Or was that unspoken thing still tethering him and Sahar together until the very end?

Sol, who'd only been on the surface for a few months and had seen the worst it had to offer. The cold loneliness, the icy despair, and the bitter grief. Would she still look up to the sky in wonder if they got her out alive? Or would she stare down at the ground, bitter that she couldn't return home to a city she'd sacrificed it all for.

And then there was Gyda.

Evren tried not to think about her. All it did was hurt, and she wasn't sure why. Gyda had walked away from her more than once, and yes that was terrible. But she'd found Evren when she was wandering after the blizzard. Before that, she couldn't forget the night bandaging each other after hunting the wraiths. Or her easy smiles and laughter in the baths at Serevadia.

Gyda was terrifying. Both in battle and in the sense that Evren didn't know what to *do* around her. She made everything fuzzy and confusing, but the kind of hazy that was intoxicating. There was never enough time with her, the woman with the broken sword and quiet past.

Evren couldn't be angry at Gyda for coming back to the Expanse and drawing them all with her. She hadn't meant to involve them. And it wasn't like Evren didn't have her own troubled past she was running away from. They all did. But there was something gnawing at her that grew with each nail hammered down. No matter how much force she put behind her swings, she couldn't shake it. It rose and rose, filling her lungs and making her hands shake.

This energy, this *rage*, it wasn't for Gyda. She wasn't even sure it was for Gail. But she'd hone it into an arrow and aim it at him anyway. Regardless of how it happened, she was going to put him down. Whether she left the Expanse alive or not.

Evren wasn't sure when it happened. There was no massive celebration or even a collective sigh of relief. She just walked out onto the ice with the new harnesses to fit to the ship, and it was finished.

It was a mere fraction of the size of the one it was scavenged from. Its sail was dirty and rolled up, but Evren knew there would be patches from everyone's blankets sewn on it. The mast was stubby, and the rudder Sorin had designed looked hilariously out of place in the rear. It looked like some sort of broken tail that hadn't healed properly, held awkwardly above the ice.

The ship itself was rather lumpy and mismatched with all its different wood. But there were no holes in its hull, and the sled runners underneath looked sturdy enough to carry it to the bay.

"This might actually work," she whispered to herself. She didn't realize she was smiling until she felt the cold wind on her teeth.

Sorin came up behind her and wrapped his arm around her shoulders. He no longer smelled of warm seas and salt. Now it was just the musk of wood and iron. "She looks good, eh?"

"She looks sturdy?" Evren offered.

"You wound me!" he gasped. "And *Alkimos*!"

She shot him a flabbergasted look. "What?"

"I named the ship *Alkimos*."

She started to laugh. "Why?"

He shrugged and gestured to the ship. "I don't know! It reminded me of the bastard!"

Evren cackled, nearly doubling over as she held the harnesses to her chest. And oh, did she hurt. Everywhere was sore and aching, and laughing just made it worse, but she couldn't stop it. Every time she looked at the dinky little sled-ship contraption they'd made, she saw Alkimos's massive body squashing it into tiny splinters. It took her far longer than it should've to calm down. And even when she straightened up, little fits of giggles would still worm their way past her lips.

"I think he'd like it." Sorin looked like he was on the verge of pouting.

Evren looked at the *Alkimos* again and grinned. "You know what? I think he would."

"So says the Worm-Rider." He elbowed her.

The wind picked up and swept a sheet of tiny, almost dagger-like, ice crystals across their legs. Unconsciously, Evren followed the ice as it swept east. Towards the White Cairn and Gail. Towards an army of undead and, hopefully, three still living souls. If she was the praying sort, she would've been on her knees begging the Divines or the Elders for some sort of stroke of luck. But she never was one for whispering to beings long dead or gone.

"We'll make it," Sorin said, following her gaze.

"Odds are we don't make it back out, you know."

His arm tightened around her, like he was afraid she'd drift away with the wind. "At least we'll be with them if we don't."

There was that smile again. Only this time, tempered with realism and not boundless optimism. *Yes*, she thought as the sky bloomed green and blue again. *I'll be with them all again. And this time, I won't let go.*

Out loud, she made sure to sigh heavily and tear her eyes away from the imposing glacier. "Let's get this over with, yeah?"

She slipped out of Sorin's grasp, and he gazed longingly at the *Alkimos*. "You get the dogs and I'll get the others?"

Evren nodded, and they got to work.

Herding the dogs back outside was easy enough. One look at their altered harnesses and they were ready to go. They ran over each other, barking and yapping as they tumbled out into the ice. A few of them sniffed the *Alkimos* curiously, while others ran fast circles around it a few times before settling down. Evren let them get their jitters out before whistling sharply. All eyes and pointed ears turned towards her, ready and eager.

Three teams worth of sled dogs lined up. The biggest and strongest dogs in the back to pull the sled, the ones in front of them to maintain the speed, the next row for the ones that would steer the sled, and then finally the leaders. They were the smallest and the smartest. Evren's injured one was one of them, and while she still favored her paw, the look in her eyes made it clear she wasn't going to sit this one out.

Evren tightened the harness on her and made sure it was secure. Then she cupped the dog's face with her hands and rubbed her ears. "You know the way home when we let you go. Just be sure to get your friends there too."

The dog whined a little and rewarded Evren with slobbery dog kisses. She booped her snout one more time before standing up and dusting the snow off her legs. She checked all of the harnesses again, and the disconnection when she needed it. She didn't want to think about it all failing and the dogs tumbling into the frigid waters as the boat dragged them along.

Everything checked out. It would work as well as it could, given how quickly it was put together. Before she knew it, the entire ship was packed and ready to go. Everyone was onboard, fixing the falling sail and taking their places. Evren climbed on board while something like excitement burned in her belly.

"Think it'll hold?" Arke asked as she settled down.

"We built it well, thanks to Sahar and Sorin." She tried to be reassuring. "Why? Are you worried?"

His yellow eyes narrowed and he hugged his spellbook. "Sure, 'cause our last boat ride went so well, right?"

Evren grimaced. "Okay, that's . . . , fair. But this is different."

"Yeah, I doubt there's any murder-maids waitin' for us in those waters. Too damn cold."

"At least we'll die quickly in those temperatures."

"Not helpin'," he growled.

They sat still, side by side as the *Alkimos* was prepped for its first, and most likely last, voyage. Sahar sealed some more gaps with some sticky paste she'd made, and Nerezza dried it with some fire behind her. Abraxas tied everything down, and kept Keres glued to their seat in the very middle of the ship. All the while, Sorin ran up and down the deck what must've been a thousand times to make sure everything was all right. Finally, he passed by Evren, and she grabbed his arm and pulled him to a stop.

"It's ready, Sorin," she said. When he started to protest, she cut him off. "So are you. Let's go."

He closed his mouth and nodded. She squeezed his arm one last time before letting go. Sorin continued walking back to the rudder at the very rear of the ship. He sat down beside it, gripping it hard enough for the wood to creak. "Anyone wanna get off?"

Halfhearted murmurs rose up, but everyone shook their heads. They were all looking at Sorin, and Evren watched his chest swell with pride. His eyes swam with tears as he smiled.

"Let's go get this bastard. For *our* family."

He nodded to Evren, and she whistled again, sharp and clear. All at once, the dogs barked in response and then leapt forward. The *Alkimos* shuddered underneath her, and then started to move. Slowly, just inches at a time, until the wind was whipping through her hair so fast her eyes were tearing up. Arke huddled behind her to get out of the wind, but the more speed they picked up the more it felt like flying.

Mortova's Maw fell away until it was little more than a dark speck on the horizon. The *Alkimos* sped across the ice with abandon. The dogs rushed forward, the landscape becoming a white-and-black blur.

Evren clutched the railing and pulled herself to her feet. The whipping air took her breath away and snaked into her clothes, chilling her to her core. Overhead, the stars wheeled behind the brilliant aurora, snaking ever forward towards the White Cairn.

She closed her eyes and felt her stomach flip. It really was like flying. She could've laughed if the wind didn't steal that from her as well. But it was exhilarating all the same. The feel of the sky as she imagined it rushing below her, the world falling away from her with each passing moment. It was almost magical.

No wonder Sorin missed sailing so much.

Evren forced herself to pry open her eyes. She watched the Expanse tumbled past them in a whirl of snow and churned ice. They passed packs of running wolves hashing reindeer, ruins of cold, empty villages, and dark skeletons of creatures she couldn't name, with vertebrae as long as the *Alkimos*.

There was still so much she didn't know about in this cold wasteland. Life that found a way, and the remnants of what didn't. How many secrets did this corner of Eith keep hidden behind its cold grasping fingers? Was she still the same woman who'd risk everything to pry them open?

No, she thought with a twinge of pride. *No, I'm not. And I can live with that, if I live at all.*

The next hour was a blur of speeding past landmarks and watching the horizon darken with the black water of Myrefall Bay looming ever closer. They weren't far from the water. She could smell the sea in the air again. With each passing mile, the lights of the aurora continued zipping into the White Cairn. Its white expanse of towering ice rose higher and higher, until she couldn't see the sky behind it without looking straight up. Slowly it grew, like a predator rising to meet its foolish prey.

Evren's throat was tight, and she had to force herself to look away from the glacier. Soon that's all she would see. Soon, it could very well be the tomb that held her body with hundreds of others. She looked down. She broke eye contact. Until she saw something else, and her blood ran cold.

"Sorin!" She turned around. He was still guiding the ship from the back, but at her panicked voice, he stood up. "Undead!"

She pointed, but they all saw them now. A single line, stretching across the coast. Bodies with unblinking glowing greenish blue eyes. The aurora seemed to swirl in their sockets like it did the sky above. They were tightly packed, shoulder to shoulder, and getting closer by the minute.

"They were waiting for us!" Abraxas shouted.

"There's no way around." Sahar confirmed her fears.

And they were all looking at Sorin. Their time was dwindling. The dogs wouldn't stop unless they told them to, and even then, they hadn't built brakes into the ship. They didn't think they'd need them.

Sorin hesitated long enough for half a mile to pass before locking eyes with Evren. "Let the dogs go."

She nodded, even while Nerezza argued, and scrambled to the front of the ship.

"Are you insane?" she cried. "We're not close enough to the shore!"

Sorin pointed a jerky finger at the sail. "It'll have to be enough."

"Over the undead?"

Evren heard Arke cackle in the wind. "Inertia's a bitch!"

All other arguments faded from her ears. Evren bent over the edge of the ship and tugged off her thick gloves. Immediately the air stung her skin like a thousand bees. She stuffed her gloves between her teeth and bent over further. The ice was rushing past her at a dizzying speed. She had to squint to ignore it. The dogs were moving incredibly fast. She worked on the latches. One for each team.

One latch fell off easily, and she threw the loose leather to the side. The dogs veered off with it, slowing down to a trot as the ship whizzed by them.

The next latch was harder. A piece of ice was welded into the metal, and she had to slam her fist down on it one, two, three times before it finally snapped off. Her hand was bleeding. The second team joined the rest, and she passed them by.

The last team. The one helmed by her injured dog. Evren made a point not to look up to see the undead. She didn't want to see how close they were. But her fingers were numbing in the wind. Raw and red and angry, they were fumbling with the latch too much. She cursed around her gloves, her vision blurring as panic started to seep in again. She wasn't going to lose the damn dog, too!

Screaming in frustration, Evren attacked the latch one more time. So hard she felt like her skin was peeling off. But with a satisfying snap, it broke free. She tossed away the leads and pulled herself up just in time to see her leader pull her team away from the undead.

She let herself smile and relax. No sooner had she slipped her gloves back on, did one of the undead leap over the bow of the ship and slam into her.

Evren was knocked onto her back. Her head smacked against the wood and her eyes sparked with stars. The undead gave a sucking screech and lunged for her throat. Her numb hands were all that held it back. She could feel the cold seeping through its bones as her hands dug into its rotting flesh. She tried not to gag.

Those eyes. Those aurora eyes. It was all she could see. Beyond the black gums and chipped teeth. The flesh just sloughed off the bones with every jerky movement.

Every stolen breath Evren heaved was laced with decay but felt like a victory. It snapped at her throat, teeth gnashing close enough that she could feel the air push through them onto her bare skin.

Then she smelled fire, and she bared her teeth.

She shoved them back with all her might and let them go. They immediately rushed back towards her but were thrown backwards by a ball of fire. The hungry flames engulfed their dead flesh, and Evren kicked their writhing body over the railing.

She flipped over and pushed herself to her knees. Arke stood only a few feet from her, his hands still smoking as ash fluttered down to a pile at his feet. They nodded to each other sharply before turning back to the rest of the ship.

Undead were crawling over the edges. Not a horde, but enough. Abraxas and Keres fought back-to-back. His black sword slashed through the hearts of the corpses, and Keres's fingers grew long and pointed like talons before they ripped hearts out with their bare hands. But the cold made Keres's slow, and they were hard pressed to keep the undead away. Nerezza and Sahar kept the undead off the side as much as they could, spells and jars shattering fire with every passing second. Sorin was still standing at the rudder, eyes wide, but locked on the fast-approaching water.

Evren drew her bow without thinking. Beside her, Arke was crumbling fists of paper into fire again. She shot down at an undead as it threw itself at Sorin and watched it reel backwards until it fell. The next one burst into flames so hot it was reduced to ashes in a matter of seconds.

Ice-cold hands raked along her scalp and yanked a fistful of her hair. Evren yelped, her next arrow going wide and narrowly missing Keres. She grasped at the hand over her head and felt teeth sink into her forearm. She screamed in pain; her vision suddenly sharp once again as blood seeped into her armor.

She gritted her teeth against the sudden surge of strength and smashed her head backwards. She felt the skull behind her crack under the impact, and her own head riot in pain. But it was enough. The teeth let go, the grip on her hair loosened. She whirled around, brought her fist up, and slammed it into the already cracked skull of the undead. It tumbled over the edge, still clawing at her.

Evren was gasping for breath, trying to ignore how close its teeth had been to her throat, when she saw another problem. The water was only a few feet away, and there were no more undead. And no beach either. The drop into the water was at least twenty feet straight down.

"Sorin!" she screamed.

"I see it!" He sounded like he was in pain, but Evren couldn't tear her eyes away from the ledge. "Hold on!"

Without thinking twice, Evren grabbed Arke by the scruff, and ran away from the front of the ship. He didn't fight her. Not even as the undead piled over the edge. Not as the floor started to tilt underneath her feet.

She slammed to the floor as the ground fell out from under them, and gripped Arke hard enough to bruise. She'd left her stomach on the cliff's edge, her breathing too quick to be useful. She watched the undead fall away from the boat as it plummeted down, down, down, and her friends grasped for the railings, some rope, and even each other.

The fall wasn't a long one. Even so, the impact was enough to tear what little breath she had from her lungs. Her teeth clacked painfully as her chin slammed into the wood. Water flew up from the bay and then rained down on them like sharp, ice-cold daggers. The ship bobbed dangerously back and forth, tipping to the point where Evren could see the water over the railing, until, bit by bit, it steadied out.

Soaked through, bleeding, and incredibly sore, Evren pushed herself up on her elbows. Arke wiggled out from underneath her. She looked around, counting heads, and relaxed when she saw everyone was cold, wet, and scared shitless, but alive.

From the very back, Sorin shook the water out of his hair and laughed. "We made it!"

21

Myrefall Bay reeked of cold and death.

Abraxas let down the sail. It unfurled its patchwork canvas in all its splendor, already catching some of the wind. Evren could see the spots where they'd used each of their sleeping bags, and some of their cloaks. She saw Vox's deep green cloak taking up the right corner, and Keres staring at it with a strange look.

The *Alkimos* cut slowly through the icy waters.

Evren had expected the ice. Pockets of jagged icebergs poking out like massive missing teeth from the pitch-black waters, or even solid, dagger-thin sheets blocking their path. The waves rocked the *Alkimos* steadily back and forth, and the chunks of ice Sorin couldn't avoid bumped into the hull with dull, scraping thuds that made Evren's teeth grind. It was like each piece was a separate tooth of a massive predator, slowly tearing the ship apart.

"Good thing I got them runes on here." Arke buried himself deeper in his furs until only his eyes were visible.

"That's what they were for?"

"I don't mind dyin' for a cause, but I'd like to get there first. Not drowned before I can do shit."

"Thanks," was all she said. That's all she could muster in the cold light of the glacier.

Evren didn't hear Arke waddle off as she stared into the water. She didn't hear Keres approach either, but she smelled them. She wrinkled her nose and scooted over as they settled next to her at the bow of the ship.

Stretched ahead and towering over them was a sheet of deep blue and white. They were close enough now that Evren could see a glow emanating from within the White Cairn, pulsing blue and green with every passing minute. They inched ever closer, knocking away more ice with every gained foot.

"Something you said has been bothering me." Evren finally spoke.

"Oh?" Keres looked over at her with mock surprise. "Just the one?"

She ignored the jab. "Back in Direwall. You called Sol King slayer. You told me to prick my finger to kill Mortova. It's like you knew more about us than even we did. So, how?"

They flicked a chip of wood off into the water. It landed with a soft splash, and the ripples were eaten up by the waves the *Alkimos* left in its wake. "It seems like you have a working theory."

Evren worried her lip. "Maybe. Maybe you haven't been completely honest with me. Maybe you've been watching us since the very beginning."

"Before the Black Pass?"

"Before Dirn-Darahl."

This made Keres freeze. They stopped picking at the wood with their twitchy fingers and finally turned to look her in the eye. Try as she might, she couldn't read them. No emotion was given away in those cold, dead features. Nothing except a plain, blatant curiosity. Evren's skin started to crawl as they just stared at her.

"What manner of creature have you been consorting with?" they asked.

"I was hoping you could tell me."

The floor shuddered underneath their feet as they hit another piece of ice, but neither of them broke eye contact.

Finally, Keres shrugged their bony shoulders. "I haven't left this place, Evren. I do not travel beyond the Black Pass for many reasons. The first and most important is because I am not whole. I'm missing my soul, my power, and a great deal of the history of my people that I had stored in my memories. Whatever you think I am, whatever you've seen, I can assure you I've had nothing to do with it."

Evren bit back a hiss of frustration. "Then how did you know those things about us?"

"The same way I know Sorin has lost his magic and feels helpless. The same way I know that Lady Al-Fasil carries enough regrets to drown this whole boat of people ten times over. And that Nerezza is more worried about you than the task at hand."

Evren opened and closed her mouth a few times before something came out. "*How?*"

"You're thinking about it." Keres waved their boney hand in the air. "No, it's not mind reading. Vernes is known for its necromancy, but divination goes hand in hand with such magic. And when you become something other than living or dead, and have been that way for a long time, you can hear things. Your thoughts are loud, and they are like music to my dead ears. You think about your blood a lot, and your friends. The number of times you think abouts dogs and sugar rolls is honestly disturbing."

Evren's ears would've grown hot if they weren't freezing. But Keres went on as if nothing was wrong.

"Solri was always thinking about the King and the mistakes she made. The only thing louder was her loyalty to you." Keres looked her up and down. "You seem to tie it all together, Evren Hanali."

She blew a piece of hair out of her face. "So I've been told."

"Abraxas thinks his gods are back," Keres noted.

"I know."

"They aren't."

"I know that too."

"And yet, Sorin lives. Not without consequence. Not without scars both on the surface and far deeper. But he lives. Does that concern you?"

She hesitated and drew her eyes to the water. A chunk of ice as big as the ship was drifting closer. "Yes."

"But not as much as whatever was behind his resurrection."

Evren pressed her lips together in a firm line. She refused to look at Keres. "I was always taught that death was final. That there was no coming back from it. But now, ever since I started adventuring, it feels like the balance is off. Death isn't permanent, life isn't always good. I can't tell if that's because I'm finally seeing Eith more wholly than before or if it's not a coincidence."

"And the being you thought was me?"

"They know too much," she whispered. "They knew about Serevadia when no one else did. They warned me about the aurora. And they always show up before these adventures, all melodramatic and cryptic. I just . . ." She sighed and bowed her head. "I want answers but I'm working with the pieces of ten different puzzles and none of them seem to fit."

"Either that, or one very large puzzle."

Despite it all, Evren felt herself smile. She watched the water as thoughts of what came next crept ever closer.

"If you make it out of the White Cairn with your body and mind intact, perhaps you should sit this being down and interrogate them."

Evren wanted to laugh, but nothing came out. "Maybe I will. Or I'll just toss you at them."

"Bold of you to assume I'm leaving with you."

"Where will you go?" Evren asked as she peaked back up at them. "Eith has changed a lot since you've been here. It'll be confusing."

"Everything is confusing if you're dead. Life is too fast and bright; everyone won't stop talking and thinking at the same time. More often than not, I'm always confused. But I plan to be whole again after this, and perhaps go home." They gave her a long look. "You don't think Abraxas will let me."

She shook her head. "I think he'll kill you before you have the chance to leave."

An almost human smirk found its way onto Keres's borrowed face. It almost looked like Vox again. "I'd like to see him try."

"I won't let him."

Keres blinked at her as the smirk fell. They looked truly and completely baffled. "Why?"

Evren thought for a moment and let the idea of her words floating out her ears and into the air simmer for a moment. She smiled over at them. "I think you already know."

Their face softened. "I . . . Yes, I suppose I do."

The piece of ice finally bumped into them and nearly knocked Evren off her feet. She picked up an extra piece of wood from the floor. It had been warped too much by Arke, but he'd stubbornly kept it in the boat for a reason only known to the goblin himself. She took it in her hands and brought it up to push the boat away from the ice. But as she was bridging it down, Kere's rotting hand wrapped around her wrist and pulled her back.

"Don't." they hissed.

She reeled back. "Why?"

They pointed towards the ice, and for the first time Evren truly forced herself to look deeper into the iceberg. She saw swirling white and deep blue sea ice. But as it rocked back and forth against the waves, the light shifted. Suddenly, the ice wasn't clear anymore. It held a frozen corpse, mid-swim, eyes wide as he stared at her with an open, gaping mouth.

Evren yelped and dropped the wood. Keres carefully nudged the iced away, their face grim as the *Alkimos* continued its steady course towards the White Cairn.

"No respect for the dead." They sneered towards the glacier. "The boy is a monster."

"None for the living either," Evren pointed out.

"That's why you're here. Among other reasons." They looked back at her. "We get back my soul and power, you get Gyda back."

Evren frowned. "And Sol and Drystan."

Keres smiled wryly. "You weren't thinking about them."

~

EVREN's first thought when they saw the massive slit in the base of the glacier welcoming them in was that Gail was expecting them. Her second thought was to take the long climb up just to spite him. No one else agreed.

The entrance into the White Cairn was tall and slender, barely wide enough for the *Alkimos* to fit into without the sides of the hull scraping the ice walls. The cavern reminded her of a cathedral, with its tall, pointed ceiling and hollow emptiness. Her quickened breaths could barely be heard bouncing off the walls as the sea water lapped against the hull. The chill settled deep into her bones long before the view of the bay slipped out of sight. Before long, it was nothing but a long, achingly tall tunnel of water leading them deeper into the White Cairn. No one dared to say anything to break the fragile silence.

The ice turned a deep, enchanting blue the further they went. Shimmers of green danced in the ice, like the aurora was captured in the glacier itself. The same way she used to catch fireflies in jars. The thought didn't calm her.

Sahar's fingers grazed the ice as they passed. "Beautiful." Her voice echoed across the waters.

"Dangerous," Abraxas countered. "Be ready for anything."

It was a good order. It kept Evren busy for a whole two minutes as she got her bow out and checked her arrows. Another minute passed with her making sure her armor was on right. The only hole she had was on her forearm, and she'd take that over a missing throat any day.

As they sailed ever deeper into the glacier, Sorin was practically itching in the back. "Shouldn't we see more undead?" he asked. "After that show at the shore, I expected more security."

"That's because it was a show," Nerezza said. "He wants us here."

Sorin shivered. "I hate that."

But Nerezza was right, and no one argued with her. Gail wanted them to come to him. For revenge for killing Mortova or to add to his growing horde. But so long as they weren't being overrun, Evren told herself that it was a good thing. Over and over.

Looking at Keres, they didn't seem to believe her.

Her grip on her bow was tight enough to break bones. It only got worse as the hull started scraping, and their slow inch forward turned into an agonizing crawl. Looking into the water, she saw the black had cleared to water she could actually see through. It was shallower, and growing more so by the foot. The sled runners still attached to the bottom didn't make that much better.

"I can see a beach," Keres announced as they peered ahead.

"Any palm trees?" Sorin asked. "Coconuts? White sand?"

Keres ignored him. "We'll run aground unless we pull it to shore."

Evren looked down at the water. "I don't think that's healthy for any of us."

They stood up. "Maybe not for you. Lady Al-Fasil, are we in need of the sail? No? Then let's use that rope for something better."

The ship had come to a complete halt before Keres was wrapped in a length of rope and splashing through the water. They pulled the ship up the icy shore, inch by inch, as the sled runners met solid ice. It was slow going, and Evren could see pieces of Vox's body tearing under the strain. But Keres gave no signs of discomfort, and before long the *Alkimos* was out of the water completely.

The shore was as narrow and slick. Evren's boots slid dangerously underneath her with every step. Beyond the shore, was the mouth of yet another tunnel. This one was blissfully devoid of water.

"Did I mention I hate caves?" Arke asked.

"Yeah." Sorin picked him up and put him on his shoulders. "You mentioned it a few times. And water."

"Perfumes and incense," Abraxas added.

"Don't forget spicy foods." Evren grinned. "And dwarves."

"The outdoors!" Sorin said. "Oh! And very nice taverns."

"Uneven ground, rain, and the quiet."

Sitting on Sorin's shoulders, Arke's scowl got comically deeper with every comment. "I hate all of y'all too."

"Adding it to an already long list." Sorin shrugged and the goblin bounced up and down. The jovial atmosphere dampened the moment silence fell. The small tunnel ahead of them looked inconspicuous of the horrors they knew lay past it.

"I really don't," Arke said, suddenly sounding smaller than he looked. "Hate you, I mean."

"We know." Evren swallowed the lump in her throat.

She took a step forward and ignored the shiver that went through her whole body. The tunnel's walls closed over her, and the air seemed to get even colder. With every step, she felt like she was walking into a grave. Her friends followed her, until the little beach they'd left their ship was hidden behind one, two, three winding corners. Until they were walking forward through the veins of the glacier, where the living most certainly shouldn't be.

The walls shimmered and pulsed. The floors and ceilings too. It was dizzying, and more than once Evren had the sense that she was walking into dead-ends rather than going anywhere. She was suddenly reminded of the little festival Orenlion would hold once a year, and the maze of mirrors she'd run into and get lost for hours in. Running with a dozen different copies of herself while her father called her name outside and she giggled with wild excitement. Until the excitement ebbed away, and she still wasn't out of the maze and her father was no longer calling for her. Until fear creeped up in her throat and threatened to choke her.

This was no maze. There were no mirror copies of herself, and her father wasn't waiting outside with a basket of treats and a relaxed smile. The threat was real this time, but she wasn't alone.

In the far back, Nerezza's voice sounded like it was miles away. "Keep straight, Evren."

"No branching paths so that's not a problem. Why?"

"Glaciers are moving, remember? I'd hate for us to defeat Gail and free our friends only to have lost our way and the ice cover us in a matter of days"

"We won't be down here that long," she countered, but doubt had found its way in her mind. She kept one hand on the ice, and one of her bow. Just like she would've done in a maze. A part of her wanted to mark the wall every couple of feet, but she kept thinking of the frozen body in the drifting ice. She didn't see anything in the walls yet, but she didn't want to tempt fate.

With every slippery step deeper, every sucking, painful breath, something foreboding ate at her resolve. She heard nothing, saw nothing, and yet she could feel herself being watched. It wasn't the same uneasy feeling as with Keres. This made her body revolt in fear. Every bone of instinct she'd gathered over the years was screaming at her to leave. It was like her whole skeleton was pulling her in the opposite direction.

Don't go forward, it seemed to beg. *Don't keep walking. Turn around!*

It was like an itch she couldn't scratch creeping across her skin. This deep, burning anxiety that wouldn't leave her. Without her permission, her lungs started to constrict. Her breaths were too short, the air too thin. She couldn't breathe.

314 | GILLIAN GRANT

She needed to turn around.

Evren gave in to her fear. She whipped around, hands latching on to both walls to steady herself. An apology was already at the tip of her tongue for Sorin, who was going to run into her and throw Arke into a heap on the ground.

But there was no one behind her.

Evren's breaths came faster now. Too fast to be of any use. The tunnel was empty, devoid of all life and one snarky corpse. Where had they gone? How had they left without her hearing them?

Why?

"Sorin?" her strangled voice cried out. "Abraxas?"

Nothing but her own echoes bouncing back to her.

"Arke?" Her voice was barely a wheeze at this point. What little air was in her lungs had gone into that one name, and then they deflated.

She fell on her knees, gasping for air. Her fingers clawed at her throat, and her chest. Her scar burned like it was a fresh scab being ripped off. She wished she had claws so she could do it herself. She wished she could tear a hole out in her throat so she could *breathe*. But all she had were dull, useless fingernails scraping against her skin.

Hot tears pricked at her eyes. Her vision started to blur. From the lack of air or the tears? She coughed and squeezed her eyes shut. It didn't matter. Her lungs were burning. She could feel the fresh air against her skin. She could taste it on her tongue. But it never found its way into her lungs.

I'm dying, she thought with enough panic to send another useless gasp crawling up her tight throat. *I'm dying and I can't even fight it.*

A pair of hands were shaking her shoulders. When had that happened? They were warm. Bright, like twin suns. Shaking her gently.

". . . Evren?" The voice came to her ringing ears. Soft, but scattered. She only heard pieces. ". . . ren, look at me. Open your eyes!"

That she could do.

Evren snapped her eyes open, and nearly fell on her back. Her eyes were flooded with color. Warm reds and golds, browns and bronzes. Pure, rich sunlight fell on her, filtered only by the red of the leaves still clinging to the massive trees that soared above her head, taller than the lighthouses. Wide enough for several people to link arms around and still not all touch.

"Evren!"

She started, staring at the man before her with wide, unbelieving eyes. He was crouched in front of her. A young elf. Round face and high cheekbones. Warm, heavy-lidded eyes full of concern. Strawberry-blond hair falling out of the hasty braid down his back.

"Aster?" she wheezed, and then coughed more.

He rubbed her shoulders, helping the fit pass. "Hey, you're back! You're all right. Just-just take deep breaths, okay? Nice and slow. With me. In and out. In and out. Good, one more time."

With his guidance, Evren forced her quivering lungs to open, one breath at a time. With each successful lungful, she felt herself starting to relax. Her tense muscles were loosening, the stress falling from her like melting snow.

"There." Aster let go of her, and the warmth instantly faded. She started shivering. "Better?"

No.

"I think so." She looked around, eyes drinking in the colors as if she hadn't seen them in years. "What happened?"

Aster shrugged. "Moon above, I have no idea. We were walking along and suddenly you collapsed. You haven't had one of those fits in years, Evren. Are you sure you're all right?"

"I don't know." She shook her head. "I can't remember what we were doing."

He let out a bark of laughter. "You drag me out of bed and through the woods and you can't remember why?"

Little pieces of memory started flashing back. Sneaking into
Aster's room. Throwing his boots at him. Urging him to hurry
up and *for the love of the Elders be quiet!*

"A little . . ." she admitted. "I guess that fit was a really bad
one."

"I guess so." He stood up and held his hand out to her. At
her sour expression he said, "Oh, come on. You can accept help
every once and a while."

"I'm fine," she retorted, but took his hand anyway. As she
was pulled back to her feet, she had the sudden thought that she
wasn't supposed to take his hand. She brushed off the leaves
clinging to her pants. Her hand came back damp.

Aster turned around and started walking forward. "Right,
well, come on! We have a forest to save and all that. Can't keep
lagging behind."

"Right," she said slowly. She followed him, eyes still on the
trees above her. She didn't think she'd see them again. Then she
frowned. What an odd thought to have. She *lived* in the Deep
Wood. There was nothing but these trees to look at.

She picked her way over roots bigger around than she was,
hopping down into their little valleys of fallen leaves before
climbing up another one. Always ahead of her, Aster made good
time, as if he could see easier paths that she couldn't. Which was
ridiculous because Aster barely left Orenlion and was usually
always stumbling behind her.

As if reading her thoughts, he paused panting at the base of
the tree and waited for her. When she finally joined him, he
threw his hands up.

"I give up!" he exclaimed. "I have no idea where I'm going."

"You seemed very sure of yourself a couple minutes ago."

"Well, of course! You weren't up to leading. Are you still
okay, by the way? You look a little pale."

She thought about it for a moment. "I'm cold."

"It's autumn."

"I'm colder than that." She shook her head. "I can't explain it."

"It could be the Heart's magic, you know," Aster offered. "I don't feel it, but you've always been more connected to the forest. Maybe we should follow it."

Evren felt a flash of irritation. She was tired of being cold. But as soon as it sparked to life, it was gone, and she was just tired again. She racked her brain for ideas, memories. Why was everything so damn slow and fuzzy?

"The Heart," she murmured, rubbing her eyes, and trying to focus. "We have to find the Heart. Cure it, heal it . . . or something."

"Yes, that's why we're here." He frowned. "Well, partially. I know you're also delaying the inevitable."

"Funny word for wedding," she said and turned away from him. Find the Heart. Cure it. Go home. Use it as leverage against the wedding? What a terrible plan. But it's all she had.

She took a step forward and let her boots slide along the piles of dying leaves. The cloying scent of sweet, earthy decay filled her nostrils. She was suddenly reminded of hot sands and deserts, and some absurd story about a city at the bottom of an oasis. Odd.

At the bottom of the roots, she looked ahead. Two paths from what she could pick out. All her life living in these woods, and they bent to her will. *Show me the way out.* She urged them, and they did. One path leading west, and another leading sharply north.

The western path looked promising. Deeper into the forest and getting more and more choked with vines and massive tree trunks as the trail went on. If one was to find the Heart, it would be there.

The northern path made her feel sick again. Like her lungs were already constricting for some unknown reason. It was colder there, too, like she was drawing closer to a pile of snow. It felt wrong, and yet she found her feet going that direction anyway.

"Hey!" Aster's voice stopped her short. "Where are you going?"

"This way." She pointed.

"That's not the right way."

"Not for you." She didn't know where the words came from, they just felt right. The look of hurt in his hazel eyes made her stomach twist into knots. "I'm sorry, Aster. I just can't follow you that way."

Something was tugging her north. More than one thing. It was like she had a bunch of ropes tied to her waist and they were all tugging on her incessantly. While she knew west was the right way to the Heart,—she knew it deep in her bones—she also knew she didn't need to go there. Not yet. Not anymore.

"So, this is it?" he asked. "This is how you leave? *Again*? Because you're always leaving me, Evren. I know the situation is terrible but . . . am I really that awful to be tied to? I can think of worse people to marry."

"You're my best friend," she said, and felt like she was reading a script. "But I don't love you."

"You don't have to! We'd just be partners. Us against the world, like it always is. One ceremony won't change that."

"It'll change everything," she insisted. She could feel the northern cold creeping up her back and shoulder blades. "And you know it."

"You won't even give me a chance, will you?" He laughed bitterly, his eyes uncomfortably bright. "You'll just run off and leave. Like you always do. Never mind that we could make it work. That I would never push you to do something you weren't comfortable with. We could grow to love each other but you refuse to allow yourself that."

"Goodbye, Aster."

She turned and walked away. North. There were a million things she'd said, a thousand more that she didn't. She kept both options locked behind her tight lips. With every step she felt that dread creep back up her spine, and Aster didn't stop yelling.

"I know I was never enough, but you could've given me a chance! One chance, Evren! Out of the thousands I gave you! And you still turn your back on me like everyone else!"

She blocked him out. As she'd done before. The first time she'd left him. The fifth. The last. Although she knew she'd found the Heart before that. Somehow, even though she couldn't remember. She knew that without a doubt.

Evren couldn't remember when the Deep Wood suddenly turned to ice. One minute she was among trees and birds and golden leaves, and then next she was plunged into an icy tomb alight with the fire of an aurora. And she was still utterly alone.

Gritting her teeth, Evren rubbed her face over and over again.

"Mind games," she seethed and glared at the ice. "You want to play like that? I've had my head toyed with by a priestess who makes your attempt feel like a pleasant stroll. And I beat her! What do you think I'll do to you once I find you?"

The walls pulsed but didn't answer.

Evren swallowed and looked around. She needed a plan. She needed to find her friends. But there was only one way forward, and she couldn't go back.

She picked her bow back up and let air hiss out between her teeth. And then she set out to find the heart of the White Cairn.

22

The glacier was moving.

With every passing minute Evren could feel it. The ice cracked and heaved, so audible now that she was alone. It wasn't enough to knock her off balance. She could barely feel it at all. There was just this keen knowledge that stood her hairs on end after what Nerezza had said. That the doorway out was going to swallow them whole like the mouth of a whale. That they could win and it wouldn't matter. The White Cairn would become their tomb.

The ice was easier to listen to than Aster's voice. It was still there, echoing in the ice, calling for her. Sometimes pleading, other times furious. A tiny part of her broke every time she turned away. That wasn't her friend, not really. She couldn't waste time searching for a phantom when she had real people to find.

There was never a break in the tunnel. Never another path to choose. It was always the same curling, slippery path she'd been following since the beginning. She always kept one hand on the ice though. It didn't look like a maze, but she'd lost her whole team to it anyway.

It seemed like she walked for hours and she grew colder and

colder. Her teeth chattered constantly, until that's all she could hear. Bones against bones, no more shifting ice. She couldn't stop her body from wanting to curl into itself. Try as she might, the farther she went, the more hunched she became. Her core muscles spasmed and grew tight, and each breath was a victory, albeit a small one.

The light started to grow brighter, but there was nothing warm about it. If anything, the cool blues and greens made her feel like she was drowning in a glowing sea. But she pressed on, eyes forward, hand on the ice wall.

Until it fell out beneath her fingers completely. Evren shouted in surprise as her whole body tumbled where she'd been leaning only seconds ago. She barely caught herself; legs and feet tangling uselessly as they slid until she skidded to a stop.

Panting, she took a moment to calm down. Bit by bit, she forced her core to unlock and let her straighten up. She groaned with the effort, but soon stood in what she realized was a small circular cavern. The ice dripped water periodically here, in tiny little pools in the corner. The sound was so strange after nothing but bone and ice.

Evren's breath stopped for a few short seconds as she saw who sat in the middle. A dwarf with white-blonde hair and eyes like the sky. She was shivering in her seat on the ice, and staring listlessly in the distance.

"Sol?" Evren couldn't believe her luck. She wanted to laugh and cry. She knelt down beside her. "Sol! It's Evren."

She didn't answer. She just stared ahead, unblinking. Unmoving. Evren's short-lived smile faded.

Sol didn't look dead. There was red in her cheeks and nose from the cold. Her lips trembled and her eyes were wet but not quite teary. Her hands were clasped tightly in her lap. But those eyes were hers. No glowing, just pure sky.

Evren lifted her hand, hesitation and fear and the damned cold making her shake like she'd never done before. She tried to steady herself, looking her friend in the eyes as she did. "Sol, I know you can hear me. Maybe I don't seem real. But I'm here now. And I'm not leaving without you."

She touched her shoulder. To wake her up and shake her out of it like she did every morning when she refused to get out of bed before dawn broke. As she did, she felt a wave of vertigo assault her body and she wheeled backwards.

Only now she didn't see a cave, she saw a tomb.

There were no windows. The stonework was smooth and exquisite in its detail. It was inlaid in gold and sparkling gemstones; far more wealth than most kingdoms had in a whole city. Rows and rows of heavy stone coffins were laid out along the walls. Each was adorned with different gems, precious metals, and mosaics.

But standing in the middle wasn't a coffin. It was a body, and a weeping woman.

Sol was sitting in front of a large stone pedestal, sobbing, but never taking her eyes off the body in front of her. It was a dwarven woman, old but beautiful. Her silver hair had been carefully and intricately braided and adorned with beads of stone and metal. Her frail, cold hands had many rings, and her clothes were fine but simple. Her mouth was frowning, even in death, but Evren saw her beauty, and the resemblance to Sol.

She stood there for a while, unable to move as Sol knelt beside her mother's body. She could see the numerous trinkets and gifts that would be buried with her, that would carry her to the afterlife to the rest of her family. Amidst it all, in her drab leathers and furs, Sol was the most tarnished thing in the room.

"I'm so sorry," Sol choked out between sobs. She grabbed her mother's hand. "Mama, I should've been here. I shouldn't have left you alone. I should have stayed." She bent her head over her mother's body, pressing her forehead against her ringed hand and muttering softly under her breath. "Forgive me. Forgive me, mama, I'll be by your side soon."

Was this a memory, like Evren's had been? Had Sol's mother died, and she'd been too oblivious to see the signs? But, even if

Evren's vision had been a memory, it was a wrong one. Enough to entice and confuse. Nothing felt right or wrong. The only constant was the cold always creeping up her back.

Again, Evren's hand shook as she reached out and touched Sol's shoulder. Her friend jumped like she'd been hit and whirled around so fast she nearly knocked Evren off her feet. Her eyes went wide and were brimming with tears.

"You . . ." Sol's hand went to her mouth. "But you're . . ."

She smiled gently through her own tears. "Hi."

An uncontrollable sob wrenched its way out of Sol's chest and then she was hugging Evren. And Evren, who'd been reaching out to her ghost since Direwall, wrapped her up so tightly that she couldn't tell where one of them ended and the other began.

Sol was sobbing into her chest. "How? How are you here? You were dead! I saw you die. I saw you all die . . ."

Evren shook her head as a tear fell into Sol's hair. "I'm not dead. I don't know what you saw, but I'm alive. We all are."

She jerked out of the hug, her eyes narrowed and serious through all the wet tears. "That doesn't make sense. I watched you die."

"I saw the same for you." She gripped her shoulders. "This isn't real, Sol. Maybe a part of it is something he can draw on, but what you've seen is wrong. I'm alive. I'm here. And I'm getting you out."

"He?"

"The Prime."

"I don't . . ."

"What's the last thing you remember?"

Her brow furrowed and her eyes went to her boots. "We were fighting together. Sorin had just died, and you went to kill Heliodar but she-she got you first. There was so much blood and when it was done it was just me. I was alone. I . . ." She looked up at Evren with horrified eyes. "I murdered the King. I caused all of this. All because I was angry, and I blamed him, and I took

vengeance in my own hands instead of justice. I ruined everything by killing him! My home, my honor, my friends. I'd lost it
all and now I've lost Mama and I'm so alone! Jalaa help me, I'm
so tired of being alone."

Sol put her head in her hands, openly weeping again. But
Evren was smiling. She coaxed her head back up and wiped away
her tears with her clean sleeve.

"I'm about to make your day." She grinned. "We beat
Heliodar months ago. Sorin is alive. We're all alive. Your mother
sent you with enough gold and fruitcakes to drown you when
you left the city."

"I-I left Dirn-Darahl?"

She nodded. "You did. It took us hours to get past the gates
because you took one look at the sky and thought you were
going to fall into it. You had to wear a hood for the first three
days. Do you remember?"

She sniffled. "I think so."

Evren squeezed her shoulders the same way Aster used to
squeeze hers to make her feel better. "You did kill the King."

Sol shook her head. "Why? Why did I?"

"I've been asking myself that question for a long time,"
Evren said. "But it doesn't matter. Not to me, or Sorin, or
anyone that matters. You killed a frail old man too weak to
lead his city, and maybe it was the wrong way. Maybe you
should have waited for everyone to see what he let happen.
But it's done now. You're with us, a Wandering Sol, on the
surface and saving the world one terrible decision after
another."

"I don't . . ." Sol shook her head. "The surface. Where
are we?"

"We went to Keld's Outpost for work. You never stopped
complaining about the cold and the snow."

"Keld . . ." she whispered, and then her eyes brightened.
"The demon goat!"

"Yes!"

"You set him loose on the outpost so we could get out and find Gyda." Her face fell again. "Oh Jalaa, Gyda."

"We're going to find her, don't worry."

"I know, I've seen her."

Evren's breath hitched. "You have?"

"It's all hazy, but I remember her pulling me out of the water. No . . . out of a pile of bodies. She was crying. She kept saying she was sorry. And there was another voice I think, but I couldn't understand them. Evren, Gyda saved me. But I don't think she did it without a price."

"I doubt it," Evren agreed. But it confirmed what Keres had said. Gyda was strong enough to save Sol. Maybe she was strong enough to survive the rest. "Come on, I have a feeling everyone is in a dream like this. We have to get them out."

She held out her hand, and Sol gripped it so hard she felt like she'd never be able to untangle their fingers. "Okay. Everyone is here?"

"Except Drystan, but if you're alive he might be too."

They started to walk out, towards the cold and the way she came. But Sol tugged her back. "Evren?"

"Yeah?"

"How did you get out of your dream?"

She hesitated, guilt worming it's way like a nasty snake in her chest and tying her up in knots. But she couldn't hear Aster's voice anymore. She couldn't tell if she was relieved or upset.

"I'm good at walking away," she said, letting her voice break. "Maybe too good. But it brought me to you, so I can live with that."

She smiled. "Me too. Don't let go?"

"Never."

~

PAST SOL'S CRYPT, the world fell into ice again. They were both shivering now, but they clung to each other. Sol looked at it all with wide-eyed astonishment. A part of Evren had hoped she'd seen enough of the glacier to get them through it faster, but Sol was little help there. Every chunk of ice, every glowing light, was new and dazzling.

Evren explained all that she'd missed as they walked. Who the Prime was, the ship they'd found, and Keres' role in the story. Sol didn't like it. Her eyes were darkening with every passing minute. But she nodded anyway as the story fell into place.

Their plan was far too simple. Find their friends, get them out of their dreams, and then take the fight to Gail. And hope beyond hope that Gyda and Drystan were alive to be saved.

They walked for a couple minutes, or maybe an hour. Maybe two. Until, just like she had in the mirror maze as a child, Evren nearly ran into herself.

She scowled at the iced-over dead-end and gave her warped reflection the middle finger.

"I guess we turn back?" Sol offered.

She didn't want to. She'd had one shoulder plastered to the side the whole time and it was numb. She didn't find any secret rooms like she had for Sol. But there wasn't another choice. So, she shrugged, and they carefully shuffled on the slick floor until they turned around.

And then they were faced with the sight of Nerezza with her back to them, staring at the wall of ice.

"She wasn't there before," Sol whispered. And although it wasn't a question, Evren shook her head. "Good, I thought I was losing it."

Evren licked her lips, trying to find something other than the taste of blood and ice but coming up empty. She took a step forward, and Sol stayed behind her.

"Nerezza?"

"I wish you wouldn't." Nerezza's voice was crackling like lightning in a storm, powerful but barely leashed emotion leaking through.

Evren stopped in her tracks. "What do you mean?"

"What I said." She didn't turn around. "What I meant. I wish you'd turn away."

"Well, we need to stick together," Evren said. "And there's a dead-end anyway."

"No there isn't."

Evren started to argue, and then thought better of it. "Okay. But we still need to stop Gail. Together. I don't know what he's shown you in your head."

"He showed me nothing I didn't know."

"And you got free. Right?"

A pause, heavy and thick. And then, "Yes."

Evren sighed in relief. "Great. Let's go. We still have a lot of people to get to."

"There's no need for that, Evren."

She frowned. "I'm sorry?"

"I can take care of Gail. I know how to take his power away from him. But I need to do it alone."

Ice crept inside Evren's lungs again, but she squashed it down. There was something eerily familiar about Nerezza's tone. Not her voice, but the way she was talking reminded her of another woman with a voice too soft for the power she wielded.

"Nerezza, turn around," she said. She forced iron into her spine and her voice. Sol's hand tightened her grip.

"It wouldn't change anything for me," Nerezza said. A low humming filled the room and it took Evren a minute to realize that she was laughing. She held up her left hand and pulled off the glove. It fluttered to the floor, forgotten when it revealed a metallic skeleton of a hand. "To think I relied so heavily on this thing for so long, and now it won't matter."

"You have a metal hand," Evren said, feeling rather stupid as she did.

"Terevasans are nothing but ingenious creators. Did you know that they can work enchantments into their metal? Small things like warming a cup of tea, producing sparks of electricity, and even minor illusion spells. It has helped me immensely. I find I liked this hand better than the one I cut off."

Evren blanched. "You what?"

"I told you, Blood magic requires sacrifice."

"That little girl you talked about was you, wasn't it?" Evren was hit with realization not like an oncoming tide but like a flash flood. All at once she was drowning in the barely covered truths she'd been fed.

Nerezza's shoulders shrugged. "It wasn't a lie that she died. She needed to die so I could live. But I suppose now . . . now she doesn't need to anymore."

The metal hand snapped off with a sickening click and clattered to the ground. The ice cracked like a spider web around it. Nerezza didn't turn around, but her whole body shuddered as if a massive weight had been taken from her.

Evren looked at the ice. So smooth and clear, it was like a mirror. It wasn't easy, but slowly she started to see pieces of Nerezza's features. Her hooked nose, her wide round eyes, and pointed chin. None of that had changed. But her skin had changed from being pale and rosy, to pure white. Her hair wasn't cream anymore, but the color of untouched snow. Her eyes were as black as the night sky.

A cry of shock twisted out of Evren's mouth. For one horrifying moment she was looking at Ainthe, fearsome and commanding shadows as well as an army. But looking again, Nerezza wasn't that old. She couldn't be any older than Evren's twenty-three years.

"You're the lost Mora," Sol said, breaking the silence. And Nerezza flinched. "You were the one Ainthe was looking for."

Then Nerezza turned around, and Evren couldn't believe how fooled she'd been by a simple illusion. All it did was subtly change her skin and hair to not be so blindly white. And her eyes had been changed from black to a normal color. But all the rest was the same. The girl they'd been looking for. What she'd thought to be a child no older than the one Ainthe had, was an adult.

"How long have you been on the surface?" Evren breathed.

"Since I was young enough to be stolen." Her eyes flicked to Sol with disdain. "By your kind. Young enough to be molded, and then sold, and then escape. Old enough now to know I don't owe you an explanation."

Evren held her hand up pleadingly. "This doesn't change anything."

"It doesn't?" squeaked Sol.

"Not right now! We still have the same goal. And we can take you back to your people."

Nerezza frowned and looked her up and down. "Who said I wanted to go back? This is where we're meant to be."

Her protests died before they reached her mouth.

"And besides." Nerezza shrugged. "I don't need you to take down Gail. I just need you out of the way."

She flicked her good hand, and Evren *felt* the blood inside her veins lurch backwards. Her body followed, even as the veins pressed against her skin, and she was thrown off her feet and against the ice wall. The ice cracked. Her vision blackened. Her lungs forgot how to work, and all of her veins stung like they'd met fire.

She gasped until the air found its way back inside her. She blinked away the black spots in her eyes quick enough to see Nerezza disappear down the tunnel, her hand on the ground pointing after her.

Beside her, Sol was struggling to get up, her face was splotchy and red, and her fingers were twitching. Evren's were too.

"What the hells?" Sol cried out.

"She's going to eat Gail's soul."

Sol shook her head as if she was trying to clear out cobwebs from her hair. "She can't do that!"

Evren turned to her and didn't bother to keep the fear out of her voice. "She studies magic, Sol. She told me. We were on *Mortova's Maw* for so long, there's no telling when she figured it out. And she just said she knew how to take Gail's power. Not kill him, take his power."

Slowly, Sol's face paled. "Evren, every dead soul in here is tied to him."

She was getting sick again. "I know."

"She wouldn't just be getting Gail's . . ."

"She'd get them all," Evren finished grimly. "Keres' and all their power. Gyda and Drystan too." Evren shot to her feet. "I have to stop her."

Sol scrambled up, chest heaving. "Evren, you can't!"

"I have to try."

"But what about the others? They still need us."

"Stuck in their heads, they're still connected to Gail. I have to at least keep her busy." She threw her arm in the direction Nerezza went. "I have to get to her, Sol. I have to try, or we will lose everything."

"You don't think she'll give the souls back?" Sol asked.

"No. No one eats souls and comes out the same," she said with certainty.

Sol hesitated, looking torn. Her eyes went to the metal hand gleaming on the ground, and then back up to Evren. "Go get her," she said, "I'll get everyone else."

Evren's shoulders sagged in relief. "Be careful, Sol."

Her eyes were storm clouds now. "You too. I can't mourn you a second time."

23

E vren ran, her veins burning and icy air cutting her lungs, through the White Cairn. With each twist she slid into a wall. With every corner she'd just lose sight of a flash of white hair. Always a step behind, her body full to the brim with adrenaline. She wished now, more than anything, that she really could fly. Instead, she half ran, half slipped her way through the maze of ice.

One corner turned into a dozen, and then a hundred. She saw flashes of dark figures. Maybe more of her friends. She couldn't stop. The only thing that kept her going was the knowledge that no matter Nerezza's intentions, she wouldn't let the souls go.

Keres's alone had corrupted Gail. Even if he'd been mad when he'd done it, he'd been twisted into something else entirely. Now Nerezza would take Gail, Keres, and the countless Ikedree people he'd gathered over the decades?

Evren tried not to shiver. She'd seen what Ainthe was capable of, and a fraction of Nerezza's true power. All of it combined would make her far too powerful to stop. Maybe too powerful to talk down.

The light got brighter, almost blinding. The ice pulsed around her like a heartbeat, the waves of blue and green light chasing her feet as she ran. Leading her forward. She gave chase, or they nipped at her heels. Either way, she ran with fear making its way up her throat.

She narrowly avoided slamming into another wall when the tunnel abruptly opened up. The ceiling rose fifty feet above her head. The walls stretched on for just as long. They hummed with a constant, fast pulse of dazzling blended, turquoise light. The ice beneath her feet thrummed, like a heartbeat. The heavy stink of rot was overpowering and intense enough to have Evren coughing, but it was the cause of the stench that nearly made her vomit what little food she had left.

In the middle of the ice cavern, the heart of the White Cairn, was a massive, writhing pile of bodies. They were oozing blood, their glowing eyes looking everywhere at once. Arms flailed wildly. Some mere bones, others fresh enough to still be bleeding. At first, Evren thought it was just a pile, maybe a ball, that stretched up to the ceiling. But she watched in horror as an arm made up of at least thirty bodies, each finger being two to three undead, reached over and plucked something from the ground. A body was crawling towards it, its legs taken off. Burned off. The "hand" picked it up and gently placed it inside the mass of undead. Arms and twisted legs wrapped around it until it was consumed.

"WELCOME HOME."

The deep booming voice shook the cavern and rang her ears. Like before, it was all their mouths speaking as one. But somehow it sounded like an individual.

It was him, she realized sickeningly. There was nothing left of Gail the Vasa. He was just a pile of bodies now, and they were all him.

Evren stood frozen for too long. The moment all the eyes snapped to her she felt fear like never before. But before she could move, her head exploded with pain as something heavy slammed against her temple.

She crumbled to the ground like a sack of grain. Her bow skittered along the ice, out of her reach. She touched her temple, and her fingers came back red. But there was no power in this pain. Just numbing, bone-chilling fear. She flipped over on her back, ready to get back to her feet, until her neck was met with cold steel.

The blade was achingly familiar. She'd been in this position before, under the mercy of Gyda's sword. But looking up at her now Evren could've wept.

Her eyes were glowing the same hellish turquoise as all the others, and they were cold and unflinching. Her hair scarf was gone, her hair was wild and free around her shoulders. The mass of brilliant red stood out so starkly from the rest of the room it was all Evren could see. It felt wrong to stare at it. She forced herself back to the rest of her friend. Her bare arms, devoid of her usual ink. Her hide armor ripped and falling apart. The sword, still deadly, but with none of its glowing runes.

"Gyda." Her voice cracked, and she wasn't sure if it carried over the clicking of bones. "It's me. It's Evren. You don't want to do this."

"Gyda does what I wish, Evren Hanali."

Evren winced as the voices bounced inside her tender skull. Gyda did not speak. She didn't move. Evren looked sideways at the mass of bodies.

"Gail!" she called. "I know it's you. I know what you did!"

"You know nothing!"

"I've been to your ship! I saw what you wrote on the walls."

"Then you know my suffering. You know I am building a family, not an army."

"This isn't a family!" she protested. "You're killing people and robbing them of their freewill and afterlife. You're trapping hundreds of innocent souls."

"They want to be here!"

336 | GILLIAN GRANT

"They have no choice!" she shot back. "You don't give them one."

"YOU ARE WRONG." The corpses used their many legs to shamble forward, like an insect. "I GIVE THEM ONE HOME, ONE FAMILY. THEY WILL NEVER HUNGER LIKE I DID. THEY WILL NEVER WANT FOR COMPANY. I TAKE FAMILIES AND MAKE THEM WHOLE AGAIN. GYDA HAS BEEN REUNITED WITH HER CLAN, AND SHE IS HAPPY."

"I'd like to hear that from her," Evren spat, then shrank back as a dangling arm got too close. Gyda's cold steel kept her from going as far as she wanted.

"TELL HER, DAUGHTER. TELL HER HOW YOU LONGED TO COME BACK HERE EVEN WHILE YOU SLEPT BY THEIR SIDE. TELL HER YOU ARE WITH YOUR ONE TRUE FAMILY."

"My family." Gyda's voice was low and monotone. "My family is here in the White Cairn."

The last little bit of hope in Evren died. Gyda had always been the strongest person she knew. Seeing her as little more than a shell tore her apart.

"That's not true," Evren choked out. "You saved Sol. She told me how you pulled her from death. You kept her from being in that." She pointed accusingly at Gail's monstrous form. "Because you knew it was wrong!"

Gyda said nothing above her. Her sword didn't waver, the cold blade biting ever so gently into the soft skin of her neck.

"I know you!" Evren yelled up at her. "I know what you're capable of. You are better than this. You're stronger than some mad kid. And if I have to beat it into you, I will."

Evren raised her leg back and kicked against Gyda's knee. It jerked to the side, bringing her down briefly. If it had been anyone else it would've snapped their knee, but Gyda barely flinched. Evren rolled out the way as the sword came down with a crack against the ice she'd been laying on.

She leapt to her feet and immediately latched onto one of her arms.

Get the sword from her, she told herself. *You stand no chance if she has it.*

Her fingers had barely touched the bone hilt before Gyda's elbow slammed into nose. A spray of blood and a spark of pain sent Evren reeling backwards. She spit the blood out of her mouth as Gyda got to her feet, her expression neutral and unchanging.

"At least be a little angry I touched your sword," Evren said.

"I am."

The arc of steel was far faster than it should've been considering its weight. Evren barely ducked out of the way, rolling on her back as Gyda followed up with a backhand swing that would've carved her in half.

She got on her knees and barely had time to catch her breath before Gyda was running at her again. Evren dove between her legs, wincing as the ice scraped up her cheek. But Gyda tumbled past her, and her blow missed by a mile.

Evren tried to get up, but had no traction. Her boots kept slipping on the ice, and she could hear Gyda recovering. She scrambled forward, her fingers clawing for her bow and was mere inches away when Gyda grabbed her ankle and yanked her sharply back.

She was lifted off the floor effortlessly and thrown across the room. Sailing through the air, Evren barely had enough time to cover her head before she struck the wall with enough force to crack her ribs. Her whole body was on fire as she crumbled to the ground, every breath agonizing. She peeled herself off the floor and, through her curtain of fallen hair and hazy eyes, she could see Gyda slowly approaching, her sword dragging along the ice emitting painful screeches and sparks.

She used the wall to pull herself to her feet and pressed against it. Her mouth was coated with blood, but she refused to taste it. One hand cradled her cracked ribs and the other she put out between them; palm outstretched.

Gyda stopped a foot from it, unwavering. She half expected

her to cut it off, just to prove a point, but her sword point still rested on the ice.

"You're not going kill me." Evren smiled through her blood and pain. She shook her head. "I know you. You won't."

"As I said, Evren, Gyda does what I wish. With your death, she will have you as a part of our eternal family. You will have everything you ever wanted—love, security, a family that will never leave you, and a home eternal."

She spat a bloody wad of saliva on the ground. "I don't care for cages. I'll slit my own throat before you take me."

"That wouldn't make a difference. And wouldn't it be sweeter if Gyda did it? She could make it painless."

"I want that pain," she snapped. "I need it."

Evren turned back to Gyda and softened her gaze. The sword was inching off the ground now. The light of the cairn glinted off the steel like lightning. It bathed Gyda in a heavenly light and, despite it all, Evren couldn't get past how beautiful she looked with her hair down.

Her fingers stretched out, and her voice was soft as a feather. "Gyda, look at me. You don't need to do this. You're not alone. You have all of us waiting for you. You have me. All you need to do is take my hand."

Gyda didn't move, but her sword did. It was level with Evren's chest again. Tears welled up in her eyes and, feeling childish, she closed them. She didn't want Gyda to see her cry, even as a tear slipped down her cheek.

"Please," she begged.

No, she prayed. But not to gods or Divines. Not to corpses of long-dead powerful people. Evren prayed to Gyda. One last childish stab in the dark with her eyes closed, her hand outstretched, and a sword at her chest.

At least it'll be clean, she thought numbly as the sword pressed against her leathers.

And then a hand was in hers. The sword was gone, and she was being pulled forward. Evren's eyes flashed open just in time to see Gyda pull her into an embrace. She pulled her out of the way, just as one of Gail's massive arms crashed into the spot she'd just been in.

"No!" he wailed.

Bones and pieces of bodies were flying everywhere as he tore up the ice around them. Gyda's body shielded her from any flying objects, and she hissed and flinched with every hit. But she never let go. And her eyes, now blissfully normal, were on Evren.

Evren choked back a happy sob. "You're back!"

Behind her, Gail's twisted form raged and cracked the ice with jagged black crevices. One was spreading towards them. Gyda saw her widening eyes and rolled them out of the way. They both landed on their backs, dazed, still holding each other. Gail loomed over them.

"I WILL HAVE YOU!" he cried. "ALIVE OR DEAD, I WILL HAVE YOU!"

A massive hand made of corpses reached out as if to pluck them up. Instead, the fingers curled inward, as if he was coaxing someone towards him. Physically, Evren didn't go anywhere. With Gyda holding her down, there's no way she could've if she wanted to. But some*thing* inside her did.

For a brief, blindingly painful moment, Evren was reminded of what Nerezza did against her blood. Only this was excruciating. Like he was tugging on her very being and ripping it out of her body.

My soul.

It was all she thought before the ice faded. The cold feeling faded as well. She felt . . . nothing. The haze of blue and green light remained, swirling like an ocean around her, but she was the light and she could see everyone else that made it. Hundreds of crying, screaming souls. All reaching out and fighting, but it was useless. She glimpsed someone in the middle of it. Someone calm and small. A boy with shaggy black hair and eyes like the depths of the sea.

"Gail."

And there it was. The answer to all her problems. She took a step forward, if a soul could even step, but then stopped. She was falling backwards. The same tugging she felt before, only this time in the opposite direction. Gail met her eyes as she was flung out of the light and slammed back into her body.

Evren gasped for breath and clawed at her chest. Gyda had her hand there, and her brow was beaded with sweat, her eyes bloodshot.

"What did you do?" Evren barely got out, before Gail threw a mound of bodies in the air that might've been his head. He wailed even louder.

"YOU MISUSE MY GIFT, DAUGHTER! GIVE HER BACK AND I WILL LET YOU JOIN HER."

Gyda leapt to her feet and put her sword between herself and Gail. One of the runes started to flicker to life. Her hair flew around her from the wind Gail was kicking up.

Evren thought Gyda had never looked more fierce.

"I will rip every soul out one by one if I have to," the warrior seethed.

Gail took a staggered step forward. Gyda was tall and always imposing, but next to a mountain of rotting flesh and corpses, Evren had never seen her so small. She was frozen, watching as Gyda faced Gail down by herself. Until something glowing caught her eye from the side.

The ball of fire streaked through the air and slammed into Gail just as he started to swing at Gyda. He stumbled back, a thousand voices hissing in pain even as the flames were sputtering out. All three of them turned to see the source.

Arke raised his clawed middle finger and crumbled another spell. "I'm gonna crisp you, boy."

Gail turned towards him in fury. If Gyda had looked small

next to him, then Arke was minuscule. But as fire reared up from his palms, other figures darted out from behind him.

Abraxas's black armor caught the green and blue light and seemed to swallow it. He charged in, sword and shield raised with a war cry that echoed Gyda's. He took the brunt of the blow meant for Arke, his knees crumpling for a moment before he pushed back and cut the bodies off. Next to him, Sol whipped out her daggers and slid under one of Gail's many massive appendages. She cut and sliced, her mouth in a grim line as bodies fell around her.

Gail started to shake bodies loose. They fell off him and ran towards the party individually. They were met with Sorin's flashing rapier. He dodged nimbly and stabbed so quickly into the hearts that it looked like he was barely poking them. Sahar came up behind him and let out a fierce yell as she threw out one of her white bombs. It would've hit Gail, but a mound of bodies leapt off him to intercept it and the fire consumed them. No flame touched him.

Amidst all the corpses, one flew into a frenzy and was ripping hearts out left and right. Keres was fighting tooth and nail to get to Gail, their eyes alight with fury and passion. Their teeth and tusks were bared, but with every undead killed, another ten took their place. And Keres was no match for them all.

Nearly half of Gail's bodies went to deal with the party. He had no face in this form, but Evren saw all the rest of the eyes turn back towards her and Gyda. They were on the opposite side. She heard Sol scream in frustration, but they couldn't get through. And there was no Nerezza to be found.

Gyda raised her sword and took a menacing step forward.

"No!" Evren got to her feet and had to grab onto Gyda to steady herself. Gyda glanced at her with a look of heavy concern, but never stepped away from her spot.

"Keep back, Evren," she said, "I'll keep him from taking you."

Evren gripped her arm tighter. "Look at me!"

Reluctantly, Gyda did, and Evren saw fear clear as day, but also resolve. Whatever means Gyda used to take souls away from Gail must've been how she saved Sol. She couldn't let her do it again.

"Let him take me."

"*What?*"

"YES. SHE SEES NOW! SHE WANTS IT, DAUGHTER. DO NOT FIGHT IT."

Gyda was turning back to Gail, but Evren forced her to face her. It was like tugging on a stubborn mountain and caused white-hot pain to shoot up her side. She breathed through it, looking up at Gyda.

"I can stop this," Evren said, "But I have to get inside. He's the connection to all of this. If I get him there, it all falls apart."

Gyda looked lost. "I can't . . ."

"Trust me," Evren said firmly. This wasn't a plea or a prayer. It was a demand. "I can do this."

For a moment, it was just the two of them staring each other down. A mountain's resolve against the wind's. But even the wind could chip away at stone, bit by bit. Evren saw the moment Gyda gave in. Her shoulders drooped and her sword fell to her side.

"I will pull you back if this takes too long," Gyda said softly, so only the two of them could hear. "I swear it."

"I know."

Evren squeezed her arm gently and tried to smile. But she felt her lips quivering even as she did and turned away. She swallowed down her tears and faced Gail fully.

"I'm ready," she said.

"GOOD, GOOD. IT IS ALWAYS LESS PAINFUL WHEN IT'S NOT FORCED."

The same, agonizing tug tore her soul free of its earthly binds. It did *not* hurt less. Evren was dimly aware that she was screaming, but she couldn't feel her throat. She couldn't feel anything.

The next thing she knew, she was back in the blue. The sea of souls swarmed around her, angry and riling like the ocean. Unlike last time, she couldn't see past them. She couldn't see Gail. All she saw was pain, frozen faces as their phantom hands clawed at their air. Above her, below her, all around her. There was no end to them.

Then, she wasn't alone.

Evren turned and, standing beside her like he'd never left, was Drystan. Ghostly blue tinged with green. A scowling phantom dripping sea water. Of course, he was scowling.

"Drystan." Her voice wasn't even a whisper. It wasn't even a voice, but he heard it all the same. He turned towards her, and the scowl lightened slightly.

"Evren." He inclined his head towards her.

"You're here. I thought . . ."

"She could only save one at the time. I don't blame her."

"Oh." Evren sank back, thinking of the bodies her friends were fighting. Which one of them was Drystan's? Would Gail be cruel enough to send him after Sahar and make her kill him? Or had that already been done?

"I need to get to Gail," Evren said.

"So, you can stop this?"

"Stupid question."

He rolled his eyes. "I'll help you then. Follow me."

He didn't wait for her. He never did in life, why should he in death? He floated forward and squeezed between the numerous souls. It was hard to keep up, let alone keep her eyes on him. Everything was blue and green, and he blended right in. The only thing that stuck out was the streak of white in his hair. Evren kept her eyes on that, never blinking, as she followed him.

The deeper they went, the bluer it got. From turquoise to light blue, to a deep unyielding sea blue. The crowd of souls stopped, and so did Drystan. She paused beside him, looking out at the open space of blue where a little boy sat huddled on the floor.

He was the only spot of color. Rosy cheeks, suntanned skin. She could even see freckles on his gangly limbs that he never got to grow into.

Evren turned to Drystan. "What happens to you once I do this?"

He paused, mulling over her words. "I suppose I would die."

"But if I do this, I can get you out, right? You won't have to."

He smiled sadly. "Evren, I died in the water. If there is a second life for me, I don't want it. All resurrections come at a price, and I have been dead far longer than Sol was when Gyda dragged her back to the living. As we know it, her heart had barely stopped before she was brought back. She was lucky. The rest of us?" He gestured to the sea of souls. "We have no such luck."

She wanted to argue and rage and tell him to fight. Isn't that what he was good at? Fighting and pissing her off? Instead, she looked him up and down. He was him, but also not. He was . . . content. She realized with a jolt that she'd never seen him not on edge. But here he was a completely different person.

"You want this?" she asked.

He smiled ruefully. "Stupid question."

"But you love Sahar."

He faltered for a moment, his soul flickering. Then he blinked and shook his head. "Obvious statement. Everyone loves her."

She nodded and took a floating step towards Gail. Then she turned around and caught Drystan before he could disappear. "She loves you too, you know."

"That is the most magical thing, isn't it?" he asked. "To love someone and have them love you in return. She should develop better taste when I'm gone. Would you . . ." He hesitated. "Would you make sure she's all right after this? Take care of her?"

"Of course."

He sighed, and his form started to drift backwards. His eyes sparkled with a light he didn't have in life. "End this then. For all of us."

Then he disappeared into the souls, and Evren was alone with Gail.

24

T he boy who ate souls looked completely and utterly
human as Evren got closer to him. He looked up at
her, with big sea-blue eyes, and it was there that she
saw the weight of so many lonely, neglected years. He stood up
to meet her, and somehow managed to look down his narrow
nose even though he was nearly a foot shorter than her.

"You're not afraid anymore," he said. He sounded like a boy
and not the monster that was killing her friends as she spoke.

"No, I'm still afraid," she corrected him. "I'm just not letting
it win right now. Are you afraid, Gail?"

He hesitated, his brow scrunching up as he thought, before
finally saying, "I was for a long time. I don't like being alone.
But I'm not anymore, and neither are you."

"I wasn't alone before," said Evren.

"But you will be. People die, people leave. And then it's just
you and it hurts. But it shouldn't have to."

"It's life."

"It shouldn't hurt," he repeated, and the whole world trembled at his tone. She suppressed a shiver and nodded.

"It shouldn't," she agreed. "But it always will. Gail, what
you're doing right now is hurting people."

He scoffed at her. "No, it's not."

She turned and pointed to the souls all scrambling to keep away from him. "Look at them. They're in pain. They're alone and scared. You took them from their lives and forced them into something they didn't choose."

"But they have their family here," he protested. "I made sure to get whole families every time so no one would suffer. I missed Gyda last year, and that was my first and only mistake! Honest!"

"I believe you," she said. "But are any of them going to their loved ones?"

He looked out and confusion spread across his brow. "No?"

"They're terrified, Gail. They don't see their family. They only see a jumble of torn souls like themselves. But I'll let you in on a secret."

He looked at her skeptically. "What?"

"These people all have places to go when they die. They go to the stars with their families. All their past ancestors are waiting for them up there. By keeping them down here, you're keeping them apart."

"Then, I-I'll," his lip trembled, "I'll go to the stars! I'll get their family too!"

She shook her head. "No, Gail."

His mouth twisted into a pout. "But why?"

"You can't go with them because you're not their true family." Evren watched his face crumble and felt a twinge of regret at the hurt in his eyes.

"But . . ." he started, and his eyes welled up with tears. "But what about me? I don't have anyone!" Hot tears tumbled down his cheeks. "You killed Mortova! He was my last friend, and you killed him! I won't let you take them away from me. I won't!"

The souls started to writhe at his tone. The whole world of blue shook and shuddered. And in her gut Evren felt a tug.

Come back, it said.

She pulled away from it. *Not yet.*

Gail was sitting back down and holding his knees to his

dripping chin. He sniffled angrily when she sat cross legged beside him and shot her a withering glare.

"I can't take them away from you," she said, and he brightened at that. "But we can't stay here."

"But it's safe here," he insisted. "No one can hurt us."

"That's not living, Gail. This," she swept her hands out at the frightened souls, "this isn't family. I know Vasa believe that you make a family wherever you can, and it's a beautiful thought. But family chooses you, not the other way around. Family is a group of people, or maybe just one person, that feels like home. They're your shoulder to lean on, the person who always has your back, and takes care of you. They're also the ones that teach you right from wrong. They make you a better person, and you do the same for them. It's a give and take, you see."

He wiped his nose with his arm. "You have people like that." He said it bitterly.

She smiled, warmth fluttering in her chest. "I do. That's why I'm here." She leaned forward. "Would you like to be my family, Gail?"

He blinked up at her wide with eyes. "W-what?"

She shrugged nonchalantly. "I've never had a little brother. Maybe I'd like one. Maybe," she shot him a look. "If you let these people go. You and I stay."

"Forever?"

"As long as you want."

He sat, his chin on his knees again, and looked out over the people he'd gathered. Warriors and fishermen. Children and old couples. Every color, every emotion, every range of person. So wide and beautiful. For a moment, she could see the appeal, but she blinked and forced herself to focus.

"No one's ever chosen me for me," he mumbled against his knees. "Not even Mortova."

"I am."

"I know, and it's strange, considering you're heartless."

Evren feigned hurt and placed her hand on her chest. "Ouch! Already taking that sibling part seriously, huh?"

"No," he said, sounding tired. "You just are."

Her smile fell and she let her hand join the other in her lap. Gail looked over to her, at her serious face, and perked up.

"But that's okay! I don't mind that you don't have a heart! Honest!"

She held a hand up to stop him. "No, explain. What do you mean I don't have a heart?"

"Isn't it obvious?" He cocked his head to the side, and a dark curl fluttered across his forehead. "You don't have one. That's what heartless means."

"But if I didn't have a heart, I'd be dead," she protested. "I have blood, and a pulse. I am—well, I *was* alive."

"Have you felt your pulse, though?" he squinted. "Really felt it?"

She floundered. "Well, I-I never focus on it . . ."

"People can live without things." He shrugged his bony shoulders. "Hearts? Not really. I'm guessing that's why you're sick. You need your heart back. Before you die. Or before you do heartless things."

She swallowed nervously and her hand went to her chest. But she was nothing but mist now. Of course, she didn't have a heart. She put her hand back down. "Will you help me then? Find my heart?"

"Only after I let them go, though. That's what you're going to say?"

She nodded, and he sighed dramatically and threw his arms and legs out like a starfish. "I guess I could. But you promise to stay?"

"Well, you're helping me with my heart, right?"

"Yes." He nodded once, sharply.

"Then I'm staying."

Gail wrinkled his nose like he was going to change his mind and then he closed his eyes. His hands splayed out in front of him and his lips moved around strange words. With every passed word, Evren saw a soul flicker and disappear. One, and then ten, and then twenty more. The sea of souls cleared out, bit by bit as she watched, fascinated and strangely sad. As more left, Evren found Drystan watching her and smiling sadly. She waved her hand in goodbye, and he did the same before his form turned into mist and he too disappeared.

There was only a couple dozen left, their faces turned towards Evren and Gail with unfiltered hope. Suddenly, Gail stopped and his face grew tight with pain.

"What's wrong?" Evren asked, reaching out for him. But he was drifting away from her.

"I-I don't know!" He started crying again and his eyes flashed open. "Evren, it hurts! Make it stop! PLEASE!"

She launched to her feet and ran after him, but the tether on her gut pulled her back. Sharp, painful, insistent. A lifeline home. But she strained against it, reaching for Gail even as he screamed and writhed in pain.

"Gail! Reach for me!"

"I can't!" he wailed. His eyes locked with hers and she could see the brilliant whites of his eyes even from a distance. His next words were soft. "She's eating me . . ."

Realization dawned on Evren like the cold light of day. But Gyda was pulling her back. She couldn't fight it. The world turned from deep blue to more and more green. Gail screamed for her, and other souls tried to grab her, but she slipped through their fingers like she was nothing. The last thing she heard before the light faded was Gail's sobbing.

"Don't let her eat me, Evren! Don't leave me too! Please . . ."

~

SHE WAS CRYING when she woke up. Her tears were freezing to her face. And she was so cold. Hells, was she tired of being cold.

She blinked against the light, trying to clear something up. But it was fading. Was she dying?

No, the light of the Cairn was dying. It was plunging everything into shadow.

Evren tried to sit up but found a cold hand pressing her back down. She wrinkled her nose at the smell. "Keres?"

"Such disdain." They shook their head. "I thought you'd be happy to see me."

"Where's Gyda?" She mumbled wearily. Then a shot of panic flew through her. She pushed Keres away and sat up. "Where's Nerezza?"

Her head was pounding like someone was driving a knife repeatedly behind her eyes, but she ignored Keres' attempts to get her to lay down. The aurora glow was fading fast, and everything was shadowed. But torches were lit, and soon the cheery orange glow of fire lit up the heart of the glacier.

The room was piled with bodies, but they were all still and lifeless. Making their way out of the pile were her friends. Arke was burning away any of them that had gotten close to him and tottering up to Sorin. Abraxas was picking through the bodies, his torch held high. Sahar was right behind him, her eyes fearful and hopeful all at the same time. Gyda's tall form was easily visible as she pulled Sol out from under a mass of bodies. Sol hugged her tightly, and she went stock still underneath the touch. But Nerezza was nowhere to be seen.

"Where's Nerezza?" Evren repeated, and this time she got onto her feet. The whole room swayed, and she tipped over again before Keres caught her and helped her up.

Sorin shrugged and wiped his blade off. "She was just right here." He turned beside him to see Arke, but no sign of the elven mage.

"I saw her!" Sol was gasping through her tears as she pulled away from Gyda. "I tried to stop her, Evren, but she pushed me into the dead. I couldn't get to her."

"Stop her?" Sahar waved the torch around to glare at them. "She saved us! She killed him."

Evren was very suddenly and irrevocably tired. All the fight drained out of her and all she was left with was a broken body and a corpse holding her up. "No, she didn't."

"What are you saying?" Sahar spat, and she looked as close to angry as she'd ever seen her.

"Nerezza found out how to do what Gail did," Evren explained and pinched the bridge of her nose. "She told Sol and I when we saw her in the caverns. She wanted to get to Gail first, to take him and the souls he'd gathered for herself and eat them. Sol and I split up. Me to stop her, and her to get the rest of you. But I didn't see her when I got here."

Abraxas let out a long, shaky breath and leaned heavily on his sword. "She entered the battle after you collapsed. When she was doing a spell and the lights were fading, we thought she was killing him."

"She was." Evren tried to shake the sound of Gail's panicking screaming from her ears. "She ate him. I was there with the souls and him when it happened."

Gyda stepped forward and nodded to her. "Evren was trying to get Gail to stand down on his own. It was the only way we would have won."

Sahar shook her head furiously. She was crying, but every tear that fell was wiped away fast enough to fling it in the air. She left traces of soot on her cheeks. "No. No! She wouldn't do that! I know her, she would never . . ." She faltered and then the tears came too fast for her to wipe away. "She wouldn't . . ."

Evren met Abraxas's eyes. "She was Serevadian. The girl that Ainthe said was stolen is her."

He bowed his head. Beside him Sahar just sobbed and fell to her knees. Her torch fell out of her hands and Gyda picked it up before it rolled into any of the dead. Sorin picked his way over to her sobbing form and immediately settled down next to her.

Evren was tired enough to sleep there, but Keres kept her upright.

"Evren," they said under their breath. "Nerezza has my soul."

Her shoulders sagged. "I know. I'm sorry."

Keres, bloody, dead, lost-soul Keres had nothing else to say. They just herded her back to her friends, where Gyda took her arm and silently looked through the dead with her.

Evren knew what they were looking for, but that didn't make it any easier. It took them thirty minutes of halfhearted searching until Gyda's boot unearthed the body of a man with a streak of white in his hair.

Evren turned away from his bloated corpse, her eyes already pricking with tears she thought were spent. She found nothing but Gyda to go to, and without hesitation fell into her waiting arms.

Gyda held her without complaint. Evren felt her voice vibrate as she called Sorin and Sahar over. Sahar's sobbing turned to cries of anguish nearly immediately. Evren peeked out of Gyda's arm to see her huddled over Drystan's body.

It was silent as a graveyard except for Sahar's muffled sobs. She fisted her hands in his shirt and shook him as if that was enough. His eyes were mercifully closed. One by one they all turned away from her to give them some privacy, but they all heard loud and clear her tear-filled words as they echoed through the glacier.

"Don't leave me, you bastard! You said forever! You swore! Please don't leave me alone. Please, please, please . . ." Her voice broke again. "Listen to me just this once, you stubborn man. Come home to me."

Sahar Al-Fasil went unanswered, and the White Cairn became a tomb for a lover she never had the chance to have.

25

The dead couldn't remain in the White Cairn.

It took numerous trips back and forth to Direwall to make sure they laid them all to rest before the White Cairn swallowed them. Long after the tunnels they'd walked had closed up, Evren felt the imprint of the ice on her skin, like a memory that would never leave her.

Under the vast night sky, Sorin laid to rest what was left of Gail the traditional Vasa way. There wasn't much left of his body —a barely recognizable mangle of bones and torn skin. Despite it all, the Wandering Sols set his body adrift, surrounded by the scales of Mortova. Wherever the water took him was where he belonged.

As the water took Gail, Sorin began to sing for the first time in months.

"Take to the stars ye lost soul of water,
Where your salt-laden spirit cannot falter.
Oh, spirits to ash, and bones to the thunder,
We wait for the day our souls meet in wonder."

The words had meaning again. Evren found herself singing along and thinking of the boy who befriended a sea serpent.

"Leave behind your home of salt

and the sea,
Forget the ending of life you didn't foresee.
The Bond that holds us has never been stronger,
I wait for the day our souls meet in wonder.
Swim in a sea of stars and ride waves of wind,
Your brilliance in life such death cannot dim.
Just don't forget who waits for you under,
I cherish the day our souls meet in wonder."

THE REMAINING Ikedree people of Direwall resigned to burn their dead, not unlike Etherakians were used to doing with every funeral. But pyres were rare so far north. The Ikedree normally left the dead to the elements, so they could feed the next cycle of life and their soul could be returned to the sky and all its stars. But there were too many bodies, and the night was too cold. Fire and smoke laid the dead to rest.

Pyres burned throughout the night. The wind swept the ashes into the sky. When the aurora returned, the Wandering Sols, Keres, and Sahar shivered in their furs. The Ikedree rejoiced.

"It is the light of our ancestors!" one said in passing, his eyes shining with the same heavenly glow. "They shine brighter than they have in years. They must rejoice in the souls of the lost being returned to them, for our skies would not be so bright otherwise. Rejoice, southerners! Winter is breaking soon."

None of them did. In the following two weeks of darkness, all they did was recover. Bandage and heal their physical wounds, maybe even try to talk out some of the mental ones. The conversations were soft, and short, and didn't heal much. It was a start to a very long road, but the first few steps were taken.

Keres was kept locked away since Vox's steadily decaying body couldn't be hidden. Sahar kept Drystan's body on ice and preserved. She refused to talk to anyone except Keres for days on end.

Evren slept. Far longer than she should've. She woke only to eat and get her wounds checked before she wearily collapsed back into bed. As drowsy as she was, she didn't miss the worried tones that whispered above her. No matter the salves, or potions given to her, she was healing slowly, if at all. Everyone else was back to full health by the time Evren refused to keep drinking the potions they shoved down her throat.

There wasn't any point in wasting them, she told herself. The major parts were mostly healed. The broken ribs, the multiple head wounds, and the bite from one of the undead. There was no risk of infection and no fever. Just lingering tenderness and an all-around lethargy that wouldn't leave her. Her cuts were still swollen and pink, and she felt better bandaging them. And she always felt better asleep.

Her friends wrote it off as exhaustion. They had all passed out for days on end after the funerals were done. And Evren always allowed herself to get beat to the hells and back. They let her heal and rest, and occasionally dropped in to talk or make sure she'd eaten. Sol stayed for hours, even when Evren couldn't keep her eyes open. She'd wake up later to find the dwarf passed out next to her, bundled in as many furs as she could find. Sorin would go back and forth between loudly talking about anything and everything, to letting silences drag when he couldn't force words past his tears. Arke always came in when he thought she was asleep, when the candle was out and the room was so inky dark that the glowing of his eyes was barely visible. He never said anything, just scooted a chair up and sat for a few hours. He was always gone by the time Evren woke up. Abraxas had finally put his armor away, although at the cost of becoming a fretful nurse. He scowled and cursed at every slowly healing wound. He seethed when she refused to take more potions and argued until they were both blue in the face. Eventually, he let her win. Evren knew it would come at a cost eventually, just not yet.

Gyda never came. At least, not that Evren saw or heard. She

asked how she was, and if she'd come by, but she always got the same answers.

"She's been distant." Sol would shrug. "She barely even talks to us."

Sorin would shake his head. "Won't even look me in the eyes. Any of us. You'd think it wouldn't be hard to find a woman that large, but she always disappears on me."

"Don't worry about her," Abraxas would say. "She's healed physically. The Divines only know how long she'll let the wounds of her heart fester."

It hurt a little more than Evren thought it would to not see her. After working to find and save her for so long, it was strange to feel like she was still not there. Like there was an empty space where she used to be, both in the room and in her mind.

Still . . .

There was a moment back in the White Cairn where she felt like Gyda wouldn't let her go. Her arm was wrapped so tightly around Evren's shoulders, she was sure she'd stay like that forever. And yet, every time she'd woken up cold and alone, her eyes looking at the doorway and finding it empty.

But there she was again, shifting restlessly in her bed and looking towards the dark doorway with barely contained hope. She stared, unblinking until her eyes burned and the flame of the candle swam in her vision. She blinked rapidly, ignoring the drip of false tears as she turned her back on the doorway and the candle.

The furs were heavy across her body. She tucked them up to her chin and let the shadowed other side of the room comfort her dry eyes for a bit. She could feel sleep tugging her weary too-warm bones down for another black nap. Another few blissful hours where she could hide from her steadily throbbing body and wherever her mind happened to drift off to in her waking hours. But she chewed on the bottom of her lip instead, forcing herself awake. Downstairs she could hear talk, laughter, and best of all, music. She could even smell the warm hearty food from her room.

She should go. Force herself downstairs and let herself smile and be happy. But how could she? She didn't feel like she'd won, that she deserved to celebrate. All she could feel on her chest was the weight of the lost souls. The crew of *Mortova's Maw*, Gail, Drystan and Vox, the dozens Nerezza managed to steal before Gail could let them go.

She'd lost them. She'd let Nerezza slip away. She hadn't been able to save Drystan and couldn't even look Sahar in the eye. Yes, the undead threat was gone. Yes, she'd gotten Sol and Gyda back. But at what cost?

Evren couldn't get Gail's voice out of her head. His screams of agony as Nerezza ate his soul, his pleading sobs. And most of all, what he'd said about her.

People can live without things. Hearts? Not really. I'm guessing that's why you're sick. You need your heart back. Before you die. Or before you do heartless things.

Heartless things. She shuddered under her furs. She was kind, wasn't she? Compassionate and forgiving? Unless someone didn't deserve that kindness. Surely, she wasn't actually heartless. He was a boy driven mad by power and years of loneliness. Surely . . .

Her fingers crept up to her throat, as they'd done a dozen times before. She nestled them against the soft flesh right under her jaw, and she waited.

Nothing.

No pulse, no flow of blood and life. She pressed harder, willing herself to find what she was steadily realizing wasn't there. Tears pricked her eyes again, and she sucked them back with a shaking breath.

If she didn't have a heart, what did that mean for her? Was she doomed to get sicker and sicker, only feeling strong when she drew blood? How much blood did she have to bleed before she didn't have any left?

Where had her heart gone?

Magic could do amazing things. Terrible things too. It could lift mountains or raise armies of the dead. It could heal the sick or burn whole cities to the ground. Could it also remove a heart and keep the body living? And erase the memories of what happened, because no matter how many times Evren dug at the scar on her chest, she found nothing but thick, raised flesh and a blank space in her mind.

Evren flicked her fingers away from her still throat. She laid there for a moment, brimming with too many mixed emotions. Longing, regret, confusion, grief, and above all, anger. Her skin felt hot and itchy with the surge of unwarranted rage that rushed through her. It was not going to let her sleep.

She threw off the covers and forced herself onto her feet. Her body protested weakly in the form of shaky hands and unstable feet and eyes that blurred whenever she moved too fast. But she forced her clean clothes on layer by layer. She brushed her hair and pulled it away from her face with her clumsy fingers. She splashed chilled water on her face to wake herself up more, and the anger recoiled slightly as she scrubbed the sleep and grit from her eyes.

Evren still felt awful, and once the anger had dulled down to a throb in her empty chest, she had half a mind to collapse back into the furs and snooze until the sun rose. Whenever that would happen. She'd completely lost track of time.

Instead, she marched past her bed, opened the door, and walked out so purposefully she nearly trampled the goblin laying over the threshold.

"OI! Watch it—WATCH THE EARS!"

Evren yelped and jumped around until she was thoroughly out of breath and halfway down the hallway. She turned around to see Arke scowling and picking himself off the floor. His ears were intact.

"You're awake, eh? Good. I was—"

"I think there's something wrong with me," she blurted out.

His mouth snapped shut, the little pointed teeth that never managed to stay behind his lips poked out. He looked her up and down, his expression blank.

"Yeah?" he said slowly. "You need me to get Abraxas?"

She shook her head. "No. No I just . . ." She found her fingers wringing themselves into knots and stuffed them into separate pockets. "The blood thing we talked about before?"

"Yeah?"

"Nerezza has it too."

"Ah . . ." He tugged his ears down like he was pulling his hair, and it made his face stretch out comically until he let go and they snapped back into place. "Shit."

"And it's killing me," she added quickly. "The magic."

His expression instantly softened. He tottered up to her, those full-moon eyes brimming with concern. "You sure?"

"Yes." She looked down at her feet. "Nerezza said that to get blood magic I needed to sacrifice something. I think," she took a deep breath, "I think I sacrificed my heart. Don't ask me how I'm still standing because I don't know. Don't ask me why I did it because I can't remember. All I know is that I have no heart-beat, a massive scar on my chest, and a magic that is slowly killing me each time I use it, and I don't understand any of it."

Her words were so rushed they slurred together, and so fast she didn't even breathe between them. When she was done, she gasped air back into her empty lungs and had half a mind to go back to her room. But Arke put his hand on her knee, as gently as the goblin knew how, and forced her to meet his eyes.

"I ain't gonna let you die," he said firmly. "Do I have an itchin' clue what you're talkin' about? No. But I'm gonna get you through this."

"How?" she asked, feeling helpless for even leaning on him but also incredibly grateful that she didn't need to stand alone.

"No clue." He shrugged. "Might wanna try with not bleedin' for a while."

"That's good advice in general."

"Then try takin' it and listenin', all right? We'll work this through."

"All right." She nodded and breathed in and out a few times. She squashed the mild panic down next to the ever-present anxiety and deep-seated regret. "All right."

He squinted up at her. "Want me not to tell the others?"

She thought about it for a while. She'd kept her problems to herself for so long. Partly because it was just easier. Partly because she didn't know how to tell them. It wasn't their weight to bear, why should she force it on them? And yet, she was so sick of secrets and feeling alone around the people she cared about.

"I'll tell them," she said, "In time. I need to figure out a better way than just blurting out that I'm dying."

He patted her knee and shuffled away. "Please do. That's terrifyin'." Then he waved her away from the doorway and closer to the stairs. "Come on, the party is in full swing. You should enjoy it."

"What's it for?" she asked as she took the stairs slowly after him.

"Sunrise."

Below in the feasting hall, everything was loud, hot, and full of laughter. Fires roared and stained the ceiling black. Mead and steaming spice-wine were handed out. Jaunty music filled the air while people who Evren knew previously as solemn and serious had taken to dancing on the tables, tossing food at each other, and singing bellowing songs that followed a dozen different mismatched tunes.

The heat was nearly stifling enough for Evren to take off her coat. She allowed herself to at least unbutton it. She lost Arke around the same time she found a warm mug in her hand. She sniffed the contents, and her nose was filled with warm spices and something distinctly alcoholic.

A warm arm wrapped around her shoulder, and Evren nearly spilled her drink all over herself as Jarl Eirunn guided her through the crowd. She smelled of mead and sweat, and her eyebrow glistened above her new eyepatch.

"You do not sniff it, Worm-Rider, you drink it."

"What is it?" Evren kept her mug close as a dancing trio jumped from one table to another.

"Goat's milk." Eirunn laughed at her wrinkled nose. "Spiced and spiked. Do not worry, it will fill that empty belly of yours and warm you almost as well as a lover."

Evren drank even while her ears burned with embarrassment. The thick milk was strong, and the spices stuck to the back of her throat. But she could feel the warmth blossoming in her belly and let herself drink more.

"Me and my people owe you much," Eirunn said seriously. "I have never seen a Daybreak quite so happy as this."

"Even with all that you lost?" Evren asked, dumbfounded. "These people all lost someone. There's so many widows and widowers and orphans and childless parents now. How can they celebrate?"

"Because the time for mourning has passed." Eirunn stopped her and put her hands on her shoulders. Her one good eye stared at her intensely. "We remember, as the ice remembers. But it does the dead no good to wallow. So, we will rebuild and be stronger for it. We will remember the Long Night where Mortova was killed in our harbor, and we will sing songs of those who fought him and his master. But we will live, Evren Worm-Rider. That is something to remember when you leave us."

Evren drank some more to keep her mouth from staying something stupid. When she swallowed, her throat burned. "I'll try."

"Very good." She clapped her on the back hard enough to kick up some of the milk Evren barely choked back down. "Remind your friends as well. Grief looks so dour on them. I'd like to see a genuine smile before they leave tomorrow."

"Thank you for your generosity, Jarl Eirunn," she said, "We won't forget it."

"Yes, I know well you won't. Just tell that skinny little rat with the glasses and the goat that we tried to skin all the newcomers, hm? Keep him and his kind away."

Evren snorted a laugh. She'd almost forgotten about Elend. "Oh, definitely."

"Good, good." She let go of Evren. "Enjoy the party!"

Eirunn started to disappear into the crowd, but Evren caught her arm before she could go. "Wait. I have a question."

Eirunn just raised her eyebrow, still poised to walk away but giving her time to talk.

"Before the battle you called Gyda 'Soul-Dust.' What does that mean?"

Eirunn sighed a little and kicked back the rest of her mead before tossing the mug away. When she turned back, her good eye was soft. "To lose one's entire clan is to lose one's soul. Gyda lost all of that but could've been taken into any of the others. She is a powerful warrior and a good woman. When she came to Direwall after losing her clan, she could've found a new home in any other clan. I myself begged her to stay. But she refused. By turning her back on all of her people, her soul turned to dust. Without a family to nourish it, it is nothing but ash. There is no kindling there, no fire behind her eyes. Therefore, she is, as we call her, Soul-Dust. unless she changes her mind."

"What do you mean?"

"Well, I made the same offer once she returned with you. Less begging, of course. She said she would make her decision once the sun rose."

Evren's stomach sank, and the milk started to curdle. "You asked her to stay?"

Eirunn regarded her strangely. "Of course. Her people are here. And without the Prime to dog her steps, she is free to come back to us. One day she will have her soul again."

"But . . ." Evren struggled for words. "She's our friend. She's a part of our party, a valued member. We came here to find her and bring her back to us."

"An admirable deed to fight so hard for a warrior in arms." She nodded gravely. "But Gyda does not belong in the south. The mountains are her home. She knows this. Why else would she not simply tell me no again?"

The world was far too fuzzy and warm for Evren to focus. She set her drink down, and barely registered when someone else immediately picked it back up and finished it off. She tried to shake her thoughts free, to untangle them, but they just sat muddled and tight. Eirunn simply watched her with a curious expression.

"Excuse me," Evren managed, before shouldering past the Jarl and walking into the crowd.

Everything was too hot. It didn't matter that everyone who saw her gave way. She never bumped into anybody or had to worm her way through a crowd. They all stopped to watch her pass. Some even waved at her or held drinks in the air as she passed. She was dimly aware of Sorin and Sol telling stories by the fire and cackling loudly. A shadow in the corner might've been Abraxas nursing a cup of mead. Sahar might've been sitting beside him. Evren ignored them all, marching her way through the hall until she saw the doors at the end.

She sighed in relief, her skin itching for reprieve as she pushed one open and slipped out into the night air.

Immediately, the chill stung her to the bone, but she didn't bother to button up her coat or put on her gloves. She just stood on the steps, her hands stuffed into her pockets and her breath steaming out in furious little bursts.

She was angry, and she wasn't sure why. The cold air did little to calm her, but she drank it in anyway. Her hands were balled into fists at her side, and she couldn't tell if she was shaking from the cold or the fury in her veins. Thankfully, her tears stayed away. This was a dry anger, and she was more than thankful for it. She'd shed enough tears for a lifetime.

She had a right to be upset, didn't she? If Gyda stayed, then it almost felt like she went through it all for nothing. Which was stupid, and wrong. She would've done it regardless. But the idea that, after everything, Gyda wouldn't be coming back with them still stung. Worst of all, it made sense why she wouldn't visit Evren then. If she already planned on saying goodbye, why not try to widen the gap between them even further?

And Gyda didn't owe her anything. Not an apology, not an explanation, not even a goodbye. Evren just realized far too late that she wanted all those things. More than that, she wanted her to stay. Everything felt so hollow without her. The silences were empty if she wasn't there to fill them. The nights were lonelier when she was on watch. There'd be an extra bowl and cup rattling in their bags until they either got rid of it or replaced her.

No.

There would be no replacement. Evren knew that as surely as she knew the sky was lightening. Slowly, but surely, navy blue turning lighter and warmer with each passing minute.

People were out on the streets, bundled up and holding cups of steaming milk as they watched the sky. Evren took the stairs two at a time to get away from them, heedless of her side twinging at every other step. Her boots crunched on the ice as she took to the streets, going nowhere, but too furious to stay still.

The sky was lighter when she caught sight of a familiar woman leaning against a building and watching the sunrise. Evren stopped short.

Her hair was tied back again, this time with a new headscarf. It had a plethora of colors. Evren hadn't bothered to memorize each clan, so she had no idea which one shared Gyda's new scarf. She wasn't wearing armor, just simple wool clothes with a blanket of fur tossed over her shoulders. Her eyes were blood-shot, but a serene smile was on her face as she watched the sky.

The mere sight of her sent a million jumbled thoughts

crashing into each other in Evren's head. She had no idea how long she stood there staring until she felt her feet moving. Before she knew it, she was right in front of Gyda.

Gyda straightened up quickly, her eyes bright and startled. "Evren, what are you—"

"Come with us," she blurted out. *Again* with the word vomit. She wanted to throw herself against the wall. But the damage was done.

Immediately, Gyda closed herself off. Her arms crossed over her chest, and she took a step back.

Panic rose like bile in Evren's throat. *Stupid, stupid, stupid!* "I-I mean, we could . . ." she stumbled. "We could really use you out there. Down there. South, you know. And-and I know it's a lot to ask. This is your home and all."

Gyda said nothing. She just stared down at her.

Evren's ears were on fire. She rubbed the back of her neck, not even feeling the bite of winter as she continued to stumble over her words.

"There's just so much to do. Nerezza could be anywhere, and we have to get Keres back their soul. Who knows what she's going to do with it! And then there's the problem of just the team falling apart without you. I mean, we barely made it through all this by ourselves. Sorin thinks he's useless, Sol won't open up to anybody, Abraxas is conflicted about his Divines, and Arke is . . . well, Arke is fine. But you get my meaning."

Nothing. Just ice-colored eyes, as cold as frost.

Evren shifted her weight from foot to foot. She bit her lip again, then stopped when she felt blood. "Are you going to say anything?" she asked, frustration mixing with anger, like a dangerous cocktail.

"Are you going to let me?"

She blinked up at Gyda, who still hadn't changed her expression from cold neutrality, and Evren found she couldn't keep the bite of anger from her voice. "I'm sorry, I'm kind of used to you not talking to me. How long have we been back in Direwall?

And you haven't once said a word to me. After we left the glacier, I haven't heard a peep from you until just now. I had to hear from Eirunn that you were planning to stay here. Which is fine!"

It wasn't. But Evren shook her hair free of her leather tie and tried to make it seem like it was. "It's fine! You can obviously do what you want. This is your home, after all."

The more she talked the more she became aware of how acutely selfish she was being. She wanted to snatch back every word, retrace her steps, and drown in more of that spiced milk. Her hair brushed the back of her neck as a chilling breeze swept through the street. It seemed to separate them further.

Finally, Gyda sighed. "Are you done?"

Evren startled back, half angry and half hopeful. She bitterly told the ice, "Yes."

"Good."

Gyda pushed off the wall and closed the gap between them. Evren looked up at her, trying to read her but just got lost in those glacier eyes.

"I have a home, Evren," she said, and Evren wanted to shrink away. "I have a family. I told you that back in the glacier."

"I-I know," Evren muttered, shame coloring her cheeks red, as the sky started to turn pink. "I wouldn't take you away from that, I'm sorry."

"I have a family," she repeated, and put her hand on her shoulder. Evren flinched despite herself, but her touch was warm and comforting. She met her eyes again. "It's the Sols."

Her breath hitched. "You mean . . ."

Gyda smiled. "I follow you. My home and family is where I make it, and it is no longer in the ice."

Evren's mouth flapped open and closed like a dying fish. "But . . . your clan's weave?"

Gyda shrugged. "I made it. A new weave for a new clan."

Evren could see it then. The colors all matched the Sol's. Black for Abraxas, blue for Sorin, gold for Sol, orange for Arke, and green for Evren.

Relief bubbled up into nervous laughter, and Evren couldn't stop it. "That's great! I mean, less so for Jarl Eirunn. But great for us! We-I mean, I am glad to have you back."

Gyda raised an eyebrow down at her, and Evren shrugged.

"I missed you."

"Yeah, strangely enough we *all* missed you." Sorin's voice made them both snap their heads down the street. He was holding Arke on his shoulders again, a steaming cup of milk on his head in Arke's hands. Abraxas and Sol were not far behind him.

Gyda stepped back from Evren, looking at them all quizzically as they gathered around her. "You did?"

Arke, who was now as close to eye level with her as he'd ever be, barked a very goblin-like laugh. "Damn straight! None of them knew what to do in a fight without ya."

Sol protested loudly. "Excuse you! You burned off most of your hair in that last fight!"

"Not the point."

Abraxas waved them both off. "It has been awful without you, Gyda. Lonely on the frontline for sure."

Sorin rolled his eyes. "Sure, don't mind me and my sword."

Gyda smiled. "Mine's bigger."

"*You're* bigger." He shook his head. "I missed having that giant ass as a shield. Abraxas's is so tiny in comparison."

Sol snorted. "His ass or shield?"

"Both."

The elf looked like he was aging years before their eyes, and Evren couldn't help but laugh with Sol and Sorin. "Maybe it's time for some squats, Abraxas." She snickered.

"Only if Arke joins in."

"Hey! My ass is fine by goblin standards! I am a paragon of beauty among my kind."

They laughed like that for a long time, making up for so many lost hours. Sol passed out drinks, and warm furs were given to those too mindless to bring their own—namely Evren.

They chatted until they found a spot with a sweeping view of the horizon. Huddled together, their breaths steaming the air as they shared their warmth, they watched the sky blossom. From blue to pink, with streaks of orange and gold, until finally the sun broke over the mountains.

Pure, golden light spilled over Direwall. Evren's eyes watered from staring at it. She closed her eyes, tilting her head up to bathe in the sun's rays. Everything felt more colorful and lighter with the sun back. As if the Long Night had bleached the world just for the sun to show up and reveal all they'd been missing.

Daybreak came, and the decision was made. In the golden light of day and the waning winds of winter, the Wandering Sols were whole again.

26

Gyda

Gyda hadn't looked back walking from Direwall. She sure as hells didn't look back crossing the Black Pass again. But being back in Keld's Outpost was strange. Strange because nothing had changed since she'd left. Elend definitely hadn't, except he looked stiffer. As if he'd managed to shove another pole up his ass.

Gyda stood stock still in his study as he glared at her over his steepled fingers. She didn't know many brave enough to glare at her. She tried not to squirm under his gaze. Without the rest of the Sol's to back her up, the heavy weight of her sword was little comfort against a man that weighed half as much as it. There was just something in his watery gaze that unsettled Gyda. Sol was cunning, but Gyda always knew her schemes worked out in her favor. Arke was intelligent, and she didn't understand half of what he said, but she trusted the goblin. Sorin was insane and infuriating. She was starting to like that about him.

But Elend was just an ass who liked being smarter than everyone and making sure they knew it. Gyda wanted to turn him inside out so he wouldn't have a chance.

"The whole team?" he finally asked.

"Yes."

He scowled as if he expected a bigger explanation. The firelight glinted off the sweat on his brow.

"How?"

Gyda blinked at him and very honestly asked, "Why are you asking me?"

Elend stood up and stuffed his hands in his robes. "Because you are the only one left in this damn outpost who I can trust."

Debatable.

"The rest of my team saw more," she said instead.

"Sahar Al-Fasil is the last of the Ashen Bond, and that's all you have to say to me?"

She nodded curtly.

Elend marched around his desk, his spectacles flashing in the firelight. "Three seasoned adventurers gone! And if your story is to be believed, one of them has eaten souls and is out there doing Divines know what!"

"Yes."

He hissed through his teeth and pushed his glasses back up his nose. "Gyda, you must understand how bad this looks. The Ashen Bond were premiere adventurers, and you were their guide."

Gyda didn't show how her heart sank. She remembered giving herself up to them, hopeful that they could take her home and keep her friends away. She'd used them, hadn't she? Now, one was dead, another's body was possessed and circling the outpost out of prying eyes, and another was gorged on power unfathomable to her. Sahar Al-Fasil was delicate, but strong in her own way. Gyda remembered the kind warmth in her eyes before Lostwater. She looked hollow now. Was Gyda to blame for that? Was the guilt that weighed as heavy as her sword earned?

She raised her chin and looked down at Elend. "You heard my story. If you need another, there are others."

He sneered. "Yes, your friends who broke every rule to get to you. How did that work out in the end?"

Gyda took a menacing step forward. Anger brimmed untapped below her sternum, and she let it shine in her eyes. Elend, to give him credit, didn't back away. But she saw the fear in his eyes. That's all she needed.

"Professor, in what way is it a good idea to piss off a woman who could snap you in half without breaking a sweat?"

Gyda stood frozen as Sahar swept into the room, and Elend rushed to make himself presentable. Sahar looked like she'd never been on the road traveling. Her hair was neatly combed and oiled, pulled back into a twisted bun. Her new jacket was rich and gleaming, and the air smelled like jasmine wherever she walked. She brushed past Gyda and gave her a warm smile. Her eyes still looked cold.

"Lady Al-Fasil!" Elend laughed nervously. "I was just about to call you."

"You should've called me first."

"Yes, but—"

"It is Collective protocol to speak to any remaining adventurer of a dead party before speaking to witnesses, correct?"

"Well, yes—"

"Then you can stop tormenting the woman who saved my life and reward her."

"*What?*" Elend shook his head in disbelief.

"What?" Gyda said, sounding much duller than the two of them.

Sahar rounded on Gyda with a flourish of perfume and practiced grace. "Gyda, you saved my life more than once during that awful adventure. Furthermore, your team did as well. Despite the atrocities that took place, I have never been in the company of people more driven than your friends. Had you been at the very bottom of the hells, I have no doubt they would've come for you."

Gyda cleared her throat awkwardly, looking anywhere in the room other than Sahar's intense gaze. "Uh, thank you."

She nodded and then turned back to Elend. "The issue up north could not have been rectified without the Wandering Sols. Given that Gyda is very good at explaining gruesome details, I'm sure I can spare you the details of the outcome that would've happened had her people not intervened."

Elend was recovering. "Be that as it may, my lady, they still defied orders. The Collective can't reward—"

"The Collective can, and they will." Sahar brought herself up tall, and Gyda noted with a little jealousy that he feared Sahar more than her. "My father sits at the head of the Collective, Professor. No doubt he could have you removed from your cold little exile here with one good word from me."

Elend's eyes flashed hopefully.

Sahar leaned forward, one hand braced on the desk. "Imagine what a hundred bad words will get you."

Elend gulped, his throat visibly bobbing up and down. Gyda had the sudden thought to take it out, but she was enjoying watching him squirm. He dabbed his forehead with his sleeve before nodding.

"What is it that you wish, my lady?"

Sahar smiled, and it was like watching a tiger circle her prey. She straightened her back and brushed phantom dust off her perfect sleeves.

"I want the reward you meant for us split between them. Vox's share will go towards his family, so you needn't worry about that. Nerezza's and my share, as well as Drystan's, will go to the Wandering Sols. I would also add a few key items in there, Elend. They deserve it. Oh! And a full, complimentary report on their heroism and bravery. Shining marks across the board, or so help me I will ruin your reputation with the stroke of a quill. Understood?"

Elend's jaw was tight, and he stared down Sahar as if he wanted to say no. Everything she said was the exact opposite of what Gyda knew he wanted to do. It was like telling Gyda she had to sit and have a cup of tea with him instead of wringing his neck. His face crumbled in a way that would've sent Evren into a fit of laughter right before he nodded.

"Done."

"Good," Sahar waved a flourish with her hand. "And good mounts for all of them. Yes, even the goblin. He's got a bigger brain than you do."

"With all due respect, my lady." he said through gritted teeth. "Is this really necessary? I understand they saved your life, but they are a band of bumbling idiots playing at being heroes. Surely your judgement is a little clouded after everything you've been—"

"My judgement." She cut him off coldly. "Has never been clearer. Two of my friends are dead. Another is gone with enough power to break her. And the only ones who can find her and stop her, the only ones I personally trust, are the Wandering Sols." She picked up his quill and he visibly shrank back. "Do not make a habit of questioning me, Professor. It tends to be very bad for your health."

Elend nodded once, sharply, and then moved behind his desk. He rummaged through what Gyda assumed was his safe before dumping out four bags of gold. He then separated them as Sahar watched, counting them dutifully whenever she so much as raised an eyebrow. Gyda put those all away in her bag.

From there he laid out a bunch of baubles.

"Extra treasures." He nodded to Gyda. "Bonuses, if you will. There's not enough for seven . . ."

"Nonsense, Professor." Sahar waved him off. "We're not thieves. Two will more than suffice. What do you say Gyda?"

Gyda wanted Arke. He would know what shit was magical and what just looked shiny and fancy. She walked up to the desk, peering down at the various trinkets. A swirling glass bottle that seemed to shake on the table, a cracked hand mirror with a rusted handle, a necklace that looked too fine to be practical, a glowing potion bottle, and a piece of black rock. Gyda froze when she saw it, and Sahar immediately snatched it up.

"Good choice." She tossed it over to her, and Gyda caught it with little effort. The giant rune started glowing immediately under her touch, and she brushed the pad of her thumb along the edges.

"What does it mean?" Sahar asked.

"Binding." Gyda shook her head. She had wrath already. "I don't know what it does."

"But it matches your sword?"

Gyda nodded, not hiding her surprise. She mentioned her sword and it's need for runes once before to the Ashen Bond. She wouldn't have expected Sahar of all people to remember.

"Well." The noblewoman smiled. "I'm sure you'll figure it out. Get Arke to help you."

Elend opened his mouth like he was preparing to offer the same help, but Sahar talked over him.

"Now! Which one would you like next? They're all very good, I have to say."

Gyda shifted from foot to foot, still clinging to the rune. It was all she could think about. How could she pick anything else?

Sahar's face softened. "Would you like me to pick for you?"

Gyda hesitated. Then she heard Sol's voice in her head, telling her she needed to accept help more often. She nodded.

Sahar took no time in snatching up the hand mirror. Elend made a choking noise, and Gyda decided she liked it simply because it distressed him. She took it from Sahar, making sure to be gentle around the edges. Her cracked reflection stared back at her.

"What does it do?"

Sahar smiled. "It's a Fey gift. They're common in Terevas, less so up north. To find one without a contract is incredibly rare. You could keep it for yourself and see what properties it holds, or you could gift it to another."

Gyda pocketed the mirror, knowing exactly who she was giving it to. "Thank you." She turned to Elend. "Are we done?"

He nodded gloomily. "Yes, thank the Divines. See yourselves out, if you will."

Sahar swept out without another word, Gyda trailing behind like a cold shadow. As she did, Elend called out behind her.

"And do leave my goat alone while you're here! He's sensitive!"

The door shut on him, and Sahar dropped the mask. "Sensitive? More like evil." She massaged her temples. "Are you quite all right, Gyda? Handling slugs like him is what I do, but you were alone with him for a while."

"I'm . . . fine." She fell behind Sahar again as they climbed the stairs. "Why did you help me?"

Sahar scowled, and somehow it made her prettier. "I detest men like him. After everything you and your party did for me, I wasn't going to let him drown your reputations."

To the hells with reputation. She could give a shit about the opinions of others. Eith was a mess that was going to be fixed by chaotic people. No one sane started adventuring. The Collective was a piss-poor way of trying to make order and money from a bunch of people who had nothing better to do than save the world, over and over again. Gyda was insane for following her friends south because they were going to do it again. Somehow, they'd find themselves in more trouble. Someone would get hurt, they'd nearly die, and maybe they'd get paid shiny baubles for it.

Only now, Gyda knew that whatever they did would involve the mage Nerezza. And certainly, a lot more pain.

As they cleared the next landing, Gyda stopped Sahar. "What will you do?"

The noblewoman shook her head. Now that her mask was gone, no amount of perfume or hair oil could disguise how tired and broken she was. Her eyes were still puffy and red from crying, her lips cracked and peeling. Her nails were torn and dirty from biting. She looked hollow, like a shell of the woman who'd been full of warmth and hope.

"I don't know," she said. "I have to look for Nerezza in any way I can. I hope she went back to Terevas. She has a home there that I plan on checking. If it makes a difference, I'm taking Keres with me. They're just as adamant about finding her as I am."

Gyda frowned. "The corpse?"

Pain flickered across her face. "I'll find them a different body. For now, I'll have to deal with Vox and Drystan on my own."

"We can help."

"No, no." She shook her head sadly. "This is my burden to bear. I will do right by them in death since I couldn't in life."

Silence clamped down on Gyda's mouth before she forced it open. She cringed even as she said the words. "I couldn't save him."

Sahar flinched. "I know."

"I'm sorry."

"Gyda, if I blamed you, you'd be a pile of melted marrow and leather right now."

Somehow, she believed her. But Gyda still blamed herself, even if Sahar didn't. Strange that she couldn't unshoulder this weight like she used to. Would it stick with her forever?

"Regardless of the past, I'm leaving in the morning." Sahar patted her bicep. "I'm so damn sick of the cold I could scream. And I'm all out of my face cream. If I am to retain my youth, I need to hurry south quickly."

Gyda knew the Sols weren't leaving for another two days. "Will you say goodbye?"

Sahar pressed her lips into a firm line. "No. I think it is far too painful. But I will keep in touch. We all have a common goal, you know."

Gyda nodded. Knowing this wouldn't be the last time she saw Sahar Al-Fasil, she started to make her way up the steps to the next floor. Sahar cleared her throat daintily enough that the creaking wood nearly drowned her out. Gyda stopped anyway and looked at her over her shoulder.

"Don't be a fool, Gyda," she said, her lip quivering. "Not like me. Time is precious whenever you do what we do. You might not always have the time to . . . well, you know what I mean. Speak your heart, is all I'm saying. And be well."

Then she was gone, but left so many confusing words left in the air that Gyda was left standing dumbfounded on the stairs for five whole minutes. She shook her head and put them in the same pocket she put the mirror. But they burned a hole in her thigh, those words. They wouldn't leave her be. With each step her mind tugged a little harder, her heart pulled a little more, in a direction she hadn't planned on going.

Soft, dark nights like this were normally spent outside. She knew there was no fear of her feet taking her back to Direwall, for they had no desire to. Amidst the gently falling snow and coyly curling breeze, she could enjoy winter, true winter, one last time. She doubted she would see it again.

But nights where the heart was heavy and troubled shouldn't be spent alone. On those nights, Gyda would stick inside her shared room with Abraxas. He was quiet and calming in his own way. He never asked for an explanation or prodded her for the weight that so obviously slumped across her shoulders. At most, he told stories of his past, which were far too sweet and soft for the man that carried them. Abraxas and Gyda understood each other in some silent way that neither ever had to worry about. She could always count on his shoulder, should she need it.

Neither the crisp night nor the warm bedroom was where she was headed though. Gyda was dimly aware, with each passing step, that she was just heading up. Up to the mess hall with its deep shadows and expansive windows. Back to where she first told the living, somewhat, of what had happened to her clan in Lostwater.

Evren had been different then. So hopeful and kind in the way she'd reached across the table and made her sweet promises.

She was much changed now, as Gyda stepped into the mostly empty room. She couldn't tell what it was that changed; something small that didn't ruin what made her Evren, but enough to switch the way she held herself or looked others in the eye.

And she was waiting for her.

That was a foolish thought that Gyda shook from her head. Even so, she stood by the stairs as still as stone for a while to simply watch the half-elf.

Evren hadn't noticed her. She was sitting next to the frosted window, silver starlight caressing her hair and cheeks. No fire kept her warm, no tea steamed in her hands. There was just a blanket around her shoulders, partially fallen and carelessly held together with her fingers. Her hair was a mess, like she'd just gotten out of bed. It was always so beautifully tangled in the morning, as if she spent all night running instead of sleeping.

"Are you just going to stand there?" Evren asked suddenly, still not looking away from the window.

Gyda did just stand there, but for only a few more seconds before she walked across the room and sat opposite her. Her sword clanked uncomfortably against the bench, but she didn't unstrap it. She was keenly aware that this was the same table they'd been at the night before Gyda left. She could almost smell the sharp tang of ointment in the air and feel the bandages as Evren tied them with swift fingers that burned on her skin long after they'd stopped touching her.

There had been an easy smile to that Evren. A warmth Gyda hadn't seen since. She felt a cold pit in her stomach open like a yawning mouth. Had she caused that change?

Across from her, Evren tapped her thumb on her chin, her eyes still glued to the trees outside. The frostbite scar was white on her nose. "What did Vaughn say? Are we all stripped of our lowly status and doomed to wander away again?"

It took Gyda a minute to realize she was talking about Elend. The bitterness in her voice should've clued her in sooner.

"No," she said softly, not wanting to break the odd quiet in the room.

"No?" Evren finally looked at her, her thumb resting just below her lip, forgotten. "What happened?"

"Sahar stepped in." Gyda shifted uncomfortably in her seat. "We have our reward, a good recommendation, and a few other prizes."

Evren looked at her knowingly with those pitch-black eyes. "Did you get another rune?"

Gyda nodded.

"That's exciting!" And Gyda knew she meant it, even if her face didn't quite show it.

"Confusing," Gyda corrected. "And a little underserved."

Smiles from Evren used to be easy. A little crooked, always showing a too-sharp canine, but always friendly. Now a scowl pulled at her lips instead.

"What do you mean?"

Rune, mirror, and Sahar's words burned like a forest fire in her pocket. She tried to ignore them. "I don't see how I deserve to add another piece to my sword after what I did."

"Gyda, no one blames you."

"I do."

Something flashed in those midnight eyes. Anger, maybe, but oddly not towards Gyda. Stiff determination set her jaw as she leaned forward. She smelled like cedar even now, and a flower Gyda couldn't name.

"What happened up there wasn't your fault," Evren said firmly, her eyes blazing. "Would it have been easier if you'd told us everything? Yes. Would it have stopped everything from going wrong? No."

Gyda frowned and put her elbows on the table as she leaned forward, too. "Are you saying that I couldn't have done better? I couldn't have saved Vox or Drystan by warning them? Or Sol from the horrors of the White Cairn if I—"

"You saved Sol." Evren cut her off. "Vox died at Gail's hand, not yours. Drystan made his choice, again and again. We all did. At any point we could've turned around and gone home, but we didn't. We stayed."

"Why?" The cold iron edge to her voice couldn't disguise the deep confusion that made it waver.

Evren sat back and stared at Gyda the way she always did when she didn't understand something. Hard and unflinching, as if she was trying to pick her apart bone by bone. Gyda didn't move.

"You're everything to us," she finally said. "There was no way we'd leave you behind."

It didn't make it better. It didn't make up for the hundreds of corpses Gyda saw crying out in silent agony, or the souls that continuously plucked at her brain to set them free. The new power of ripping souls from their bodies, and shoving them back in again, was Gail's gift to her, and she kept it locked in her chest. She would *never* use it again. That promise didn't change anything either. It didn't fix the dark look in Sol's already shadowed eyes, or the very fresh wound of loss Gyda couldn't seem to stop bleeding. But Evren's words did change something.

Gyda looked at Evren again. She took in her messy hair that barely hid the points of her ears. She took in the black eyes, paired so well with the dark circles that never seemed to leave her. The scar above her eyebrow, on her nose, a very old one on her left cheek that all gleamed in the starlight. She looked smaller, colder. A little less alive and a little more like she was clinging to life. Her skin was paler, her cheeks less full. Her fingers shook as they clutched the blanket tighter around her chest, hovering over that massive, mysterious scar on her chest.

She'd changed, unwillingly it seemed. But it was still Evren. Her voice was clear, her eyes were sharp, and if she smiled it would be crooked.

Gyda needed to see it, just to be sure.

"When you said you would always find me, I never expected you to follow me in death as well as life," Gyda said slowly.

"We're not dead yet."

"No." Then Gyda let herself smile. "You look dead, though."

Smile for me, she begged internally. *Show me you're still there.*

And across the table, Evren laughed. She threw her head back and her whole body shook as she did. The sound and the movement broke what little soft peace there had been. Gyda crushed it under her heel.

There it was. That crooked smile that warmed the room better than any fire. Her eyes were warmer too, and she shook her hair out from her face. She said very slyly, as if sharing a secret meant only for Gyda, that drew her in against her will, "I do, don't I?"

Her shoulders still shook from the laughter, almost feverish. It was like getting a sudden shock of pure Evren that she'd been missing. A rainstorm in a drought. Gyda had deserved the dry silences. She missed the rainstorm laughter, though.

Like soil parched and thirsty, she drank up the sound. It wasn't enough, and she had a feeling it never would be. They sat there until Evren's fingers turned blue and she couldn't keep her eyes open, until the stars started winking out and the sky was lightening for another beautiful dawn.

All Gyda could think, each time she looked over at Evren, were the same three words in her head.

Do it again.

THE END

Thank you for reading WHERE THE NIGHT CONSUMES.

The Blood of Eith series continues next with
WHERE THE HEART FESTERS.
available at
www.GillianGrant.com

Keep reading for a excerpt from
WHERE THE HEART FESTERS...

EXCERPT OF WHERE THE HEART FESTERS
THE BLOOD OF EITH, BOOK THREE

The ghost only came by moonlight, and only to Evren.

At least, she assumed it was a ghost. Either that or she truly was going mad, which wouldn't be that much of a leap for her. Not now.

She didn't like how it looked. The way it glided instead of walked, the way it shimmered and spun like moving mists in the pale light of the moon and barely tried to take the form of a person, irritated her. As if it was trying to remind her, gently, that she couldn't do anything rash to it.

On the nights where it said things that stoked the ever-growing fire of rage in her chest, its etherealness made her scratched red welts into her arms. She always stopped herself before she could bleed, but her skin caked under her fingernails was a poor substitute for what she wanted to do to the ghost. Those were dreadful nights. She never spoke back on them.

There were never any good nights, however. Just ones where the ghost's words weren't so barbed and cruel, and where her fingers stayed steadily on her thighs without the urge to hurt. Those nights, she didn't mind it with her. At least she wasn't alone.

Tonight was one of those nights. Bright moonlight filtered in through the tavern window, pooling in silver streams over the two beds. One, the farthest from the window, was empty and cold. The dwarf that had slept in it still hadn't come up for bed. It was well past midnight. In the other bed, Evren sat curled up next to the window. She rested her forehead against the cool glass, shivering at the reprieve it gave her fever heated body. She didn't look away from the view of the sprawling village outside, but she felt the ghost when it appeared.

"It's too close." She murmured. To the ghost, the glass, and the dark smudge of forest beyond.

The ghost was quiet for a while before it whispered, "It's a large forest. Orenlion isn't as close as you think."

Evren pursed her lips. The voice always threw her off at first. Deep and soothing, even when it spoke harshly. She never could bring herself to hate it.

"We'll leave soon." She said.

"Will they let you?" it asked.

Always with the obvious fears. It seemed able to pick out what she dreaded most and say them aloud. Evren shivered again.

"They'll leave if I ask."

The floorboards didn't creak to show it was moving. The air just got a little damper and cooler, as if she was passing through a soft patch of morning fog. It was by her bed now.

"They brought you here, even when you protested." it said. "They think being near will convince you to go back."

"It won't."

"Why?"

Evren shook her head. Under her nightshirt, she could feel the massive scar on her chest throbbing. If she had a heartbeat, she would guess it was in time with that. But the hole where her heart should be was just that, a hole. The strange throbbing only made the dull fever she'd had for weeks now more prominent.

Outside her window, the village of Angel's Fall stood stocky and proud against the night. The last piece of Etherak before the towering trees of the Deep Wood swallowed the earth. She couldn't see the stars unless she craned her neck up. The black of the Wood blocked them out and left nothing but a shadowed wall at the edge of the forest.

"I can't go back." Evren said. "I'm not like them. Orenlion isn't home. If I go back, I'll never leave."

"And if it could save your life?"

"Whatever took my heart isn't the kind to give it back." she said. "I won't find it again."

"How can you be so sure?"

She scowled, and irritation bubbled in her empty chest. "I'd rather die out here among people I care about than trapped in there for the rest of my days."

"What if your friends won't let you? They won't watch you die."

"They'll be fine."

"I won't watch you wither away."

Finally, she turned away from the window. Her head throbbed as she rounded on the ghost. The absence of cool glass made her feel stuffy immediately.

He looked as he always did. Long white hair, elegantly braided away from his face. His dark grey skin was softer now that he was a specter. His moth wing robes fluttered in an invisible breeze. The ghost looked like the Viggo she remembered, the one she left behind in Serevadia and sealed the tunnels over him. He hadn't wanted to leave his home, but it still felt like she'd killed him. Even more damning to see him like this. She'd cried the first night. Now she just narrowed her eyes at him.

"You don't get a say." She said hotly.

He frowned at her, like he always did when she bit her words at him. That was more often now, the sicker she got.

"I know that." he said gently. "I'm merely trying to help you."

"Then you're not playing your role as Viggo very well, spirit." She said. "Viggo only helped when it suited him."

"You still don't believe it's me." he said flatly.

"It's not."

"I've explained this—"

"And I'm done listening." She snapped. "Either you're a spirit taunting me with whatever form you think is easier, or I've lost my mind and I'm arguing with myself."

"You haven't lost your mind. Not yet."

It wasn't a threat, but the harsh truth of the words settled over her like a sticky blanket, anyway. She rolled her shoulders, now constantly sore, and tried to think a little clearer. Anger normally helped. If not that, then pain. But she was too tired to be truly angry at the ghost tonight. And if Sol found her with any fresh marks, she'd be furious.

Instead, Evren put her head in her hands and tried to massage the ache from her temples. Her hair, now past her shoulders and long enough to irritate, fell around her like a waterfall. It blocked Viggo from view.

"Whatever you are," she said. "I'm too tired to argue. With you, or anyone else. I just want to rest."

"No you don't."

She laughed darkly. "Sure feels like I do."

"You don't remember, Evren." the ghost said. "What took your heart?"

As always, a blank wall of nothing greeted her when she tried to remember. Nothing but a few splintered memories of traveling in the leaf dappled sunlight, and then darkness. The memory that Ainthe had clawed up was painful; a nightmare she hoped wasn't real. The claws in her chest felt real, though. The storm, the screams and blood in her throat too. But where that ended was more black.

"It doesn't matter." She said.

"Liar. You never could resist a good puzzle."

She snapped her head up, an argument already forming on

her dry lips. But it was gone. The room was still and shadowed, and she was alone.

She took a shaky breath, and let her heavy eyelids close as she slipped underneath the blankets again. It was mostly for show. Whenever the ghost suddenly left, it usually meant she wouldn't be by herself for long. And, just as she predicted, soft footfalls crept outside the door. The latch clicked up, and the hinges barely made a sound as Sol slipped quietly into the room and shut the door behind her.

She was always quiet and careful, but even more so in the past few weeks. Evren could smell the ale and smoke on her from the table the Wandering Sol's preferred right by the fireplace. She felt, more than heard, Sol's hesitation at the edge of her bed.

But Evren forced herself to breathe deeply, and slowly. She tried to let her eyebrows relax, so she looked more like she was sleeping fitfully. She couldn't tell if it worked or not, but Sol's soft sigh filled the room as she traded her clothes for her nightshirt and slipped into her bed. It took all of five minutes before the dwarf was snoring, her earthly worries forgotten in the blackness of sleep.

Evren didn't sleep. She rolled over, her face in the moonlight and the dark wall of trees looming in her vision. She was closer to home than she had been in over a year. Why did the dread in her stomach feel so heavy when Orenlion was all she could think about while she was in Serevadia and the Reino Terminan? Hadn't she been dreaming of the woods and warm breezes to lessen the blows of the harsh adventures she'd been on? Shouldn't she want to at least try to fix herself?

That weighted dread dragged her down. She wondered, dimly, if Gyda had felt the same way on the edge of Enrial Wilds. Closer to home than ever, and the darkness she'd left. Gyda had faced it, and came out whole.

Evren had a feeling that if she went into the Deep Wood again, she wouldn't come back at all.

* * *

By day, it was easy to see where Angel's Fall got its name. Anyone not familiar with the village would think someone named it after a beautiful waterfall tumbling from the sweeping river it sat beside. But the Glasgus River was very gentle and wide. The land it carved though would dip into a few rapids the farther West it ran, but next to Angel's Fall, and coming from the Deep Wood, it was calm enough to swim in during warmer months.

No, the village got its name from the small, but impressive crater it was built around. It was old and weathered, but the imprint of a large humanoid in the rock hadn't been erased by time. There were debates on what made the crater. Of course, the popular theory was a fallen angel, if one believed in them. Unlike devils, who made themselves known and were frighteningly real, angels were even harder to imagine than gods.

"You think someone did it?" Sorin asked, peeking over the side to glimpse the imprint of the body below.

"What?" Evren asked.

"That." he gestured to the imprint. "They could've carved it into the rock."

Beside him, Sol shook her head. Her blonde hair gleamed in the bright spring sunlight and hung down to her shoulders. She played with it idly. "I don't think so. It looks old."

"Well, the crater is old." he argued. "Some crusty priest could've done it when he first found it."

"But why?"

"I dunno. Why do priests do anything?"

"The mayor said the crater has been here for thousands of years." Sol said. "If you believe Etherak's history, then humans weren't around yet."

Sorin frowned. "Why does the priest have to be human?"

"Because only a human would go through the trouble of taking an already mysterious crater and adding an angel to it." Evren said with a small smile.

The Vasa snorted. "We wouldn't. At least, no Vasa human would."

"Would a Vasa know what to do with a rock if he had it?" Sol joked.

He threw his hands up in the air. "You know what? Forget it. I feel attacked. I shouldn't have dragged you two out here. All I wanted was to do some *normal* sightseeing like a *normal* person before something inevitably crawls out of the ground and demands we answer its riddles three or get destroyed."

"That's specific." Evren raised an eyebrow.

"I had a weird dream last night." He waved her off. "A giant made of cheese said if I didn't answer its riddles, he'd make me into his next block of rariso."

Sol balked. "His what?"

"The cheese!" he said. "You know, it's really pale. Red veins. The good kind has holes in it."

"Why would there be a cheese giant?" Sol asked. "That makes no sense."

Sorin pointed to himself. "It's my dream."

"Did you win the riddles?" Evren asked.

He scowled. "They weren't riddles! They were stupid philosophical questions. The ones that have no right or wrong answer but you'll end up pissing someone off, regardless? Somehow that also centered on cheese."

"Well," she breathed. "That explains your breakfast."

The three turned away from the crater and walked back into town. Angel's Fall was like any other Etherakian village. Small, brown houses with thatched roofs divided by dirt roots and plenty of mud. It was bigger than most, though. There weren't many hunters who routinely made trips into the Deep Wood, but those who did found great game. That, the crater, and Glasgus River giving an easy ride West towards the coast made Angel's Fall a bustling tourist spot.

The smell of wood smoke and cooking meat permeated the air. The laughing of children overshadowed the sound of the river flowing in its bed. Barking dogs chased after treats while hunters shouting back and forth at each other. It was almost picturesque.

With the river curving around the village on one side, the crater on the other, the towering forest of the Deep Wood to the north and rolling hills of green to the south, there was an unrivaled sense of beauty and peace in the village. Like all things Etherak, it held a wild edge. Something barely civilized clinging to a land that refused to be tamed, even after centuries of cities, villages and roads being built. The people were the same way. Their tongues were as sharp as their blades, and smiles were warm but guarded. Living on the edge of the Deep Wood, far from any city, meant danger. From beasts, monsters, or ravaging storms.

And yet, they thrived. Evren had respected it the first time she set foot in Angel's Fall, when she'd left Orenlion. That respect hadn't waned.

"Any word from Sahar?" Sorin asked casually, as if the question itself wasn't enough to send spikes of anxiety through all of them.

Sol shook her head. "Nothing much. Her last letter said she's back home in Rhienwall. She visited where Nerezza said she grew up, and the people running the orphanage didn't know who she was talking about."

Evren grimaced. That wasn't new information, but it at least confirmed another one of Nerezza's lies. Sahar had gone south to Terevas, determined to find something there to find her old friend and last remaining member of her adventuring party. The letters she sent were all the same; uncovered lies and no new leads.

It should've been easy to track Nerezza. A mage with that much power, especially if she was using it, would be noticeable. But long after Evren and her party had left the Reino Terminan, it was like all traces of her had vanished.

"Do you think she went back to Serevadia?" Sol asked as she stepped around a pack of hunting dogs.

Evren gave them each a passing scratch behind their floppy ears. "I don't think so. We still don't know how she got away from her kidnappers. Why join the Ashen Bond? Why didn't she go back immediately? She has a plan; we just need to figure it out."

"No chance it's easy and right in front of our faces, right?" Sorin chuckled. "With our luck, she's all the way in Melkarth. Wouldn't it be nice if she was hiding out in the Deep Wood, huh? What a perfect place to hide. With all those . . . trees."

A soft hiss escaped Sol's lips, but the damage was done. Evren stopped in the middle of the road, her back purposefully facing the towering wall of trees. She didn't want to glare at Sorin, but a familiar hot prickle of anger was heating her already sweating body. Sorin had the good decency to look ashamed and shuffled his boots in the mud.

"I take that as a no?" he offered.

Evren took a cooling breath. The morning air, while quickly warming, was still damp with last night's mists. "We've been over this, Sorin."

"Have we, though?" he asked. "I feel like every time we get started, you cut us off."

"We need to focus on finding Nerezza," Evren said. "And nothing points to her being in the Deep Wood."

"What we need to focus on is you." he argued, and some iron leaked into his words. "You're our best chance at finding her."

"What do you think I'm doing?" she snapped.

"For starters? Suffering."

Evren pursed her lips together. The villagers gave them a widow berth, but she could see them eyeing her as they walked past. Arguing in the middle of the street was not one of her finer decisions. Between her and Sorin, Sol was fiddling with her hair again, and the stark worry etched across her face was clear for all to see. She flinched at Sorin's words, but didn't dispute them.

Sorin took a step closer, and Evren was all at once hit with a wave of déjà vu. In an icy tavern at the edge of an eternal night, they'd stood like this. Only the roles had been reversed. Sorin grappling with his mortality and suffocating fear, and her trying to comfort him. How had things changed so drastically? He was far from fixed. Evren still saw a darkness in his honey eyes that hadn't been there before Heliodar plunged a dagger into his chest. There were still dark bags under his eyes, and his smiles weren't quite the same.

But now he was feeling strong enough to force her into an argument she was sick of having.

"You look terrible, Evvie." he said gently. "And I know you don't feel well either."

"I'm fine."

"No," he shook his head. "You're not. Why don't you want to fix this?" Sorin pointed at her chest. Her shirt hid the scar on her chest, but seemed to burn hot against the fabric when he mentioned it.

"It's not that simple, Sorin." she said hollowly. "I can't even remember how I lost it. Going into the Wood now would have us wandering aimlessly for years."

"Trollshit," Sol finally spoke. "You can track anything, and you know those woods."

Evren shook her head. "It's a waste of time. We're focusing on Nerezza."

"We came here to focus on you," Sol said. "The entire party did."

Evren's eyes throbbed, and she struggled not to rub the pain away. "We came here to resupply before heading down to Terevas. Passing through the Vanguard Mountains won't be easy. Sahar is waiting for us."

"You've been repeating that so often lately it's losing all meaning." Sorin said.

Something in Evren finally snapped, and she whirled on him. "What happens to me is nothing compared to what Nerezza can do if we don't find her. Am I in the best health? No. But I can still fight. I can still get you to Sahar and from there we can find Nerezza before she does any actual harm. Or have you forgotten what Gail did?"

Sorin's eyes flickered over to Sol, who was forcibly ignoring both of them now. He looked back at Evren. "I haven't." he muttered. "But Nerezza isn't Gail."

"No." Evren stepped back. "She's more powerful than him now. She still has Keres's soul, and Gail's, on top of the dozens we didn't save in time. That kind of power broke Gail. What can it do to an already powerful mage?"

Sorin shook his head again. "But Gail was isolated. He lost his entire crew, his family, and was starving and desperate before he turned to Keres. Nerezza—"

"Lost her party." Evren finished. "She watched Vox die for her. She knew Drystan was dead before we went into the Cairn. And she's been isolated ever since they took her from Serevadia."

"But she had Sahar!" he argued.

"Exactly." Evren said. "She'll go back to her eventually, fractured mind or not. Which is why we need to be there when she does instead of wasting time *here*." She waved her hand around at Angel's Fall, taking in the villagers, huts, dogs and the sweeping river in one gesture. "Please, Sorin. Let the Deep Wood go. For me."

He looked like he would argue. Knowing him, he could go on until the sun set and the stars wheeled overhead. But Sol gave him a knowing look and gave a soft shake of her head. He sighed, his shoulders drooping.

"Alright," he said. "You win this one."

It didn't feel like a victory. Not when he looked at her with barely disguised worry, and Sol had already started walking away. But she took it anyway and followed the dwarf further into the village.

There was a part of her, not so easily buried, that knew they were right. She'd pushed herself too far during the Long Night, dipped into magic she didn't understand, and she was paying the price. The fever she'd dealt with once they left the mountains and the constant headaches were irritating but manageable. But how long before she *couldn't* manage them? She only felt herself when she was in a fight. The sudden crisp clarity had her blood singing and all her pains forgotten. But afterwards she crashed, hard. And she was getting worse.

She spared an upward glance at the Deep Wood. The leaves aching to brush the sky, the trunks supporting the twisting branches thousands of years old. No tree in the Deep Wood had been cut, ever. They rose and fell as time allowed. And there was a time Evren knew them like her own mind. Even when Orenlion felt more like a prison than a home, they'd always been there to offer solace when she snuck away.

So why did the mere sight of them now send a spike of fear through her?

She tore her gaze away from the shadowed forest as they came closer to the village's biggest tavern. The Gilded Feather was an impressive three stories tall, and sturdy as all things Etherakian made. Springtime meant another season of hunting, which meant it was packed with hunters, both noble and peasant. The other three taverns as well. It was only by Sol's charm they could get enough rooms for the party to stay.

Already the smell of baking bread and bacon was in the air, getting heavier the closer they got. Evren's stomach rumbled with hunger, and she inwardly winced. She'd forgotten to eat breakfast, again. She'd have to sneak a plate before her friends noticed.

"Sounds like a party in there." Sorin commented.

Evren frowned and drew her thoughts away from breakfast. As she did, she picked up on the sound of raised voices, the cracking of wood and the breaking of glass.

"That sounds like a fight." She corrected. "Who—"

The nearby window shattered in a spray of sparkling glass. The trio barely staggered out of the way as a man tumbled through the broken window. He collapsed on the ground, groaning and holding his bleeding nose.

"Oh, look!" Sorin said cheerfully. "How much gold do you wanna bet that Gyda's made some new friends?"

~

WHERE THE HEART FESTERS
available at
www.GillianGrant.com

ACKNOWLEDGMENTS

I wrote a little novel when it came to acknowledgements last time according to my friends, so I'll try to keep it short and sweet this go around.

If there's one thing this book has taught me (and Evren), it's perseverance. I'd heard that sequels were harder to write, and *Where the Night Consumes* lived up to that promise. But the amount of pride I have for this book shocked me, and seeing it come to life as the next adventure for the Wandering Sols was well worth the blood, sweat and tears.

Of course, it wasn't just me alone in this marathon to get Book #2 published, and I couldn't have done it without everyone below:

• Laura, I was so nervous to give not one but *two* of my babies to you at once. But they couldn't have been in better hands. Your little stories and snarky comments in the margins never failed to make me laugh and learn new things. I'm looking forward to every comment and critique on the future problem children.

• Stef, for such a gorgeous cover that seemed to come straight from my noggin and onto the screen. Every new cover feels like Christmas!

• Charity, for the patience, schedule squeezing, support, and gorgeous teasers and graphics. I know as forgetful and scatterbrained as I am that I'm not the easiest to work with, but you make it look like a breeze.

• To all the survival guides, youtube videos on how to

survive blizzards and build shelters, and backpack vloggers I watched in between chapters. Half this book would be nonsense without you.

- To my blood family, ever supportive and understanding.

- To my found family, which includes step-sisters, a bonus mom, and many crazy nerds who found their way into my life. You make the days brighter and the nights warmer. Or, cooler in my case, since I can't stand to be hot.

- And, of course, to every reader, writer, Dungeon/Game Master, D&D player, burnt out gifted kid looking for an escape, and trash goblin out there. Thank you for another whirlwind adventure!

ABOUT THE AUTHOR

Gillian Grant was born in Texas and grew up enthralled with fantasy stories of all kinds. As she got older she often traveled with her family and imagined wild adventures while exploring the mountains of Colorado and the glens of Scotland. Back home in Texas she took her love of fantasy to the next level and sat a group of friends down to play Dungeons and Dragons. From there, they built the world her first novel, *Where The Shadows Beckon* was set in. When she's not writing Gillian is normally juggling too many D&D campaigns, grooming dogs, and imagining her next adventure. She still lives in Texas with her two cats.

www.GillianGrant.com

facebook.com/GillianGrantAuthor

instagram.com/gilliangrantauthor

amazon.com/Gillian-Grant/e/B09J94DBHP

CPSIA information can be obtained
at www.ICGtesting.com
Printed in the USA
BVHW091936020123
655423BV00007B/25

9 781737 224563